D0000066

Miracle Creek
CHRISTMAS

OTHER CONTEMPORARY PROPER ROMANCE TITLES

Check Me Out by Becca Wilhite

Glass Slippers, Ever After, and Me by Julie Wright

Lies Jane Austen Told Me by Julie Wright

Lies, Love, and Breakfast at Tiffany's by Julie Wright

Miracle Creek
CHRISTMAS

PROPER ROMANCE

KRISTA JENSEN

SHADOW
MOUNTAIN

For my dear friend Carmen and our hours in the dialysis center. You joked that one day I could use the experience in a story and we laughed. Who knew? You are a light.

And for the firefighters of the Pacific Northwest, who work so hard to preserve this beautiful chunk of Earth.

© 2020 Krista Jensen

All rights reserved. No part of this book may be reproduced in any form or by any means without permission in writing from the publisher, Shadow Mountain®, at permissions@shadowmountain.com. The views expressed herein are the responsibility of the author and do not necessarily represent the position of Shadow Mountain.

This is a work of fiction. Characters and events in this book are products of the author's imagination or are represented fictitiously.

Visit us at shadowmountain.com

PROPER ROMANCE is a registered trademark.

Library of Congress Cataloging-in-Publication Data
(CIP data on file)
ISBN 978-1-62972-787-5

Printed in the United States of America
Publishers Printing

10 9 8 7 6 5 4 3 2 1

Chapter 1

I n another life, Mark Rivers would've focused on the woman who'd just entered the bakery and nodded in her direction with a smile of appreciation. The new art teacher had turned more than a few heads in town. But this wasn't that life, so he took the bag of apple fritters Lette Mae handed him, pulled his hood farther over his head, and ducked past the new customer and out into the chill of November third.

He brushed off the lingering feeling that she'd looked his way. Everyone looked. It had taken months for the locals of Miracle Creek to stop staring at him like he wasn't who he'd always been. Like he hadn't gone to their schools and played in their conference championships and been to their weddings and funerals and anything in between. Eighteen months had passed since the summer fires had devoured a large portion of his family's orchards—and a portion of Mark, too.

Rivers Orchards hadn't been the only property devastated by the fires. A lot of families were hit with loss. But while orchards were replanted, homes were rebuilt, and new growth covered charred ground—even in the skeletal remains of the Cascade Forest—Mark was still scarred, and, in some ways, still burning.

He passed James Dean, Lette Mae's basset hound sprawled on an old quilt in the winter sun, and climbed into his truck, still careful of the healed burns on his body.

Town wasn't much. Main Street made a sort of "J"—the bakery, the auto shop, and gas station on the corner, the IGA and Ace Hardware across the street, the Grill-n-Go drive-thru next door. The street meandered past the K-12 school and a park, a few blocks of homes, some "town" orchards, and then out of town.

Pick a valley. Pick a hillside. Almost any road led to orchards. Acres of apple, peach, pear, apricot, and cherry trees along with the occasional vineyard had been tucked into the curves of this foothill region just east of the Cascade Mountains. The coastal weather from the west kept things mild, and the mountains siphoned off just enough rain to keep things irrigated. Usually.

Two summers ago, a rare drought had settled in, and without the rain, everything had crackled on the ground. Midsummer greens had turned yellow and brown. A spark—campfire, cigarette, broken glass in the sun—nobody knew for sure how the blazes started, but once they began, high gusty winds out of nowhere had pushed and pulled until—

Mark shuddered and clenched his right hand. That kind of thinking used to end with him in a sweat, screaming, his body feeling phantom flames. Even now, sometimes, the heat burned in his dreams. Not as much as it used to.

He took a deep breath and let the truck follow its own way out to the old homestead.

Several minutes later, Mark realized he was sitting in front of the house, his truck idling in park. That happened more often than he liked. He cut the engine and took in the stark reality of the fire's hunger. The property north and west of the house remained charred except for what had greened up this past spring and summer. It had looked hopeful for a couple of months. Now with winter set in, it only looked bleak. The hillside was still pocked with mounds of blackened apple tree limbs—skeletons—and was traced with rows where irrigation pipes, twisted from the heat, had been dug up and hauled away. The acreage sat like a primitive battlefield in the morning mist.

Only forty yards from the house, a large outbuilding had stood for decades. Now, nothing but foundation remained. His dad had started building a new orchard shop, office, and storage building all-in-one where equipment repairs could be made and the workers could eat lunch. They'd selected a plot down the east side near the irrigation pumps. Just in case. His dad hadn't said as much, but Mark knew. The fire department's response couldn't be relied on. Not when half the force were volunteers—good volunteers, sure—because the full-time firefighters were out miles away in all directions, fighting other fires. Moving the outbuilding made sense when their only water came from irrigation pumped from the river or the house well.

The house sat untouched, thankfully. The wind had turned the flames back on themselves, and with no more fuel, the fire had burned out. But only after destroying thousands of acres and a dozen homes in the county alone.

Mark reached for the bag of apple fritters and made his way to the front porch.

"You make those fritters from scratch?"

He looked up and found his dad holding open the front door.

"No," Mark answered.

"Took you long enough. I wondered if Lette Mae put you to

work in the kitchen." Cal Rivers smiled, deep grooves along the sides of his mouth proving he did it a lot. Irritatingly.

Mark pushed the bag at his dad, who took it in the chest, still grinning. "I got 'em and came right back."

He entered the house, and his dad shut the door behind him. The smell of his childhood home filled him like it always did, reminding him of the contentment of a nine-year-old boy running outside to play in the dirt after eating a stack of syrup-drenched pancakes and gulping down a cold glass of milk he'd squeezed from Ol' Maize all by himself.

Dad pulled a fritter from the greasy white bag. "See anybody you know?" He took a large bite on his way to the kitchen table, where two glasses of milk waited next to two plates. Maize had long passed, and so had Mark's milking days.

"It's a small town, Dad. Everybody knows everybody."

His dad waited patiently, brow lifted.

"I saw Lette Mae," Mark answered. "And James Dean."

Dad gave him a look and plunked down onto a chair. "Anyone else?" He pulled out the chair next to his and motioned for Mark to sit.

Every Friday morning, Mark was sent to the bakery for apple fritters and anything else his dad might request. An attempt to get him out of the house, Mark knew, and maybe see a few people. "Nope."

His dad gave him a long look, then nudged the other chair with his foot.

Mark sighed and sat at the table, pulling out a fritter and shoving a third of it in his mouth. "There." He chewed the word. "Happy?"

Dad nodded, still watching him. "You got something there, on your shoulder."

Mark glanced at his shirt. "I don't see anything."

"Hard to miss. Mighty big chip. Right there."

Mark frowned, but his dad leaned back with a look that challenged Mark to respond. Mark just bit into his fritter.

"We're putting up framework today. Ivy's school play is at six."

Mark swallowed his last bite and took a long drink of milk. It had taken a lot of practice to master the task without dribbling down his front. He wiped his mouth with a napkin.

"You're going with me," Dad said.

Mark fought the urge to tell his dad to stop ordering him around. But he knew his dad was the reason he'd come so far in his rehabilitation. If his dad didn't prod him into stuff he was expected to do, Mark wouldn't do it. He wouldn't have done anything. Besides, Ivy had begged him to come, and he couldn't let his niece down.

He nodded and pushed his chair away from the table. "I'll meet you down at the site."

"Thanks for the fritter," Dad said. "Delivery makes 'em taste better."

Mark grunted in reply.

❄ ❄ ❄

Riley Madigan looked over the backdrops and the painted props she and a handful of students from art club had worked on for weeks after school. She reviewed the spreadsheet on her clipboard, mentally checking off the order the props would be used in each scene and when each backdrop would be lifted to reveal the next, hoping the mechanics would all work smoothly. Rehearsals had been hit-and-miss.

She found Yvette Newsome, head of the drama department

and director of *Peter Pan*, helping the four mains check their flight gear—basic theater harnesses for "flying"—as the set of the nursery window was pulled away and the background filled with stars before the curtain dropped. Fairly effective and low-risk as long as everything coordinated properly. At least stunt rehearsals had gone well. Dropping backgrounds was one thing. Dropping kids? Never good.

Yvette spied Riley and dismissed the students. "Hey, just the person I need to talk to."

"Why do I get nervous when you say that?"

Yvette laughed. They'd been working together on the play practically since the day Riley had moved into the tiny orchard community of Miracle Creek. As soon as Riley had been hired as the new art teacher and word got out she was revitalizing the defunct art club, Yvette had spread out her far-reaching wing and pulled her into the frantic carnival ride that was a high school play.

Yvette dragged a foam-and-fiberglass prop toward center stage. She shaded her eyes against the glare of the stage lights and called out, "Can I get the lighting for the Lost Boys scene?" She waved to Riley. "Follow me."

Riley followed her into the auditorium seating.

"Now, what do you see?"

Riley narrowed her gaze. "What is it supposed to be?"

"It's *supposed* to be a rock," Yvette said.

"Well, with this lighting, it looks like a pig."

"Like the *rear end* of a pig."

"I can't un-see it," Riley said. The shadows the students had painted had to have been unintentional, but still. "Is that a tail?"

"I can't have a pig's rear end on my stage, Riley. Wendy sits on this rock."

"What if you turn it around?"

Yvette yelled to one of the kids on stage to turn the prop around.

After a moment, Yvette broke the silence. "Now it looks like a roast turkey." She threw out her arm. "It's too distracting."

"I'll fix it," Riley said. "If I do it now the paint will be dry in time."

"Thanks," Yvette said. "You are the Smee to my Hook. Don't take that the wrong way."

She laughed. "Smee is charming in his own way. I'll take it."

"Hey, who brought the turkey?" a student called from a row of seats. Giggles followed, and the lights on the prop went out.

Riley hurried to the stage. She'd need to move the prop to the art room; no easy task given its awkward shape and size. After enlisting a couple of students to help her, she led the way off stage and down the hall, exchanging the bright hum of the auditorium for the quiet art room.

They set the prop down on a covered table used for painting. "Thanks, guys," she said. "Back to work." They grinned and left.

Riley tilted her head at the rock. "Start at the start." She selected her acrylics and brushes, filled a water jug, and went to work. This rock would look like a rock, no matter the lighting.

❋ ❋ ❋

Mark hung back as the crowds surged forward to congratulate the actors on a successful opening night. He found a dark corner to the right of the stage stairs to wait. From there, he could see his family—his dad, his older sister, Steph, and her husband, Brian, their baby—Mark's namesake—and his seven-year-old niece, Ivy.

He could also see backstage, behind the closed curtains, to the backdrop hanging from the last scene. The play had been entertaining, even with the occasional mistake, but the painted scenery had caught his attention. He wondered if the school had bought the backdrops premade, or if they'd hired someone to do them. He knew of a muralist who did work over in Leavenworth, but the style wasn't his. He wondered if the new art teacher had done them, and if he had the nerve to ask her about them.

"Uncle Mark!"

Only Ivy could make him forget it was difficult to smile. She ran to him, lunging at his waist and squeezing him.

She looked up. "What did you think?"

He pulled out a rose wrapped in cellophane from behind his back. "I think you were the best Tootles ever."

She beamed and took the flower. "Thanks." Her smile faded, and she crinkled her nose. "I forgot a line when Wendy was telling us a story."

"I didn't even notice."

Her smile returned.

"Are you ready to do it again tomorrow?" he asked.

Her eyes grew round. "Oh yeah! We do it again!" She nodded. "Maybe I'll remember my line tomorrow."

"I bet you will," he said.

She leaned against his side, smelling her flower.

The rest of the family approached, and his dark corner grew suffocating. He moved along the wall toward the auditorium to create more space.

"Thanks for coming, Mark. You know how much it means to Ivy." His sister, Steph, pulled the little girl into an embrace.

Mark nodded, keeping one eye on the crowd of people drawing nearer. "Wouldn't miss it." He pulled at the hood on his jacket.

Brian ruffled Ivy's hair. "That's a pretty rose."

"Uncle Mark gave it to me." Ivy turned. "He's coming tomorrow to watch me remember my line."

Steph looked at him, surprised. "You're coming tomorrow, too?"

"Uh . . . I didn't—" Mark hadn't planned on coming again. It'd been hard enough to face the crowds tonight. He caught Ivy's hopeful expression and released a breath. "Yeah, I'm coming." He poked Ivy in the shoulder. "You better get that line, or else."

"Or else what?" Her eyes danced.

"Or else . . ." His voice became menacing. "Or else Captain Hook will be the least of your worries." He made a pretend grab for her.

She squealed and shrank back into her mom, smiling at him. He caught his sister's eye.

"What?" he asked.

"Nothing." She smiled. "It's good to see you."

Mark sobered.

He glanced at his dad, who shrugged. "I see you all the time."

Mark rolled his eyes.

A group of people began making their way between Mark and his family, heading toward the exit. He pressed back against the wall, dropping his head, watching his feet, only nodding when people addressed him.

"Hey, Mark."

"Hi, Mark."

"Nice to see you out, Rivers."

They shuffled past.

"Good to see you, Mark."

His head came up faster than he wanted. He quickly adjusted the angle of his face so the right half was shadowed by his hood.

Caylin Clark blinked at him uncertainly. Some guy stood next to her, his arm around her waist.

"H-Hey," Mark said, hating how his voice halted.

"I saw you from across the auditorium and thought I'd say hi." Caylin turned to his suddenly reserved family. "Hello."

They muttered hellos back.

She turned to Mark, and when he didn't say anything, she shook her head. "I'm sorry, this is Nick. His cousin was Peter Pan."

Nick nodded. "Good to meet you. Caylin told me what you did, saving those kids. That's really cool, man."

Mark never knew how to respond to stuff like that. That day in the fires hadn't been cool. It had been a nightmare.

Nick glanced between him and Caylin. "Well, take it easy." He whispered something in Caylin's ear and left.

Caylin turned back to Mark. "So, what's it been—a year?"

A year and four months, Mark thought. She'd stuck around a whole two months after he'd landed in the hospital.

"Well," she continued, as more people shuffled past, "you look great. I mean, really. Look at you. How are you feeling?"

Look at me.

Out of the corner of his eye, he saw his brother-in-law try to pull the others away, but Stephanie shook her head, handing Brian the baby and placing her hands on her hips. His dad stayed where he was.

How am I feeling?

This girl had been his girl. His future. His anchor. Then the fire burned everything down, including her interest in Mark.

"I'm feeling good, thanks." He turned his face from the shadows and saw her flinch, ever so slightly. "You look great, too." It wasn't a lie, with that strawberry-blonde hair falling past her shoulders and blue eyes to go with it. Same pouty lips. He held out his hand, which was covered by a fingerless compression sleeve. Stephanie had suggested he get black so it looked tough. "Don't be a stranger."

She glanced at his hand and hesitated just long enough.

A knot tightened in his chest, and he withdrew his hand. "Still can't touch me?"

Her face reddened. "I didn't mean—"

"What? What exactly did you mean?"

Her mouth set in a line, and she glanced at a few more people who excused themselves as they made their way to the exit.

"Hey, Caylin. Mark." Jeff Cranston mumbled the greetings.

"Hey," Mark replied.

After they passed, Caylin stepped to his side of the wall. "I didn't want to cause you more pain. I couldn't be what you needed. I'm sorry for that."

He gritted his jaw and steadied himself. "Hey, it's history. Everyone got what they wanted in the end, right?"

Her brow furrowed as she deciphered his meaning. Slowly, she nodded. "Right. Well, you're the hero." She turned to his family as if to say more, then, with another uncertain look his way, took her long legs off to find perfectly undisfigured Nick.

"That wasn't very nice," his dad said.

Mark shrugged, hiding the emotion her presence had kicked up, her final words cutting more than he thought they would. "She never was very nice, was she?"

"I wasn't talking about her."

Mark frowned. "Excuse me?"

"C'mon, Ivy," Brian said. "Let's go get your coat and things." He took Ivy's hand and disappeared up the stairs with the baby. Steph stayed put.

"Dad, give him a break," she said. "What was she thinking, coming over here and telling him he looks good?"

"Gee, thanks," Mark said.

She looked at Mark. "You know what I mean. It took all I had not to tell her what she could do with those boots—"

Dad cut her off. "Nothing gives Mark the excuse to use what he's been handed to . . ." He trailed off.

"Hurt someone?" Mark finished for him. "Make them uncomfortable? Ashamed?" He fought to lower his voice as a few people looked their way. He stepped closer. "Like they're not worth the effort?"

Dad folded his arms across his chest. "The word is *intimidate*. And no. Never. Do you feel any better?"

Mark didn't have to replay the look of aversion on Caylin's face. He felt like he'd been kicked in the gut twice over. He was over her. She'd just made an easy target for the anger that still roiled up inside him on occasion. And no, he didn't feel better. Bugs on a windshield felt better than he did.

"If you ask me, she had it coming," Steph said.

Mark and his dad turned to her.

"What?" she asked, wide-eyed. "Sure, he could've taken it on the chin, helped her feel good about her magnanimous journey all the way across the auditorium. But our boy's got some fight. I, for one, am happy to see it."

Dad sighed.

Steph reached for Mark's arm. "Forget her. She's not worth a fraction of you."

He lifted his gaze, the right side of his face to the shadows. "I bet you say that to all the burn victims."

"Only the heroic ones."

Mark remembered his time in the burn unit. "That's all of them."

❋ ❋ ❋

Later at the house, Mark pulled an envelope from the pile of bills on the front table and retreated to his old room. After leaving the hospital, he'd moved out of the apartment he shared with Jay in Wenatchee and back home to focus on his recovery. Twenty-seven years old and living at home. He was waiting for a sign that it was time to move out, but he couldn't bring himself to look for an apartment—or a roommate. Besides, his dad needed his help with the property. It was a big house for just one man; it was a big house for two.

He clicked on the desk lamp with a flick of his finger. He opened the envelope and pulled out the contents. Smoothing out the paper, he saw a boldly scrawled picture of a man in a yellow shirt and hat holding a small boy on his hand like a tray of dishes. Around them, a giant red fire loomed with tiny scary faces drawn on each flame. Above the figures in blue crayon it read, "Firefighter Mark saved me from the fire."

Mark pulled out a shoebox from the top shelf in his closet. He added the picture to the nearly full box and put it away. He brushed his teeth and undressed for bed. After sitting for some time with his head in his hands, he pulled himself up, twisted the lid off his skin cream, and began the necessary ritual of tending his scars.

❋ ❋ ❋

Riley shut the front door of her new-old house and locked it. She'd been lucky to even find a house in this tiny town, let alone one on this avenue with its small but stately old homes. The house was definitely "historical," complete with a solid oak front door and a real glass doorknob that occasionally fell off on the outside. She'd have to get a dead bolt for better security, though she suspected she was the only person on her street who bothered with locks. Miracle Creek seemed to be stuck in a past decade, and she liked it that way.

Unlike other homes on the block, Riley's house hadn't been kept up, languishing for years on the market. Her parents had been skeptical, but she knew what she was doing. She'd gotten a great deal on the house, and her family had renovated a few fixer-uppers before. Plus, she'd studied the real estate market in Washington. The location might have been rustic, but being surrounded by national forests, skiing, and just a few miles from the alpine destination village of Leavenworth reflected in property values. Riley was sure she could make a profit, whether she stayed here long-term or not.

She shivered and rubbed her arms. The old place needed a lot of work. The previous owner had considered getting new vinyl windows retrofitted to replace the drafty originals but had hesitated because "they just didn't make dimpled glass like that anymore." She had to agree; they did not.

As charming as the original windows were, winter had come to the Cascade Mountains, and she was going to have to get some of those plastic insulation kits from the hardware store to cover up the dimpled glass. She had a lot of things in her skill set, but changing out hundred-year-old windows was not one of them. She'd have to hire someone to update the windows. In the meantime, she'd wear more sweaters.

That feeling returned—the one that had her questioning her decision to take this teaching job in a tiny town in the middle of a state she barely knew and buying this old house when she wasn't even sure she wanted to stay.

You know exactly why you left. You're right where you need to be. Maybe. For now.

She rolled her eyes at her stalwart resolve as she removed her coat and hung it up in the closet. She checked the thermostat. At least she had central heat, though a few more inches of insulation in the attic wouldn't hurt.

The play had exhausted her, and nothing sounded better than sleep. She turned, and the house across the street caught her attention through her big front window. Innumerable Christmas lights had blinked on, covering not only the house but the detached garage, picket fence, several trees, shrubs, and—Riley narrowed her eyes—the mailbox? She crossed the room. Mr. Taggart waved at her from his driveway and gestured toward his house.

She waved back and gave him two thumbs up. He seemed to appreciate that, even as she closed her curtains.

"It was just Halloween," she murmured. "I don't even *own* Christmas lights."

Her gaze roamed over her own space. She'd decorated sparsely, but the things she owned she loved: the old maple rolltop desk with someone's initials carved on the inside, three small canvas paintings she'd left frameless, and a green velvet couch she'd grabbed from an estate sale in Cashmere. She'd found the dinette set in the kitchen at an antique store in the valley. Her rocker, of course. All a little dinged up but solid and, she thought, perfectly aesthetic. Add her equally simple bedroom furniture and kitchen things, and the art stuff she kept in the second bedroom, and she could pack up and move in a day. Maybe two. If she decided to rent out the house, the furnishings she'd leave behind were charming and inexpensive. A great combination. And so different from the sleek, modern style she'd been heading toward in Studio City. Different, but more *her*. Like a favorite pair of jeans and a comfy sweater after a long day.

To be honest, Riley wasn't sure how long she'd be here. Thinking of the future made her uneasy. Like standing at the top of a waterslide and trusting there was a pool on the other side of the turns and tunnels.

Nobody in California had heard of Miracle Creek or Wenatchee Valley. Which was perfect. Start at the start.

Maybe after putting enough work, enough of herself, into something like this house, she'd have more of a reason to keep it. Or not. But the option would be there.

She sighed. She liked Miracle Creek. She'd rarely lived in one place for more than a year, and she'd liked a lot of the places her nomadic upbringing and schooling had taken her. And she'd liked Studio City, working with her dad in Hollywood. Her parents had even been getting along, but then, after a string of dead-end relationships, she'd made the mistake of giving her heart away and allowing herself to believe love could be different.

She'd been wrong.

Miracle Creek was where she could nurse her wounds in obscurity, teaching at little Mt. Stuart K-12 where nobody had ever heard of her and nobody cared.

She appreciated the job. Art departments were already obsolete in elementary schools, and more were being cut out of middle and high school curriculums—along with home ec, woodshop, and orchestra. Art had been her favorite class in second grade, and yet now it was possible to find kids who had never been in an industrial, hodgepodge, color-chaos, clay-and-turpentine-smelling art classroom. But it was what Riley loved, and of all the things she'd left behind, she loved returning to this. She'd missed having a classroom and students. Her classes at Mt. Stuart were small, and her art room felt timeless. And she couldn't deny, between the busyness of the school play, her classwork, and the town's absolute non-Hollywood atmosphere, she'd done some forgetting and some healing in the last few months.

Maybe she'd stick it out and find a bit of peace in Miracle Creek, Washington.

Apprehension bloomed in her chest as it did whenever she thought about settling down.

A knock at the door broke her from her thoughts.

She opened it to see the entirety of her student art club—all four of them.

"Hey, Ms. Madigan," Justice said. "We were making cookies, and we thought you'd like some." She held out a paper plate covered in plastic wrap.

Riley spied chocolate chips as she took the warm plate. It had been hours since she'd eaten. "Thanks for thinking of me."

"Thanks for bringing back art club," Holly said.

"My pleasure. You guys have been a great help."

"We messed up the trees," Paulo said, nudging Jack.

She smiled. "Oh, I'm sure somebody somewhere has successfully grown a palm tree in London. Besides, we have tomorrow to get it right. Right?"

They nodded and waved goodbye.

Riley watched them walk down the street. Two more houses turned on their Christmas lights, and her mouth dropped open. Seriously?

She peeled back the plastic wrap and bit into a cookie, peering at her own eaves and wondering if a wreath on the door would be sufficient enough decoration.

Chapter 2

Mark pounded nails into the framework of the new out-building. Trusses were going up Monday, and they needed to be ready. He paused and wiped his forehead. They had a nail gun, but Dad had made Mark do it by hand to build up strength and coordination. It had been painfully slow going at first. A few swear words had been shouted, and the hammer had been dropped—or thrown—more than a few times, but eventually, Mark had been able to pick up his speed and accuracy.

He'd spent most of the day focused on the work in front of him, but just now, sitting up on the frame, listening to the sound of his dad's electric screwdriver and overlooking the gentle slope to the trees, their various shades of fading orange, yellow, and red, and the mountains climbing in the background under a pink sky . . . He breathed in the fresh orchard air and drank in the last of the colors.

The apple trees to the south had produced like mad this season. Harvest was over, but remains of dropped fruit—those the deer hadn't eaten yet—tinged the air with a tangy sweetness he'd known his whole life. That, mixed with crisp mountain pine, was the smell of winter coming to Miracle Creek. He closed his eyes, and his nose picked up the faint scent of woodsmoke. His gut lurched, an automatic response to the warning and a call to danger. His pulse raced to fight-or-flight mode.

He scanned the area but saw no definite signs, no billowing black clouds or even thin traces. *It's a woodstove. Everyone has a woodstove. They'll be used all winter. Get used to it.* His senses, on high alert, finally listened to his logic, and backed off.

Prying his hand from the frame, he wiped sweat from his brow.

"You okay up there?" His dad was moving the ladder under him.

"I'm okay."

"Liar. Get down here before you fall."

"I won't fall." He picked up the hammer and tried placing a nail. "I was just taking a break." His fingers shook, and he hesitated.

His dad took off his ball cap and rubbed his head. "Mark, please come down."

If his dad had said it any other way, Mark would have argued. But when Cal Rivers spoke with patience and fatigue in his voice, Mark had to obey.

Once on the ground, he sat on a ladder rung and watched the concrete. "I'm fine, Dad. I just . . . smelled smoke." He hated to admit that. It was the tail end of autumn. People burned their rubbish piles and woodstoves and backyard firepits.

"Ah, son." Mark felt his dad's hand heavy on his shoulder, keeping him from blowing away like a leaf.

"Caught me off guard." He shrugged. "I spent most of last winter inside." He'd been in and out of hospitals and clinics with skin grafts, reconstruction, and recovery.

Dad nodded. "Do you need to call the doc?"

"No." He knew what his therapist would say. *Did you do your exercises?* Yes. *Did you place the emotions in their proper box?* Eventually. *What do you need to change to make it better?*

"I'm going to smell smoke out here. Next time I'll be able to sort it out faster."

His dad watched him a moment, then seemed to accept his answer. He looked up at the framework. "Okay. Good plan. Let's stop for today."

"We don't have to stop just because I lost it up there for a minute."

"We're stopping because I'm starving, and it's your turn to make dinner. We gotta eat before Ivy's play." He started to walk toward the house. His dad always walked back to the house, even if they'd driven the truck there.

"But we've got a lot to do before the trusses come on Monday."

His dad turned, walking backward and pulling off his work gloves. "Then I guess we get up extra early in the morning." He grinned. "Your favorite. Meet you at the house."

Mark sighed and pulled off his gloves. When they'd had Maize and a couple other cows, Mark and Steph had to milk morning and night. His dad's definition of "extra early" was ungodly. They'd be working by the light of construction lamps before the neighbor's rooster crowed.

All because he couldn't keep it together when he smelled a little smoke.

He put away the tools and got the site ready for morning, then climbed into his truck and drove up to the house, beating his dad by a couple of minutes.

Ham sandwiches and canned soup made up dinner. The men

ate steadily without many words. When they finished, his dad pulled out a ledger while Mark cleaned up the dishes.

"What're you looking at?" he asked.

"The last of what we lost in the outbuilding. Just going over it for the insurance company so they can wrap this up."

Dad had that same masked look on his face he always got when they discussed the loss from the fire. Half the stuff in the storage building had been equipment, tools, and machinery, easily replaced by insurance. But the other half had been memories. Boxes of baby things, stuff from Stephanie's wedding, his parents' old photos and keepsakes, holiday decorations, and, of course, nearly all of Mom's original oil paintings. Some had stayed in the house, thank goodness, but the rest had been carefully stored, waiting to be treasured by future kids and grandkids. Steph was still sick that she hadn't picked up the paintings when she and Brian got their house. It had been on her to-do list. Now they were gone.

And then there was the nativity.

Dad suddenly shut the ledger and rubbed his eyes. "I'm going to lie down for a minute before we leave." He pushed back from the table and left without another word, walking with an age he rarely showed.

Mark pulled the ledger over and opened it up. There in his dad's neat, blocky handwriting were lists of items and their estimated values. Some had check marks next to them, some didn't. The list was made up of orchard equipment and machinery. Then irrigation stuff. He turned the page. More business items already compensated for.

His dad had dealt with all this without him.

Then his finger stopped on the opposite page.

Leah's Paintings:
Sunflowers
Barn
Old Oak
Apple Blossoms
Mt. Stuart

The list went on. He'd catalogued all of her paintings by name. Mark could picture many of them, but his dad had known them all.

Mark ran his finger farther down the page and stopped again.

Leah's Nativity:
Mary
Joseph
Baby Jesus in Manger
Star
Shepherd with 2 Sheep

Mark noticed the monetary value column on the page was empty. How did you put a price on something priceless? The insurance company probably had some method to put a base value to a painting, but Mark knew his dad. The column was blank because base value didn't matter when it came to the nativity. All that mattered was that it was gone.

Last Christmas was a blur for Mark. Even now all he remembered were lights and some music. Cards that Steph or his dad had read to him. Pictures Ivy drew. He hadn't considered it would have been the first Christmas without the decorations that allowed them to include Mom in their holidays.

It hadn't even crossed his mind until now.

He closed the ledger. Dad had been there for him almost every minute. Even when he was pushing Mark out of the house and into social situations, no matter how agitating, he did it for Mark. And Mark wanted to repay him in some way.

He glanced at the time. They'd be leaving for the school in a few minutes. Anxiety raised its head, and Mark told himself that he'd done this before. He could do it again. He'd enjoyed the play. He pictured Ivy grinning in her Lost Boys costume. Breathing a little easier, he remembered the painted backdrops for the school play, and it occurred to him why he was drawn to them.

They were familiar.

The final performance had gone well, minus the last-minute hang-up, literally, with Wendy's harness. Backstage was bustling with the stage crew and their families, and a few actors who hadn't left for the after-party. The janitors were cleaning the back of the auditorium, working their way down to the stage.

Riley studied the backdrop she'd painted of the Darling nursery. Though she'd loved how the London night skyline, Neverland forest, and the pirate ship backdrops had turned out, this was her favorite. She'd researched toys and furnishings from the Edwardian era and reproduced them for the Darling children as though they'd been well-played with, wanting to make this a place where magic happened.

Movement in the shadows caught her eye. To her left in the darkness of the wings, a hooded figure leaned against the far wall. He seemed to be watching her, but she could be mistaken. She glanced at him, and he straightened, looked in both directions, and took a few steps toward her.

Riley's pulse quickened with concern while telling herself she was overreacting. This wasn't Santa Monica.

"You coming to the after-party?"

Riley jumped and turned as Yvette padded toward her, shoes in one hand and a large satchel on her shoulder.

"My treat. Well, the school's treat." Yvette paused and gazed over Riley's shoulder. "Well, what do you know?" she said quietly. "He ventured out."

"Who?" Riley looked behind her, hoping that whatever unease she'd felt at the stranger's attention could be explained.

But the stranger was leaving, slipping out the exit door into the night.

"Who was that?" Riley asked.

"A local hero. Mark Rivers. Good for him."

Riley busied herself checking her bag, making sure she had everything. "Why good for him?"

"Oh, he's a bit of a recluse." Yvette pressed her lips in a smile. "I'm glad he came. Hope it made him happy."

Riley paused, wondering what a recluse would want with her.

"Earth to Riley." Yvette snapped her fingers and adjusted the strap of her bursting bag. Tonight, Riley knew, it held a makeup kit, a first aid kit, a sewing kit, a hairdo kit, duct tape, a screwdriver, and a stapler. "Come on. Get your things. We'll get this cleaned up tomorrow."

Yvette dropped her shoes on the floor and wriggled her feet inside each one as Riley collected her coat and bag. She couldn't help but glance at the exit door where the "hero" had lurked and—if she wasn't mistaken—had almost approached her.

Yvette motioned to the backdrop. "Best we've ever had. I had a teacher tell me once that the best sets draw the audience to the stage and then fade into the environment of their new reality. Tonight, you gave us that."

Riley smiled. "You're just saying that so I'll share my onion rings with you."

"Whatever works." Yvette winked.

They left the building, and Riley strode across the nearly empty parking lot to her car, arms full of her own backstage emergency tote and a bouquet of roses the kids had given her during bows. She called out to Yvette. "I'm going to drop my stuff at my house first. See you at the restaurant."

Yvette gave her a thumbs-up and climbed into her own car.

After Riley stowed her stash in the trunk, she came around to the front of the car. She'd parked along the edge of the lot, and across the street from her, a truck idled with its lights on. By the streetlamps, she spied the hooded figure watching her from inside the vehicle. After a moment, he pulled away.

A shiver ran through her. She got in her car, glancing around. She'd never felt like she was in danger in this small mountain town, but her adrenaline kept her alert all the way back to her house. Hero or not, if this person had become a recluse, who knew what could be going through his head.

Mark shook his head, furious with himself. Here he sat, three homes up from the art teacher's house, away from the nearest streetlamp and the Taggarts' annual Christmas lights spectacular, watching like a . . . like a stalker. He'd heard her say she was going home before heading to the restaurant, and he'd been stupid enough to think that he'd be able to work up the nerve to ask what he wanted to ask by the time she came out of her house. But he hadn't left his truck yet or even parked in front of her house, which would be the normal thing to do if someone simply wanted to catch a person and ask them a question.

He huffed out a breath and looked away. Why was this so hard?

He rubbed his jaw where the skin often felt tight, then ran his hand against the rest of the right side of his face, feeling the map of scars.

That was why.

"Phones," he mumbled. "This is why we have phones."

He shook his head at himself again, determined to find her number and call her tomorrow.

A knock on his window nearly sent him through the roof. "What the—?"

And there she was, the art teacher, holding a baseball bat like she knew how to swing it. Hard.

"No!" He rolled down his window. The cold night air rushed in. "No, no, no, no, please." He held his hands up like she was aiming a gun. "Please don't hit my truck."

"I'm not looking at the truck," she said without blinking, her breath puffing in the cold. "Why are you following me?"

He felt heat creep up his face. "I—I didn't mean to follow you. I'm not—I mean I don't usually—" He took a deep breath and let it out. "Look, I know it seems like I was following you, but I was just . . . getting up the nerve to ask you about something and it's been a while since I've spoken . . . to people. At all."

She shifted her weight but kept the bat ready to swing. "Who are you?"

"Mark Rivers."

She narrowed her eyes and shifted her stance again.

"My family owns Rivers Orchards. I was at the play—at the school—the school play—and I wanted to ask you . . ." He hesitated again.

She waited, seeming to mull that over. "Yes?"

He straightened his shoulders and gathered himself. "Principal

Grant told me you painted the backdrops, and I wanted to ask if you'd be interested in painting something for me. For Christmas."

Her grip relaxed on the bat, but she didn't lower it. "So you followed me to my house and waited in the dark? Have you heard of doorbells? Or phones?"

He closed his eyes, his hands still in the air. "I was just reminding myself of phones when you knocked on my window." He eyed her bat. "Look, I'm not a bad guy. Just . . . forget it. I've clearly made a mess of this."

He lowered his hands to put the truck in gear, and she tightened her grip, pulling the bat back as if to swing.

He lifted his hands again. "Whoa, wait a minute. I'm leaving."

"How do I know you don't have a gun down there?"

He frowned. "Really? You think I might have a *gun*, and you come at me with a baseball bat?"

He could see the foolishness of the situation hit her. But he'd been just as stupid. Even more so.

"Listen," he said. "I don't have a gun. I'm a firefighter. If anything, I'm going to have an ax. Isn't that what firefighters have? An ax and a dalmatian?" His weak attempt at humor didn't seem to make a difference. He kept his hands where she could see them and huffed out a laugh at the idiocy of the situation. "Look, you want to know if I have a weapon down here? You're going to have to come and check for yourself."

She blinked, and he thought he saw her biting back a smile—or maybe it was rage—when the blip of a siren sounded and red-and-blue flashing lights bounced off his rearview and side mirrors. They both shaded their eyes, and she finally lowered her weapon.

"You called the cops?" he asked.

"No," she said. "Though that probably would've been the smarter thing to do."

He groaned, pulled his hood off, and leaned back against the headrest as the crunch of boots approached the truck. A flashlight shined first at her, then at him.

"Hey, Mark."

"Hey, Lester," Mark answered.

"Ma'am."

The art teacher nodded.

"Could you drop the bat please?"

She did. "What about him?" she asked, tipping her head at Mark. "He said he had an ax."

"I did not," Mark countered. "I said if I *had* something it would be an ax."

Lester looked between them. "Is there a problem here?"

They both started talking at the same time, and Les put his hand up, quieting them both. "We got a call from a neighbor about a possible assault with a baseball bat—"

"I *thought* he was—" she began.

Les held up his hand again. "And a call from another neighbor worried about a possible stalker or burglar, and I quote, 'casing the joint.' Although he said he thought it was your truck, Mark, and wondered if you'd reported it stolen."

Mark sighed. He looked sideways at Les, who motioned toward the houses. Several neighbors had gathered on their front porches, huddled in small groups, trying to be inconspicuous in the glare of their porch lights.

"Great," Mark said.

"You want to tell me what's going on? Ma'am, your name?"

"Riley Madigan." She flicked her gaze toward Mark.

"Ms. Madigan, if you'll go first, please?"

Riley rubbed her forehead. "I saw him in the stage wings at the high school, watching me after the play, and then again in the parking lot. But he took off both times. So I was careful driving home, and when I saw him park here after I went into the house, I got my bat and . . . I thought he might be planning to attack me . . . or something."

Mark ran his hand over his face and deflated into the seat. "You will never know how sorry I am that I gave you that impression, but anyone who knows me—*anyone*—Les, tell her I would never—"

Les held up his hand again. He turned to her. "You thought he might be an attacker, so you came out to his truck with a bat?"

She stared at him. "Have you ever been a single woman living alone in a big city?"

"No," Les said with sympathy. "I can't say that I have."

She shrugged. "Some of us sleep with guns under our beds, some of us have bats."

Les nodded. "Fair enough."

What had Mark been thinking? He hadn't. Just like with his dad. He'd been living the last couple of years in a self-centered bubble.

"What do you have to say, Mark?"

Mark rubbed his hand over his mouth. Then he leaned toward Les, speaking quietly. "You remember Mom's nativity?"

Les nodded. "Of course."

"It was lost in the fire."

He frowned. "I know. I was sorry to hear that."

Mark nodded and glanced at the teacher, who frowned too, but in an angrier sort of way. He focused on Les.

"I was getting up the nerve to ask the art teacher here if she

29

would consider painting a new set. I was thinking of surprising Dad with it."

Les smiled. "Oh, hey, that's a great idea." He looked hopefully at Ms. Madigan, but when she didn't smile back, he sobered again. "So why didn't you just call her?"

"That's what I asked him," Riley said, glaring at him.

Mark gritted his teeth. "I swear, on my mother's grave, I would never think of harming you."

She studied him, and he was grateful she could only see the left side of his face.

"Ms. Madigan, can I have a word with you, please?" Les motioned toward his unit.

She nodded and followed him. Mark watched them in the side mirror, stewing over what a mess he'd made. And now Les was probably telling her Mark's sob story and how pathetic he was and to show a little mercy. She stood—all 5'4" of her—arms wrapped around her torso in an attempt to stay warm, glancing Mark's way. Finally, she shook her head, and as Les left her and approached the truck, she turned away.

Les rested his arm on Mark's window frame. "Well, she's not pressing charges."

Mark swallowed, considering for the first time that that was even an option.

"You understand why she thought what she thought, right?"

Mark nodded, fully ashamed.

"She's pretty shook up. I'd give her space if I were you. Just until things settle down."

Mark pressed his lips together in a line. "That shouldn't be a problem." He wanted nothing more than to head home and lock himself inside. "But she believes me about never hurting anyone, right?"

Les nodded thoughtfully. "I think so. Most likely your reputation will eventually change any ideas she has about you."

"You mean the one about being a deformed, unhinged recluse?" Mark grumbled.

Les furrowed his brow and looked him in the eye. "I mean the one that you're a hero." His words were measured and filled with conviction. "You saved those boys' lives."

Mark looked away.

"Like it or not, that's what people say about you." He sighed. "Gotta be tough, though, all that admiration." He waited for Mark to respond.

Mark didn't.

"Okay. Well, you're free to go. Tell your dad hello. And again, I'm sorry about your mom's nativity. That was a county treasure. Come to think of it, so was your mom." He glanced Riley Madigan's way. "Maybe she'll still consider it."

Mark huffed.

"You never know," Les said, backing away from the truck. "Miracles happen."

It took Mark a moment to realize Les was waiting for him to leave and would stand there until he did. He looked back at the art teacher, and she returned his gaze. He gave her a quick but sincere nod, shifted the truck into gear, and pulled into the street, driving past the neighbors still standing on their porches. Roger and Beth Simons waved enthusiastically. Mark couldn't help raising his hand in return. Everybody knew everybody in this town.

The kids had chosen the '59er Diner in Cashmere for their after-party. There weren't any actual restaurants in Miracle Creek, just the Grill-n-Go drive-thru, the bakery, and a bar called Jake's.

Riley almost hadn't come, but after all their hard work—and the evening's events—she would at least have a milkshake. On the school's tab.

Hit with the fortifying smell of onion rings, Riley slid into a vintage red vinyl booth across from Yvette. Most of the kids had eaten. A few greeted her with enthusiasm, wired from the success of the performance, sodas, and ice cream.

"You made it. Here." Yvette pushed a menu at Riley, who glanced over it half-heartedly. She motioned a waitress over.

"Can you mix milkshake flavors?"

"Yes, ma'am."

"I'll have onion rings and a peanut butter, marshmallow, hot fudge milkshake."

"Anything else?"

"I'll let you know."

"That was decisive," Yvette said after the waitress left.

"It called to me."

Yvette smiled.

Riley tried to relax into the atmosphere of the '50s-style diner, complete with black-and-white checkered floor, posters of Marilyn, Frank, and Doris on the aqua-blue walls, a jukebox, and a life-sized statue of Elvis standing in the corner. But Riley's mind was replaying her evening so far. Not in a good way.

When her food came, Riley started with the milkshake.

"Hittin' it hard tonight, huh?" Yvette ventured.

She swallowed and pinched the bridge of her nose as the brain freeze struck. "I just did something horrifying and humiliating at the same time."

"What happened?"

Riley shook her head, hesitant to share anything. Finally,

she leaned heavily on her fist. "What do you know about Mark Rivers? The man we saw tonight after the play?"

"Why do you ask?"

Yvette wasn't a gossip, and Riley respected her for that. She wouldn't share anything Riley didn't need to know, but she would give her the truth.

"He followed me to my house tonight and scared the heck out of me."

"After the play? But why would he do that? I mean, I can understand being scared, I guess. It's a little startling at first. But what did he want?"

Riley paused. "What do you mean you can understand being scared? Has he followed you home?"

Yvette covered her mouth. "Oh, heavens, no, I didn't mean that. I'm just saying that it doesn't sound like something Mark would do. Are you okay?"

Riley couldn't help the twinge of anger growing in her gut. "I'm fine. But what if I wasn't? What if something had happened and he'd done something? Is this the kind of town that holds their *heroes*"—she made finger quotes—"so high they're immediately exonerated of all guilt?"

Yvette frowned, watching her. "What exactly happened?"

Riley covered her eyes. "It's all so lame." She told her the story, and as she did, she became sure of the stupidity of it all.

"I guess he wanted to ask me to paint him something for Christmas, and for some reason that was difficult for him. And I, obviously, misunderstood. I'm a single woman living on my own. I had to think like that in LA, Denver. Anywhere." She picked up an onion ring, but then set it down. "Am I that unapproachable?"

"Maybe with a baseball bat in your hands," Yvette suggested.

Riley smiled at her.

Yvette sighed. "Honestly, that doesn't sound like Mark Rivers. At least the old Mark. Good family. Good kid. Top of everything. So much going for him and a smile that stole hearts in a second." She paused. "He's been through a lot. I'm not saying you had no reason to be concerned. His actions were . . . odd. But truly, I'm not putting him on some heroic pedestal. He's kept to himself after those horrible fires. Considering his situation, I'm not at all surprised he has trouble approaching anyone. Especially a woman like you."

Riley raised her brow. "Like me?"

"Oh, don't tell me you haven't noticed the number of eligible males in this county turning their heads your way. That thick black hair of yours and big green eyes."

Great, just what Riley wanted to hear. Not the compliment to her hair, but that "eligible males" part. Yvette was divorced. And Riley knew her friend would be happy to settle down with an eligible male again. "Settling down," however, was not in Riley's scope at all. Not after what happened in LA.

"And you're smart but unpretentious," Yvette continued, "all jeans and big sweaters over a rockin' figure, kickin' around in your Chucks. This is a small town, Riley. You're new and noticeable. Speaking of which—my son will be home from his deployment in six months, you know. He can't be more than three years younger than you." She winked.

Riley chuckled. "Great. And congratulations."

Yvette grinned.

Riley drew her arm around the middle of her "rockin'" figure. Her mother called it "shapely." Riley called it "can I please find a pair of jeans to fit my hips *and* my waistline?" Her father—well, her father photographed movie stars.

"If I'm so approachable then why would Mark Rivers have a

problem talking to me? He doesn't seem to be short on looks or brains—aside from the stalking thing. In fact, for a moment there I thought he might be . . ."

"What?"

"Well, flirting with me. I didn't know whether to smile or swing." She shook her head. "It was dark, and tensions were high."

Yvette seemed to choose her words carefully. "Mark was in a serious accident a while back. He saved lives, but he was critically injured and another firefighter—his best friend—died. And while he was fighting fires miles away, his family orchard here was nearly lost. It struck him down for sure. He's barely begun making appearances in town. If he was trying to get up the nerve to ask you for something—in person—well, that's a big deal."

Riley stared at her shake, this new information weaving its way into the old. Weaving its way around the guy in the truck. It explained a lot.

Yvette took one of Riley's onion rings. "No one will blame you for being extra vigilant. Especially at night in a new place, even in our very small town. The world is what it is." She dipped the ring in ketchup. "All I'm saying is that you need to make up your own mind about Mark Rivers."

Riley stared at the wall of vintage album covers, replaying the evening's events in her head through a new lens.

After a contented sigh that only eating a good onion ring could evoke, Yvette pushed the basket closer to her. "Here. You need these."

Riley didn't argue.

Chapter 3

Mark drove down the dirt road to the new outbuilding site in the dark hours of the morning in a frustrated stupor. He'd barely slept. Next to him, his dad pointed out potholes—each one too late—and remarked on the good ol' days.

"Being up this early kinda makes you wish you had a cow to milk."

Mark threw his dad a dubious look and hit another pothole. The truck rocked.

"Good gracious, son, you trying to break some sort of record?"

"Maybe if you put in a decent road, I wouldn't have to treat this stretch like a godforsaken minefield." He swerved, barely missing another dip. "It's dark out," he added.

"I hadn't noticed," his dad replied. "You want this road improved, you do it. Great idea. You can start as soon as the outbuilding's done."

Mark kept his grumbling to himself. It wouldn't do any good. He pulled into the clearing and parked, his headlights shining on the site. He'd have to keep them on until the construction lights were plugged in. Soon they'd have motion-sensitive floodlights on the building. But first they had to put up walls and a roof.

Mark hadn't told his dad about his run-in with the art teacher. When he'd asked why Mark was home later than expected, he'd just said he'd gone for a drive. Now, after going over and over in his head what he should have done differently, he knew he couldn't talk to his dad even if he wanted to. The nativity, if it were to happen, had to be a surprise. Mark hadn't thrown the idea away. Yet.

Something about the way Riley Madigan had looked at him during their confrontation had struck Mark. The street had been dark, and she probably hadn't seen him clearly in the truck. But still, she hadn't flinched, or worse, looked at him like he was an injured puppy. She'd just held her bat and dared him to move.

He couldn't help the smile that came to the corner of his mouth.

"You okay?" his dad asked.

Mark rubbed his eyes. "No. Man wasn't made to work before sunup."

His dad positioned a construction lamp and flipped it on.

"Gah." Mark turned, blinking in the sudden brightness.

"Behold," his dad said. "The sun."

"Nice," Mark said, pulling on his gloves. He went to turn his truck lights off, pulling his coat collar a little higher. Even with his hood pulled over his beanie, the chill crept in.

"So, Lester called last night," his dad said.

Mark stopped. "Yeah?" he asked without turning around.

"Yep. Wanted to make sure you got home okay."

Since when was Lester Healy his babysitter? Mark waited, measuring how much more to ask. A few moments ticked by. "Anything else?"

"Not really."

Mark allowed his shoulders to relax.

"Who's Riley Madigan?"

Mark froze again. "Uh, I don't know." That was the truth, sort of. He didn't know her at all.

"Hmm. Lester says there was a misunderstanding between the two of you."

"Is that right?" He reached into his truck and turned off the ignition.

"Yep."

Mark picked up his tool belt and a box of nails. "Anything else?" He didn't want to give anything away if Lester had kept things to a minimum. When he'd mentioned the nativity to Les, he'd specifically said it was meant to be a surprise. But more than that, he didn't want his dad to know what an idiot he'd made of himself.

"No. And maybe it's none of my business."

Mark cinched his belt on his hips and climbed the ladder to the spot where he'd been working the afternoon before. "Maybe." He'd become really good at this game. If he didn't want to answer, he didn't have to. "It was just a misunderstanding. Mistaken identity."

"She thought you were someone else?"

Mark considered that option. "Yep." Riley Madigan had thought he was a stalker. "It's fine."

"Okay." His dad left it alone, and Mark finally focused on the work and keeping his hands warm in the morning chill.

"Nice for you to be talking to a woman, though."

Mark just about hit his fingers with the hammer. "Dad. Knock it off."

"I hope you were nice. Les said she's new in town. Single. Smart. Is she good-looking?"

Mark scowled. Like that even mattered anymore. "She's a teacher, and she looked strong." He hadn't been able to keep from stealing glances at the fierceness in her eyes. When he wasn't watching the bat.

"Bodybuilder, eh?"

Mark laughed outright. "*Dad*. Let me work."

❄ ❄ ❄

Friday morning, Mark stood in the back of the bakery, hands shoved into his coat pockets, waiting to order his fritters. The temperature had dropped, and the forecast was teasing the idea of snow, but the bakery was warm and full of people. Still, Mark kept the hood of his sweatshirt up. The counter was on the right side of the bakery, so his right side faced the door and anybody coming in. He didn't like startling people.

"Uncle Mark, why is it taking so long?" Ivy asked, pulling on his elbow, waving their ticket in the air.

"Because they like to make little kids wait," he teased. "If you'd stayed home, I'd have our order by now."

She looked skeptical. "I'm not little."

"Little enough for me to do this." He scooped her up over his shoulder like a sack of potatoes, Ivy squealing with giggles.

"Put me down," she said.

"What's the magic word?"

"Please."

"Nope."

Whenever Ivy was home from school for a teacher prep day, he took her along to get fritters. Ivy made everything easier.

"Donuts," she tried again.

"Nope."

The bell jingled on the front door, and he felt the too-familiar sensation of being stared at.

"Pickles," Ivy squealed.

Mark lowered Ivy to the ground.

She scrunched up her nose. "The magic word was pickles?"

He lowered his head, allowing the hood to fall forward a little more, and smiled at her. "This time it was."

The bell jingled again.

"Mark!"

He peered up. Nate Crandall and Gus Pratt hailed him and walked around a few customers to join him. As they approached, he spied Riley Madigan by the door; she averted her eyes.

"Mark, good to see you out and about." Nate fake-punched him in the arm. He looked down. "Hey, Ivy, what's up?"

Mark had known Nate since fourth grade, and Gus since freshman year in high school. Nate was in Spokane now, and Gus was in Wenatchee just down the valley, but they'd both visited him in the hospital and then again after he'd moved in with his dad for recovery. The three of them—plus Jay—had spent most of high school trying to figure out cars, girls, and life in general.

"What are you guys doing home?" Mark asked.

Nate shrugged. "Came to see my little brother play in the game tomorrow. Joslyn is having a girls' weekend with her sisters in Seattle."

Mark shook his head. "I'm still not used to the idea of you being married. I'm sorry I missed the wedding."

"No worries. You were a little busy."

Nate had married last year in Pashastin, right in the middle of a round of Mark's painful skin grafts.

Gus folded his arms. "Oh sure, he gets off easy."

Nate turned to Gus. "Dude, you were forty minutes away. You could've at least come to the reception."

"I told you, I had to take my grammy to Emerald City Comic Con. You try turning down a ninety-year-old woman who demands to see Zachary Quinto. It's not like I could've dropped her off at the door with her walker and her Iron Man compression socks." He waved to the air. "Bye, Grammy. Pick you up at ten. I'll meet you out here by the giant Eye of Sauron."

Mark stifled a laugh.

"Okay, fine," Nate said, chuckling. "Grammy wins."

Gus winked at Ivy. "She always does."

Ivy giggled.

"You going to the game, too?" Mark asked Gus.

"Naw, I'm helping my parents get the vines mounded before winter sets in. My in-laws have the kids; Heidi needed a break."

Mark nodded, sobered. Gus's parents had lost an entire vineyard to the fires. They'd been able to replant early this spring but the young vines needed to be heavily mulched for winter.

"How is Heidi?" Mark asked.

"Good. Baby has another month so she's getting the house ready and generally going nuts."

Ivy swung on Mark's arm. "Is she having a boy or a girl?"

Gus grinned. "Which do you think it is?"

"Umm . . . a girl!"

Gus made the sound of a buzzer. "Wrong. Try again."

"A boy?"

"You got it."

"I guess boys are cute, too."

"Oh, they are, are they?"

Ivy shook her head. "*Baby* boys."

Mark half-smiled at the exchange. He sensed he was still

being watched. Closely. He dared a glance in the direction of Riley Madigan and caught her gaze. He would've looked away immediately, except that she didn't look away first. People usually did. She continued to study him, her expression one of questioning more than morbid curiosity.

And then she smiled.

Mark dropped his gaze and smiled back. Sort of. He suddenly felt like swinging Ivy up in the air again and laughing at her squeal. And letting Riley Madigan look on.

Thankfully, he wasn't given the chance.

"Number twenty-seven," Lette Mae called. "Mark, that's you, hon."

Ivy jumped toward the counter, and Lette Mae handed the bag of fritters to the girl while Mark paid.

"I threw in an extra one just for you, Tootles." She winked at Ivy.

"What do you say?" Mark prompted his niece.

"Thank you," Ivy sang.

Mark took her hand. "Thanks, Lette Mae."

"Don't be a stranger. Number twenty-eight?"

Just as Mark and Ivy turned, Riley stepped toward the counter. To avoid colliding, Mark had to yield, giving her his right side. He quickly ducked his head. "Excuse us," he muttered.

"My fault. Too eager to get to the Bavarian cream."

He raised his gaze at the normalcy of her comment.

She met his eyes easily. "I'm a sucker for Bavarian cream."

For reasons beyond his comprehension, he said, "I'll have to remember that."

Her eyes narrowed a fraction, but not in anger. It was that thing she'd done the other night. Daring him to move.

"For the next time you're waving a bat in my direction," he said.

Her mouth twitched into a smile. He nodded goodbye, trying desperately to ignore that warm mix of awkward and pleasure in his gut.

She stepped up to the counter to collect her order.

"Hey, Mark," Nate called. "We're having a bonfire at my folks' house tonight. You should come."

Mark froze. Any pleasure he'd felt shattered on the floor. Gus immediately hit Nate in the arm.

"What was that for?" Nate asked Gus.

Gus gave Nate a significant look that Mark both appreciated and despised. But he didn't blame either of them.

"I might have to pass on that," he was able to say. "But thanks."

Understanding broke across Nate's face. He slapped his forehead. "Dude."

Mark raised his hand. "Tell Joslyn I said hi." He looked at Gus. "And Heidi. Good to see you guys."

Gus waved.

As Mark opened the door, the bell jingled, and Ivy asked, "Why don't you want to go to the bonfire?"

He held his breath, then let it out. "Because fire and Uncle Mark don't get along too well these days."

"Aww," she said, clearly dissatisfied. "Dumb ol' fire."

"Yep." The door closed behind them. "Dumb ol' fire."

❄ ❄ ❄

Riley both liked and loathed prep days. She got a break from the usual daily grind and was able to plan assignments and inventory materials. It also meant hours of teacher instruction and menial tasks like grading projects and entering those grades into the computer.

But as she drove to school, her mind wasn't on the stack of game boards she'd had the kids design for their mixed-media unit, or the box of clay and glazes she needed to order, or even the photography club proposal she was considering.

It was on Mark Rivers.

The bakery had been cheery and bright with customers. A far cry from that night on her dark street a week ago. She'd recognized the hooded figure right away but was captivated by the small girl who flitted and jumped around him as they waited, pulling on his arm and calling him "Uncle Mark" all while he absently twirled her around and . . . smiled.

And then his friends had entered, and he'd lifted his face and . . .

Yvette's words came back to her.

Mark was in a serious accident . . . He was critically injured and another firefighter died . . . It's a shock at first.

Riley parked her car in the teacher's lot and cut the engine.

He'd been burned.

That's what she'd missed that night as he'd sat in his truck in the dark, avoiding looking at her outright. That's what she'd missed when she'd threatened him with a bat.

Riley closed her eyes and groaned. "I threatened him with a bat." She leaned against the seat. Shame had filled her in the bakery, but it had faded some as she watched Mark interact with people who obviously cared about him. He was careful. Self-conscious about where he looked and where he stood. Who he faced.

His hood had fallen back as he'd laughed. Red scarring outlined his eye, cheek, and jaw along the right side of his face, seeming to continue down his neck. More than anything, though, Riley noticed the laugh. The laugh had bubbled out of him like a solid reminder that behind whatever made him wear that hood was only surface. The laugh was who he was. The smile that broke across his face when he'd caught her studying him was who he was.

A smile that stole hearts.

❅ ❆ ❅

A couple of teachers were talking over their coffee in the staff room as Riley entered. She greeted them and set the box of pastries on the table next to another. As she turned to go, Dalton Gainer entered and smiled brightly.

"Hey, new girl."

"Oh, hey," Riley said. They were almost past the first semester, but that never stopped Dalton from using the greeting anytime he saw her.

"Ready for the weekend?" He drew closer and leaned against the table next to her. The scent of his aftershave filled the air, mixing with the smell of maple bars.

"I will be after today," she said.

"Isn't that the truth?" He reached back and grabbed a donut from one of the boxes with a napkin. "Got any big plans later?"

"Nothing specific." Riley didn't know what to think of Dalton. He taught history and coached both football and basketball, and, she had to admit, was very easy to look at.

"The Crandalls are having a bonfire at their place tonight, and a bunch of people are going. I thought maybe you'd like to go."

She cocked an eyebrow. "With you?"

He laughed, tossing his fair head back. "Don't look so skeptical. I just thought that with you being new in town, this might be a good chance to get to know people."

"And you," she challenged.

He shrugged, not the least bit concerned. "And me. What could it hurt?"

"Don't you have a football game to coach?"

"It's tomorrow. We play Entiat."

She vaguely remembered. These smaller schools didn't have lights on the fields, so a lot of games were played Saturday afternoons before dark.

"Are you chaperoning the dance after?" he asked.

She shook her head. "I think with all of the play hours I logged, they let me sit this one out."

"Shame," he said, his gaze lingering.

"Yes," she said. "Chaperoning high school dances is the absolute highlight of my career."

He arched a brow. "Touché."

Riley had heard of the bonfire. Just that morning in the bakery, Mark's friend had invited him, and Mark had graciously turned him down. "Where do the Crandalls live?"

"Just up past Sunvale Vineyard on High Road. Does that mean you'll come?"

"I'll come."

He grinned. "Great. I'll pick you up at seven?"

"I'll meet you out there," she said.

His grin dropped. "Really?"

She smiled. "Really." She turned, and he followed.

"Maybe I was too subtle. I thought we could, uh, go together." He threw a glance toward the other teachers, who attempted to look like they weren't listening.

She faced him. "I did catch your subtlety. And I appreciate the offer. But I have this rule about men."

"What's that?" he asked, narrowing his eyes.

"I always drive myself on the first date. That way I have a way out if I need it."

Dalton grinned. "So, this is a *first* date."

She'd walked into that one. She smiled at his transparency. "I'll see you in the auditorium."

"Great," he said. "I'll be the one falling asleep."

"The *one?*" There were always several nodding heads during the often-dry presentations.

He laughed as she walked out of the room.

A bonfire might be fun. Out in the country under a cold November night sky. She'd gotten over her anxiety of meeting people within the first few weeks. Miracle Creek seemed wonderfully oblivious of Hollywood gossip.

And Dalton was a nice enough guy. He'd led a few teacher staff meetings and seemed pretty on the ball when it came to his career. She knew little about his private life, and experience had taught her not to assume anything. A lot of women in her situation had the same rule for meeting a guy on a first date: drive yourself.

Too bad there wasn't a clear rule for what to do when things didn't go so well with someone you thought you knew.

As she unlocked the door to the art room, Yvette approached, file folders in one hand and a huge scarf around her shoulders.

"Good morning, Riley. Last day of the week."

"Yes, thank goodness."

Yvette followed her into the classroom, switching the lights on when Riley didn't. "Something wrong?"

"Oh." She set her stuff down on her desk. "I had my eyes opened this morning, and it didn't feel very good."

Yvette raised her eyebrows, waiting.

Riley sat down at her desk and rested her chin on her fist.

"Remember how you told me to make up my own mind about Mark Rivers?"

Yvette nodded. "You figured it out, huh?"

She covered her face with her hands. "Yes."

"So that's a good thing, right?"

Riley slapped her hands on her desk. "Yvette! I threatened him with a baseball bat!"

Yvette chuckled, but stopped when she saw Riley's expression. "True, but it didn't go beyond that, and he had you spooked, so no harm, no foul. What happened this morning?"

Riley sighed. "I saw him this morning at the bakery. He was very gracious."

"He spoke to you?"

Riley nodded, pulling a water bottle out of her bag.

"What did he say?"

"Something about Bavarian cream and using it to stave off my ferocious swing."

Yvette chuckled again. Riley joined her this time.

"Well," Yvette said, "Lette Mae's Bavarian cream is miraculous."

"I know, I ate an entire *bollen* in the parking lot." Riley had discovered the round, cream custard-filled pastries topped with fudgy chocolate the day after she'd moved into town, and she was hooked. Lette Mae had told her they were a specialty in the region, brought over by the Dutch. She lifted the water bottle to her lips and drank, hoping it would help wash down the pastry sitting in her gut. Or maybe that was a knot of guilt.

"It sounds like he has a good sense of humor about it, which is also pretty miraculous. Don't beat yourself up about it."

"Yeah," Riley said, not quite convinced. "He *was* smiling." She shook her head. "But you should have seen his expression when one of his friends invited him to a bonfire tonight."

Yvette clicked her tongue and grimaced. "I can imagine."

Riley nodded. "He left after that." She paused, then said, "Dalton invited me to that bonfire, though I don't think I'll be able to see it the same way ever again."

"Dalton Gainer asked you out?"

Riley looked up at Yvette, wary of the change in her tone. "Yes, just now."

Yvette looked down, sorting through some student sketches on Riley's desk. "Hmm. Are you going, then?" She glanced at Riley.

"Sure. I told him I'd meet him there."

Yvette lifted her head and smiled, but it wasn't deep. "Well, I hope you have a good time." She checked her watch. "We best get going."

"What is it? Is there a rule about dating staff that I'm not aware of?"

"No. Nothing like that. It's just . . ."

"What?" Riley couldn't imagine why Yvette would care if she went to the bonfire with Dalton. From all appearances, she and Dalton got along well enough. "Oh! Are you and Dalton—"

"Oh *heavens*, no."

"Then what?"

Yvette shook her head. "It's none of my business."

"You know I consider you a friend. One of the few I have here."

Yvette smiled at that. "Thank you. I consider you the same. And just like with Mark, you're going to have to make up your own mind about Dalton. Just . . . be careful. Masks come in all shapes and sizes, you know?"

Riley nodded. That, she knew.

❄ ❄ ❄

Mark hadn't told his dad about the bonfire or what happened at the bakery. He hadn't even mentioned Nate or Gus being in town.

But somehow his dad found out about it and decided Mark was going.

"What if I don't go?" Mark had asked.

"What if you do?" His dad folded his arms. "Nate and Gus—those boys prayed over you. They shed tears. The least you can do is go to their party and say hi. The bonfire's clear in the back away from the house, and there are always people inside with drink and food. You don't even have to see it."

"I'd smell it."

"But you'd know it's a bonfire and nothing else. Get out, Mark. Go see people. Go see your friends. They miss you."

And that was that.

Mark sat in his truck in the large circular drive in front of the Crandall home, where he'd attended birthday parties and raided the fridge and taken prom pictures, and he was shaking like a cat on a telephone pole.

"This is ridiculous," he muttered, and started the ignition. Before he could back up, a car pulled in next to him. He glanced over and saw Riley Madigan get out of the car and stare at the big house. He shifted into park.

She brushed her dark hair back with her fingers. It rested on her shoulders, reflecting the light from the house like silk threads. She popped her trunk and walked to the back of her car. Mark pulled the key out of the ignition. His truck stilled.

What was he doing? What did he think he could do?

His fingers found the door handle, and he climbed out, pulling his jacket hood up higher.

"Oh!"

He turned and jerked back. Riley was directly behind him, her hand over her chest.

"You scared me half to death," she said breathlessly.

He looked away, down, at the truck, shrinking into his hood.

She put a hand on his arm, and he stilled. "No, I didn't mean . . . I meant I'd grabbed my scarf and wasn't watching where I was going." She held up a green scarf the color of her eyes.

He peered at her. She had freckles. He hadn't noticed before.

"I thought you weren't coming," she said as she wrapped the scarf around her neck.

How had she known that? Then he remembered. The bakery.

"I'm still not sure if I'm going in," he said, finding his voice.

"Neither am I." She looked up at the sky. "It's a beautiful night, though." She shivered in her vest jacket.

"You're cold."

"I didn't want to be stuck wearing a heavier coat if the bonfire was too warm." She rubbed her arms with her hands. "California spoils a body. I should be fine though. Reminds me of—" She stopped herself.

"Of what?" he asked.

She shrugged. "Of home, I guess."

He wasn't sure what to say. Should he offer her his jacket? Ask her about California? Was that her home?

"I wanted to tell you," she said, saving him from the silence, "that I'm sorry I was so quick to judge you the other night. I think I was wrong."

"You're sure about that?" he asked.

The corner of her mouth lifted. "Well, I can't be absolutely sure."

"So *now* you're being cautious?"

"I'm always cautious."

He looked down, toeing the ground. "Except when you've got a baseball bat in your hands."

"Caution shows itself in many forms."

He peeked up at her. She was watching him, studying him again.

"I get it," he said. "Why you thought I was . . . you know."

"No, you don't," she said, lifting her chin. "I've been in scary situations before. I've been followed by men in the dark—"

"Aw, man. I'm sorry." Regret surged through him.

"No, it's okay. I mean it wasn't okay. But you never know . . ." She trailed off. "So, I'm careful."

"And I'm an idiot," he said.

She laughed quietly, then stuck out her hand. "I'm Riley Madigan. I teach at the high school. But you knew that."

He hesitated, then placed his hand in hers. "Mark Rivers. Stalker extraordinaire."

"It's nice to meet you, Mark."

He looked down at their hands, and her gaze followed. He wore his sleeve, but the mottled skin and scarring on his fingers was visible, ragged, and he fought the urge to yank his hand away.

"Is this okay?" she asked. "It doesn't hurt, does it?"

Her questions somehow eased his anxiety. He shook his head. "A lot of it's numb, actually. I can't feel much here or here"—he showed her the places on the back of his hand and fingers—"except for some pressure." He lifted her hand and opened it in his left. "But I can feel this." He ran his right fingertips over her palm. It was soft, smooth, and warm.

He glanced at her, and she caught his gaze. Neither of them moved.

He lowered her hand, letting it go. She blinked, looking back up at the house. He put his hands in his pockets, still feeling the silk of her skin on his fingertips.

"Everyone's getting ready for the holidays," he said lamely. The Crandalls had put up their usual display of colored lights and a big star above the front door. This year they'd added an inflatable snowman—slightly out of place on the leaf-strewn lawn. The little snow they'd had hadn't stayed.

"Does everyone put up their Christmas lights so early?" she asked. "We just had Halloween."

"You don't like Christmas?" he asked.

She drew her gaze from the house. "I like it in December."

He nodded. "It gets cold here pretty fast after Halloween. Weather can be unpredictable so close to the mountains. Most people get their decorations up before it freezes."

"Oh. I was beginning to think you all were Christmas zealots."

"I never said we weren't."

She smiled slowly, and he had to look away, glad the thump of his heart couldn't show through his jacket.

He kicked his toe at the ground, considering the topic of Christmas. "I wanted to ask you something," he said. He took a deep breath. "I was wondering—"

"There you are." Dalton Gainer came striding down the lawn. From the goofy grin on Dalton's face, Mark guessed he wasn't talking to him. He met them at the drive, eyes on Riley. "Were you coming up? I've been waiting."

"Of course," Riley said. "Mark was about to ask me something."

"Hey, how's our hometown hero?"

Mark kept his face partially hidden. "Great. You?" Dalton was a few years older than he was and had made high school All-American in their division in football and State in track. Mark had idolized the guy, then had shattered all his records. Dalton had never liked that.

"Perfect," Dalton answered, displaying white teeth. He refocused on Riley. "Are you cold? Here." He pulled off his leather jacket and put it around her shoulders. "You're not in LA anymore."

Riley shrugged under the weight of the jacket. "Thanks. I'm sure it will be warm closer to the bonfire."

"People are already peeling off layers." He winked, then turned to Mark. "You coming, Rivers?"

"I was just about to leave."

Riley turned to Mark. "Didn't you just get here?"

Mark lifted a shoulder. "I got farther than I thought I would."

She dropped her eyes and hid a smile. He liked that.

"Now that you mention it," Dalton said, "it's been a couple of years since I've seen you—well—at anything." He chuckled. "You've become quite the hermit, Rivers. Welcome back."

Mark saw Riley look at Dalton with what he hoped was annoyance. She turned back to Mark. "What did you want to ask me?"

"It can wait."

She hesitated, then smiled and nodded before Dalton led her away.

"Don't be a stranger, Rivers," Dalton called behind him with a raised hand.

Riley waved.

Mark kept his hands in his pockets. "I might take you up on that, Gainer," he muttered.

Chapter 4

Riley let Dalton guide her up to the house. She'd wanted to keep talking to Mark. Wanted him to keep revealing pieces of himself.

Which was why she let Dalton pull her away.

She'd done what she'd set out to do. She'd apologized to Mark about the other night, and he'd accepted it. The memory of his fingers running across her palm like feathers made her shiver, and she looked back. The truck was gone.

"Are you still cold? Come on, new girl. Let's get you to the bonfire." He placed his hand on the small of her back to direct her through the house and outside again. He grabbed drinks along the way and offered her one.

Smooth. She'd heard that much about Dalton. Divorced. Two kids. Competitive. Kind of a player. No matter how exceptional he thought he might be, those were pretty average stats in the adult dating world.

She was counting on those stats to be accurate. Dalton wasn't looking for anything lasting.

"Hey, Gainer, looks like you found your date."

One of Mark's friends from the bakery hailed them from the perimeter of a large bonfire built in a giant tractor wheel rim turned on its side.

"I did. Nate, this is Riley Madigan. Riley, Nate Crandall, our host."

Nate smiled. "I saw you at the bakery this morning."

"Teachers love their donuts," she said.

"We keep Lette Mae in business," Dalton said, raising his drink.

Nate raised his back. "Pretty sure Lette Mae's *bollens* keep her in business."

"To Lette Mae's *bollens*," Dalton said. "May they always be light and creamy, and never fall flat."

Riley rolled her eyes, and Nate caught it.

"How many of those have you had, Gainer?"

Dalton chuckled. "My apologies. My feelings for Lette Mae and her confections are pure, I assure you. And, for the record, this is my first."

Nate raised his brows at Riley. "A word of warning—he's like this sober."

She smiled, deciding she liked Nate. "So, you're a friend of Mark's?" she asked, despite her silent vow not to think about him for the rest of the evening.

"We've been friends since we were kids." He narrowed his gaze. "How did you meet him? He's been pretty antisocial."

"We met after the play on Saturday." *Kind of.*

"Oh, right. His niece was one of the Lost Boys."

That's where she'd seen the little girl in the bakery before. "It's too bad he left the party early."

Nate frowned at her. "He was here?"

"I just talked to him down at the driveway."

Nate looked behind her as if expecting to see Mark in one of the groups of guests. He took out his phone and started texting. "Excuse me," he said, glancing up. He nodded to them and walked toward the front of the house.

Dalton chuckled, shaking his head. "Babysitters."

"What was that?" she asked.

"Oh, nothing. Just Nate and a few other people like to mother our local hero as if he were a stray puppy. I bet you Nate's calling around to get a location on Rivers to make sure he gets home safe, or you know, doesn't drive his truck off a cliff."

Riley gasped quietly.

Dalton shook his head. "I don't mean to sound cold. Geez. That kid's been through things beyond imagining. But I saw who he was before, what he's made of. He's tough as nails. He tackles a challenge. Thrives on loose reins. Just get him going in the right direction and *bam*. He'll knock down whatever wall is in front of him. He's one of those guys who can carry the world on his shoulders and make it look good. At least he was. All this mothering and quiet corralling and Big Brother watching him—" He took a drink. "It's gonna undo him sooner than anything."

Riley considered the turn his words had taken. "It sounds like people care a lot about him."

He nodded. "Can't help that, I guess."

They watched the fire for a time. Riley shrugged off Dalton's leather jacket.

"Getting warm?" he asked, taking it from her.

She nodded. Too warm. Anger and unease knotted inside her, and though she appreciated Dalton's take, his callousness unsettled her. He was probably right in some ways. If what he said about Mark's tenacity was true, then no wonder people corralled him, even if he didn't want to be. But she didn't like Dalton's glib remark about driving off a cliff.

She watched the fire as it snapped and hissed. Tiny explosions popped here and there, and red-hot ashes whirled up into the sky. Heat warmed her skin even from six feet away. "I don't blame him for not coming up here."

Dalton took another swallow of his drink. "Neither do I."

Another guest hailed Dalton and came over. They started up a conversation about retirement plans—401Ks versus the DRS— so Riley excused herself to the house to freshen up. But as she walked, she scanned the crowd. She roamed the open areas of the house and headed out the front door, finding herself on the front lawn again.

A couple of people caught her eye, and she drew closer. Nate was in deep conversation with Mark's other friend from the bakery.

Nate lifted his head at her approach, and she slowed, not sure she'd be welcome.

"Hey, Riley, right?" He motioned her over. When she joined them, Nate clapped his friend on the shoulder. "This is Gus Pratt. Another friend of Mark's."

"Hey," Gus said. "I saw you at the bakery."

She raised a brow and looked at Nate. "And here I thought I'd done my best to blend in."

Gus shook his head. "Mark Rivers spoke to you. He *smiled* at you. These days that stands out anywhere."

"I didn't know it was a big deal."

He held his hands out wide. "Huge," he said.

"Why is that? A big deal, I mean?"

"You're new," Nate said. "Mark's barely coming out of his shell after the fires and all the surgeries. He's been a ghost for years."

She looked from him to Gus, who nodded in agreement. Yvette had said the same, but Riley had dismissed it as exaggeration.

"That's why I was surprised when you said he was here. I had to see if I could catch him or convince him to come back."

She glanced toward the cars. "No luck?"

He shook his head. "It seems you're the only one he talked to."

"You mean I'm the one who scared him off."

Gus huffed a laugh. "Doubt it."

"So, did you hear from him?" she asked Nate.

He nodded. "He said he thought he'd just drive by. Said it was good to see the house. Looks like you lucked out."

She recalled her conversation with Mark and had to agree.

Nate folded his arms. "Can I ask you something?"

Riley shrugged. "Sure."

"We've known Mark most of our lives. We tried to help when he got hurt, but then he closed himself off from everything that made him who he was. That's been rough. But you—you didn't know him before."

"I barely know him now," she said, wary of her part in this conversation.

"But you've met. A few times. You have nothing to compare to who he was before."

"What's your point?"

"What do you think of him?"

She paused, taken back by the question. "Why are you asking me this?"

"He seems to like you. Trust you at some level. I'm just wondering what it is that helps draw him out."

As flattered as she was by Nate's observation, she was reminded of Dalton's opinion. "Why does he need to be drawn out? Surely there are citizens of Miracle Creek who live quiet, private lives?"

Gus looked doubtful.

She proceeded with caution. "Maybe if he didn't feel like he was under everyone's watch, he'd find his own way. Maybe if this town didn't consistently remind him that he's some kind of hero, he could focus on being himself. Whoever that is now."

Gus elbowed Nate. "That's what I said. The hero thing, I mean."

"And maybe that's it," Riley continued. "Maybe he talks to me or whatever because I'm new. I have no preconceived notions about Mark Rivers. He was burned. He's healing." She stared out past the cars. "I heard he lost his best friend. That's big." She shivered and turned back. "Mark seems like a good guy. He's trying. He has a great smile. That's all I know about him."

The men studied her, Gus nodding his head.

Riley bit her lip. "Actually, that's not entirely true. Last week I thought he was a stalker, and I threatened him with a baseball bat."

"Whoa," Gus said, his eyes wide.

Nate started laughing.

"So," Riley said, "I'm probably not the best person to ask. This shouldn't even be my business. It's obvious he means a lot to you guys, and you know him way better than I do."

Nate nodded slowly. "Maybe. Maybe not. But what you said, about people living quiet lives, keeping to themselves? That's not the cloth Mark was cut from."

"He does have a great smile though," Gus said, winking at Riley in a way that made her regret being so forthcoming.

Nate's gaze drifted over her shoulder, and she detected an annoyed sigh. "Gainer's looking for you."

She turned and saw Dalton standing in the doorway, his hands on his hips. She waved at him, and he headed their way.

"You're with Dalton?" Gus asked a little too incredulously.

"He asked me here tonight, if that's what you mean."

"And you thought *Mark* was a creep?" Gus rolled his eyes. "Well, Dalton got the better part of this deal, I'll tell you what."

"Hey," Dalton said when he reached them. He smiled at Riley. "You get lost?"

"What a good idea," she heard Gus say from behind them. Riley managed to keep a straight face.

"No. Just mingling. I still don't know many people."

"Well, let's fix that," he said and steered her in the direction of the house.

Riley spent the following hour next to Dalton, meeting a number of people, some whose names she might even remember. She couldn't help noticing questioning looks from several women; the kind of looks she'd get in LA because she wasn't 5'8" and as svelte as a cat. But then she noted that they seemed to be more interested in Dalton than her. They simply wanted her out of the way. Still, not a feeling she welcomed.

The bonfire had been stoked, somebody had turned on music, and as Dalton put his arm around her under the guise of keeping her warm, she decided it was time to go.

"I've got an early morning tomorrow," she said, stepping casually out of Dalton's grip. "This was fun, though. Thanks for inviting me."

He lifted his drink. "Thanks for coming. I'd try to convince you to stay, but I'm afraid I'd just sound pathetic. I'll walk you down to your car. What's the early morning project?"

"Home improvement. Drafty windows."

"Ah. Well, I'd offer to help, but I've got game films to study. Need to make those playoffs."

"Good luck."

"Thanks. Entiat's smaller than we are. Should be a cakewalk."

They reached her car. "Is that what the bigger teams say about Mt. Stuart?"

He gave her a wry smile. "My school spirit says they wish."

"Hang on to that school spirit." She made two fists. "Go Beacons." She unlocked her car and opened the door. "I'll see you on Monday."

"Yeah. We'll have to do this again. Maybe something cozier next time."

Riley smiled and ducked into the car. As she backed out, he stood for a moment before heading back to the party.

After spending almost an entire evening with Dalton, she still wasn't sure what to think of him. She guessed he liked it that way. She also guessed that, given the number of women who had been looking at him, Dalton wouldn't be alone at the party for too long.

The thought brought on bitter feelings she knew had nothing to do with Dalton. She hardly knew him; she wanted no claim on him. It was safer that way.

You know more about Mark Rivers after ten minutes than you ever will about Dalton Gainer.

She wrestled with that thought most of the drive home.

❄ ❄ ❄

Saturday morning, Dad sent Mark to the hardware store. They were short a light fixture for the new building. They were about done with it, and just in time. Snow was in the forecast, and Mark's hand didn't work so great in the bitter cold. He grabbed his coat.

"While you're out, could you drop by Riley Madigan's place and ask her if she could help me put a value on your mom's things? I don't know what I'm doing, and the insurance company is allowing us an expert's appraisal for their approval. Maybe Miss Madigan is qualified for that."

Mark's stomach flopped. "Why don't you just call her?"

His dad looked at him over his bifocals. "Because I think this is something that should be asked in person."

"Then you ask her."

"I'm not going out." His dad licked his finger and turned the page of the ledger.

Mark turned around stiffly. "I'm getting my own place. Soon."

"Good." His dad chuckled behind him. "I could use some peace and quiet."

Mark growled and shut the door.

After getting the light at the hardware store, Mark picked up some groceries at the IGA. He considered stopping at the auto shop as well, but finally caved, turned up Riley's street, and parked in front of her house. She stood in her living room, framed by her front window, arms reaching up, tongue sticking out sideways, trying to do something to the top of the window.

If she was busy, he wouldn't have to stay long. Just ask what he came to ask and get outta there.

He opened the truck door and shut it. She glanced his way at the sound. Her eyes grew wide, and she toppled over, out of the window frame.

He ran to the front door and knocked. She shouted something, and he busted the door open—which might have been unnecessary because he hadn't checked if it was locked first—and with his momentum, stumbled inside, nearly falling over a step-ladder collapsed on the floor.

Riley was already standing up, brushing herself off, staring at him. "What are you doing?"

He rubbed his arm. "You yelled. You said you needed assistance."

"I shouted 'Give me a *second*.' Who shouts, 'Give me assistance?'"

She had a point. He looked at the door swinging on its hinges, the knob he'd grabbed still in his hand, and the other half nowhere to be seen.

She covered her mouth with both hands, surveying the damage. "Oh no," she moaned. She walked past him and picked up an old glass knob from behind a green velvet couch in the middle of the room.

"I'm really sorry. I thought you were hurt." He brought his half over and held it next to hers. The brass rod that connected both pieces was bent and shorn off at the base of his end.

"I think it's dead," she said. Then she giggled.

He grimaced, and she laughed outright. "Give me assistance!" she repeated in quiet mockery.

"Knock it off."

"You've already done that."

He took the pieces from her and walked back to the door. He fit them through the hole and eyed the piecing, the cold air from outside pushing its way in. "These old glass knobs really aren't ideal for a front door."

"So you've proven."

He glared at her, but her smile only grew bigger. He shook

his head, still feeling the heat of embarrassment in his face. "I'll replace it. With something meant for an entry."

"You don't have to do that."

"Yeah, I do. I won't be gone long."

"Wait," she said. "Right now? You're just going to pick something?"

He fingered the door, needing to leave. "That's usually how it's done."

"It has to match the style of the house."

"You mean 'old'? That didn't work so well before."

She folded her arms and looked up at him with a frown.

"Craftsman, right?" he offered.

Her brow lifted in surprise. "Craftsman cottage."

"That's the one." He paused long enough to look at her with her hair all piled up messy on top of her head, a big sweatshirt nearly slipping off her shoulder, and faded jeans hinting at her curves. Her feet were bare. But her eyes—pale green and steady—held him still.

He realized he was staring and looked past her to the window she'd been working on. He frowned. "What were you trying to do?"

"I wasn't *trying* to do anything. I was doing perfectly well until you startled me."

"I was coming to your door like you suggested, instead of lurking in my truck."

She glanced out the window to his truck, sitting smack in front of her house in broad daylight. "Well, you still startled me."

"I get that a lot."

Now she glared at him, and he was the one to smile.

She dropped the broken doorknob on the couch and walked to the window. She picked up what looked like a roll of Scotch tape, except that several yards had been dispensed and she was trying to roll it back up.

"You're putting plastic on the windows," he observed.

"Yes," she said, wrestling the double-sided tape. "When I fell, this came with me. Tore off half of what I've done."

He picked up the stepladder and repositioned it for her, then watched her for a minute as she struggled. "Do you want some help?"

She sighed and then chucked the roll across the room. It didn't go far as one end was still attached to the top corner of the window. "I'll just start over." She looked above her and yanked the remaining section of tape loose, which then stuck to her in various places.

He covered a laugh.

"Stop it," she said, laughing too. "I was almost done." She sheepishly pulled the last bit out of her hair.

He looked around at the other windows in view. Sure enough, they'd all been winterized, the plastic sheeting heated and pulled tight with the blow-dryer plugged into an extension cord next to her on the floor.

"Does that plug have a ground on it?" he asked, noting the yellow cord looked aged with years of use, sporting several different colors of paint and old duct tape marks.

She shook her head. "Most of the electrical outlets in this part of the house are the old two-prong kind. I found the extension cord in the garage." At his look of concern, she added, "The outlets in the bathrooms and kitchen are grounded. The previous owners must have done that when they updated."

He nodded, looking around more carefully. "Most of the homes in this neighborhood were built in the 1920s and have been completely updated. I'll have to mention it to Alan. It's a hazard."

"Alan Gorecki? You know the people who owned this place?"

"Yep. Took their granddaughter to junior prom. Do you have lamps and things like that in the bedrooms?"

"Yes."

"How are you finding appliances that fit in the outlets?"

"Antique stores. The Goose. New2You. Old stuff fits in old outlets, go figure."

He nodded. Wenatchee Valley had more than its share of shops full of old stuff. "Are the cords in good shape?"

A smile spread across her face.

"What?" he asked.

"You sound like a fireman."

Again, Mark felt heat rise in his face. He dropped his gaze and turned away. He picked up the old doorknob pieces and walked to the door. "I'll get you a replacement at Ace."

"Could you pick up another roll of tape for the window?" she asked behind him. "This one only has a few more feet on it."

He nodded. It was the least he could do.

"Oh, and text me a pic of the doorknobs you find."

"You don't trust me?"

"No."

"I'm a certified EMT with a bachelor's degree in fire sciences, and I've helped build and restore homes and barns all over this county." She stood her ground as he stepped forward. Who knew his pride would feel a hit over home improvement? "I think I can pick out a doorknob."

"Who is the designer credited for Americanizing the Craftsman style?"

He blinked.

She took advantage of his silence. "Gustav Stickley—1858 to 1942. Furniture designer and architect. See that rocking chair?"

He glanced at an old square rocker next to the fireplace. Oak.

"It's a Stickley," she said. "Someone was throwing it out! You don't throw out an old Stickley just because it's a little beat up—" She shook her head. "You bring it home and polish it, tighten the joints, and put it in a Craftsman-style home that maybe you're only renovating but maybe you'd like to keep if you decide someday you want to actually live in a town no bigger than a Hollywood back lot, that's what you do." She had thrown out her arms and pulled in a breath.

He blinked again. "Would you . . . like to come pick it out?" She was out of her freaking mind.

She marched over to the front door and swung it shut. It bounced, shuddered, and slowly swung open again. "I would, but somebody broke my front door. I have to stay and protect the Stickley, among other things." She shivered from the draft coming inside.

He rubbed his face. This was not the morning he had planned. "With your baseball bat?"

She gave him a hard look. "Send me a pic from the store."

"Yes, ma'am."

"I am not your mother."

He covered a smile. "No, ma'am."

She growled and put her hands on her hips. "You'll need my number."

"Yes, I will. Riley."

She paused, and in that brief moment, with the banter stopped, he found it hard to breathe. Then just like that, Riley Madigan was standing close to him, putting her number into his phone.

She gave it back to him. "There. I didn't mean to be so bossy. I tend to go a little nuts over old things." She looked up at him, her freckles clear in the light streaming through the window.

He swallowed. "Your eyes are the color of moss. It's a cool, soothing color."

She blinked and looked away, her turn to blush.

"It's deceiving," he said. "You're not very soothing at all."

He watched her eyes open wide.

"You . . ."

He chuckled and made for the door.

"You . . ." she repeated.

He waved goodbye and made it off the porch.

"You are no Gustav Stickley!" she called from the open door.

He faked a knife wound to his heart and staggered into his truck. She held her hand over her mouth, her eyes smiling as she shut the door.

He started his truck, unable to wipe the stupid grin off his face, when he caught his reflection in the mirror.

He stilled. His smile weakened as he jerked his hood up over his head. It had fallen back at some point. When? Maybe from the beginning after he'd burst through her door.

A sickening cold seeped through him. That whole time he'd been exposed.

Chapter 5

Riley watched Mark drive away, biting her thumbnail, heart pounding in her chest from the adrenaline of his "visit." She'd watched him pull his hood up and drop his head on the steering wheel. So different from who he'd become in her living room. The hood had fallen back when he'd first tripped over the stepladder, and he never fixed it. For the first time, she saw what the fire had done to his skin. And for the first time, she saw what it hadn't.

When he'd left the hood off, she'd hoped he'd decided it didn't matter. But seeing his posture in his truck, she knew differently. And now she felt like she'd seen something not meant for her. An accidental invasion of something deeply private. They were, after all, strangers.

It hadn't bothered her, seeing his scars. Only in considering what he must have gone through for scars like that. Imagination was a strange thing. Most times, things imagined were far more fantastic or horrific than the reality. She had a feeling that wasn't the case this time. What happened to Mark must have been a nightmare.

He'd been a beautiful boy. The burns had transformed a portion of that, of course. But a transformation was a change, not necessarily a destruction.

She felt her own hypocrisy at the thought.

Riley sighed, gathered up the tangled window tape, and threw everything in the garbage. She glanced at the clock and realized she hadn't eaten since seven. She could use this forced "break" to make a decent lunch. If Mark was hungry when he returned, she could at least offer him food.

She washed her hands and took inventory of her fridge. She grabbed ingredients for BLTs, and soon the sizzling sounds and scent of bacon filled the kitchen as she sliced a tomato.

Then, for the first time since she'd spied him walking up to her front porch, she wondered why he'd stopped by at all.

At the bonfire, she'd told his friends she didn't think Mark needed to be drawn out of a cocoon if he didn't want to be. And from her point of view, he clearly didn't want to be. And yet Nate said Mark wasn't cut from that kind of cloth.

He used to be social. Well-known and liked. And people missed him, wanted him back. But the way Nate had said it, she got the feeling they didn't want him back for them. They wanted him back for *him*. Because it was who he was.

She puzzled over what she knew about Mark Rivers. He was funny. And smarter than she'd given him credit for. He'd wanted to ask her a question twice now. About painting something.

Halfway through removing the bacon to paper towels, her phone buzzed. He'd sent pics of three different doorknobs, each perfect for a Craftsman-style house. She chose one that closely matched the drawer pulls in the kitchen.

He responded. *Got it.*

She texted again. *Why did you stop by this morning?*

After a few moments, he answered. *Honestly?*

Yes, please.

I'm collecting glass doorknobs.

She pressed her lips in a smile.

He added, *I'll tell you when I get back.*

The sandwiches were ready and on plates with chips when she heard him come through the front door. She went out to meet him, ignoring the uptick of her pulse.

He glanced her way and averted his gaze. "Hey." He set a couple of bags and the broken glass knobs on the rolltop desk and a tool chest on the floor. His hood was all the way up, shading his face.

"Hey," she said as he knelt by the door, his back to her.

"Your tape's in that bag," he said.

She opened a bag and pulled out the window tape, but there was more. "What are these?"

"I got you a few adapters for the outlets."

She read the package. "Three-prong to two-prong outlet adapters." She found three more in the bag and a new extension cord. "Thank you."

She watched his head nod from behind.

"Your outlets still need to be grounded, but this way you can use modern stuff if you need to. I talked to Alan. The updates were professional. I can give you the name of the guy he hired." He used a utility knife to open the plastic casing on the doorknob.

"Okay. Thanks again. What do I owe you?"

"It's on me. I did break your door."

She smiled at that. "Can I offer you lunch?"

He paused.

"I made BLTs."

He turned halfway in her direction. So different from when he wasn't worried about that hood.

"It's all ready," she said. "I'm gonna eat. You're welcome to join me."

He turned back to the box he was working on.

"Or I can bring you a plate?"

He nodded again.

Okay, if that was what he wanted. She brought him his plate and a glass of apple cider and set it on the rolltop desk. "The cider's Orondo's. Yvette said it's the best."

"Yvette's right." He stopped what he was doing and turned toward the plate and juice. Finally, he glanced at her directly. "Thanks. It smells great."

She turned to the kitchen. "Tastes better."

❄ ❅ ❄

Mark swallowed the last bite of the sandwich and washed it down with cider. That lunch was about perfect, and he allowed himself to relax and focus on installing the doorknob properly. It would be tricky enough with the old door; being on edge wouldn't get the job done any faster.

Riley had turned on music, eating at the table just inside the kitchen, which worked fine for him. The nearer she was, the more he was forced to think about how much she'd seen of him. And how he'd acted like an idiot with her.

"Can I get you more of anything?" she asked from the kitchen. "More cider?"

"No, thanks. It was good, though."

She hummed while she cleaned up, and he stood to bring in his dishes. He could at least do that. He rounded the corner and paused. She was dancing. Nodding her head and moving her hips as she rinsed a fry pan under hot water. At the chorus, she lip-synced into a pair of tongs.

He cleared his throat.

She jumped so hard the tongs went flying, clanging against a cupboard and dropping to the floor with a clatter.

She rested her palms on the edge of the sink. "You really need to stop doing that."

He kept his mouth straight. "I was just bringing in my plate."

She held out her hand. He handed her his plate. Then his glass.

"Thanks for lunch," he said.

"Mhmm," she answered, vigorously scrubbing.

He bent to pick up the tongs and set them in the sink. "I never really liked that song." When she didn't answer, he turned to go. "I'm reconsidering, though."

"Don't you have a door to fix?" she asked.

He smiled to himself. The knot inside him eased a little.

Riley returned to the front room a few minutes later and began taping the window for plastic. He had the knob installed on the door and hoped it would line up once he put the new latch plate on the jamb.

"So," she said, peeling the second backing off the tape now surrounding the entire window. "Why did you come here this morning?"

"My dad sent me." He began removing the old latch plate.

"Your dad? Do I know him?"

"Nope. But he asked around and someone gave him your name."

This is something that should be asked in person, he heard his dad say. Not with his back to her, either. He put down his tools and stood, facing Riley. She had the plastic sheet spread out and was pressing it to the top edge of the taped window.

He steadied his nerves and went over to help her, holding the hanging portion of plastic and smoothing over the stretches of tape she'd already covered. Standing on the stepladder, she was a few inches taller than he was. "My mom passed away eleven years ago."

She paused. "I'm sorry to hear that. How old were you?"

"Almost sixteen. She was an artist. Oil paints, mostly. Some metal sculpture." He felt her eyes on him as her hands stilled. He was on her right side, so he didn't mind her looking. "We had a lot of her artwork in the outbuilding when it burned down."

She stepped down off the ladder. The plastic film hung where she'd left it. "That's horrible."

He nodded. "By the time my dad got to the building, it was too late."

"I'm so sorry." Her gaze drifted to the paintings on the wall. He'd assumed they were hers. They had her look.

He absently smoothed over the taped plastic again. "We had some of her favorites in the house, so at least those were saved. And most of the garden sculptures."

She frowned. "What did your dad think I could do?"

"It's the insurance. The last of the inventory. He's listed the paintings as lost items, but he has no idea how to put a value on them. He could guess, but he's too . . ." He searched for the words.

"Emotionally involved?" she offered.

"Exactly. And he's hesitant to hand it over to the insurers. They've been pretty patient with him, giving him the option to get his own appraiser. He was hoping you could come look at the ledger, listen to a description, maybe give him ballpark figures.

Honestly, I think if it were up to him, he'd just call it a loss and move on. But I think out of respect for my mom, he's got to make them count. If he didn't claim them, it was like they never existed. I think he's considering doing something she'd like with the money. Something for the arts."

"Of course," she said. "I have a friend who works at an art gallery in Denver I can use as a reference. I'd be happy to help however I can."

"Thanks. I'll let him know, and you two can decide on a time to come over to the house."

She nodded, and they went back to work. He helped her until she had the plastic film in place, and then he returned to the door while she finished the windows.

She turned the blow-dryer off. "There," she said, looking at her handiwork. "That should make a difference."

He opened and closed the door, pleased that the new doorknob seemed to be doing its job. After shutting the door tightly, he checked the brick fireplace, feeling for a draft. He peered up the chimney, checking the flu.

"Keep this damper closed unless you've got a fire in it. That will help, too."

"Thank you," she said, folding her arms and sighing. "I guess you've made up for breaking my door."

He nodded, shifting his weight, suddenly unsure. But it had been such a strange day already, he might as well ride it out. "I have something else I wanted to ask you."

"Oh?" She stuffed the trimmed strips of plastic and the rest of the mess into a garbage bag.

"Yeah. It's for me, though. Sort of."

She tossed the bag on the floor near the front door. "Okay, shoot."

"I had this idea. I wanted to know if you'd be interested in painting something for me. Well, not for me, for my dad."

"What's the project?" Once again, she was looking at him expectantly. No pity or discomfort in her expression.

He took a deep breath and decided to just get it out. "It's a nativity. Life-size. My mom painted one years ago. It's always been up at Christmastime, so people can see it from the highway as they enter town. After she was gone, it was a reminder of what she loved most. But it burned up with the fire. I saw your backdrops at the play—your painting style is really similar to hers—and I thought I—we—could surprise my dad."

She didn't answer immediately.

"I have some photos of the original," he continued. "They're not great. But I could do the wood cutouts. We've got most of the materials."

She walked past him to the couch. "That's a big time commitment."

"Yeah. I know. It wouldn't have to be complete by Christmas. Just . . . underway."

She began pushing the couch back into place in front of the window.

He stepped forward to help her. "We won't have to work together, if that's—"

"That doesn't have anything to do with it," she said, frowning. "If I don't take this on, it's because of time, not because I'd have to work with you. I have so little time with school and art club and needing to fix up this place."

"I'd pay you, of course. Whatever your time's worth. Six hundred dollars?"

"No—" She eyed the couch's position.

"Nine hundred?"

"You skipped from six hundred to nine hundred," she said, shoving the couch to the right with her knee.

"Seven-fifty?"

She laughed, and his hopes rose. But then she grew quiet again.

"Mark, thank you for asking, but I can't. I just . . ."

He frowned. "No, it's okay. It was just an idea."

"It's a good idea."

They were both silent. Mark rubbed his face, the patches and furrows that would never go away, wanting to hide his disappointment. "Yeah. I'm sorry. I can see it's not worth your time."

"Mark—"

"No, I get it. My dad'll be happy to have your help with the appraisals, anyway. Thanks." He gathered up his tools quickly, wanting to get out of there.

"Maybe you can find somebody else to do it. There are so many artists in the area."

He nodded. "Yeah." He lifted his head. "The thing was the similarity. You really do paint like her."

She said nothing, and he put his hand on the doorknob.

"What was her name?" she asked.

"She signed her paintings with her maiden name, Leah Dolan."

"Leah Dolan was your mother?"

He brightened. "Did you know her?"

She shook her head. "Not personally. But I saw her featured in *American Artist Magazine* years ago. And some of her works were in an exhibition in the Myhren Gallery at the University of Denver where I was going to school. Contemporary Women Artists of the West. Her stuff caught my eye, and seriously, I pushed myself to try to master her technique."

He shook his head. "That's . . . unbelievable."

"I'd always kept this part of the country in the back of my mind because of her paintings. When I saw the job opening, I had to take a chance."

"And here you are."

She shrugged. "And here I am."

Mark remembered that interview for the magazine. His mom had been nervous and excited and mortified at the same time. "She said giving that interview was like holding one of us kids up for the whole world to pick apart. But she was proud of it." It was the last interview she'd given. He vaguely remembered something about an exhibition tour.

"I remember her picture. You look like her," Riley said.

He nodded, feeling her gaze focus on his face. Mark had inherited his mother's olive skin, dark hair, and angular features, though most people told him he was built like his dad, broad and lanky at the same time. His mom had never seen how tall he'd gotten. He looked away. People studying his face was never comfortable.

"I look like my dad," Riley offered. "He is quite Irish."

His laugh rushed from him, brief and unexpected. "Wouldn't have guessed with a name like Riley Madigan." He met her gaze again.

She smirked.

He waited for her to say more. To call the connection a sign. To change her mind about the project.

When none of that happened, he reached for the door again. "Thanks for lunch."

"Thanks for helping fix things. Really. I feel safer. That other knob was always sketchy. Here." She went to the desk and grabbed half of the glass knob he'd broken off. She held it out to him. "For your collection."

He took it from her and smoothed his thumb over the facets. "Thanks."

He opened the door and stepped outside, taking a deep breath of the fresh cold. It had been too much to ask. After what she'd seen of him, she probably figured she could only take Mark Rivers in small doses. He shook his head. She didn't need his work, and she didn't need him hanging around, showing up and breaking things and scaring her to death. Forgetting to make sure his face was hidden. Forgetting he wasn't the old Mark anymore . . .

He was quick down the stairs and just loading his toolbox in the back of the truck when he heard her call his name.

"Mark! Wait."

He stopped, reining in his hopes that she'd changed her mind.

She ran up to him, still barefoot, carrying the garbage bag. "I could use some help with the renovation."

"The what?"

She motioned her head toward the house. "You said you've worked at restoring houses. If you consider helping me, I'll consider painting your nativity."

The breath left his lungs, and he tried to play it cool. "Okay. Yeah."

"I'd like to see the photos you have before I commit."

He hesitated a fraction. Being near her for so much time during the project—that was not a small consideration. But he thought of his dad bent over that leger. "Anything you need."

"The house needs to be done by summer."

He looked back at the house. That was a tall order. No wonder she guarded her time. "Why the deadline?"

"I'm hoping to turn it into a vacation rental."

He frowned. "So, if you do that, where will you go?"

She folded her arms and shrugged. "It depends."

"On what?"

She paused.

"Sorry," he said. "None of my business."

"I just haven't decided if this is where I want to stay. Forever."

He nodded, considering what his tiny town looked like to the seasonal tourists visiting the valley. "That's fair. Hard for Miracle Creek to compete with bright lights, big city."

"That can get old, too."

He took a deep breath. "What do you want done with the house?"

She counted on her fingers. "Open up the wall between the kitchen and front room. New light fixtures. Update the bathroom. Floors, paint. More insulation in the attic. And update the rest of the electrical outlets, I guess. Exterior paint and new gutters when it warms up in the spring. Windows."

His eyebrows rose at the length of the list.

She set the garbage bag on the ground and drew her arms tightly around herself. "Look, I wasn't completely honest with you back there. I have this thing. With Christmas. It's hard. I spend the whole season just . . . trying to look past it. It's not that I don't want to help you."

He nodded. "Christmas is hard for a lot of us."

"I guess we both have some considering to do."

"I guess we do."

As Mark pulled away from the house, he couldn't tell if the ache in his chest was from his fear that she'd say no, or that she'd say yes.

* ❄ *

Riley locked the front door, running her hand over the new hardware. She picked up her half of the glass knob and polished it in her sweater. It was still beautiful, even attached to its wrecked metal base. She set it back down on her desk and padded to the spare bedroom.

Winter light filtered through the bare lilac bushes outside the window. Her painting easel stood next to an industrial metal desk with lots of drawers for her supplies. Her camera bag sat on a shelf. The paint-smattered easel was empty at the moment. Finished and unfinished canvases leaned against the walls in a few stacks. Her paints were neatly put away, organized by color; her brushes waited in a mason jar on the desk. She opened a drawer of an old filing cabinet and walked her fingers through several files.

She paused at one. Hesitating, she flipped it open and picked up the picture on top. A little girl sat in front of a fireplace. Dark pigtails, freckles, pale green eyes, grinning. To her right, a woman with long light-brown hair and the same smile pulled her in tight for a hug. The tree, all shiny with lights and ornaments, filled one side of the picture. She shuffled through and found a few more pictures—various years, but the same woman, the same fireplace. Same light and love shining in her eyes. Riley's grandmother had been the closest thing to home she'd had. The only real Christmas she'd ever had.

With a lump in her throat, she pulled out another file. This one contained black-and-white images, clean, sharp. Different places from her childhood. Mountain flowers, city concrete, architecture, people, sky.

Her dad had taken hundreds of thousands of photos in his life. His job had taken them all over the world before landing him in Hollywood, where he became one of the most coveted still photographers in the industry. Riley had learned the art from him, but even as she was learning how to hold a camera, she was also learning to hold a paintbrush.

Painting was where she soared, losing herself in the feel of a brush in her hand, the application of line and color, coaxing out shadow, emotion, light on a blank canvas. Photography faded from her life along with her dad's presence, and she'd earned several art scholarships with her oil painting portfolio and took that path. She'd been teaching in Colorado for two years when her dad called and offered her a spot on his crew for the newest Paramount picture he was working on. The imagery of the film, her dad said, reminded him of her photographic eye. Their relationship had been tenuous, and he'd called her. Asked for her. How could she turn that down?

Had she known where that decision would lead, she knew exactly how she would've turned it down.

Dad. As much as I'd love to rebuild our relationship after so much strain, if I do this, I'll foolishly fall for the supporting actor so hard I can't see straight, and then he'll break my heart for all of Los Angeles to see—and perhaps beyond, although I'm a nobody so the articles only refer to me as "Gavin Darrow's girlfriend of eight months" and "daughter of famed photographer, Craig Madigan"—but really how many connections do we have in the greater Hollywood area, anyway? Fifty billion? Oh, and you'll be so angry about the whole thing, you'll jeopardize your career over it. Thanks for asking, though.

Riley closed the folder and put it away, pressing at the knot that had formed in her chest.

Returning to her desk in the front room, Riley opened her laptop. Her fingers hovered over the keys, and then she typed *fireman Mark Rivers Miracle Creek*.

Several articles came up. One about Mark's promotion to lieutenant of his company—the youngest in decades—and more recent stories covering the fire. He'd been in what was called the Chelan Complex Fire, where more than fifty structures had been destroyed. The blaze had charred over 56,000 acres and had forced 1,500 residents to flee their homes. And that was before the fire was anywhere close to being contained.

Mark Rivers, Jay Hendricks, and their crew had been sent up there along with hundreds of other firemen from around the state to help contain the fires raging through the area, including the lake town of Chelan and outlying rural communities.

Riley read through the articles, none of them giving her enough details. But she learned that Mark and Jay had gone after a group of young boys who had run to save their tree fort a couple of miles beyond their homes. The boys were saved, but Jay had died in the rescue attempt, overcome as they made their escape. Mark had been transported to Seattle with severe burns.

Another article titled "Chelan Fire Hero Returns Home" showed a picture of Mark in a wheelchair—the right side of him bandaged—Mark's dad, and two women she didn't recognize. The caption named the dark-haired girl as his sister, Stephanie Grady. The tall weepy blonde to Mark's left was his girlfriend, Caylin Clark.

The article didn't say much more than what she already knew. Just that Mark would continue his physical therapy in Miracle Creek, and how proud the town was. A memorial fund had been set up in Jay's name. No quote from Mark. She stared at the image. Mark was nearly unrecognizable, his look somber with half his face covered, his head shaved, but his chin up. The separate image of Jay Hendricks was a stark contrast. Smiling, blond, strong. Twenty-five years old.

She sighed. Tapping the keys, she changed her search.

severe burns, skin grafts, treatment

After reading through several medical website links, she took another deep breath and hit *images*.

After an hour of study, she closed her laptop. With shaky hands, she picked up her phone and called Mark.

"Hello?" He sounded tired. Groggy.

"Hi. It's Riley. Did I wake you?"

"No." He sucked in his breath like he was stretching.

She'd woken him. "Have you talked to your dad about when he wants to meet with me?"

"Um, yeah. I was going to call you after—"

"Your nap?"

"—after I gave you some time. I didn't want to push things."

"Arranging time to meet your dad about the paintings isn't pushing anything. I've already agreed to that."

He was quiet on the line. "We were going to talk about the nativity after, so I didn't want to push it. Push you."

"Right, well . . ."

She wasn't going to tell him she'd researched the fire, read all about the pain and rehab he'd likely been through. She wouldn't tell him the images of burn victims, before and during and after treatment, had turned her gut and torn at her selfish resolve. She wouldn't tell him that any timeline she'd given herself with the house seemed inconsequential now.

"I've been thinking. About your mom," she said. "I'm interested in learning more about her. Maybe trying to restore something of hers that was lost is an opportunity I shouldn't take for granted. Are you all right with that?"

He paused. "We don't mind sharing about my mom."

"Are you sure?"

"I'm sure. Does tomorrow afternoon work?" he asked. "I'll tell Dad you're coming before dinner to go over the ledger. Dinner is at my sister's, so he'll be leaving after you're done. We can discuss the nativity then."

"Aren't you eating at your sister's, too?"

"Doesn't look like it."

She chewed on her lip. "I don't mean to disrupt your plans."

"We eat at my sister's every Sunday. It's no problem to miss this one. Come at four. That'll give you enough time to sort through numbers and get some questions answered."

"Okay. Thanks."

"And Riley . . . I'll make us something. Can't talk business on empty stomachs."

She reached out and touched the glass doorknob. "No, of course not. That would risk disaster before we even got started."

"No disasters, then."

The quiet, deep way he spoke sent unnerving shivers through her body. She withdrew her hand from the glass. "Four o'clock, tomorrow," she said. She couldn't promise no disasters. They seemed to follow her pretty closely.

He gave her directions, and after they said goodbye, she hung up and sat back in her chair, staring at the ceiling. She hadn't expected him to ask her to stay for dinner. While she certainly wasn't trying to "draw him out" like Nate had been so concerned about, she remembered what he'd said. For whatever reason, Mark trusted her. Enough that he seemed to have forgotten his scars for a few minutes today. He seemed to have forgotten that he was trying to hide. And in those few minutes, Riley had seen who he was behind the scars.

And she was having a hard time unseeing it.

Chapter 6

Sunday afternoon, Riley drove a winding road with tall pine trees climbing the hill on her left and rows of winter orchard sloping down on her right.

She hadn't slept well, sifting through memories and dreams, second-guessing herself. She'd spent the morning huddled in her quilt, researching Leah Dolan and similar artists on the internet, perusing online galleries and making notes about valuations, getting in touch with her friend who worked at the art gallery in Denver, ignoring the clock and her growling stomach until she was forced to admit that if she didn't get up and shower soon, she'd have to show up at Mark's house in her Spidey pajama pants and fuzzy slippers. So, she showered and dressed in jeans, a thermal T-shirt, and her Chucks. Her concession to laziness had been to skip shampooing her hair, wrangling it into braids instead. She'd yanked on a parka as she'd left the house. The weather had taken a frosty turn.

As she pulled up to the Riverses' home, she was struck by the timelessness of it. White farmhouse, wide front porch, and dormer windows she guessed were functional and not the fakes people added for looks only. An old flagstone chimney climbed up the right side of the house, and trees at least thirty years old flanked both sides. They would offer nice shade in the warmer months. Flagstone steps climbed up from the gravel U-drive where she'd parked and led through an over-wintered garden.

When she stepped onto the porch, she paused. A tumbling river had been painted from the far end of the porch ceiling all the way across the covered front exterior and the front door itself to the bottom left where the siding met the porch floor. Watery grays, blues, and greens flowed over and around painted submerged rocks like a riverbed. Above the door, a painted sign read, "A Rivers Welcome."

She rang the doorbell and waited, marveling that a little-known artist she'd read about in a magazine had painted such a magnificent mural.

The door opened, and a tall man with broad shoulders, silver-gray hair, and clear blue eyes greeted her.

"Hello, Ms. Madigan. Cal Rivers. Thanks for coming." Mr. Rivers opened the door wide and beckoned her inside.

She obeyed. "Riley, please. I love this door. The whole porch is extraordinary."

"Thank you. Leah believed a doorway should make a visitor feel like an adventurer, and a family feel like they never truly left. Look here." He pointed to the lower right corner of the door where the painting gave the illusion of shallow water running over smooth rocks. On four of the rocks, she'd painted names as if they'd been carved into the stones. *Calvin. Leah. Stephanie. Mark.*

"The Rivers," Cal said with a grin. "Been there a long time. I do my best to keep it from fading."

"What a beautiful use of a name."

"I was four or five when Mom painted that," Mark said as he

came down the stairs behind them wearing a knit skullcap and pulling up the hood of his sweatshirt.

Cal shut the door against the cold. "You couldn't say your *R*s. Cutest thing—'Mahk Wivews.'"

"Aww," Riley said.

"He'd point and say, 'This is Mahk's wock.'" Cal grinned and gave her a quick wink, and it became clear to Riley where Mark got his smile when he wasn't protecting it.

"Thanks for sharing that, Dad."

Cal chuckled again and took Riley's coat. After hanging it on a hook, he waved her toward the dining room. "Speaking of pictures, Riley, we'll be working in here. Do you need anything? We've got water, juice, soda, coffee." He peered behind her at Mark, who leaned against the wall. "Don't you have something to do?"

Mark looked annoyed. "Yeah."

"Well git."

Mark turned, grabbing a coat and a pair of work gloves. "Point out a kid's speech impediment and then send him off to chop wood," he mumbled. "Brutal."

As the door closed behind him, Cal smiled at Riley. "So, something to drink?"

After an hour of calculating dimensions, frames, "gallery value," and comparing what was lost to what Leah had sold similar paintings for, Riley was able to help Cal complete the list. Cal had also taken her on a tour of the house to study the originals hanging in the rooms. Her favorite was a large oil hanging in the dining room, just above the table where they worked.

She studied it again as Cal gathered up the paperwork and adding machine. The small title plaque attached to the bottom of the frame read *Miracle Creek Bridge*.

"Her command of bokeh in the background is incredible. It

brings the subject into such clear focus. And she's bold with her contrast. It's what I've tried to do with my own work. I really had to break out of my shell, but I feel so accomplished when I just go for it. It's thrilling." She turned and looked at Cal, who was watching her with a faraway look.

"Thank you," he said. "She would've loved that compliment."

She smiled and turned back to the painting. "Is this nearby?"

"Oh, sure. Miracle Creek comes all the way down from Mt. Stuart. After it leaves our little valley here, it joins up with the Wenatchee. Pretty hike along there. The bridge is one of the few original standing structures from the early days. Used to be several mines up that way. A lot of history there."

"I can imagine."

He leaned back in his chair. "There's a legend surrounding it, you know. That bridge."

She turned back to him. "What legend?"

He gazed at the picture. "Just some stories about wish-making. Goes back for generations." He looked at her and chuckled. "Don't look so impressed. Our little bridge isn't as big a draw as the ski slopes or Leavenworth. I'm guessing you've been over to the Bavarian village to see all the hubbub?"

"Not since I moved here, no." Riley had looked up the nearby German-themed village and vacation destination online when she'd applied for the teaching job. With its Alps feel and abundance of festivities, Leavenworth had the makings of a romantic storybook getaway in any season, which had fired her idea for a vacation rental.

"Why not?"

"I don't know. School started up as soon as I got here, and then there was the play. Yvette wanted to take me over there for Octoberfest, but it didn't happen."

He scratched his chin. "Yeah, I bet the both of you have been a bit busy." He picked up the ledger and took it to a bookshelf in the front room. "Well, we'll have to remedy that. Here in Miracle Creek we shine pretty well for the holidays, but Leavenworth . . . that's the dazzler."

The front door opened, and Mark came in, wiping his feet on the rug and pulling off his gloves.

"Mark, this lady has never been to Leavenworth," Cal exclaimed.

"You don't say," Mark said, unimpressed, as he hung up his coat. His hood had fallen off but his knit cap stayed on, his right-side mask toward them. His complexion was rosy in patches from the cold.

"Christmas tree lighting's coming up in a few weeks. Shame to miss it her first season here." Cal smiled at Riley. "Most festive thing you'll ever see."

She politely smiled back.

"It happens every year, Dad. A billion people show up, they light the tree, and everybody crowds into the shops to get warm while the owners hope to sell a hundred more nutcrackers than they did last year."

Cal looked affronted. "You did not just say that."

Mark folded his arms. "What if I did?"

"I'd take you out back and tan your hide."

"Too late, fire already did that."

Riley's eyes grew wide until she saw the two men exchange smirks.

Cal turned to Riley. "I knew this guy once. He'd get so excited for the tree lighting that he'd go early and save a place for his family with camp chairs. Once in the pouring rain." He thumbed not-so-secretively at Mark.

Mark looked at her. "Don't believe him."

Cal cleared the water glasses from the table. "He'd pack a thermos of hot cocoa and bring mini candy canes for everyone. And I mean *everyone*."

A real smile crept across Riley's face as Mark shook his head, glancing at her. "I'd throw them at people."

"Yeah," Cal called from the kitchen. "Hit 'em right in the Christmas spirit."

"Are you done?" Mark called back.

"Just about." He returned to the dining room and offered a hand to Riley. "Thank you for your help. I feel like a weight has been lifted. I owe you, so anything you need, you name it."

She took his hand, touched by the sincerity in his offer. "I'm glad I could help. It's not often I get to study firsthand the work of an artist I admired."

He placed his other hand over hers and gave her a second shake. "You're welcome any time."

He headed for the front door. "Well, I'm going to go have a roast beef dinner with mashed potatoes and gravy. I'd invite you, but I've been told you two have other plans." He pulled on a wool peacoat and a bomber hat. "I'd say that was great, but I know how this guy cooks. So, I'll just wish you luck."

"Bye, Dad."

"Goodbye." Cal waved and shut the front door.

Riley held back her laughter, and Mark let out a low sigh.

"That seemed easy enough, getting him out of the house," she said. "What exactly did you tell him?"

Mark shrugged. "That I was making you dinner. It's the only way I knew he wouldn't argue."

"You knew that, huh?"

"Been a while since I've made anybody dinner."

Riley imagined where Cal's thoughts had gone with that information. "Maybe that's a good thing. Your dad didn't exactly build my hopes."

"My dad didn't know I bought steaks. I thought we'd grill. Is that all right?"

"It's been a while since I've had a good steak."

"Well, it might still be a while. I haven't grilled since before—" He looked away, putting his hands in his pockets. "Anyway, I thought I'd give it a shot."

"I can help," she offered. "Maybe light the grill or something." Inwardly, she cringed.

After a barely detectable pause, he nodded, though she couldn't read his expression. "I'll get the steaks," he said, turning toward the kitchen. "Grill's this way."

❄ ❅ ❄

She lit the gas grill with a pop and hiss and closed the lid to let it heat up. The chill in the air nipped at her nose and cheeks as she eyed Mark through the back-door window. Inside, he washed and prepped the steaks. His compression sleeve was gone, and he rubbed in some kind of seasoning and slapped the steaks on a plate. He washed his hands at the sink and looked up to catch her watching. He looked away immediately.

Riley slipped her hands in her pockets and studied the backyard in its winter darkness.

The sliding door squeaked open, and Mark brought out two New York strips and tongs. She took the plate from him and put one steak on the heat, the sudden sizzle a welcome sound in the quiet. She held out the tongs for Mark.

He looked at her and narrowed his gaze.

She lifted her chin. A little motion, but he read it correctly.

He took the tongs, and with a deep breath, he gripped the remaining steak and placed it on the hot grill. The tongs clattered on the plate where he returned them.

She smiled, casual. "Now what?" she asked, as if he'd merely dropped a letter in the mailbox.

He opened the back door and waited. As she stepped past him into the house, he touched her arm.

She looked him in the eyes and saw unease beneath his dark brows. She'd overstepped her bounds. It wasn't her place to make him face his fear. Not now, not ever.

He shot a glance toward the grill where a few flames licked the undersides of the steaks. "Thanks," he said, his voice low.

She nodded, searching his face for irritation, his tone for sarcasm, but she found none. She entered the warm kitchen, and the sound of the door closing followed soon after.

"How are you with scrubbing potatoes?" he asked, placing a couple of bakers next to the sink.

"Oh, sure, give me the dirty work."

While the meat sizzled outside, the potatoes steamed in the microwave, and Mark dumped a bagged salad into a serving bowl.

"I can do better than this," he mumbled.

"Better than iceberg lettuce and shredded carrots?" She grabbed the empty bag and held it up, reading the label. "It's a classic. Says so right here."

He gave her a look that challenged her soft gibe and grabbed the bag, tossing it in the garbage can, then disappeared behind the fridge door. "Ranch okay?" He stood, looking more closely at the bottle. "It's bacon ranch. My dad's branching out."

"Sure," she said with a smile.

He set it down on the table. Shaking his head, he put his

hands on his hips. "Living with my dad, I've learned that the kitchen is not his . . . strength."

She looked around. "It's clean."

He turned and opened up cupboard after cupboard, ending with the fridge.

"Okay, so it's clean and empty," she said.

He closed everything back up.

"So, fill it up," she said. "With as much as . . . two men living on their own need to eat. Does he cook?"

He shook his head. "Not if he can help it. Not if *I* can help it."

She smiled. "Do you cook?"

He turned to get plates out of one of the cupboards. "Used to."

She watched him, his hand and arm back in its sleeve. "You're cooking now."

He paused as the microwave dinged, and he arched a brow in her direction.

"I'll check the steaks," she said.

He continued to set the table while she turned the meat. The scent of whatever he'd done to them before they hit the flame made her mouth water. Inhaling deeply, she took a minute, chilly as it was, to drink in the moment. Not a sound could be heard except for the small noises from inside the kitchen and the sizzle from the grill. She could just make out the silhouettes of mountains against the night sky. Everything was still up here. And the stars . . . They didn't show up like this in the city.

The back door opened. "You okay out here?" Mark held out a jacket.

"Thanks. The steaks are about done." She took the jacket and wrapped it around her shoulders. It smelled like wool and aftershave. "I was just noticing how dark and quiet it is up here."

He nodded and hitched his shoulders up as if trying to warm

himself. "Not much in the way of streetlights or neighbors. The highway is a couple miles that way." He nodded in a northern direction. "You can see it from the new outbuilding, but not from here. It's one of the reasons Mom picked this place when they left Tacoma. Their apartment had been right off the freeway. The traffic noise drove her nuts."

"I can imagine it would be hard to create with that in the background."

"Exactly. Her studio is upstairs in the attic. Did my dad show you?"

She shook her head. Cal hadn't taken her up that far.

"She and dad converted the space when they first moved in. I'll take you up there after dinner."

"Did you keep it as she left it?"

His eyes narrowed in thought. "Most of it. Dad keeps saying if he ever sells this place, he'll need to show the room in its best light. He keeps it clean."

"Would he ever sell this place?" she asked. She couldn't imagine giving up something like this house, after being here so long.

He shook his head. "No. He keeps my mom's studio the way it is because they built it together. It's as much a part of him as she is. He's not fooling any of us." He nodded at the house. "This place would be my sister's when it gets too much for Dad. But she and Brian don't want or need the work that comes with it, so I'll be taking it."

"You need the work?"

He shrugged.

She drew the coat more tightly around her. "Can I say something?"

"Haven't stopped you yet."

She watched him, remembering how he'd been himself—his

real self—with her yesterday, once again wishing he wasn't always so careful about giving her his left side. "You guys talk about your mom," she said, "like she's still a part of things here."

"She is. That's why I'm asking you to help me with this project. My dad still loves her, but he's the kind of person who sees the big picture. 'Get through the grieving and live on.'" He looked into the darkness. "I've heard that a hundred times."

"That can be easier said than done," she said.

He nodded. "Time has helped."

He watched her, his dark brown eyes unwavering. She knew the smile they were capable of. Knew there was more to him than she should hope to learn.

The weight of Mark's request settled on her shoulders like a blanket. The weight of keeping her emotions out of this project. The weight of potentially stepping into his mother's shoes as an artist and replicating something that connected her to this house. To their lives. To Mark.

"The steaks are about ready," she said. "Medium-ish?"

He handed her a clean plate, and she grabbed the tongs, her pulse flighty in her veins.

"Can I ask you something?" he said, turning toward her so the light from the porch lit the left side of his face.

"Haven't stopped you yet," she answered, bracing herself for the possible questions he could hurl at her now that she'd given him permission.

His high cheekbones and full mouth were the color of a Big Sky sunrise. The knit cap hid the dark mess of hair she'd seen when his hood had fallen at her house. Burns masked his face, but fingerlike scars stretched back from his temple in smooth stripes where no hair grew, and his ear was a patchwork of healed reconstruction.

"How do you do that?" he asked.

"What?"

His brow furrowed. "How do you look at me like that? Like . . ." His voice quieted. "Like you see this every day. Like it doesn't bother you."

She frowned and turned off the grill, wondering if she was so different from everyone else in town that he had to ask.

"Lette Mae doesn't look at you differently. Neither do Nate or Gus. Or your niece. Ivy adores you."

He gave her a weak smile. "It's taken a long time for people in this town to look me in the eye, even Nate and Gus. Sometimes people look me so hard in the eye I know they're trying not to look anywhere else." He shrugged. "Ivy's a kid. She was afraid at the beginning. Until she heard my voice." He lifted his gaze out to the yard. "From that point on, I was her Uncle Mark again. That space, where she didn't know me, where she cried and hid . . . that was rough." He cleared his throat. "But you're the only adult besides my family and my doctors who didn't shrink back from the beginning. Who didn't turn away quick when I caught them staring."

"But you did catch me staring," she said.

"You didn't turn away."

"In this whole town, I can't be the only one who . . ." She wasn't sure how to end that sentence.

He helped her out. "In this whole town, you're the only one who looks at me like a person with burn scars, instead of burn scars walking around like a person."

She met his gaze, and a few seconds stretched between them. She knew that wasn't true, but the way he said it, she could see how it could be. The people he grew up with were blinded by who he used to be. The memory of the old Mark got in the way of seeing him now.

"Everyone thinks you're a hero. That's who they see."

"If seeing me as a hero helps them look at me, fine." He shook his head. "But that's not me, either."

Her mind raced for something to say. She hadn't expected the conversation to go this deep when she agreed to come over. "Well, maybe I'm insane. I'm the insane artist who moves to a small town and turns it upside down because I see people with burn scars instead of burns with people scars. I'm a freaking M. Night Shyamalan movie." She clamped her mouth shut.

Oh, please, don't let him be offended by the words that just came out of my mouth.

A smile appeared around his eyes, easing her distress.

"So," she ventured, "in this movie, do we ever get to eat?"

He stepped back, opening the door for her and letting her pass through. She hadn't really answered his question, but it seemed to be enough for him.

They sat at the smaller table in the kitchen.

"This smells great," she said. "I haven't grilled in forever."

"That's a really long time."

She gave him a wry smile, and he gave one back as he reached for the water pitcher.

His smile turned to a frown of concentration as he carefully filled their glasses. "I've had to learn to do more stuff with my left hand. I'm strong enough. It's the agility. Nerve damage. Pouring water was one of the things I took for granted. Seriously, pouring water." He shook his head.

"I had a friend who hurt her back. She said the same thing about pouring water. She didn't have to switch hands, but she had to adjust her balance differently."

He nodded.

She lifted her glass for a toast. "To pouring water. May we never spill."

"Or be thirsty," he said.

"That, too," she conceded. "Important."

He smiled fully, then, and she felt a flush of warmth hit her cheeks as she sipped her water. She focused on cutting into her steak.

"So," he said after a few minutes of silence, "where are you from, Riley Madigan?"

She paused and swallowed her bite. "I'm from a lot of places. I tell people I'm from Montana."

"Are you from Montana?"

"Once I was from Montana."

He stopped his chewing and gave her an odd look. He swallowed. "And the other times?"

She sat back and sighed. "Wisconsin, Illinois, New York—twice—Florida, Germany, DC, Maine, Louisiana, Sydney, Ontario, the Philippines, Colorado. And then California."

He stared at her, all self-consciousness gone. So that was the trick. Stun him with her nomadic history.

"Your family moved around that much?"

She shrugged, uncomfortable. "My dad's a photographer. A driven, ambitious man. It was important to my mom to be with him. We went where the job was. Sometimes. Sometimes he went without us."

"I can't imagine what that would be like."

She looked around the kitchen where he'd probably eaten dinner since first grade. "No, I suppose not."

He turned his attention back to his food. Almost. "Was it hard?"

"I spent as much time as I could with my grandma in Montana. Holidays, mostly. It's all I knew, so . . ." She stabbed some salad. "You sure are talking a lot for someone who was afraid to come to my door to ask me a question."

"I did come to your door." He jabbed a piece of steak with his fork.

"Yeah, and then you broke it."

His fork paused, and he narrowed his eyes at her, then took his bite.

She fought to hide the smile that surfaced from that one small action. She worked on her potato.

Mark sat back. "How did you learn to renovate houses?"

He was definitely getting more comfortable asking questions. She swallowed her bite of potato, wanting to shove more in her mouth. "My mom. If she knew we were going to be in an area for a while, she'd get her hands on a diamond in the rough in a good neighborhood and challenge herself to flip it before we moved again. My dad would help sometimes." She stabbed another forkful of salad, remembering it was usually better when her dad didn't help. "I learned a lot from her." She glanced at him, painting on a smile.

"I'm sure you were a big help."

She pulled in a deep breath. "Oh, I don't know. There were times when I definitely did not help."

"Like when?"

She lifted her glass. "C'mon. I can't tell you all my secrets."

"I'll remember you said that," he said, leaning forward to put another bite of steak in his mouth.

She finished her drink. "Fine. We both have secrets. There's nothing wrong with mutual understanding between friends."

"Is that what this is? We're friends?" He kept his expression neutral.

She shrugged. "Why not? I'm new in town with a shadowy past. You're the uncertain town hero coming out of hiding. Sounds like we could both use a friend. Now that you're being talky and all."

He shook his head. "You *are* insane."

"I told you so."

After a few more bites, she said, "You aren't wearing your hood."

He didn't look up. "Nope."

When they finished dinner, she moved to start clearing the table.

"Stay," he told her, standing. "We're not finished."

"But I'm so full."

He ignored her, but she stayed and waited until he returned with a plate.

"Are those—?"

"Tender, flaky pastries? Yes. The best Bavarian cream you've had outside Bavaria. Wait, you've lived in Bavaria."

She grinned up at him. "Munich. You are evil."

"I'm not gonna lie. I'm trying to soften you up."

"Literally?"

He chuckled. "For the project."

"Very cunning."

"You gave me the weapon." He offered her the plate.

"And you chose to use it," she said, taking one of Lette Mae's *bollen*.

"Better than a baseball bat."

She licked the cream off her finger, smooth and cold and infused with vanilla and sugar. "Mhph" was all she could say.

After they cleared the dishes, Mark led her upstairs. At the top, he walked past several rooms and, at the end of the hall lined with family pictures, he pulled down a set of folding stairs from the ceiling. He stepped back and motioned her up.

As Riley climbed the stairs to the attic, anticipation tickled the back of her neck. It was an art room, for heaven's sake. She had an art room. It didn't give her tingles any time she walked into it.

Maybe it should.

She emerged from the stairs into darkness and stepped aside for Mark. He flipped a switch, and the room lit up.

The track lighting was no surprise, but the floor-to-ceiling window draped with white Christmas lights made her gasp. "I bet this gets great light during the day." Riley approached the easel in the center of the room. She glanced at Mark, who nodded.

A few tubes of oil paint, old and bent from being squeezed, lay in the easel tray. Umber. Chrome Green. Cerulean.

Riley smiled. "Sennelier."

"She used other brands, but mostly this." Mark watched her, his arms folded, his expression unreadable.

"Monet painted with Sennelier. And Gaugin, Matisse."

"Picasso," he added.

Riley nodded. She shoved her hands in her pockets, afraid if she didn't, she'd pick up the tubes just to feel them.

Mark inhaled deeply. "It used to smell like her in here. The paint, of course. Turpentine. But she had this perfume. Sunflowers. Dad always got it for her for Christmas."

"I remember that one."

His head ducked. "Go ahead. Look around."

She lightly ran her hand over the worktable to her left. Small boxes of feathers and hooks littered the top.

The attic walls rose about four feet before they pitched up to the roofline. A long shelf of cubbies pressed against the wall, each one stuffed with books, magazines, jars of brushes and sponges, old linseed oil, spatulas, and rolls of newspapers. Several palettes were stacked vertically into taller slots. She pulled one out a few inches. Blobs and smears, mixes of colors still covered the surface, cracked and dried after so many years.

She looked at Mark.

"I don't think Dad knew what to do with that one. Mom had cleaned the others like she always did after a project. That one was what she was working from until the end."

"What was she painting?"

He nodded toward the opposite wall where two dormer windows let in more light. Fixed to the wall between the dormers was a painting of the house and the orchard behind it, tall mountains, a shimmering cerulean sky.

Riley stepped closer to have a better look. Leah had included a couple of copper metal sculptures in the summer gardens— tooled with a blade—and the mural on the front porch.

"That's me on the tire swing," Mark said behind her. "Steph's in the window, reading. Mom knew this would be her last one. She didn't finish."

The children were shadows. A portion of the tree remained in charcoals, the rough sky painted in around it.

"So much movement," she said. Even unfinished, the painting was filled with vibrant life.

"Sometimes I wonder what she'd think of Dad keeping the room like this. Is she shaking her head thinking this would make a great playroom for the grandkids?"

She smiled. "Who's to say what we hang on to and what we let go?" She looked around, eager to redirect. "It's not really hurting anyone, is it? Keeping this?"

He shrugged. "Eleven years and I'm the one asking you to recreate something of hers that we lost."

"True," she said.

She felt him study her, like a puzzle piece.

She wondered if Cal Rivers took his own advice about moving forward. Would he always be alone? She bit back the question. It wasn't her place to question anyone about moving on after losing someone.

She turned to the large window. "Southwest facing?"

"Yep."

"Does it catch sunsets?"

"Sometimes. Sunsets are tricky with the mountains so close."

She nodded. "I miss the coastal sunsets in the Philippines, and Montana's big sky. Miles of sunsets."

"You'll see plenty of sky come summer."

"Surrounded by all these mountains?" she teased.

"We'll get you up the mountains. See how you like that."

"At sunset?"

"If that's what you're after."

The confidence of his challenge stirred up her competitive side, and she imagine a hike up these beautiful mountains with Mark. For a sunset.

They locked eyes for a moment before he turned away. "I've got those pictures of the nativity downstairs."

She nodded, glancing around once more. "Thanks for showing me this. She must have loved to work up here."

"She did." He paused as if to say something more, but then motioned her down ahead of him.

Stepping away from the stairs, she took the opportunity to glance over the family pictures in the hall, and one in particular drew her eye. The family of four lounged on a riverbank, parents seated under a tree, a young woman posed behind them. Next to her, one arm reaching up to a low tree limb, stood Mark, looking casual and confident, probably thirteen or fourteen years old. He was on the verge of laughter, whole and carefree. His mother had the same look of laughter, of joy in her family.

The bang of the stair door folding back into the ceiling startled her, and she spun away from the portrait.

"Can I get you anything?" he asked, brushing his hands on his pants. "A drink? More pastries? Are you warm enough?"

She brushed a stray lock of hair back from her face, her heartbeat returning to its normal pace. "I'm fine, thanks."

He nodded, seeming distracted.

"Are you all right?" she asked.

"Yeah. Why?"

They descended the stairs to the main level. "You asked me if I wanted another pastry, and we both know I'm about to bust."

He shook his head. "Just nervous, I guess."

She nodded carefully. "About what?"

"About convincing you to do this project."

"Ah."

"Should I be nervous?" he asked, glancing at her sideways.

She drew in a deep breath. "I'm here to consider something I already told you I was interested in."

"But there's still a chance you might say no."

She smiled. "Just show me the pictures you have, and I'll decide for sure."

He led her down another hall. "I shouldn't have pushed the *bollen*."

"Let's not go that far."

The corner of his mouth lifted.

Chapter 7

Mark led Riley to a small room behind the garage. A washing machine and dryer were tucked into one corner, and a cot and desk sat in another. He grabbed a pile of folded clothes off the cot and shoved them into a basket.

"I used to sleep out here when we had a lot of company for Thanksgiving or whatever." He went to the desk and opened the top drawer. "These were all I could find. They were shots I took as a kid with my cheap-o camera, so they're not the best quality." He held out a small stack of photos.

"Your mom didn't take pictures of them when they were completed?"

"She did, but they were in the outbuilding . . ."

She took the photos from him.

"We kept most of the photo albums here in the house. A lot of family pictures. But we lost several boxes of pictures that were stored. Pictures of her childhood, and Dad's. Their wedding. Mom had some framed here in the house, but when they turned the attic into her studio, the outbuilding became a storage unit. Can't blame them. It was as insulated and weathertight as this house and had plenty of room in the loft for all kinds of stuff. Including the Christmas decorations."

Riley tried to wrap her head around that kind of loss. Her family had so few possessions she hadn't known they'd even had a storage unit until she was older. Her parents' brief separation when she was a kid had shed light on a lot of things. One of those was a storage unit in Bozeman, and another in Madison, Wisconsin.

Riley leafed through the pictures, studying each one. They'd definitely been taken from a lower angle. She turned one in her hand, trying to see what the photographer had seen.

"I told you they were lousy."

"They aren't that bad. I can see most of Joseph in this one. This one of Mary is good."

He peered over her shoulder.

"There isn't a clear one of the baby," she said, sorting through the pictures again.

"I was trying to get a close-up, I think. With a flash."

"That explains the big shine over his face."

A shiver of recognition ran down her back as she studied the figures, understanding why Mark had seen his mother's style in her own. "The boards were painted black first."

"She did that often. Used gesso. She said the colors didn't have to fight so hard to glow."

She turned her head, startled by his nearness. A few more inches and she could've reached up and touched her nose to his jaw. He must have felt it too, because he stepped away, leaving a blend of aftershave and grilled steak and pastry in his wake.

She drew in a breath and cleared her head. "You know a lot about her painting." He'd recognized terminology and showed familiarity with the art; she couldn't help being impressed.

He studied the floor. "I asked a lot of questions."

She could imagine the exchanges—probably similar to the ones she'd had with her dad about photography. The trick of priming, or gessoing, a surface matte gray or black instead of leaving it white was used when—like Mark said—an artist wanted the colors to pop. Blues shimmered, reds flamed, greens came alive. Whites shone. Leah had used the black base to create a dense outline and add depth to the figures. And—as Mark said—they glowed. Riley had used the same technique in the Peter Pan backgrounds and props.

"You see it, don't you?" Mark asked.

Yes. She saw it. "They're stunning."

"Every year I told myself I needed to take better pictures after they were set up. And every year when I finished, my mind was on getting back to the house to warm up or getting to town or . . ." He looked away, his hands resting at his hips.

"You never know when something special is going to be gone," she heard herself say.

His expression clouded. "I've learned that lesson too many times." He took the photos from her hand and shuffled through them. "I drew up some sketches and dimensions, too." He set the photos on the desk and lifted his gaze to hers. "Will you help me do this?"

She wanted to have some valid excuse to back out. To say, no, she couldn't take on something of this magnitude.

But that wouldn't be the truth.

He noticed her hesitation. "What makes it a hard decision?"

The obvious answer was time, but he'd offered to help her with the house. She'd painted three backdrops for the play in a few weeks, and she'd been just as busy. She couldn't deny the spark she'd felt looking at the images and feeling challenged to create again. But the knot in her chest was made of fear, deep and familiar.

She shook her head. "I want to have the house done by the end of the school year, and Yvette's already talking about next semester's play, and art club twice a week and—I just don't know if I could take on a project this size and have it finished for you when you want it," she lied. "I don't want to promise you something I can't deliver."

"I told you I can help with the house," he said.

She folded her arms. "I'd like to have it ready as a vacation rental by summer."

His gaze narrowed a fraction. "While you're somewhere else."

Watching the cement floor, Riley shrugged. "Like I said. I'm still deciding if I belong in Miracle Creek."

A few uncomfortable seconds ticked by.

"You belong," Mark said quietly.

Riley lifted her gaze to find him focused on the wall. His words echoed through her.

"It's the Christmas thing," he said. "Right?"

He'd paid too close attention last night. "It's complicated."

His brow pulled forward. "I know the best guys who can do the electrical and plumbing. And the windows. I'll do everything I can to help you with the rest of the house."

"Just like that?" she asked.

"Just like that." He kept his left side to her.

She shook her head, but could feel herself caving. What was she getting herself into?

He stepped to the doorway. "Take all the time you need to consider. I'll get you another donut—"

"Mark."

He paused.

She took a deep breath. "I'll do it."

He turned back to her. "What?"

"You heard me—whoa—" In two steps, he'd reentered the room, held her arms, then kissed her cheek.

"Thank you," he said, holding her gaze, his face close to hers.

She caught her breath. His eyes weren't as dark as she'd first thought. Not that she'd been thinking about his eyes. Even if they were a true walnut-brown ringed in black.

"I'll help you," he said. "I promise."

Her gaze followed the scars trailing from his eye down to the corner of his mouth.

He abruptly stepped away. "I-I'm sorry," he stammered, his voice low and quiet. He didn't look at her. "I don't know where that came from. It won't happen again."

"It's okay," she said, her heart still recovering from his sudden show of gratitude. "I know this is important to you."

"I really didn't know if you'd say yes."

"Well, I could use the help with the house. And I like your dad. And your mom."

A moment hung in the air where she should have said, "And you." They'd declared themselves friends. But she didn't say it, and the space was filled with nothing. Awkward nothing.

"I'll get you the notes I made." He left her in the cold room while he returned to the house.

Riley folded her arms against the chill and walked over to the desk, grabbing the stack of photos again. She sat on the cot and shuffled through the pics. She shook her head.

This was not in the plan, Madigan.

Mark returned and set some drawings and a pad of graph paper on the desk. "I've got the boards. I can get the figures cut tomorrow if we draw them out tonight. And I can paint them black, or both of us can. That would speed things along. You probably have family stuff planned for the holidays, huh?"

She huffed a laugh, his nervous energy contagious. "No. I don't have any plans for Thanksgiving or Christmas. That should help."

He sat down next to her on the cot. "No family stuff?"

She shook her head, staring blindly at the top photo.

"Can I ask why?"

She shrugged. "My parents are traveling over Thanksgiving. They'll be in California for Christmas, but I need to . . . not be in California." She gave him a smile. "It's just me."

He shook his head, as if he couldn't understand.

Her smile remained, though sharing even that much with him felt like it cost her something. "I'm okay with it. Really. I prefer quiet holidays."

"You better not let word get out that you're on your own. The town will adopt you and make you their project."

"Then I'll trust you not to say anything."

He looked at her sideways. "I don't know. I'm the current project. Might take the spotlight off me."

She suppressed a laugh, and he smiled.

After a few moments, he graciously changed the subject. "I meant it when I said you paint like my mom. Not exactly like her, of course. But I'm not wrong."

She nodded at the photos. Most artists would cringe hearing someone tell them they painted like someone else, but from Mark it was a high compliment. "Thank you," she said. And she meant it.

She'd take this challenge. She'd keep it together, keep it strictly business, get the house fixed up, and be done. All the while working closely on a *Christmas* project with Mark Rivers, who'd told her she belonged . . .

He handed her his drawings. "We can refine these on the graph paper for better scale."

She sorted through the rough images he'd penciled out. "They're not bad."

"They're no Riley Madigans."

"You can stop with the flattery, I already took the job."

He grinned, and she remembered the touch of his lips high on her cheek. The knot in her chest flipped.

That's trouble.

They went back into the dining room and spent the next couple of hours sketching out figures on graph paper, keeping to Mark's dimensions. Joseph stood. Mary knelt. The baby nestled in a manger. A shepherd knelt, too, cradling a lamb. Another lamb stood on its own. Then there was the star.

"What about the stable?" She picked up a photo and squinted at the simple frame arching over the figures.

"I'm making that." He pulled a sketch from the pile. "It won't be exactly the same, but I'm thinking I can make it sturdier than the last one." He handed her the drawing of a simple wood frame faced with natural branches, the star at its peak.

She nodded. "When did you work construction?"

He shrugged. "Out here, summer jobs are either orchard work, construction, or working at the IGA. I was always working the orchard, but my dad made sure we got some other experience under our belts. He believed if we were busy working, we'd stay out of trouble."

"Was he right?"

"For the most part. He still thinks that way, unfortunately."

She smiled. "When did you decide to become a firefighter?"

His expression dimmed, and he slid the plans for the stable from her fingers. He stared at the page for a few seconds. Finally, he spoke. "I don't remember *not* wanting to be a firefighter. I saw a fire truck in a parade when I was a kid, and I knew that's where I needed to be." He set the page down. Then he lifted his head. "I'll go get the boards and meet you back in the laundry room. It would be better if we were out there in case my dad comes home. Like I said, if we can get the silhouettes drawn tonight, then I can cut them out whenever he's not around."

"Do you need help?"

"I got it."

His sudden departure left an emptiness in the room. Obviously, the demons Mark fought didn't end with the scars on his face. How would it be to excel at something you loved, only to have it so violently snatched away?

Things needed to lighten up.

On the way out to the laundry room, Riley checked her phone. At some point, Dalton had called and left a message.

"A few of us are heading over to Seattle next weekend before the passes get dicey again. Hoping to celebrate winning regionals. Also hoping you'd like to come along. Think about it."

A couple of days in the city sounded great right now. Cool restaurants, great shopping, attending the symphony or maybe hitting a club. Wearing real shoes. Or maybe not, because of the rain. Did people wear Jimmy Choos in the rain? But crowds and city lights, food and the music of the streets—

With Dalton.

She laughed at herself. Dalton probably shouldn't have been an afterthought on that list.

She texted back. *Got your message. Just took on a commissioned art piece with a deadline. Gotta pay the bills. Maybe next time?*

He answered immediately. *Your loss.☺ Definitely next time.*

Mark arrived, shouldering a stack of heavy-looking boards like they were nothing. He knelt down and dropped them with a smack. "This should cover the smaller figures."

"Do you go to Seattle often?" she asked as she put her phone away.

"Used to." He slid the pile more toward the center of the room. "It's been a while."

"Is it as rainy as they say?"

He paused. "You haven't been to Seattle yet?"

She shook her head. "You sound like your dad. Dalton just asked me to go next weekend. I told him I had a commission to work on."

"You didn't tell him what it was, did you?"

"No. It's a secret, right?"

He nodded. "Small town. Word gets around." He stood and walked over to the desk, grabbing the stack of sketches. He dropped four of them down on the wood: Mary, the baby, the star, and the lamb.

"It rains a lot in Seattle," he said. "Mostly during the winter. But there's a lot to do, no matter the weather. If you go, take a rain jacket."

She considered that and knelt down next to the stack of wood, picking up a pencil. She'd start with the star. Get down the simple symmetrical piece and move on to the more organic figures. "What are the dimensions for this one again?"

He glanced at the graphed sketch and grabbed the yardstick. "Two and a half by three feet." He knelt across from her and measured it out while she made the marks on the board.

"Are you and Dalton a thing?" he asked quietly.

"No," she answered. "Hold that this way."

He pressed the ruler at the angle she needed. She leaned forward and ran the pencil along the hard edge. It moved slightly, and she looked up at him. Grilled steaks and aftershave.

"Sorry," he said.

She adjusted the ruler and pressed it down herself, her hand between both of his, and finished the line. Her bangs had fallen in her face, and she pushed them back. "Here." She pointed out the next line and he positioned the ruler again.

"Can I say something?" he asked.

"You can say anything, just keep that edge still." She pointed to the next line, ignoring how much he smelled like something she wanted to eat.

He pressed the ruler down. "Be careful with Dalton."

She looked up at him, but he remained focused on the ruler.

"I'm always careful."

She expected him to follow up with a few accusations aimed at Dalton. She was ready to shut him down and make it clear that she was a big girl, and could handle herself, yada yada, but he stayed silent. Where had his warning stemmed from? She'd gotten the same feeling from Yvette. Of course, asking Mark his reasons was out of the question. It went against her whole "I'll judge for myself" platform. Then again, the last time she'd judged for herself she'd been flat-on-her-face wrong.

She glanced at him again and caught him smiling. "What?"

"When your head gets spinning like that, you purse your lips and get a dimple. Right there." He reached and nearly poked her in the spot next to her mouth.

She brushed his hand away. "I do not. And you don't make my head spin."

"I didn't say I did."

She paused and felt heat creep up her neck. "What did you say?"

"I said when you start thinking about things really hard you get that look. *You* said I make your head spin."

"No, I said you *didn't* make my head spin."

"You sure about that?" he asked. "Because that dimple is back." He pointed again, and she swatted his hand away.

"Enough with the dimples." She picked up the yardstick and repositioned it. "If you're making my head spin, it's because you're exasperating."

"Is that right?" he said, clearly not believing her honest evaluation.

She sat back on her heels and met his dark eyes straight on, a rare thing with him. Humor played in their depths like Puck hiding behind dark-stained glass. She liked it, and she didn't want it to go away.

She swallowed. She had to keep this professional. "Get me the dimensions on that lamb or nobody's getting anything for Christmas."

He attempted to hide his amusement but said nothing, which left her conflicted because wasn't him coming out of his shell a good thing? But this . . . this . . . magnetism . . . She hadn't counted on that. And dang if he wasn't hitting too close to home.

She finished the star and was able to fit the standing lamb on the other end of the same board.

She glanced at him to see what he thought of the outline.

He nodded. "I can see it."

"Yeah?"

"Yeah."

She smiled. *Stop smiling so much, or he's likely to kiss you again.* She stopped.

She was able to get most of Mary on the next board when Mark's phone buzzed. He looked at the text. "My dad's on his way home. You keep going, and I'll get the rest of this stuff under the cot."

In a matter of minutes, she had Mary's outline done, and the room looked as it had before. Mark found a blanket and spread it over the cot so the edge reached the floor, hiding their work.

He held the door for her. "My dad doesn't get off the property much. I'll need to come up with some excuses for him to leave so I can use the saws without him getting curious."

"Why don't you use the shop equipment at the high school?" Riley asked. "Tom Staley helped us out with the play props. I bet he'd let you use whatever you needed."

"I don't know if that's such a great idea," he said.

"Because it's a surprise? I'm sure we could trust Tom. Especially if he knew it was for your dad. You said the nativity was a special thing for the whole town. He'd respect that, wouldn't he?"

Mark shrugged, shifting his weight. "Probably."

"And I'm guessing your dad wouldn't ask too many questions if he thought you were meeting friends. He got out of your way tonight, right?"

"Are you implying that I don't get out much?"

"Do you?"

"No."

She put her hands on her hips. "And does he worry about that?"

He paused. "You're nosy."

She lifted her brow and counted on her fingers. "It's away from the house. We can work after school when everyone is gone. I can sketch the rest of the figures right there before you cut them out. And it will give your dad the impression that you're out making friends or whatever. Tell him you're helping me with the reno. So, bonus getting him off your back for the day." She waited for him to agree.

He rubbed his neck. "Nobody else can know."

"We can't exactly put the school on lockdown."

Finally, he shrugged. "I guess it would be easier than trying to hide stuff anytime he comes around."

"Call me if you want to try."

He nodded.

That was enough for her.

Cal returned as she was putting on her coat. "Hey," he said. "You don't have to run off on my account."

Riley smiled, seeing the same gleam in his eyes that Mark had showed her once or twice. "I have school tomorrow."

"Well, I hope you two had fun." He looked curiously at Mark. "You staying out of trouble?"

"Planning my escape," Mark deadpanned.

"Ah. Well, let me know how it turns out." He turned to Riley. "His bedroom window sticks, so it might be best to cut loose through the bathroom. Beware the climbing rose bush."

"Got it," she said. "Bathroom window. Avoid the roses."

"There's a decent ladder in the garage," Cal said. "I'll be sure to turn a blind eye."

Riley stifled a giggle.

"Are you two done?" Mark asked.

Cal hung up his coat and hat and threw Mark his jacket.

"What's this for?" Mark asked.

"Aren't you going to walk her to her car?" He turned toward the kitchen without waiting for an answer, mumbling, "He knows this stuff. That fire didn't get to his brain—"

"I can hear you," Mark said, shrugging into his coat.

"—didn't get to his hearing, either."

Riley bit her lip, hiding her grin.

Mark grabbed the door and pulled it open. "After you."

She stepped outside. The Christmas lights on the porch blinked blue and white. Mark shut the front door behind them.

"I can see why you're doing this for him," she said.

"If you're being sarcastic, I don't blame you."

She laughed. "I'm not. I think he'll love it."

"Christmas will be a lot brighter this year, for sure. And we'll take you to the tree-lighting in Leavenworth, show you how we do things here in the valley."

He'd said it offhandedly, she knew, and she hesitated to respond as they walked down the stone path. "I'm not sure I could handle it. What if it doesn't measure up to the hype?"

He laughed quietly. "Now I know you're being sarcastic."

"Yeah, well, maybe I am, maybe I'm not."

"So, what is it? About Christmas, I mean." They stopped at her car and he shoved his hands in his pockets, toeing a rock out of the lawn and onto the drive.

She shrugged, not wanting to pursue it, but not wanting to put him off.

"Is that the real reason you didn't want this job?" he asked.

"I didn't say I didn't want the job."

"Yes, you did. Your first answer was no, remember?"

Her smiled faded, and she looked off into the trees. Her breath came out in puffs, and she shivered.

"You don't have to tell me," he said. "I'm just wondering if it will help me navigate this project better. It's all Christmas—*life-size*." He watched her expectantly.

"Okay," she said, bracing herself. "Let's say I learned at a very young age that Christmas is about wishes and hope. It's about home, right? So I'd wish for a home." She shrugged. "A real one—you know, one we weren't tearing down or putting back together. One where I didn't have to tell the friends I'd just made that we were leaving again. Don't get me wrong, I know we had a lot. I saw a lot of the world. We had food, clothing, beds. When we were in the country, I'd spend Christmas with my grandma . . . Sometimes with my parents. Sometimes not. Most times they were busy."

He winced.

"My grandma's house was the closest thing to a permanent home I ever had." She pulled her jacket closer, swallowing her emotions. "By the time my parents settled in California, I'd left for college. My mom started writing for travel blogs and magazines, so she was off again, all over the world. It was hit or miss. Then my dad invited me to come work for him." She bit her lip. "But that didn't work out. So here I am."

His eyes narrowed in concern. "I'm sorry."

She shrugged. "I just learned I was better off not hoping, you know? It was easier that way."

She couldn't tell if she saw pity or disapproval in his eyes.

"Hope is one of the big ones," he said.

She frowned. "The big ones?"

"Hope. Faith. Love one another."

"Ah," she said. "Those big ones."

He shrugged. "Christmas." He leaned forward. "The *Nativity*."

She nodded. "Yes, my point exactly. You asked why I hesitated about the project."

He smiled at her sideways. "You know, I'm not going to judge anyone on the Christmas thing. For all I know, you're an atheist."

"I don't know what I am."

"Okay. I get that. But really? Hope?"

Riley folded her arms. "I told you."

"So, you've chucked hope."

She nodded. "Mostly." The last time she'd allowed herself to freely hope, it had crashed around her like a building demolition.

"So, then what? What's left?"

"Work," she answered, sure of it. "Work hard. See your life come together under your sweat, your stipulations. Things go wrong, you know why. It's not because of some silly desire for miracles."

His smile was gone.

A sick feeling grew in her stomach as she realized who she was talking to.

His eyes darkened. "How nice to be in charge of what happens to you. Shielded from pain. From disappointment." He stepped to her, his gaze intense. "But what happens when hurt and pain come after *you*? What happens when they tear at you and take everything you know and explode it into a thousand pieces?" His voice was hoarse with emotion. "What happens then, if you refuse to *hope*?"

She opened her mouth to answer but nothing came out. She knew the tearing pain of helplessness. Her heartbeat felt taut, like the plinking of a guitar string held against the fret.

"Nothing," he said, quietly answering his own question. "You don't work. You don't look for tomorrow." He shook his head, his jaw tight. "You don't *want* a tomorrow."

Warm tears pooled in her eyes. "I'm sorry, Mark," she whispered. Seconds passed.

"No, I'm sorry," he said. He stepped away. "And I'm sorry life has made you think hope is worthless. I've been there, too."

He looked away, toward the house. "Sometimes I'm still there, I guess."

"Not if you come at it like that, you're not." She quickly swatted away her tears. "Wow," she said. "You don't hold back, do you?" She sniffled and forced a laugh, but her heart still cut that sharp rhythm, and she still couldn't look at him.

"I should've stopped talking eight minutes ago."

She couldn't argue with that. "I shouldn't have opened up." She turned to the car, her emotions all over the place. She fumbled with her key fob, finally getting the door to unlock—as if she needed to lock her doors out here.

"Riley, wait."

"Call me about using the school," she managed to get out.

"Riley?"

She waited.

"Be careful driving down."

She nodded and got in the car. She should have thanked him for dinner. She should have assured him that she was fine. Told him he was a stronger person than she was. He stood there as she drove away, watching even as she turned down the winding slope.

She couldn't keep her emotions in check, though. She was no good at relationships. Not ones that mattered.

Making friends with people like Mark Rivers was dangerous. People like him drew you in deep, made you feel like you could believe. That you were connected. Part of something that said, "Stay." The Dalton Gainers of the world allowed freedom.

Be careful with Dalton, Mark had warned her.

Be careful with Mark, she told herself.

Chapter 8

Mark put off calling Riley about using the school all day. The way things had been left last night made his stomach turn. He'd hoped he could manage to grab some time to work on the boards while his dad was away. The trouble was, his dad never went away.

They'd spent the morning fixing potholes in the dirt road down to the new outbuilding. His dad had loaded gravel onto the flatbed, and while he drove, Mark sat on the back, waiting for the next stop to fill the hole.

Once they got to the outbuilding, he was put to work installing shelves, moving in equipment, and organizing tools, including moving the band saw from the garage. He tried arguing for leaving the tools where they were, but his dad had looked at him like he'd been hit too many times playing football.

And the whole time, running through the back of his mind was Riley. *Riley, Riley, Riley.* And the warning his father had given him when he was young. *Don't you make a girl cry unless it's happy tears.*

She always had this strong front. To see her vulnerable like that—he hadn't known what to do—or what she'd want from him.

By the time afternoon rolled around, Mark's stomach had tensed with anxiety, and his leg bounced under the lunch table they'd put in the shop's kitchen area.

"We're out of bread and eggs," he said, as if he'd just remembered. "And you were gonna get the oil changed in your pickup, right? Did you want to go do that now, or . . .?"

His dad spoke from behind a cupboard door. "Steph's dropping by in a while with some groceries, and I was thinking when you're done here you can change the oil for me for free."

"I can't." Mark grimaced. "I'm meeting some people."

His dad shut the cupboard quickly. "For what?"

"For meeting some . . . people . . . to meet people." *Brilliant.*

His dad stared at him. "Sounds crowded."

Mark turned away. "It's nothing. Never mind."

"No, go. We'll get the oil changed another day. Go meet your people."

Mark paused. Was it really so predictable that his dad would want Mark to get out of the house? "Thanks."

He texted Riley.

I'm sorry about the way things were left last night. I'm hoping you still want the job. If so, can I come use the school? There's no avoiding Dad out here.

He waited for a response, knowing school would just be getting out, nervous that she'd back out. After a few minutes, she replied.

I talked to Tom. Today will work if we're done by six. Bring everything to the shop as soon as you can so we can finish drawing the characters.

She wasn't backing out.

He excused himself while his dad was still deep in work and returned to the house. He cleaned up a little then packed everything he and Riley had worked on into the back of his truck, wrapping the boards in an old blanket and securing them with bungee cords. He might be overprotective about keeping the project a secret, but he would feel better once the pieces were cut and inside Riley's house.

Once more, he chastised himself for coming down so hard on her about the hope thing. It wasn't his right to preach to her or anyone. They'd agreed at dinner: mutual understanding between friends. And then he'd laid into her like a preacher at a pulpit. He promised himself he'd back off and respect her privacy, even though something inside him itched to know more of how she'd given up the one thing in life that had kept him alive.

And this place? He shook his head as he drove into town, the streetlamps adorned with lit garlands and tinsel snowflakes hanging from every traffic light. Santa's Workshop was already set up in the corner of the IGA parking lot, waiting for Santa to hold court for portraits and hand out candy canes and a coupon for a free ice cream cone at the Grill-n-Go. Christmas carols would blare from the Christmas tree lot between the hardware store and the IGA as soon as it was filled, though the Salvation Army bell ringers were already working their posts in front of the Main Street stores.

For someone who wanted to avoid Christmas, Riley Madigan had picked the wrong place to live.

But it sounded like she'd picked it partly because of his mom.

He parked the truck in the school parking lot.

Maybe if he could show her what this town meant to his mom—what *hope* meant to his mom—maybe she'd have a change of heart. But he'd have to stop the preaching.

He was hefting the pieces of wood under his arm, deep in thought, when he heard a voice behind him.

"What are you up to, Rivers?"

Mark glanced to see Dalton Gainer closing the trunk of his car.

"Just bringing some stuff in for the shop." He adjusted the backpack containing all the drawings and photos and nearly lost his grip on the boards.

"Good for you, getting out. Need some help?"

Mark let the patronizing statement drop. "Nope. Got it." And he did. Gainer shut the tailgate to the truck for him anyway. "Thanks."

"I saw Ms. Madigan heading for the shop, too," Gainer said, a question in his tone.

Mark met Dalton's steely blue gaze. "Ms. Madigan? You mean Riley?"

Gainer smiled. "During the school day, she's Ms. Madigan."

"Ah," Mark replied, gladly turning to go. "Well, I'm not a student. And school's out." He headed toward the school, but before he could take three steps, Gainer called to him.

"Rivers."

Mark paused despite everything in him telling him to keep walking.

"When it comes to Riley, this is one record you won't beat." The subtle warning in Gainer's tone came through loud and clear.

Mark took in a long, deep breath, trying to douse the wave of insecurity and anger flaming up inside him. It's not like he'd felt any encouragement last night, but that wasn't the point.

He turned, and Gainer stepped aside to avoid the swing of the boards.

"What do you mean?"

Gainer shrugged. "I mean I'm interested in getting to know her better, and let's be honest, your game's a little off."

"How so?" Mark knew exactly how so, but he was curious to hear Gainer's answer.

He lifted his hands as if in defense. "I'm only saying that I've been working on something here, and maybe you should take your warm-up somewhere else."

Mark shook his head. "Is everything a sports analogy with you?" He squared himself against the man he'd once idolized. "I've got no game plan. No warm-up concerning Ms. Madigan. If you've been working on something, I'm sure you have no need to worry about the likes of me." He almost turned, but stopped. "Oh, and if you're going around referring to her as one of your goals on the scoreboard, I'd be very careful."

Gainer chuckled. "Oh yeah? Why is that?"

Mark kept his own voice even, his gaze steady. "I happen to know she sleeps with a baseball bat under her bed."

Gainer's self-confident expression faltered slightly. Mark regretted that his words implied he and Riley had something more than a working relationship, but the guy was asking for it, so he made no correction. He turned, making sure the jerk had to duck out of the way of the boards once more, and headed toward the shop.

"Thanks for the heads-up," Gainer called after him. "And challenge accepted."

"Unbelievable," Mark muttered under his breath.

Any illusion of self-assurance he'd gained from his exchange with Gainer fizzled when he entered the shop. Tom Staley, who'd been the shop teacher since before Mark was in school, lifted his head and smiled. Riley, however, turned away with a box she was carrying and deposited it at the far end of a long worktable without so much as a "Hey."

"Mark Rivers, good to see you." Tom extended his hand, and Mark took it, painting on his smile and giving Tom the better half of his face. He'd left his hoodie at home, but kept a knit cap pulled over his ears.

"Mr. Staley. Thanks for letting us use the shop."

"Just Tom. And you're welcome. Riley tells me it's a secret, but it's one I'm happy to be in on. You can count on me."

"Thanks, Tom." He looked around the large industrial room. The smell of fresh-cut wood, machinery, and wood glue took him right back to freshman shop class. "Hasn't changed much."

"No, it hasn't. I'm a bit dustier, but the shop's the same. Same rules. Same kids doing what they can to break them." He gave Mark a wink. "You and Jay nearly gave me a heart attack a couple of times, if I remember."

Mark smiled, a real one. "Are you kidding? That safety movie you showed at the beginning of every semester scared the crap out of everyone."

"Still, I recall someone not paying attention and nearly sending a block of mahogany through my office window."

Mark grimaced. "Oh yeah. The table saw." He chuckled and glanced toward Riley, who was closely examining a handful of pencils. "Sorry about that."

Tom shook his head. "Job hazard. Still, I'll miss it."

"Miss it? Are you leaving?"

"Retiring. After next year."

"Wow. Congratulations. I can't believe that."

"Me neither. But it's time." He rested his hand on Mark's arm. "Good to see you here. Go on, and set your load down." He nodded toward Riley. "You know where everything is."

"Thanks." Mark watched Tom retreat to his office, then turned to the worktable.

He noted a change in the air as he approached Riley. It was stiff and distant, and he didn't like it. Not with her. He dropped the boards heavily onto the worktable, and she jumped.

"Ms. Madigan?"

She cast her green eyes his way, questioning his address like he knew she would.

He'd considered his next words over and over, but she hadn't been staring at him when he'd practiced. "I need to apologize. To you."

She tucked her hair behind her ear and folded her arms.

"I think it's twice now I've left you feeling like I've let you down in some way. Or maybe I've come across as a self-righteous blowhard."

She bit her lip.

"I give you this song and dance about wanting to be treated just like everybody else, and then when you open up like I am anybody else, I use what I've been through to put you in your place. My dad would call me a fool. I'm sure you have better names."

Her mouth pursed. Yeah. She had them, all right.

He shifted his weight and pushed on. "I was only trying to help. And I screwed up. Can you forgive me?" His fingers tightened around the strap of his backpack like he was a high school kid asking out his crush.

She studied him, her eyes round and her lips parted, and he allowed himself to consider how soft those lips might be.

Thoughts like that are trouble, Rivers. He quickly drew his gaze back to her eyes.

She blinked and looked away again, organizing the pencils

on the table into an orderly row. "Thank you, Mr. Rivers." She glanced at him sideways. "I wasn't entirely undeserving of your . . . opinion," she said quietly. "I was insensitive. At least, I didn't consider—" She took a nervous breath. "Some of the things you said were hard to hear. But it wasn't because of you." She touched the last pencil on the table and faced him. He saw what he'd hoped to see.

A light behind her reserve. Acceptance of his lame apology. A willingness to make things right—or at least bearable—while they worked together.

"Friends?" he asked.

She clasped her hands in front of her. "Friends."

He nodded, feeling a weight lifted, and slung his backpack onto the table while she unwrapped the boards. He hung up his coat on the peg next to hers and grabbed two work aprons. With a nod of thanks, she took one and tied it on.

They worked in silence for a time, sorting boards and sketches. Just as he was reaching to gather up the boards ready for the big cuts, she reached in the same direction and their hands met. He pulled away before she did.

"If you don't mind me asking, how long were you in recovery? For the burns, I mean?"

He paused at the unexpected question, unsure how to answer.

"I'm sorry," she said. "I didn't mean—"

"Almost a year," he found himself saying. "At first, I mean, with the physical therapy and everything. Then more skin grafts. More physical therapy. I'm still—" He paused again, hesitant to say more, or not knowing what to say. "I'm still recovering, I guess." He picked up the boards and began to walk to the band saw. Then he stopped and turned back to Riley. "I don't mind if you ask me about it." He was pretty sure he meant it. At least he wasn't spiraling into a dark place with his back pressed against a wall.

She nodded. When it didn't look like she was going to say anything, he turned.

"My grandma died on Christmas Eve," she said.

He stopped.

"I was thirteen. I was alone with her."

He turned slowly.

She stood looking at the floor, turning a pencil in her hands. She straightened up taller. "My parents had been having these horrible fights and decided to go away together to try to work it out. My grandma and I shared some milk and cookies, and then . . . she had a heart attack. I tried everything, but . . ." She shrugged, looking everywhere but at him. He was used to that from other people, but not from her. "I lost the one place that felt like home to me, and I lost it on Christmas. That was when I stopped believing. I couldn't wish for anything more after that. I just thought you should know. So you'd understand why I said what I did last night."

He took a step and set the boards back down. He put his hands into his pockets and shook his head. "Why didn't you say something then?"

She swallowed. "I'm saying it now."

He took another step to her, but she took a step back.

"It's okay," she said. "I mean, I'm a grown-up. But Christmas—It's been a long time since I've been able to find meaning in it. I'd go through the motions to please my parents when I still lived with them. I thought I'd grow out of it after I left home. You know, leave stuff behind. But some things are still . . ."

"Hard," he said.

She let out a breath. "Yeah."

"So, you're still healing."

A small smile touched her mouth as she met his gaze. "Yeah."

He nodded. He looked over their work, trying to focus his thoughts on what to say or do next. Her grandma died on Christmas Eve? And Riley had been alone, without anyone to help? Holy crap. He gestured toward the drawings. "You don't have to do this."

"I want to. For your family."

He nodded again. He fought the urge to gather her up in a big hug, which he was sure she didn't want.

"For you," she added.

He looked at her, giving her his left side. Again, her gaze darted everywhere but to him. Even so, he was warmed by her words. He hadn't realized how much he'd wanted them. Gradually, she met his look, and something passed between them. An undeniable rush of heat pulled at his gut, and he found it hard to breathe. She took a step toward him.

He backed up and started to turn away, grabbing a breath of air without showing it. He felt her hand on his arm. The pressure of it, anyway. He couldn't feel the actual touch of his sleeve, and he wouldn't feel her skin on his. How soft it would be on his. Not on that arm.

"Mark?"

He looked down at her hand. "I'm sorry," he said. "I can't imagine." His Christmases, for the most part, had been everything he wished for. "I'm glad you told me."

"Thanks. I'm sorry about your . . . about what you've been through."

He nodded, fighting the idea that had been sitting in the dark corner of his head since he'd met her—that maybe this was charity work for her. Pity. Would she have stuck around after last night if he didn't have a road map on the side of his face?

Gainer's veiled message came to mind. Maybe he was a little "off his game," but Riley wasn't like that. Still, the possibility crawled under his skin.

"We all have stuff," he threw out there. "Hard stuff." He turned around, grabbing the boards. "Thanks for doing this. It will mean a lot to my family. To the town, I hope." He gave her a smile, though it felt detached.

She smiled back. But whatever had passed between them, or what he *thought* had passed, was gone.

"Well," she said, "what are friends for, right?"

He felt a knot constrict in his chest. "Right." *Friends.* Because he was who he was. And that's all he'd ever be.

❄ ❄ ❄

Riley finished outlining the last figure—the baby in the manger—to be cut. She glanced toward Mark, working steadily at the saws. He was now making the finishing cuts with a jigsaw, the noise filling the room. She'd felt the heat between them dissipate as soon as they'd ended their earlier conversation. But they were making good time on the project, so maybe this was better.

But there had been heat. It had drawn her to him despite her desire to stay away. Despite the pit growing in her stomach that told her she'd overshared.

And then he'd extinguished it. *Just like a fireman*, she thought. Putting out fires that weren't supposed to be there. Fires that were growing dangerous.

She picked up the board and made her way to Mark and the jigsaw. He looked up when she drew near enough, his safety glasses bringing a small smile to her face. He smiled back, reserved, and she noticed that what she'd taken for a sly, sort-of-crooked smile was probably caused by damage to the muscles on the right side of his face. It was scarcely noticeable—the scars barely reached his mouth—but that didn't mean damage hadn't been done to the muscles that had once pulled his face into a full grin.

"Last one," she said, setting the board down.

He nodded and went back to work, finishing the shepherd's crook. On the table sat a stack of neatly trimmed life-size figures they would paint entirely black. It would be up to her to bring them to life with shape, color, and shadow.

The saw paused, and she glanced up.

"Here," he said, shoving a small hand-sander in her direction. "If you can finish the edges, we can get these ready to paint by six."

He went back to the saw, and she plugged in the sander, but she didn't turn it on.

Why had she just blurted out such private things? She rarely told anyone about her past. He'd been moved once the words had left her lips, but then he'd withdrawn like she was the damaged one. Ha. *She* was damaged.

She glanced at Mark.

No.

He'd said she was still healing, like he was. He'd given her that option.

He glanced at her, and then turned off the jigsaw. "Is everything okay?"

"I hadn't thought of it that way," she said.

"What?"

"What you said—'still healing.' I hadn't thought of it that way."

He removed his safety glasses and watched her, waiting for her to continue.

"I'd mostly thought of it as still wounded," she said. "Still hurting."

He looked down, absently wiping away sawdust from the figure he was working on. His brow furrowed. "That's understandable."

"If I'm still hurting, after all these years, it makes me feel like . . . like . . ." She frowned, unable to explain it.

"Like you're doing something wrong," he answered. "Like you're not trying hard enough to fix something you had no control over. Or you're just . . . damaged beyond repair."

She lifted her chin. "Yes. Exactly. But saying you're still healing, that changes it."

He shrugged. "It's proactive. Moving forward. Working on it."

"That's very wise."

"Well, my therapist is very wise, so . . ."

She smiled at that.

He watched her another moment, wary, but patient. And there it was again. That sensation of being drawn in.

"I'm not sure how to work on it," she said.

He reached for something on the workbench and moved toward her. She steadied her feet, bracing herself, though his motions were smooth and unhurried. He stopped in front of her and lifted his hands.

"Here." He gently slid a pair of safety glasses over her ears and onto her nose. "Those eyes need protecting."

His fingertips brushed the soft skin just in front of her ears.

She shivered, and he dropped his hands. "Thanks," she managed to say, watching him, her mind dizzy with what she should be saying or doing or—

"You start by helping someone else, even if you don't want to."

"Is it okay if I want to?" she asked.

He nodded, looking away. "Of course. Even if it's a charity case."

"This isn't a charity case," she said, studying the beautiful left side of his face.

His gaze returned to hers. "No?"

"Of course not. Who do you think I am?" She folded her arms in front of her and leaned forward. "I'm trading you for backbreaking labor, remember?"

He broke into a smile at the same time she did.

"That's right." He put his safety glasses on. "And I'm not pulling up your carpet so you can stand around, lollygagging. Back to work, Ms. Madigan."

"Lollygagging?"

He stepped back to the saw and switched it on. Once again, the room filled with noise. He brought two fingers up to his eyes, then pointed them at her.

She grinned and switched on the sander. Movement drew her eye to the window of the classroom door, but she looked at the pile of wood and decided no one would be able to tell what they were up to. Then she got back to work, still grinning.

❄ ❄ ❄

Mark smoothed his hands over the boards. After he'd finished cutting out the last piece, he and Riley had both sanded and finished up just before six. They gathered everything they were taking with them, and Tom locked the door behind them on their way out.

"Looks like you two made good use of the shop," he said.

Mark nodded. "Can't thank you enough."

"Hey," Riley said as they walked down the hall, "we should use the art room to paint these. They're going to take up a ton of space as they dry, and my house doesn't have much of that, even in the garage. I've got all the drop cloths and brushes in my classroom, and they'd be dry by the next morning. I could have them gathered up and out of there before school starts so nobody asks about them."

"I've got the paint in the back of my truck," he said. "Just tell me when."

"If we start tomorrow after school, we'd have time for two coats. You could pick them up Wednesday morning and then drop them at my house for the real painting."

Mark nodded. That would definitely move things along. They paused as Tom unlocked the exterior door to let them out.

"You two have a good night," he said with a nod as he walked to his car. "And good luck."

Riley waved, then faced Mark. "So, you'll just bring the cutouts tomorrow—Oh, wait," she said, her hand going to her forehead. "I've got art club from three to five." She stepped off the sidewalk, and he followed her.

"It's up to you, but if we started right at five, we'd probably still have time for two coats. We'd just be here later." He waited on her reaction. He'd already spent one evening with her. He didn't want to push another too soon. It wasn't like they were dating or anything. It was the project. But still. "I could bring dinner," he suggested, wondering what was going on with his brain. "Nothing fancy or anything. Drive-thru. Just burgers or something. Not even burgers. Just something quick." *Stop talking, Mark.*

"Wow. Not-even-burgers. That sounds amazing." Her eyes lit with humor. "Maybe we could get some not-even-fries with that."

"They come with the whole not-even-a-meal."

She laughed, and it did something to his insides.

"Okay," she said, stopping next to her car. "Be here tomorrow after five with the cutouts, the paint, and two not-even-meals." She looked around. "Where's your truck?"

He thumbed to the far side of the lot. "Over there. The lot was full when I got here."

"Then why did you let me keep talking while we walked this way?"

He looked at the ground, then peered up at her. "You heard my dad. Always walk a lady to her car."

She nodded. "Thanks. I'll see you tomorrow."

He backed away, watching her duck into the driver's side of her car. As he walked across the lot, his thoughts starting spinning about tomorrow night. As soon as he'd pushed away any rising hopes about the work session—it was a work session, *not* a date— they'd come right back. Like those static Styrofoam peanuts. As soon as he'd get rid of one, five more turned up.

He put the cutout figures in the back of his truck and glanced toward Riley's empty parking spot.

She'd laughed with him. She had a great laugh. The kind of laugh you wanted to keep bringing around.

He rolled his eyes. *She's just a* friend, *Mark.*

Still, there had been moments . . .

Gah. Styrofoam peanuts.

Chapter 9

The next day, Mark was sweeping up the loft space in the new storage building when he heard a voice bellow from below.

Gus strolled in. "And here we have a three-bedroom, single bath, split-level with a great view of Mark's dad's house and an irrigation ditch out back for the kids. No kitchen, but it has this great pulley system for when your in-laws come to visit, if you know what I'm saying, right, Nancy? And take a look at those beams, Carl. A man's castle is nothing without exposed beams. Kind of hits you right in the tenders, am I right?"

Mark chuckled and brought the broom to the top of the stairs. "You trying to sell this place out from underneath us?" he asked.

"Somebody's gotta make a living around here." Gus, alone on the main floor, beamed up at him. "Your dad told me where I could find you."

Mark came down the stairs. "I wish he'd said you could find me in Mexico."

"You want to be in Mexico?"

"No, I want *you* to be in Mexico." Mark smiled at his friend.

Nate could be intense, but Gus had always been easy. Easy to talk to. Easy to mess with. And he gave as good as he got.

"I'll take that as the good wish it was meant to be."

"Suit yourself," Mark said. "Can I get you anything? Tequila? Sombrero?"

"Ha. No, thanks. I haven't talked to you in a while, and I found myself with some free time. Thought I'd come up and see how you're doing. So . . . how're you doing?"

"Good."

"That's the short answer," Gus said.

"Long one's the same."

Gus studied him. Mark started sweeping the floor.

"You're not wearing your hood."

Did the whole world notice whether or not he wore his hood? "Sweatshirt got bulky under my winter coat."

"Whatever. It's a good move."

"Why's that?"

"Because, dude, one—you're not a rap star. Two—the scars are fading. And three—you're not freaking seventeen years old. I get it. I do. But this is a good move for you. So, good on you."

Mark shook his head, debating on whether he wanted to put Gus in a choke hold or hoist him up with the pulleys.

Gus must have felt the vibe because he put his hands up in defense. "The hat looks great, though. Wear the hat. Own it. You know, until summer comes around 'cause then you'll just look like one of them hipsters over in Leavenworth, and I'd have to kick the whoop out of ya."

Mark grinned at the image of Gus trying to do that.

"Ah," said Gus. "There's that devilish scamp we used to follow around, hoping to catch his leftovers."

"Knock it off. That never happened."

"It did until Caylin came along."

Mark glared at him, then rolled his eyes. Not worth it.

"Whatever, dude," Gus said. "How about we go play some pool at Jake's and then get dinner at Visconti's. I'm jonesin' for some pesce risotto."

Mark went back to sweeping. "I can't."

"Why not? The kids are with Margot and Art. Heidi has her feet up, reading a book. I've got the minivan. We're free and easy."

Mark kept sweeping.

"Aren't we?"

Mark stopped and looked at his friend. "I have something."

"Something? No offense but since when do you 'have something'?"

"You're a real jerk, you know that?"

Gus shrugged. "And?"

"And I'm sorry I can't hang tonight. I've got a . . . thing." He stepped past Gus to put the broom away.

"Does this thing have a name?"

Mark couldn't hide the slight pause in his step. The question had thrown him. He cringed.

Gus jumped on it. "It does, doesn't it? Would it happen to have a *woman's* name?"

Mark took a deep breath and blew it out. Gus was his friend; he didn't deserve a punch in the face. "Look, it's not what you're thinking."

To Mark's frustration, Gus's grin grew wider. "It's that teacher from the bakery, isn't it? The one we talked to at the bonfire."

Mark frowned. "You talked to her at the bonfire?"

Gus's eyes grew wide, and he exploded into a celebratory dance. "I knew it!"

Mark ran a hand over his face. "Look, she's just helping me

with something. A project. I'm trading her for some work on her house." He shook his head even as Gus kept nodding his. "Please don't make more of this than it is. It's nothing."

Gus stopped his awkward dance and scratched his head. "I thought she was with Gainer. On the other hand, all she did was talk about you."

Mark's head came up. "What?"

Gus shrugged. "She wouldn't stop. Just went on and on about—well, you probably wouldn't be interested."

"Gus, so help me—"

"Nah." Gus made a face. "It's none of my business anyway."

Mark stepped within reach and swung at him. Gus ducked and popped up to his left.

"You call that a swing? My grammy swings better than—" He ducked just as Mark swung again, but Mark recovered quickly and put him in a headlock.

"What did she say?" he asked.

"I take it back. You *are* seventeen."

Gus was shorter than Mark but stockier, and Mark wouldn't be able to hold him very long. "Tell me what she said, or I'll tell Heidi about the time you left Gabi in her baby carrier in the shopping cart at the IGA."

"You would not."

"Or the time you ran over the diaper bag, and Heidi's camera was in there so you bought the exact same camera and said nothing when she couldn't figure out how she'd lost all the pictures on it."

"Hey, that's—"

"Or the time you left the dirty diaper behind the—"

"That's enough!" Gus shouted and twisted out of Mark's grip. He straightened his shirt and ran his hand over his head. "See if I ever tell you anything about the joys of fatherhood ever again."

He stretched his neck. "That's quite a grip you've got there. You been working out?"

"It's all this manual labor my dad's been having me do."

Gus reached and squeezed Mark's bicep. "Hey, that's coming along."

Mark flexed. "Yeah, I—gahh!" In a blink, Gus had Mark in a half nelson.

"*This* is for threatening my happy time with Heidi. You never threaten a man's happy time with his wife."

"Okay," Mark shouted. "Okay, I give."

Gus shoved him away. They both bent over, out of breath, and laughing.

"I can't believe you still fell for that," Gus said.

"*Happy time?*" Mark asked, not wanting to know more. He stood and walked over to the couch they'd set up by the utility sink and mini-fridge. He collapsed against the cushions, gesturing to the small counter. "You were wrong. We have a kitchen."

"Nice." Gus eased himself onto the couch. "I'll have that tequila now."

Mark laughed. Then he quieted and shook his head.

"So," Gus said, serious. "What's going on?"

Mark considered the question. "I don't know. I don't. She's just helping me with a project—something for Dad, for Christmas. A surprise, so don't say anything. But I just . . ." He turned to Gus. "Was she really talking about me?"

Gus studied him, probably deciding if he should make a joke or not. He must've chosen not. "Yes. And she had some pretty insightful things to say, considering she kept insisting she didn't know you that well."

"Like what?"

"Oh, Nate was asking her some questions about you—as

Nate does—and she answered him really thoughtfully. And besides totally agreeing with everything she said, I couldn't help but get the impression that she sort of digs you, man."

Mark shook his head. "Shut up."

"I'm serious. I wouldn't pull your chain about this. There was something."

"What something?" Mark was sitting on a wall of frustration with reality on one side and hope on the other.

"I don't know. She was just different. It was like she knew you better than I do."

Mark leaned forward, his chin on his fists. "She is different. From anyone I've ever been around."

"And she's kind of hot."

Mark shot him a look.

Gus chuckled. "Well, she is. Or have you not noticed from behind your hood?"

Mark was too tired to swing at him again. "Yeah, I noticed." He'd noticed how she filled out a thermal T-shirt and a pair of jeans better than anyone he knew. He'd noticed how her cheeks blushed the same color as her lips. He noticed how one small lock of hair near her temple curled even though the rest of her hair was straight. And he remembered the touch of his fingertips on her palm, and again just in front of her ears when he'd put her safety glasses on. That had been a reckless move, but he couldn't stop it.

"Hey, Ground Control to Major Tom." Gus snapped his fingers in front of Mark's face. "Come in, Major Tom."

Mark swiped his fingers away and rubbed his face. "I'm meeting her at five for this project, and I'm bringing dinner."

"Sounds like a date to me."

"It's not. It's not that easy."

"Uh, sure it is. You asked her to help you tonight. You're bringing dinner—"

"Actually, meeting tonight was her idea."

"Even better. But dinner was your idea, right?"

Mark hesitated, remembering his botched job at offering to bring food. "We need to eat. But Gus, this isn't a date." He frowned. "At least not the kind I'd like to ask her on."

"So, you do want to ask her out."

"I want to do a lot of things, that doesn't mean I'm stupid enough to do them."

"What's stupid about it? Just ask her. You're already miserable, so you've got nothing to lose, right?" Gus elbowed Mark's arm.

"I still have my pride."

"Maybe that's your problem. I'm telling you, you'll be surprised when she says yes."

Mark's stomach knotted. "*If* I ask her, and *if* she says yes. Which I won't, and she wouldn't."

"Why not?"

Mark stood and walked a few steps, filled with too much restless energy. "Because I'm not the kind of guy someone like her goes for." Even as he said it, he remembered the way she'd looked at him in the woodshop, and the way—for a few minutes—he'd forgotten who he'd become while he was with her.

"My friend," Gus said, "there's only one way to find out if that's true."

"I don't want to find out."

"That is definitely *not* true."

Mark let out the breath he was holding.

"If you don't ask her out," Gus said, "it's going to drive you crazy."

Mark turned away, his hands in his pockets. He was halfway there already. "I can't do it."

"Sure you can. Rumor is you're some kind of hero, not that I listen to gossip. And while it's mostly old ladies who have an unfortunate crush on you—sorry, dude, it's true—the Mark Rivers I know never backs down from a challenge."

Mark looked back over his shoulder. "You're challenging me?"

"I'm not. But I think Dalton Gainer might be."

Mark turned. "What?"

Gus folded his arms. "He's been talking down at Jake's. You know Dalton. Any woman who turns his head must be up for a piece of the Gainer. He's all but taking bets on how easy it will be to divide and conquer. Not *whether* he'll do it, mind you, but how *easy* it will be."

Mark's blood heated, recalling Dalton's words in the school parking lot, territorial and competitive. *Challenge accepted.* "She's not like that."

Gus laughed. "Then what's she like?" He raised his brow expectantly.

"I don't know."

"Well, find out."

Mark stood there, torn between wanting to strangle Gus or remind Dalton of who broke all his records. Not just broke. Obliterated. "I can't treat her like Dalton would. She's not a prize. She's the one—"

"The one?" Gus asked, grinning.

Mark wanted to wipe that smirk off his face. "She's the one you want next to you on the field. The one you want to get the ball to. You just need to be enough to . . . to make her want to keep playing. Someone like Gainer—he's not even playing in her

147

league. He's just looking for a pickup game." Great. More sports analogies.

"And what are you looking for?" Gus asked.

Mark paused. He hadn't seen that one coming. He wasn't looking for anything.

Gus watched him, his grin fading. "Whoa, you are so gone."

Mark grabbed an empty water bottle from the counter and flung it at Gus.

Gus ducked, his grin back. "Mark wants himself a tight end. For keeps."

"Shut up, minivan."

❄ ❄ ❄

A couple of hours later, Mark left the Grill-n-Go drive-thru with two not-even-meals and a brick in his stomach.

What did he want?

Gus's question echoed through his thoughts as he considered what Riley would do if Gainer made good on his talk. The jerk had already asked her to Seattle. For a weekend.

What could Mark do to compete with that? He parked in the empty school lot, close to the school doors this time. He sat back in his seat.

What do you want, Rivers?

He couldn't get past the fear of what wanting brought with it. Wanting someone meant asking them to want you back, and he couldn't let himself hope that much.

He wanted to help Riley get the nativity figures painted. That's all. He had as much claim on her as he did the sky.

Mark wants Riley. For keeps.

A knock on the window jolted him, and if he hadn't still been wearing his seat belt, he was sure his head would've hit the roof of the truck.

Riley stood, laughing and hugging her arms around her in the cold afternoon dusk next to his truck door. "I'm sorry," she said through the window.

He undid his seat belt, grabbed the bags of food and the cup holder with their drinks, and opened the door.

"I didn't mean to scare you," she said.

He narrowed his eyes at her. "Sure you didn't." He got out, and she backed up.

"No, really, I was watching for you because the school doors are locked, and I didn't want you to be waiting in the cold."

"Thanks. Sorry I'm late. Happy to see you left your bat at home. Hold these, please." He held the food out for her to take.

She smiled and obeyed. "No problem. Smells good."

"Not-even-fries," he said as he opened the tailgate. "They fry them in not-even-fat."

"Perfect."

Getting a good grip around the bundled figures and sliding his arm through the handle on the can of black paint, he shut the tailgate. He glanced at Riley. "After you."

She led him to the industrial arts building and unlocked the doors. He followed her down the hall past the shop.

"I haven't been in here for a while," he said, stepping into the art room. "I took shop through high school, but I only took art my freshman year. Mom required it."

Riley led him to the chairs she'd arranged to act as sawhorses with drop cloths draped over them. "She wanted you to have an appreciation for what she did?" she asked, moving a couple of chairs closer to each other with her foot.

"Something like that, yeah." He set down the bundle and

the paint on the closest table. He took the drinks from her and followed her into the office.

"Did it work?"

"Sure. It also proved that I did not inherit my mom's artistic talents."

"I'm sure you're being too hard on yourself."

"I was quoting my teacher."

She looked back at him and smiled. "Have a seat."

He took a chair across from the one behind her desk. She cleared a space and put down two lengths of that brown paper towel all schools had.

He took the drinks out of their caddy. Two Cokes, two milk-shakes.

"I smell bacon," she said, taking her seat.

He ducked his head, hoping he'd chosen right.

Her smile widened as she pulled out the burgers and fries. "Seems to be a recurring thing with us. You can never go wrong with bacon."

He hated how much he liked how she'd said "us." One stupid word and he felt like he could be anybody he wanted. "Especially on not-even-burgers."

She nodded and pushed two fries into her mouth before he had the ketchup out. Mark took a long swig of his Coke. The joke had run its course, but it was good to be sharing a joke with someone you didn't want to put in a headlock.

"I didn't have lunch. Thanks." Her smile made his middle drop.

He concentrated on unwrapping his food. How in the world was he supposed to ask her out? He hadn't even been consider-ing it until Gus mentioned it, and now it was all he could think about. "I wasn't sure what kind of shake you'd want, so I got my two favorites, and you can choose."

"Either way, you're happy. Very wise."

"Very risky. I didn't think about what kind you'd like until the girl was taking my order through the speaker. This one's strawberry banana with marshmallow, and this one is peanut butter caramel with hot fudge."

She gave him an odd look. "You're kidding."

"Um . . . I sort of tweaked them from the menu flavors. They know what I like." He left out that the restaurant had named the unique combinations after him: "The Markmallow Smash" and "Rivers of Fudge." He didn't call them that. Ever. "You don't have to have one," he said. "More for me."

"I'm having one." She grabbed a couple more fries, then closed her eyes and swung her finger back and forth between the cups, her lips moving.

"What are you doing?"

"Eeny-meeny. Hush." She continued until her finger stopped, and she grabbed the hot fudge.

"Eeny-meeny?" he asked.

She nodded, looking up at him with those big eyes as she pulled a hard sip from the straw. After a large swallow, she sighed. "This is good. I mean, really, really good." She took a big bite of her burger and gave him a thumbs-up.

He smiled. He couldn't help it. He pulled in a deep breath. "I was wondering if you would help me with something next week. Something different, not big like this. After you're not doing anything, I mean. That is, if everything is going well with the painting and the house, and you have time." His leg bounced under the desk, and he forced it to remain still. "It would only be a morning thing. Maybe more." The words spilled out as smoothly as potholes on a dirt road.

She swallowed her bite and took a sip of soda, her brow furrowed. "What is it?"

"You'll see," he said. *You'll see? Like she'll accept that as enough to—*

"Okay. But if it's Christmas stuff, could you give me a heads-up? I feel stupid having to ask, but I have to get my head in the right place."

"It's not Christmas stuff," he assured her, though in the back of his mind, he reeled from her answer. She'd said okay. Okay as in yes.

She dropped her eyes and nodded, taking another bite, then looked at his barely touched food. "Eat. We need to get painting."

He picked up his burger, his appetite returning.

He'd just asked out Riley Madigan. Sort of. It wasn't his best work, but it was the best he could manage.

He picked up two fries and crammed them in his mouth. He was counting it.

Chapter 10

Riley watched Mark out of the corner of her eye. He dipped his brush into the paint and smoothed it along the grain of the shepherd cutout. He hadn't met her gaze since he'd rolled up his sleeves to his elbows. When he'd turned away to take off his compression glove, she'd respected his need for privacy. But now he held the brush securely and only switched to his left hand when the angle called for it.

On the forearm that had been burned, a web of scars covered his skin like pink veins, traveling from the backs of his fingers to up under his sleeve, and she wondered again about how he'd been burned, and how he'd endured it—how much still hurt, and how much didn't.

"Riley?" he asked. His arm was poised over the board, his face tight with apprehension.

She jerked her chin up, looking him in the eyes. "I'm sorry. I just . . ."

His voice was low, strained. "I needed to roll up my sleeves so I wouldn't get paint on them. If it's too much—"

"No. I like your forearms." She immediately felt heat rising to her face, and she closed her mouth.

A smile teased at his lips, but his eyes remained tense.

She put her hand on her cheek and shook her head. "I mean I like both of them. I mean, it's not a problem to have your sleeves rolled up. Forearms are attractive on guys, and I don't think something like scars detract from that. Women like forearms." Her voice trailed off. "Generally speaking, of course."

His tense look turned into one of concern for her sanity, she was sure of it.

She straightened. "All I'm saying is that I don't think you should be ashamed of your arm." She went back to brushing paint on Mary. "That's all. In case you were wondering. I mean we should be grateful we have arms, right?"

STOP TALKING.

"Yes," he said, a trace of amusement in his voice. "We should definitely be grateful we have arms."

She dipped her brush in more paint, laughing nervously. "Listen to me, telling you what to be grateful for. Between the two of us, I'm pretty sure you have a better handle on that than I do."

"On arms?" he asked.

"On being grateful," she said.

"Why is that?"

She stopped painting. "Because you've been through so much. And with your job, you've likely seen more."

"That doesn't mean it's been easy to be grateful," he said, his expression clouding.

"I didn't say that."

He nodded. "And for the record, I'm not sure that what I've been through can be measured against what you've been through.

It's different, sure. But it's all pain." He glanced at her but kept painting.

"You can't mean that," she said.

He shrugged and remained silent.

Riley went back to work, but what he said gnawed at her. The truth was, her heart had been broken a few times. With every move, with every fight, her grandma's death. A string of adult relationships doomed by her fear of commitment, followed by the most humiliating breakup she'd ever experienced. She'd be lying if she said she'd never considered what her life would've been like if her dad had been an electrical engineer or a podiatrist. If her parents hadn't fought. If they'd just stayed home.

It shouldn't matter anymore. It shouldn't still affect her this way.

She stabbed at the edges of Mary with her brush as her mind shifted unwillingly to the night they'd painted a nativity set as a whole family. Dad had brought home a ceramic set, the paints, and the shellac to make it shiny after the paint had dried. It hadn't mattered that she was five and had barely mastered paint-with-water books. She got to help paint right alongside the grown-ups.

"Which one do you want to paint?" her grandma had asked her as Mom set out the paints.

"Baby Jesus."

"Then you paint baby Jesus."

"You help me."

So, she and her grandma had painted baby Jesus. She was sure it was the best thing she'd ever attempted. It was important. She'd learned enough about this part of Christmas to know that Mary was the mother of Jesus, and Jesus would save the world. At age five, she wasn't sure what that meant, but she knew if the world she lived in with her family was in trouble, she'd want it saved.

And then her world had crashed. And nothing, or no one, had saved it.

"Riley?"

She composed her features into an expression she hoped would appear relaxed, then she turned. "Yes?"

He pressed his lips together, holding back a smile.

"What is it?" Was he mocking her? Had her inner turmoil manifested itself outwardly and he'd picked up on it? Did it amuse him?

"You have paint on your face."

"Oh." She rubbed at her cheek. "Where?"

"Well, now there. But here, too." He brushed at the side of his nose.

"Here?" She tried again.

He chuckled. "Just—don't touch your face."

She looked at her hands. Wet paint had smeared along the inside of her index finger.

"Here." Mark grabbed a roll of brown paper towels and tore off a couple big pieces. He got them wet at the sink and gave her one. "For your hands." He held up the other piece. "May I?"

She nodded, swiping angrily at the smears of paint on her fingers.

He took the corner of his wet towel and dabbed it on her nose.

"I must have itched there while I was thinking."

"It happens," he said.

Riley watched his chin as he smoothed the towel over the spot on her cheek. "Thanks."

"Not a problem." He gave her his left side, inspecting his work. "I think we got it all."

"Great." She looked away under his scrutiny.

"Sorry if I upset you. I seem to do that a lot." He took her wadded up towel and tossed it with his into the nearby trash can. "Do you want to talk more about my arms?"

She choked on a laugh.

He grinned. "No?"

She shook her head. "No." She could mention his chin, and how women dig strong chins. But she wasn't going there.

He backed away and grabbed the sheep figure and placed it on a set of chairs. He glanced at her, and she realized she was still standing, doing nothing.

"If my arms are too magnificent for you, I can move to the other side of the room."

"I said attractive, not magnificent. I'll try to control myself."

He turned away to work, but she could tell he smiled.

Riley stretched as they finished up the first coat of paint on the last figures. Working over boards was different than painting at an easel, but she always got tight through her shoulders.

"We have a good hour until we can start the second coat. What do you want to do?" She hadn't thought of passing the time between coats.

"We could go for a drive." Mark replaced the paint lid on the can and took the brushes to the sink. "Do you have something I can wrap these brushes in to keep them from drying out?"

She went to a drawer and found a container. "This should work. Where would we drive?"

He set the container with the brushes above the sinks. "There's a drive I've been wanting to take up Hay Canyon before the big snows hit. Haven't made it yet this year."

"But it's already dark outside. What would we see?"

"Depends on what you're looking for. Perspective is good."

Ten minutes later, they were driving up a narrow dirt road. They bounced and jostled—well, she mostly bounced and jostled.

Mark managed to sit firm, his hand on the steering wheel, looking like he drove roads like this every day.

After hitting a particularly jarring dip, Riley spoke up. "Are you punishing me for something?"

He shook his head, smiling. "You should see this drive in the spring. You can see the whole valley greening up. Cherry trees bloom first, and pear."

"I remember the cherry blossoms in DC."

"You'll love it. Up here you get daisies and black-eyed Susans and those purple flowers. Mom painted a ton of flowers." Mark slowed down to make a turn. "She'd bring her camera up here when the light was good and snap away. Fall's good, too."

Riley gripped the armrest. "You come up here a lot, then?"

"A few times." He glanced at her. "Mostly in full daylight. I haven't been up here at night much. It's really just a maintenance road. Power lines. We were called up here once for a small grass fire, and it became a favorite spot. But it's been a couple of years."

"What made you drive up here at night?" It was barely seven o'clock, and she couldn't see a thing past the headlights.

"Nothing you'd like to hear about," he said, eyes on the road.

"Oh," she said, knowingly. "Girls."

He shrugged.

"Did your daddy know you brought girls up here, Mister Gentlemen-always-walk-ladies-to-their-cars?"

"If he did, he didn't let on. And it was only one girl." The smile had left his voice. "And only once. Besides, there wouldn't be much to look at during the day. Everything's brown except the pines right now." His tone brightened. "After it snows, snowmobiles might be fun." He glanced at her, then back to the road.

"I've never been on a snowmobile," she said.

"Dad would say we'd have to remedy that."

She watched him in the glow of the lights from the dash, unsure how to respond. After another minute, the road leveled out, and he turned the truck around, backing it against the slope of the mountain and shutting the engine off.

He leaned back in his seat and dropped the keys in the cup holder, staring ahead of him. The overhead light that had blinked on would fade soon.

He caught her watching and turned in his seat, his back to his door, to better angle his other side to her. "Well?" he asked.

"Well, what?" She glanced up at the overhead light and squeezed her hands together.

"Well, this?" He waved his hand in front of them.

She followed his gesture and looked out over the valley below them, the hills speckled with lights from the little town, then up to the mountain peaks reaching into the black night, barely silhouettes defined by faint moonlit streaks of snow at their tips, and then up further to the stars filling the sky. So many stars.

"Snow will be coming," he said. "It might be a while before we get another clear sky like this one. Are you warm enough?"

She nodded. He'd made sure she'd grabbed her coat before they left.

"I can turn the car back on if you need the heater. I don't usually keep it running for myself."

"I'm fine. This is an incredible view. Is that Cashmere over there?"

He nodded and pointed. "You can see how the Wenatchee River winds through, lights on either side. There's the highway, of course."

She nodded. A highway with hardly any traffic. "Can we see your place from here?"

"No. It's around that way." He waved to the east.

"Oh, right."

He remained quiet.

"So who was the girl you brought up here?" she asked, trying to make conversation and keep it light.

He drew in a deep breath and let it go slowly. "Caylin. A girl from Wenatchee. I met her while I was home from college my junior year."

Riley recognized the name as the girl from the newspaper article. So much for keeping it light. "Was she . . . important to you?" Too late, she calculated in her head that they might have been together a few years.

"She was my fiancée."

"Oh." Great. She'd stumbled into his personal space. Again. "I'm sorry. Was this a special place for the two of you? You didn't have to bring me—"

"No, this wasn't special. I brought her up here soon after I found it." He shrugged.

"She didn't like it?"

"Oh, she liked it, I guess. She didn't look at the view much." He scrunched his nose at her and smiled.

Riley laughed, and after a moment, Mark joined her. That alone made her insides uncoil and relax.

"So, can I ask what happened? You didn't get married. I mean, I'm assuming you didn't. What do I know? Did you? Get married?" She quieted, wishing she'd done so sooner. Why did she always feel like she said the wrong thing around this man?

He quieted, too. "No. We were planning on getting married that fall, the year of the fires. She wanted a wedding in Anacortes, on the waterfront. The weather had been unusually sunny for the coast." He shrugged. "Anyway, one day, months after the fires, after a pretty intense physical therapy session, I woke up to find my dad waiting for me. He had her engagement ring. She hadn't been to see me for a while already. I knew it was hard for her."

"Hard for *her*?" Riley raised her brow.

He reached for the steering wheel, gripping it hard. "It was hard. For everyone. Especially in the beginning."

"But, you're not . . . it's not—" How could she say, "Your scars aren't that bad?" Even in her head that sounded wrong. She tried again. "I'm sure you'd come so far, in such a short time. Seems pretty heartless for her to just give up like that."

"It wasn't like that."

"Wasn't it? She had you, and then she gave you up. Like when someone catches a trout but doesn't want to touch it afterward. Like they'd rather have their seared tuna on a fancy plate than touch the scaly, rudimentary thing they'd worked so hard for."

It took her a split second, and the baffled look on his face, to hear her own words.

He rubbed his chin. "Well, when you put it that way." He glanced at her, his brow raised.

She dropped her face in her hands. "Oh, wow. I'm sorry. I— Why do you even talk to me?" She breathed out slowly through her fingers. "You're not scaly like a fish."

He laughed lightly. "What am I scaly like?"

She lifted her face and looked at him through the hair that had fallen over her eyes. "Nothing. You're not scaly like anything. I wasn't even talking about you, I was talking about—"

She watched his smile fade, then they both quieted again. She pushed back her hair and sunk into her seat. She hadn't been talking about him at all.

He looked back out at the view. "She was afraid."

"You must've been afraid. Did *you* back out?"

"Geez, Riley, you weren't there."

"No, but I've been there," she muttered. He stayed quiet, and she didn't blame him. A few minutes passed. "I'm sorry. You must have loved her a lot."

His brow furrowed. "I asked her to spend the rest of her life with me." His hand relaxed on the steering wheel, and he slouched back in the seat. "But when somebody leaves you like that, you learn not to love them anymore." He glanced at her, and she heard his words echo in her head.

"You were angry."

He nodded.

She unbuckled her seat belt and leaned forward, resting her arms on the dash, looking up at the stars, feeling her own scars. "'You learn not to love them anymore.' Sounds so easy." She turned to him with a bleak smile.

"You?"

She nodded. "You don't want to hear it."

"Try me."

"Oh, let's just say I allowed myself to trust, to hope."

"And?"

"Disaster."

"Working with your dad in California?" he asked.

She laughed bitterly and turned back to the stars. "He was part of it, but no." Even after all this time, emotions welled inside her like a tide she couldn't chart.

His silence made her keep talking. "When I was little, we made a family nativity set. The kind you're supposed to glaze and fire in a kiln. But we just used acrylic paint. I thought it was the most beautiful thing I'd ever seen when it was done." She laughed at herself. "I barely remember what it really looked like. It was probably a mess."

He made a quiet sound of amusement.

"The next Christmas, my dad stormed out after an argument with my mom, and I thought he was leaving us for good," she said. "I smashed it. I threw every piece of that nativity on the brick fireplace while my mom cried in her bedroom. She came, but not in time." She paused. "I remember she didn't get mad at me. She just held me and let me scream until I couldn't anymore."

She felt his hand on her shoulder, and part of her wanted to shake it off, but part of her wanted to keep it there. To keep her from falling back into that darkened room next to the Christmas tree lights that continued blinking on and off. She closed her eyes.

"As much as I can't remember what that nativity looked like up on our mantel," she said, "I remember exactly how it looked smashed on the floor around my feet. That's how this last disaster felt. I thought I loved someone—or I thought he loved me. I mean, because of my parents I'd always shied away from deeper commitment, you know?" She turned to him. "He was an actor. He said one of the things he loved about me was that I was different from the Hollywood set. In every way, shape, and form. And then, he decided that to be an A-list actor, he needed an A-list actress on his arm. But he failed to tell *me*, and I caught them making out in my dad's den during my birthday party. Everyone knew. It made the news."

He cringed.

"One of the pitfalls of having a famous father. My dad was furious that an actor in a movie he was working on had broken his daughter's heart. And he may or may not have punched said actor in the nose. That also made the news. One of the pitfalls of having an Irish father." She let out a long breath. "Now you know all my secrets."

He studied her, his finger tapping on the steering wheel.

"I don't know how you still hope like you do, Mark. I admire it."

After some time—a couple minutes or maybe twenty, she couldn't be sure—he pulled his hand from her shoulder.

"I'm sorry I asked you to help me with this project," he said.

She turned to him, leaning on her elbow. "I'm not."

"First your dad left, then your grandma passed away—both at Christmas, both tied to a nativity. I had no idea."

"I know. And I still chose to help you. We've already discussed this."

He frowned. "Yeah, but—"

"But that's all there is to it. Maybe it's good for me. Facing my demons and all that. Right?" She smiled again, but her eyes burned with unshed tears. "Like you said, you adapt."

He scrutinized her, but she didn't feel judged. "So much for taking a nice drive," he said, a hint of humor in his voice.

"Yeah," she said. "Aren't we something?"

He smiled, then checked his watch. "I'm pretty sure that paint's dry."

"Can we wait just a few more minutes?"

He nodded. "You okay?"

"Yeah." She settled back in her seat. "I just want to look a little longer."

"Fine by me," he said.

She returned her gaze to the view, this time clearing her mind of her past. She hadn't intended on sharing any of that with him. Or anyone. But it didn't feel wrong.

Chapter 11

Riley finished writing instructions for the art assignment on the whiteboard as the bell rang to end last period. She felt the collective relief from the class, as tangible as the oil pastels they'd dropped back into their boxes moments before. "Remember to have your Van Gogh projects in by Friday, and don't forget to put your names on them." She turned away from the board. "I'm looking at you, Wyatt and Charlie."

The boys groaned as the triumphant sounds of school being out for the day filtered in from the hall. Charlie stopped.

"Hey, Ms. Madigan, are you dating Mark Rivers? Because that would be awesome."

Wyatt chimed in. "My mom says you're dating Mr. Gainer and that's gonna tick off a lot of women in this town."

Riley gulped a breath and stuttered out a laugh. "I'm not dating anyone—not that it's anybody's business."

"Well," Charlie said, "I think you should date Mr. Rivers. He's awesome. Awesomer than Mr. Gainer."

Wyatt turned to Charlie. "Maybe she doesn't want to be married to a guy with scars all over."

Charlie screwed up his face. "Dude, what does that matter? The guy is a *hero*."

"Well, if she married Mr. Gainer, they would *both* be heroes, because *teachers are heroes*."

Charlie slapped his hand to his forehead. "Are you even *listening* to yourself? If she marries Mr. Rivers, they would *both* be heroes, *too*."

"That's enough!" Riley cried, glancing at the remaining students listening avidly. "Thank you for your observations on heroism, boys, but *nobody* is getting *married*. Wyatt, scars should *never* matter, and Charlie, Mark and I are just friends. That's all. Now go, or you'll miss your bus."

The rest of the class cast her sideway glances and muffled giggles until the room was empty.

Riley placed her cold hands on her hot cheeks and blew out a deep breath, attempting to ease her pounding heart. Wyatt's *mom* was discussing Riley's love life? Sixth-graders were ready to marry her off?

She turned to the table piled with boxes of pastels and pads of smooth, clean newsprint. Like a healing talisman, she pulled a pad toward her and slid open a box. If there was anything she liked better than oil paints, it was pastels. The soft, creamy crayons could put a lot of color and texture on a page in little time, and if she ever needed to do a quick sketch of something she wanted to paint later, she preferred them over pencils. The way they glided over the paper had always been soothing.

She grabbed a few colors and quickly mapped out a blue valley dotted with lit-up homes and highway lights, then darker foothills, snow-topped mountains, and a black-and-blue-and-yellow-swirled sky à la *The Starry Night*. With the thick pastel, she scattered yellow stars over the universe, a measure of tension easing inside her.

Last night, she and Mark had finished up the black paint on the figures in companionable silence, and this morning, he'd picked them up so they'd be out of the way—and unseen—for classes. She gazed down at the picture. Overall, the evening had been . . . great. But she still had that insistent feeling that she'd overshared. And now, that they were being observed.

"Hey, new girl," a husky male voice said from behind her, causing her to jump.

She turned. "Dalton. You startled me." She rubbed oily blue chalk off her fingertips.

He chuckled. "I didn't think you were the kind of woman who startled easily."

"Only when I'm deep in thought."

"Sounds dangerous."

"You have no idea."

He smiled, unperturbed, then glanced at the picture she'd sketched. "Did you do this?"

"Just goofing around before I cleaned up." She put the pastels away and stacked the boxes.

"If this is goofing around, I'd like to see what you can do when you're serious."

"I'm sure you would." She had some of her serious work in her office to show the kids so they understood that she knew what she was talking about, but something kept her from showing anything to Dalton.

"I'm not joking," he said.

She smiled and leaned against the table. She hadn't meant to come across as abrasive. "Maybe. Sometime."

"I have to earn it, huh?" He leaned next to her.

"Something like that."

"How about I take you out tonight? Dinner?"

After what she'd just experienced with her students, she hesitated. "I have work to do."

"You just finished work."

"You're a teacher. You know the work never ends."

He nodded. "All the more reason to get out. C'mon, just dinner. A couple of hours and then you can get back to work. I promise. It's a school night, so I'm contractually bound to get you home at a decent hour."

She gave him a smile for that. Despite the kids' insistence, she doubted marriage was even on Dalton's radar. She'd planned to start painting the nativity figures, but she'd put in good long hours on them already. A small break wouldn't hurt, no matter what anybody said. And a little space from a project was important, especially one so emotionally charged.

"All right," she said. "Dinner."

He smiled. "Great. I'll pick you up at six thirty?"

"Can we make it five thirty?" Earlier was better, so she could get back and work into the evening.

"Five thirty it is. I'll make the reservation."

"Reservation? Where are you taking me?"

"Ah," he said, backing away and giving her finger guns, "that's a surprise." He disappeared out the door.

She stood, scrunching up her lips. A break would be good. Last night was deeper than she'd expected. Dalton wouldn't go deep. She'd bet on it. She would go to dinner with Dalton, and hope Wyatt's mom was nowhere in sight.

❄ ❄ ❄

Mark turned the radio up as he headed to Riley's house with the nativity figures. He hadn't listened to much music lately, and this was a song he hadn't heard before. He tapped his left hand on the steering wheel. When had he stopped listening to music?

Right.

He turned down Riley's street and parked in front of her house. Rain hit the roof of his truck and bounced off the walk. A few degrees colder and this would be the white stuff.

Watching her house now, he couldn't help the hollow feeling in the pit of his stomach. The last couple nights with Riley had been great. Casual in some ways, but not in others. He'd never connected with a girl on this level before.

Maybe because you didn't have anything on this level to connect with before, Super Chief.

He shook his head and got out of the truck.

When she opened the front door, he paused, staring. Her hair was wavy all over instead of straight, and tossed back like she'd just run her fingers through it. And whatever she'd done to her eyes . . . and her lips . . .

She looked great. Better than great.

She smirked. "You want to stand on my porch all night, or are you bringing those inside?"

He moved abruptly, stepping through the doorway, careful with the nativity boards. He'd wrapped them in a tarp before coming over so they wouldn't get wet in the short distance between his truck and her porch.

"Sorry," he said. "I just—" Wow, she smelled great, too. "I just wasn't sure you wanted these dripping through your house."

"Don't worry about it." She walked toward the bedrooms wearing a skirt and high-heeled boots. That was not what she'd been wearing at school that morning. She turned and put her hands on her hips. "You coming?"

"Yeah. Of course." He rolled his eyes. *Smooth as ever.*

He followed her to the bedroom on the right, trying to keep his focus off her skirt and the way it hugged her curves. Caylin had curves, but she'd been all legs and shoulders. Riley was more—

She flipped on a light, and he blinked, his senses overwhelmed by the smells of an active art studio. He gathered himself and looked for a place to set the boards down.

"Put them over here against the closet."

He followed her instructions, glancing around as he unwrapped the tarp. His eye landed on some canvases leaning next to a metal desk. He nodded toward them. "Are those yours?"

"Why would they be mine?"

He heard the play in her voice. "See, there's that attitude I've missed since, oh, three minutes ago." He finished with the tarp and stood to fold it up.

"Oh, please."

He ignored her protest and went over to the canvases, lifting the top one with the care he knew was required. He studied it quietly. She'd painted a high cliff in orange and red, cut vertically with purple and blue shadows, a wedge of turquoise sky at the top. In the top right corner at about two o'clock stood a small, brilliant-white mountain goat. You almost missed it, but you couldn't at the same time.

He glanced at Riley, put the canvas down, and picked up the next one. A portrait of a child, bundled up in bright, haphazard colors, pink-cheeked in the snow, following an adult, holding her hand, but looking back toward the artist.

He picked up another. A bird at the edge of a puddle in the street, fallen maple leaves on the ground. She'd shown the rain.

In that bold, raw, painting-on-black style of hers, she'd somehow depicted rain.

"You're not saying anything," she said. "Should I be worried?"

He looked away. "I'm wondering why *you're* not in a magazine."

She made a *tsk* sound. "Come on."

He looked over the painting a few more seconds, then set it down with the others. He went to the easel and saw pretty quickly that she'd been sketching faces for the nativity. A few of his photos were clipped to the corners. "I'm dead serious, Riley." He gave her his full attention. "Why aren't you in a gallery somewhere?"

She shook her head, her cheeks flushed. "I've only been serious about it for a little while. I mean, I've always studied, but I was studying other things, too." She picked up a charcoal pencil from the easel tray and turned it in her fingers. "It took me a while to figure out what I really wanted to do. Painting rose to the top."

He watched her put the pencil back. "It shows."

She smiled at him. "Thanks." She looked around, then motioned for him to follow her out.

When they returned to the front room, he hesitated to leave. "I think my mom would've liked you."

She smiled, clearly touched by the compliment. "I wish I could have met her. To be able to talk to her about the industry, ask her questions . . ." She shrugged.

He nodded, feeling that ever-present loss more keenly than before. "She would've gotten a kick out of someone who actually moved to this little valley because of her interview in *American Artist Magazine*."

"They don't even make that magazine anymore," she said. "It went out of business a few years ago. Everything's online now."

"If you ever want a copy of that particular issue, we have about three dozen of them."

She laughed. "Really?"

"Yeah, my dad went a little nuts."

"That's awesome."

"Yeah, it is, I guess." He noticed the trio of paintings above her fireplace. "Those are yours, too?"

"Yep. Those are my favorite."

He stepped closer. Three different houses. Not as unique as the paintings in the art room, but still vibrant.

"They're three of the houses I lived in, growing up. Where I have the best memories."

"The yellow house in the middle looks like it could belong here in Miracle Creek."

"That's my favorite. It was my grandma's house in Bozeman. I didn't actually live there, though it feels like I lived there more than anywhere else."

She moved away from the paintings, his cue to change the subject.

"Does your mom still flip houses?" he asked.

"No. When she's not traveling, she focuses on the home she and my dad have now."

"How does that feel, after all those years?" He watched her carefully.

"You mean, how does it feel that they settled down to a real home after I grew up and left?"

He heard the hint of bitterness in her voice, but she smiled. Then her eye twitched, and he laughed.

She chuckled. "The irony isn't lost on me, believe me." She sighed. "My dad's a very charismatic person. One of those people who lights up a room and everyone in it but doesn't hold still for long. I think he's finally seeing how happy it makes my mom to be settled." She grew quiet again, studying the paintings. "Maybe."

"Sometimes it's hard thinking of our parents as just people."

"Yeah," she said. "And sometimes they make it too easy."

"Oh, so you've met my father."

She grinned, her eyes glassy.

He fought the urge to gather her in his arms. Instead, he touched her elbow. "I better get going."

She glanced at the clock. "Yeah. Thanks for bringing those. I'll start on them tonight."

"Are you going to be wearing that?" he asked, only half kidding.

She laughed and smoothed her skirt, though he couldn't see a wrinkle. "No. I'm going out to dinner."

"Oh? The Grill-n-Go again?" He teased, but he didn't feel like laughing.

She narrowed her eyes at him. "Ha ha."

"So . . . who are you going out with?" he asked, immediately wanting to take back the question.

"Dalton."

"Who?" he asked, feigning indifference as jealousy shot through his chest, shoulder to shoulder.

"Dalton Gainer."

He nodded. "Oh, that Dalton." He stood there like an idiot.

"Do you know many Daltons?"

"Sure. Loads." But only one Dalton had compared Riley to a record on a scoreboard.

She cocked her head. Then she smiled. Man, he wished she wouldn't smile like that.

"Well," he said. "Good night." He turned to the door.

"Mark?" she asked, and he winced.

He turned again, finding her standing there, wide-eyed and trusting. "What?"

"I know how you feel about him. Dalton, I mean."

"*I* don't want to date him, if that's what you're implying."

She shook her head. "You know that's not what I mean. I can handle myself, you know?"

He ran a hand over his face. "I'm sure you can. You look great, by the way."

Her smile reappeared on those rosy lips. "Oh yeah?" she asked, one eyebrow raised.

And that was when the thought of Riley Madigan going out with Dalton Gainer made him want to throw up.

Her smile faltered at his expression. "What?"

"I was just—" He hesitated. "Do you talk to Dalton about the stuff we talk about?"

After a moment, she shook her head. "No."

He let out a hidden sigh of relief.

"To tell you the truth," she said, looking back at him, "I can hardly get a word in edgewise." Humor returned to her eyes. "I'm not friends with him the way I am with you."

There it was. Again. *Friends.* He nodded. "Good night, Riley."

"Good night, Mark."

He grabbed the door and got out of there. The last thing he needed to see was Dalton's car pulling up the street. Because if he did, he might do something *really* stupid.

❄ ❄ ❄

They passed another sign, and Riley's nerves tightened a fraction. She hoped Dalton wasn't taking her where she suspected he was taking her. There were a dozen restaurants along this highway, but possibilities were running thin.

"What do you have planned?" she asked. "You're smiling like a cat with a mouse."

He chuckled. "I told you, it's a surprise. We're almost there. I couldn't believe it when I heard you hadn't been there yet."

"Been where? Heard from whom?"

"I overheard a little birdie in the staff room. Apparently, I'm not the only one who wants to get you out of our little town."

The only other staff member she knew who might want to take her anywhere was Yvette. And the only place Yvette had mentioned wanting to take her was Leavenworth, the quaint little Bavarian town hailed as Central Washington's premier tourist and honeymoon destination.

And the Christmas capitol of the entire Northwest.

Maybe Riley should have been talking to Dalton the way she'd been talking to Mark.

They passed Peshastin on the right, her last hope for any dining possibilities this side of the Cascade Mountains other than Leavenworth or Steven's Pass ski resort.

"Are we going skiing? I would have worn something warmer."

Dalton laughed again. "No skiing. And you look amazing. I told you that, right?"

"You did." She wrung her hands together. "You know, Dalton, I have this sort-of phobia—"

"Of skiing? Because trust me, that's not on the menu."

"No, not skiing. It's just—"

"I hope it's not lederhosen." He laughed, and she smiled weakly. He leaned toward her. "I promise you'll be very safe. Anyhow, close your eyes."

"What?"

"Close your eyes. Part of the surprise package."

"I'm not sure I—"

"I've practically given it away so just give me this. No peeking."

She closed her eyes. "You're not going to strap on a pair of lederhosen, are you?"

"You're cracking me up, Mads. Trust me. It's a good thing the rain cleared up. I want you to get the whole effect."

Oh, she was getting the whole something. *Mads?* She couldn't help thinking she preferred it when Dalton had other people around to talk to.

Riley concentrated on her breathing. She had a few more weeks until the big tree-lighting everyone talked about. She wasn't scared of Christmas. Just the emotions it induced. Dalton didn't know that, and he was obviously looking forward to introducing her to this town.

The car slowed, and after a couple of turns, Dalton cut the engine.

"Keep your eyes closed. I'll be right there. Don't move."

"Don't worry, I won't," she said. She waited, anticipating the click of her door as it was pulled open. She shivered at the hit of crisp air. Dalton took her hand and made sure she didn't bump her head as she exited. True to her word, she kept her eyes shut.

"Okay, follow me. Just a few more steps, I promise I won't let you fall."

The air was filled with sound: music in the distance, the swoosh of slow cars driving past, the mottled hum of people in conversation as they walked, nearby and farther away. She peeked at her shoes to keep from having to cling to Dalton's arm. About ten steps later, they stopped.

"Here's a good spot. Perfect." She felt Dalton move behind her, placing his hands on her arms. "Welcome to Leavenworth, Riley."

She told herself this was a small thing, that surely she could look down a street. Something did smell delicious. Not one thing but a hundred delicious things hanging in the air.

"How this works is," he said gently, "you open your eyes."

Slowly, she opened her eyes.

The world stirred into motion, like the beginning of a merry-go-round ride. They stood at the top of a long street. Two- and three-story Bavarian-style buildings that looked like something out of a storybook graced both sides, all lit up with Christmas lights, and exquisite tole-painted murals peeked from above doors, beneath window boxes, and between dark-hewn beams. People bundled together wearing red scarves and floppy knit hats. Jingle bells—no kidding, jingle bells—rang out in all directions.

"Holy crap," she muttered.

"I'm sorry, what?" Dalton asked, leaning closer.

"Um, it's astonishing."

"Isn't it?" he said, obviously pleased.

She took a deep breath and blew it out as he took her hand and led her to the far side of the street. Wreaths and swags and twig reindeer and old-world Santas met them at every step, yet none of it was gaudy or overdone or even overcommercialized. Somehow, Leavenworth had managed to capture the celebration of Christmas . . . and any normal person would find it *wonderful* in the true sense of the word.

"Our reservation isn't for another half-hour, so I thought we could walk first. Do you mind?" Dalton was suddenly looking at her like he'd actually consider her answer instead of talking over it.

The gears in her head clicked. "Let's walk now. Work up an appetite."

He smiled. "That's what I like to hear." He took her hand again and led her farther along the avenue. They crossed the street, and her focus lifted to a gigantic pine.

"That's the Christmas tree," he offered. "The big lighting is in a couple weeks."

"It's huge."

"Beautiful, isn't it? A whole day of festivities, and then they set off fireworks. Sounds fun, huh?"

"Mmm," she replied, banishing the unbidden image of Mark passing out candy canes to everyone.

Trees grew along the edge of a small park, complete with a gazebo framed in white twinkle lights. The gazebo glowed from within and—she realized as they approached—sheltered an oompah band, the musicians wearing embroidered vests, lederhosen, and felt hats. To the side, waiting his turn, a man stood poised in front of an exceedingly long horn.

"An alpenhorn?" she asked Dalton, leaning into him over the sound of the band.

"I'm impressed. Listen."

They waited a little longer, and then the man braced his feet on either side of the horn, which balanced on its own small stand on the ground. He took a deep breath, then blew into the horn, the melody traveling from his lips to the crowd with a rich, deep sound.

People clapped as the familiar strains of "O Little Town of Bethlehem" blended with the oompah band.

She let go of Dalton's hand and took a step back. He must have taken it as a cue to applaud the music, too. As he clapped, she stepped back again. When he realized she'd vacated the space, he simply steered her through the crowd, away from the gazebo and onto the sidewalk again.

"Not ready for Christmas music yet?" he asked.

No, she wasn't. Not ever. "I just like to take my holidays in order—have a little Thanksgiving after Halloween." She managed to smile up at him. "What's next?"

He gestured to the shops. "We stroll. Make our way to the restaurant."

Dalton led her across the street, pointing out the highlights of each shop as they meandered through the crowds.

The shops glowed from the inside, cheerful and—she had to admit—not overly filled with holiday glitz. The toy store displayed nothing but colorful block sets, puppets, puzzles, and trains, and the kids still pulled their parents inside the doors.

She found herself being steered into a bakery.

"Pick something out. Anything. We'll save it for later. They have the best *bollen*."

She looked up at Dalton at the familiar name. "Better than Lette Mae's?"

His head bobbed with indifference.

She perused the glass cases and found them: a tray of beautiful round chocolate-topped pastries split in half and filled with Bavarian cream.

"I'll have a napoleon," she heard herself say to the girl behind the counter.

"You would choose that one," Dalton said, chuckling.

"Why is that?" she asked.

"Nothing. It's nothing."

"That wouldn't be a short joke, would it?"

"I wouldn't dare," he said, looking very much like he would dare.

"Of course not," she said. "I'm sure you could come up with far more clever ways to comment on your date's physical attributes." As he opened his mouth to speak, she cut him off. "That wasn't a challenge, just an observation."

Again, he chuckled.

The girl behind the counter, who was carefully placing Riley's napoleon in a paper sack, smiled shyly.

Dalton winked at the girl. "I'll have a *bollen* and an apple strudel."

She couldn't help wondering if he had any idea how predictable he was, and what his reaction would be if he ever found out that she'd noticed.

He paid for the desserts and turned to Riley as if he'd just conquered Denmark. "Shall we go?" He offered her his elbow.

She nodded. This was easier. Easier than depth and searching and oversharing.

Except Dalton insisted on going into Kris Kringl, one of the favorite stops in Leavenworth. The sign on the towering storefront boasted "Where it's Christmas all year long!"

"We'll explore the whole store," he said. "The trains, the villages, downstairs and up. It's a requirement. You need to see everything."

"Oh, I really don't," she muttered.

"C'mon. It's like being a kid again."

As much as this playful side of Dalton Gainer was refreshing, she hung back as he pulled her along while instrumental Christmas carols played loudly through the store. She focused on the people and the floor as he steered her past displays of Santas and ornaments and mountains of miniature Christmas villages until they were climbing a staircase to the second floor, where the crowd thinned out.

Up here, themed Christmas trees took up one side, but the other half featured . . .

Nativities.

All shapes, sizes, origins, and materials—carved wood, fabric, clay, polymers, and porcelain.

She couldn't look away. Her heart pounding, she stepped toward a small porcelain set, all white, no color, just a matte glaze. Very much like the one her dad had brought home all those years ago. Carefully, she picked up the figure of baby Jesus.

"Do you like it?" she heard Dalton ask.

She set the figure back down, unable to answer.

"It's simple compared to the rest, isn't it?" he said. "I bought one of these giant sets for my mom a few years ago. She loved the ghastly thing."

Riley shook her head.

"Can I buy this one for you? Early Christmas gift."

"No." The word was rough in her throat. "I mean, no, thank you. The last thing I need is another nativity." She tried to laugh.

He joined her. "Yes, I guess it's a little trite, isn't it? As if anyone remembers this part of it anymore. You should have seen the one old Rivers used to put up off the highway, all lit up every year, cramming that down our throats. I suppose it's sentimental, though, right?"

She nodded, unable to choke down the lump in her throat or suppress the burn rising in her cheeks. "Yes," she managed to say without sounding too forced. "Sentimental. His wife painted those, did you know?"

"No, I didn't." His gaze wandered over the nativities. "Poor guy. Never remarried. You know he dated Yvette for a while."

Her chin shot up. "Yvette Newsome?"

He shrugged. "Didn't stick, I guess. Ended after Mark got himself burned up. Oh well. If it's meant to last, it's meant to last, right?"

She stared, then took a deep breath through her nose,

running a hand over her hair. "You know what?" she said, eyes wide. "I'm so hungry. If we don't get to that restaurant, I'm going to eat dessert first." She lifted her white bakery bag.

He didn't hesitate taking her hand and leading her back downstairs and outside. Even with the fresh mountain air and the drift of tiny snowflakes making the moment picturesque, she wanted to run. She wanted to yank her hand out of his and tell him where he could go.

But she knew his type. He'd blink at her. Laugh it off. Coddle her back to his side, telling her he was sorry and to at least finish dinner.

It wasn't worth the fight. It wasn't worth the possibility of tears or the attempt to reveal a deeper truth than he could grasp. Because Dalton Gainer was a shallow, selfish player.

Like so many men she'd dated.

Her pace slowed at the revelation. Dalton's hand left hers as the sounds of the world faded. He turned, concern etched in his expression. She returned the look.

"Riley, are you all right?"

The merry noises of the street filled her ears again, and she blinked. "Yeah. Yeah, I'm fine."

"C'mon. Let's get some food in you, new girl."

She nodded. She'd go to dinner with Dalton. Smile and listen. Order something light and not finish it. None of it would register on his radar as being off. He'd drive her home, try to kiss her, ask if he could come in.

And she'd tell him it was a school night.

❄ ❄ ❄

Riley shut her front door and watched Dalton's taillights disappear into the night. She closed her front curtains and tossed her little sack of pastry into the garbage can. Her boots came off next. She flung them into the hall to pick up later.

She pressed her hands to her pounding head as she headed to the kitchen, her bare feet cold on the hard linoleum. Grabbing the bottle of Tylenol out of the cupboard and filling a glass with water, she walked to her art room and stared at the easel. At the sketches she'd attempted, of Mary's face, and Joseph's, and the shepherd.

She downed two pills, not taking her eyes off the photo of baby Jesus. There was no face to study; the glare from Mark's old flash had wiped it out.

Setting down the empty glass, she picked up the charcoal pencil and grabbed the photo. Taking a deep breath, she sketched the manger, the swaddling and the hay, a round head. She paused, her heart pounding.

Next to her sketch lines, she drew a larger, faint circle. Ears. Chin. Fleshed out an infant's head and ran the pencil line in a swift arc from ear to ear to place the eyes. But she stopped.

What shape were the eyes? And how wide? Asleep or awake? Happy? Surprised?

Wise? Could babies' eyes be wise? This baby?

She put her hand over her own eyes and sighed. She took two steps and dropped down into the desk chair.

You should have seen the one old Rivers used to put up off the highway, all lit up every year, cramming that down our throats.

Riley's jaw clenched.

Ended after Mark got himself burned up.

She squeezed her eyes tight, sick.

❆ ❉ ❆

Mark grunted with each push-up. Forty regular push-ups, then twenty with each arm. Well, twenty with his left arm and as many as he could with his right before he collapsed. Which was about twelve.

Thirteen.

Fourteen—

His phone rang, and he dropped to the floor with a groan. Gritting his teeth, he reached his left hand out and checked the number.

Riley.

"Hello?" He tried to calm his heavy breathing as he fumbled his phone to his ear.

"Hi. Are you . . ."

"Working out."

She paused.

"Are you okay?" he asked, pushing himself up on his elbow. He winced, stretching his right arm.

"Could you come over?" she asked.

"Now?"

"Yes. I know it's late."

"It's only eight."

"Oh." Another pause. "Please?"

"On my way."

She hung up, and he stared at his phone, still out of breath. She'd sounded small. Riley wasn't small.

He took the quickest shower he could, threw on a fresh shirt, jeans, and a beanie, and clamored down the stairs. "I'm going out," he called, and slammed the door before his dad could begin the questions.

A few minutes later, he stood on Riley's porch and knocked on the door. It took every ounce of patience in him to stand there and wait. On the drive over, his imagination had run wild with all kinds of possibilities why she'd called. Most scenarios had something to do with Gainer and ended with Mark wanting to pound him.

Mark lifted his hand to knock again, but the door opened, and Riley stood there in a big sweater and leggings, holding a box of matches in her hand. Her hair was still wild and wavy all over, but her eyes were rimmed red.

"Hi," he said.

"Hi." She backed into the house. "Come in."

He did, looking around. She closed the front door behind him. Papers were scattered in a semicircle over the floor in front of the green sofa along with some of his old photos, but she passed those.

She knelt in front of the brick fireplace. "Can you help me with this?"

He took off his coat and knelt beside her, looking hesitantly at the couple of logs she'd piled in the grate. "You're serious? You called me over here to start a fire in your fireplace?"

She dropped the box of matches in her lap and put her hand to her head. "I'm sorry. No. I'm cold. I can't stop shivering, and I thought maybe I'd use this thing to get warm, but the logs won't catch. I should know how to do this, right?" She turned to him, and he saw what he hadn't yet.

"You're crying," he said.

She smiled, pulled her sleeve over her fist, and wiped at her eyes. "Yeah, a little."

He wanted to ask what Dalton had done, but figured he'd better take care of her first. He looked back at the sofa and spied a blanket in a heap on the cushions. He got up, grabbed that, and wrapped it around her shoulders.

"Thanks," she said, watching him.

He squatted down and checked the flue.

"I opened it up, like you said."

"Good job."

"I just couldn't get anything to stay lit. The newsprint burned right up."

She sounded so lost. So . . . un-Riley.

"Is your woodpile out back?"

"Through the kitchen."

He nodded. "Be right back." He hurried through the kitchen, out the back door, and down a few steps. He found what he needed against the house and hurried back inside.

"On the other side of your woodpile is a crate of scraps for kindling." He pushed a few pieces of tinder under the grate, arranging them so air would circulate between them and the logs above. "Do you have more newspaper?"

She nodded and stood from her cross-legged position and went to the dining table. She tore off a few pieces of paper from a large pad of artist's newsprint and returned.

She sat down again and slowly fell over sideways, staying there. "I'll just let you do that while I lie here."

"Not getting off that easy. Up." He pulled her arm, and she let him.

When she was upright again, she pushed her hair off her face. The perfume she wore earlier still lingered.

"So—" He took a sheet of paper and demonstrated how to twist it. "What happened?" He peeked up at her.

She concentrated on his twisting. "Your hand is shaking."

"It's from the workout. What happened with Dalton?" He wasn't going to let her change the subject. She'd called him over here in tears, and he was done trying to be patient.

"Nothing horrible. Well, his depth of character is about"—she held a piece of paper horizontally—"this deep, so, there's that."

"Figured that out, huh?" He took his twisted paper and showed her how to tuck it into a space between the kindling.

She followed. "He took me to Leavenworth."

He pulled back.

She finished tucking her piece of paper in and then brushed her hands. "He didn't tell me where we were going. He wanted it to be a surprise. And he didn't know my history. So . . ." She looked up and lifted a shoulder. "I'm not sure it would've mattered, though." She took another twist of paper and wiggled it under the logs.

"Maybe." He liked to think Dalton would have considered her feelings if he'd known about her thing with Christmas. "Maybe not." He handed her the box of matches, trying not to look too eager to be rid of them. "You do the honors."

She took the box from him, and he sat back. She struck a match, and a whiff of sulfur dioxide hit his nose. His pulse kicked up, and his jaw clenched. She held the match close to the papers. They caught fire and flamed up.

He pointed. "Do the same over here."

She obeyed, and in a couple of minutes, the kindling was burning, and the flames had begun to lick up the sides of the logs.

Mark retreated to the rocking chair, putting some space between him and the fire, wiping sweat from his brow. He wondered how he'd ever get past this fear.

"Thanks," she said, pulling the blanket up around her shoulders. She looked back at him. "It's hard for you, isn't it?"

He tried not to be drawn in by the orange-hot light. Instead, he focused on her eyes. "It is." He narrowed his gaze. He didn't want to talk about him. "What happened in Leavenworth?"

"I couldn't eat a *bollen*."

"What?"

She shook her head. "I don't know. *Bollen* are our thing, right?"

He stilled at the words "our thing," then nodded quickly. They had a thing.

The weight of fear from the flames started to dissipate.

She continued. "I was doing okay. I remembered what your dad said about how you used to pass out candy canes." Her smile flickered and faded. "But then we went into this Christmas store, and I don't know . . . By the time we got to the Holy Hall of Nativities, I was ready to lose it, and Dalton didn't seem to notice—or care—so I came home and curled into the fetal position."

"I'm sorry," he said, trying to sort through her explanation. But he knew the feeling of being on an emotional edge, and he didn't want it for her.

"Me, too. I actually wanted to enjoy the schnitzel." She shook her head and looked back at the fire.

"Why am I here," he finally asked, "if it wasn't to help you build a fire?"

She sighed and gestured to the drawings on the floor. "I need a face."

"You have a face."

She crossed her eyes at him, and he laughed. She crawled in front of the sofa and drew her legs beneath her. She'd dragged her blanket along with her. "I need a face for the baby. You need to help me."

He joined her on the floor and sorted through the sketches

she'd done. A page of eyes. A page of noses. A page of mouths. Hair. All babies, definitely.

"Riley, the figures are more abstract. You won't need this much detail." He lifted the page of eyes and ran his fingers over them, impressed with how she'd given them depth and even reflection. "How do you people do this?"

"'You people'?" She took the page from him.

"Artists. Painters. People who draw. Draw-ers."

She smiled at him. "We draw. A lot. Every day. All the time. We study people and other *draw-ers*. We learn. We erase. We start over. You know that."

"Yeah, I guess I do. Sounds a little like physical therapy."

She looked back down at the eyes. "I know the nativity is more abstract. This was just exercise. I've done some other images over here that take the styling into account."

She handed him another page from the floor.

Sure enough, she'd pieced together several different baby faces in his mother's style. "Any of these would work," he said.

"No. These all have a slightly different expression, and I'm not sure which to give him." She scooted closer, brushing his shoulder with hers. "This one is pretty generic, like, 'I'm a baby, but I'm kind of important, look at me.' And this one is more like, 'Whee, I'm loving this king gig.' And this one kind of— Well, I was going for wise, but he looks like he's filling his diaper—"

Mark barked a laugh, shaking his head. "I can't believe you just said that."

She grinned up at him. "Then help me."

He was grateful she sat to the left of him. They were so close he could count each and every freckle across her nose, even in the soft light from the fire and the single floor lamp behind them.

"I'll try," he said, begrudgingly turning his focus back to the page they were studying.

"This one has the right eyes, I think." He tried to picture his mom's baby Jesus. "Yeah, I think these are really close. You know, looking up but really simple. Maybe not such a round nose."

She picked up a pencil and the sketch pad and drew the eyes.

"The nose was more of just a swoop underneath. And the mouth was like this one here."

She followed his directions, filling in the space around the baby, the swaddling wrapped around the little body. She stopped and reviewed her work.

He leaned over her shoulder. "That's good."

"Are you sure?"

"That's the one."

She nodded and let out a deeper breath of relief than he'd expected. "Good."

It would have been easy to put his arm around her, to pull her closer and tell her not to worry, that anything she did would be great. But he couldn't do that and risk what he already had with her.

"You nervous?" he asked.

She shrugged, brushing her hair back. "Well, you know, Son of God, King of kings, hallelujah, and everything. It's a lot of pressure." She glanced at him like she was kidding, but he sensed otherwise. "Not to mention I'm doing this for a family who lost an awful lot and deserves something that reminds them of better things."

He watched her a moment as she began sketching out more of the image, biting her lip in concentration.

"Thank you," he said.

She nodded.

"So," he said, tapping the new sketch. "What is this one thinking?"

A small smile came to her lips as she studied the baby. "He's not quite warm enough."

He chuckled lightly, and her smile widened.

"I think he just hopes to be loved," she said. "Like everybody else."

Mark sobered and let the quiet surround them a few moments. Nothing but the pop and hiss of the fire. "I think you've got that right," he finally said. Then, in an unplanned move, he smoothed his hand over her hair. It was soft, the waves like silk under his skin. His heart played a hard rhythm beneath his ribs.

Time to go.

She blinked as he stood. "You're leaving?"

"Yeah. I've still got stuff to do, and I'm beat. I'm glad you called, though."

She stood. "Thanks for your help." She gestured to the fire. "With everything."

"Not a problem. Make sure it's completely out before you turn in."

She nodded. "Of course."

They faced each other for another moment, then he headed for the door. He stopped and turned back. "I know you didn't have the best time tonight with Gainer."

She waved her hand. "Nothing a little hot chocolate and some focused painting won't fix." She looked away, and he again wondered what exactly had happened.

"I know I've asked you for a lot of help," he said, "but I got a call this afternoon, and . . . I was wondering if you'd consider playing hooky with me on Friday."

Her eyes grew large. "Play hooky?"

"Yeah, you know where you pretend you're sick and skip school—"

"I know what hooky is." She folded her arms.

He grinned. "So you'll come?"

"For what?"

"I told you. I need help with something. It's for a friend over in Wenatchee."

"What will we be doing?"

He knew why she asked. Dalton had sprung Christmas town on her. "It's nothing to do with the holidays."

"Why don't you just tell me what it is, then?"

He hesitated. "Because if I told you, you'd think it was the most boring thing on the planet and you wouldn't come. And I could really use your help. Call it volunteer work. Please?"

She scrutinized him. "You make it sound so magical," she teased. "I'll call in a personal day. Do I need to wear muck boots or anything like that?"

He grinned. "I don't think so. But I wouldn't mind if you wanted to wear those killer boots from earlier—"

She gave him a push to the door. "Never mind. Out."

"But—"

"Out. Good night." She opened the door and continued to push, which was useless because he only moved when he stepped back himself.

"Friday morning. Nine thirty," he said.

She hid her smile, but not very well. "I'll see you then."

He'd backed out to the porch. "Maybe you could wear the skirt, too—"

She closed the door on him.

His smile remained.

Chapter 12

The silver minivan pulled up in front of the Riverses' house, and Mark stepped out to meet it. Stephanie got out and opened the side door. She grabbed the covered infant car seat with baby Mark inside.

"Hey, help me with the groceries, will you?" she asked.

"That's what I'm here for." Mark hefted a large box in his arms along with a bag of onions.

"Don't keep the onions in the garage," she said, walking ahead of him into the house. "They'll freeze and turn to mush."

"Understood." He set the box down on the counter next to her bags, then set the bag of onions on top of the fridge.

She threw him a look. "No."

"What's wrong with the top of the fridge?" he asked.

She pulled the bag down. "The bag is mesh and onion skins are dry and crackly. Anytime you move it, onion skins will flake down the front of the fridge." She opened the broom closet and put the bag on the floor.

He peeked under the baby tent on the floor. Baby Mark

seemed to sleep ninety percent of the time. "What are you feeding this kid?"

"Breast milk. Dramamine."

He dropped the cover, looking back at her. "Really?"

"No, not really. You don't give a baby Dramamine. Come on, EMT, we've got frozen stuff to bring in."

He rolled his eyes and followed her back out to the car. This time they detoured through the garage, stopping at the freezer.

"You know," Mark said, "you don't have to keep doing this."

She tossed a package of frozen burritos onto a shelf. "It's no big deal to pick up extra for you and Dad when I do the big shopping."

Stephanie's "big shopping" meant driving to Costco in Wenatchee once a month to stock up on diapers and toilet paper. And a whole case of hash browns, apparently.

"We won't eat all this," he said.

"You don't need to eat all of it. Some of it's mine. I need the extra freezer space." She pushed the freezer door shut against a huge bag of chicken. "There. Now, help me with the stuff that goes in the refrigerator."

"I can do this, Steph," he said, following her back into the house. "I don't mean just putting things away. I mean the shopping."

"Good. Next time, I'll take you with me, and you can learn what to get."

He picked up a gigantic package of toilet paper and hefted it to his shoulder. "I think I've already got the idea. Anything bigger than Ivy, I throw in the cart."

She turned to him and smiled. "Basically."

"Seriously, Steph. I lived on my own for how many years? I can do the shopping. I'm getting out more. Not sure I need to go all the way to Costco for milk, though." He turned to take the year's supply of toilet paper upstairs as she shoved a gallon into the fridge. Unlike the freezer, there was plenty of space in there.

"You're welcome," she called up after him.

When he came back down, she was dividing up fresh vegetables.

"It's like you expect us to actually cook or something," he said, taking a few tomatoes from her along with a couple of lemons.

"I do. You're feeling better, and Dad needs real food. People can't live on frozen potpies and corn dogs."

"Uh, yes they can."

She pushed a block of cheese and a box of eggs big enough for the firehouse at him. "No, they can't, Mark. Dad works hard. Make him good food."

He sighed, putting the eggs and cheese in the fridge. They sat down at the table, and Stephanie scooted the baby carrier closer.

"So, speaking of getting out more . . ." She rocked the baby carrier with her foot a few times. "Word is you've been getting over to the new art teacher's house." She raised her eyebrow at him.

Gus.

Gus's wife, Heidi, was good friends with Steph. He grunted. "For Dad."

"And she came over here?"

"For Dad."

"Um, no, she stayed, and Dad came to my house."

Oh yeah.

"And what about the school?"

He froze. "What about it?" He loved his sister, but she couldn't keep a secret to save her life.

"I hear you've met her after school a few times."

"Twice." He refused to look at the mirth in her eyes.

"And stayed late."

"Not true."

"Mark."

"What?" His leg bounced. He stopped it.

"What's going on?"

He studied the grain in the old cherrywood table. Finally, he lifted his gaze to meet his sister's. "I'm working on something."

"Is that what the kids call it these days?"

"Knock it off."

Her expression softened. "Do you like her?"

"What is this, sixth grade?" He frowned. "She's not even sure she's going to stick around here much longer."

"Okay, but do you like her?"

He shook his head, still running his hand along the table. "We're friends. And she's helping me with something, so that's why we were at the school."

"What is the thing?" she asked. The baby fussed, and she lifted him out of the carrier.

"Can't tell you."

"Why not?"

He smiled. "Because Christmas is coming, Steph."

She smiled shrewdly back, and he knew he had her.

"You should take her to Leavenworth," she said.

He laughed. "Why does everyone think Leavenworth is the place to take a girl at Christmas?"

She stared at him. "Because it's picturesque, romantic, charming, and nestled in the mountains like the Alps themselves complete with all the trimmings of the most wonderful time of the year?"

He rubbed his face and sat back in the chair. "I've got an idea.

You and Dad take each other to Leavenworth. Then everybody wins."

She frowned. "What does that mean?"

He shook his head. "It means I have a better idea." He hoped.

Her face brightened. "So, you *are* taking her somewhere."

He dropped his head. Yes. He was taking her somewhere. And if his sister knew where, he would never hear the end of it.

Stephanie rose from the table and handed him the baby. "You *do* like her." She kissed the top of Mark's head, then headed upstairs.

He looked down at his nephew, sleeping soundly again. "A word of warning, kid. I love this town, but you can't burp without your friend's wife's cousin's grandpa knowing about it."

❄ ❅ ❄

On Thursday after school, Riley entered grades into her laptop and hung the sixth-graders' interpretations of *The Starry Night* on the display board. She wanted to get home. Mark had finished framing and would be putting up drywall.

She held up the last picture in the stack and halted. It was her own drawing, the one she'd done the day after Mark had taken her up the dirt road to see the lights. She smiled, remembering the conversation they'd had, and the easy silence. Her smile faded recalling her students' argument over Mark and Dalton. As she tacked the picture up on the board with the others, her phone rang, and she answered it without looking at the name on the screen.

"Riley? Honey?"

Her stomach tightened. "Mom?"

"I know you asked me not to call—"

Riley leaned against the edge of a table. "Mom, of course you can call. I just didn't want you to try to talk me into coming back."

"I know, but . . ."

Riley could hear the strain in her mom's voice. She steadied herself. "Mom, I'm not coming back."

"Riley, baby," her mom said, "I'll be home from this trip on the first. Christmas won't be the same without you."

Riley could've argued that her parents had had a lot of Christmases without her. But she was trying to work past that. "You know why I left. I'm not ready to do all that again."

"You wouldn't have to do anything."

"We both know that's not true. Dad would insist I go to every party, every opening, every gala, with everyone there wondering how I've survived after such a humiliating breakup, but nobody actually caring that I'm doing just fine."

"It wouldn't be like that. And besides"—her voice dropped to a murmur—"Dad has someone he'd like you to meet."

Riley closed her eyes. "Mom, that's how things went bad last time."

"He's not an actor. And he's gorgeous."

"Being an actor didn't make Gavin a weak, cheating scumbag. Being *Gavin* made Gavin a weak, cheating scumbag."

"Still angry, huh?"

"I wasn't insulting him, I was merely describing him."

"Well, I would describe this new guy as perfection. You could slice an apple on his jaw."

"That sounds . . . sharp."

"I'll text you a picture."

"Please don't."

"He's an orthodontist. You have the straightest teeth."

"Because of braces."

"See? It's fate."

"Mom. Stop. I'm not meeting Dad's friend."

Silence filled the line between them. Then her mom sighed.

"I see. And how are you doing, honey? Are you really 'just fine'?"

"Yes. Really. I love my job. The house is coming along. I'm painting."

Her mom's tone perked up. "What are you painting?"

"It's a commission piece for Christmas. Which means I'm working here through the holiday. I'm staying in Miracle Creek, in my own house, with my own stupid wreath on my door, if I get one."

Her mom sighed again. "Jeremy will be disappointed."

"Who's Jeremy?"

"The orthodontist."

"He doesn't even know me. Mom, you and Dad need to stop trying to set me up."

"But, sweetheart, we have connections with so many beautiful people."

"You, of all people, know beauty isn't everything, Mom." Riley waited, knowing she'd struck a chord. "You and Grandma were the ones who taught me to see beauty in the broken things, the worn-out things. The gritty and real things. I'm done with Dad's shiny, airbrushed world. You can have it."

"I've had both, Riley," her mom said quietly. "And I've tried to do my best with it. Your dad wishes he could go back and do things differently. We both do. He's only trying to make up for how things went with Gavin."

"That's not his responsibility. I'm sorry, Mom, but I'm staying here."

After a moment of silence, her mom spoke again. "I'm

glad you're painting again. Do you remember my friend, Cheri Mathison?"

"The artist in New Orleans?"

"Yes. She's establishing an artist's residency program there this summer, and she wondered if you'd be interested in joining the faculty. Sort of a junior teacher-in-residence. Imagine, *New Orleans*."

Riley paused. She could imagine. "Did you tell her I'm teaching here?"

"I told her I would let you know about the opportunity and that you would contact her. I'll send her information along."

Her earlier conviction wavered. "Thanks."

"I can't imagine your little Creek town could hold a candle to one of the most art-fueled cities in the country."

Riley's gaze swept over her well-worn classroom. No. No, it couldn't.

❋ ❋ ❋

At home, Riley worked on the nativity while Mark cut and fit drywall onto the new, wider arched entryway between the front room and the kitchen. She glanced at her phone to find it long past dinnertime.

She came out of her art room, rolling her shoulders. "I'm ordering pizza. What do you like?"

"Everything."

"You're easy."

"Hardly."

She gave him a smirk and turned to her phone, grateful that the nearest pizza place delivered to Miracle Creek. She looked up the number and sat down at the rolltop desk, rubbing the spot between her shoulder blade and neck. After the pizza was ordered, she dropped her phone on the desk and sighed. She couldn't get the conversation with her mom out of her head.

"My neck is killing me."

"Can I help?"

She looked behind her, and Mark gestured to her hand on her neck.

It had been too long a day, and she scarcely hesitated. "Yes, please." She lowered her forehead to the desk.

But nothing happened.

"Did you change your mind?" she asked, hoping he hadn't.

She felt her hair being gently swept aside, and he began working the spot she'd been rubbing. He began almost too gently, but as his pressure increased, she exhaled and let him work the tight muscles in her neck and shoulders loose.

"Something's bothering you," he said.

"Yes." She kept herself from groaning under his firm touch.

"Hard day at school?"

"Yes." Oh. He did this well. Her breath hitched.

"Am I hurting you?"

"No." It did hurt, but in a good way.

"Do you want to talk about it?"

"Not really."

He kept working, kneading rock-hard ropes of muscle until they were smooth before moving to the next spot.

"You're good at this," she said with a tiny grunt. "How are you so good at this?"

He laughed quietly. "I've been on the receiving end of a lot of these during my recovery. I guess you get a feel for it after a while."

He placed one hand on her shoulder while he worked the

area between her shoulder blades. "So . . . my dad and I wanted to know if you'd have Thanksgiving with us."

She paused.

"My sister and her family will be at Brian's folks' this year, so it'll be . . ."

"Quiet?" she asked.

"Boring."

She smiled. "I'd like that. Thank Cal for me."

His hands rested on her shoulders. "You can thank him yourself." He slowly spun the chair to face him and crouched down. "Are you okay?"

She blinked at him, staring at his walnut-brown eyes ringed with black. She brushed her hair back off her face. "Better now."

He nodded, then stood and went back to work.

"Mark?"

He turned, waiting.

"Thank you."

He smiled and picked up the power drill.

"Mark?"

He lifted his gaze again.

"The wall is going to look amazing."

His smile widened. "So is the nativity." He nodded his head toward the back of the house.

"Man," she said, groaning. "You are such a boss."

He pointed at both of his eyes, then at her.

She pulled herself out of the chair and made her way back to the art room. Grinning.

❄ ❄ ❄

On Friday morning, Mark was back on Riley's porch. He heard a horn *beep beep* behind him and turned. Alli Kent and her sister, Liv, waved enthusiastically from their blue Bug. He lifted a hand as they sped down the street.

Yet more spectators of the Mark Rivers Show. When the pizza was delivered last night, Dave Capshaw could barely keep from gawking between Mark and Riley, and then had outright nudged Mark. "I see the rumors are true," he'd said with a wink. "Way to get after it." Mark told him they were just friends. Riley had grown very quiet after that.

He was spending time nearly every day here, though, granted, most of that time Riley was away at work. He frowned. He hoped he'd done the right thing inviting her to Thanksgiving. It was already costing him. The grin on his dad's face when he'd told him . . . The old man was going to be unbearable.

Mark knocked on Riley's front door and waited. After a minute, he rang the bell. Footsteps padded on the wood floor, and the door swung open.

Riley held her hair on top of her head, and she had something stuck between her lips.

"Come in," she said around the bobby pin. He remembered Steph holding them in her mouth like that when she'd get ready for dances.

"I'm not too early, am I?"

She shook her head, walking away from him. He closed the door behind him.

"No." She padded back to the bathroom and leaned at the mirror. She took the bobby pin out of her mouth and jammed it in her hair. "I totally slept in. I'm so sorry."

He laughed. "You slept in? It's a school day."

"Oh, don't you do that. Don't you dangle a hooky day in front of a teacher and then get upset when her body senses freedom."

He chuckled. "You hit snooze, huh?"

"I hit *off.* I didn't mean to."

"Don't worry about it. We have time."

"I just need to slip on my shoes," she said around her toothbrush. "This is okay, right?" She turned in a half circle, showing him what she was wearing—tight, dark jeans and a fitted flannel that accentuated her figure.

He had a hard time keeping his eyes from roaming. "I have those exact socks."

She glanced at her pink fuzzy socks, rolled her eyes, and finished with her toothbrush before disappearing into her bedroom.

He raised his voice. "My dad keeps throwing out the idea that you need to see Leavenworth and all the Christmas stuff going on. You know, lights, Santa, Christmas trees. A million people. You should have seen his face when I told him Gainer had beaten him to the punch."

She came out of her room. "You did not. Mark."

He nodded. "Broke his heart. I think he has a thing for you."

She shook her head, walking toward him. "You're so mean." She pulled her coat and a scarf out of the closet.

"He gives more than he gets." He lifted the side of her coat she was struggling with, and she slid her arm inside. "He cheered up when I told him you were coming for Thanksgiving."

"Thanks," she said. "I'm glad."

He watched her hands come together, fidgeting nervously. He reached out and held both her hands in his one, and she stilled. He quickly let go. "I told him what I have planned for today was better than Leavenworth."

Her brow rose. "Oh?"

He nodded. "But it's not very glamorous."

"A girl can only handle so much glamour in one week."

"Exactly. But . . . do you have a problem with blood?"

She wrinkled her nose. "Blood?"

"Do you trust me?"

She wrapped her scarf around her neck a couple times. "You're not a vampire, are you?"

He smirked. "I don't think so."

She studied him. "I'm fine with blood. But I have no idea what you're up to."

"Trust me."

❄ ❄ ❄

"What are we doing here?" Riley asked as they pulled up to a tan building.

"I told you. They called, and I thought I could use your help." He parked and turned to face her.

She knew he did that to give her more of his left side. Or less of his right. "I don't have any experience with this."

He looked out the window at the surrounding rural scenery, then smiled at her. "Won't matter."

They'd left the hills of Miracle Creek and, in a few miles, reached Wenatchee's lower orchards and farmland. The parking lot was mostly empty, and at ten in the morning, the town was quiet. She read the sign on the building.

West Wenatchee Dialysis Center.

"All right," she said. "But why are *you* here? I'm guessing you've been here before, and yet you obviously don't need dialysis."

He frowned. "Are you a doctor?"

She faltered. "Oh—"

"I don't need dialysis, Riley."

She thwapped his right arm.

He immediately grabbed the place she'd hit him and grimaced, sucking in air through his teeth.

Her eyes flew wide. "Oh no! I'm so sorry—" She leaned toward him, gripping his hand, patting his shoulder, unsure of what to do and feeling horrid. "I'm so sorry, Mark. What can I do?"

"Riley."

She paused and met his gaze, inches from his face.

"I was joking."

She pulled back and thwapped him harder.

He laughed deeply, and she fought the blush she knew was coming.

She lifted her finger. "That. Was. Not. Cool."

He covered his mouth, still shaking with laughter. "I'm sorry."

"You don't look sorry."

He relaxed against his window and reached up, touching her very warm cheek. "It wasn't nice. I am sorry." He put his hand over his heart. "You really care."

She narrowed her eyes at him. "Dummy. How am I supposed to know what hurts?"

"That's a good question." He studied her for a few moments and grew serious. "My therapist suggested this," he said, motioning to the clinic. "He set up the times and everything to start. At first, we thought maybe I should volunteer at a burn center, but the closest one is in Tacoma, and at the time, I wasn't sure I could handle it. He came up with this instead. The center was desperate for volunteers, and they're just down the road. So here I am."

"And you brought me because—?"

"Because of what I said before. Sometimes to heal, you have to help somebody else."

"But what will I be doing?"

"Just come in with me. Carmen's waiting for us."

"Who's Carmen?"

"A friend," he said. "Her husband travels for work, so she needs someone to help her off the machine and give her a ride home. You'll like her, I promise." He nodded at the front doors. "Ready?"

"Ready," she said, though she wasn't sure that was true. She hoped she didn't mess anything up.

They entered the building and put on disposable gowns and gloves at a dressing station. She followed Mark to a long front desk where a woman in scrubs looked up from a computer screen.

"Hey, Mark."

"Hi, Sheila. I brought a friend today. This is Riley."

Sheila smiled at both of them. "Great. Sign in, both of you." She pushed a clipboard toward them. "Carmen's waiting for you on number ten."

"Of course she is."

"Her lucky number," Sheila said with a wink at Riley, and went back to work.

Mark signed in, then passed the clipboard to Riley. After adding her name and phone number, she followed Mark beyond the desk. The room opened up into a large area filled with stations, defined mostly by the reclining chairs and the big machines sprouting tubes and cords next to them. Only three were occupied, and Riley felt eyes on her as they passed two men who were hooked up, their tubes filled with a red liquid.

She felt like she was intruding. Like when she'd realized Mark hadn't meant for her to see him without his hood. One of the men smiled at her, and she relaxed. If he could smile while being hooked up to whatever these machines were doing, what claim did she have to be uncomfortable?

In a corner chair next to a window, a woman with a silk scarf wrapped around her head was already waving them over.

Mark grinned. "There she is." He reached her and took her outstretched hand. "Carmen, how are you?"

She beamed up at him, pale, but bright-eyed. "Oh, I'm wonderful. Thank you. I'm so happy to see you. Tell me your name again?"

Mark didn't blink an eye at not being remembered. "Mark Rivers."

"Yes, Mark! You come to help me when they're done with me. Oh, forgive me for not remembering."

"That's all right. Carmen, this is my friend, Riley Madigan."

The woman shifted her gaze. "Riley Madigan, what a beautiful name." She held out her hand, and Riley took it. Her grip was soft, her hand cold. "You'll have to forgive me. I don't remember names well. Sometimes I forget information I've just been given, but I can remember all kinds of other things."

"That's all right," Riley said, unable to look away from the woman's pale blue eyes. She couldn't guess her age. Maybe fifty? "It's nice to meet you. Mark's been mysterious about where he was taking me today."

"He has?" She turned to Mark. "Oh, that's not very nice, bringing such a pretty girl here. And you didn't tell her anything?"

He shrugged as a nurse came over to start working with the machine next to Carmen. "I told her there would be blood."

Carmen put her hand over her mouth, covering her laugh.

Mark leaned toward her. "Nothing wrong with coming here. All the prettiest girls are here, after all."

"Oh, you!" Carmen shook her head fondly at Mark and smiled at Riley.

She was sweetness and light in a body no bigger than Riley's. Frail, maybe, but not enough wrinkles to be old.

The nurse took a seat on the rolling stool.

Carmen reached for the nurse's arm. "Mark, Riley, this is nurse Amy. All the nurses here are so nice. Oh—Mark, you probably already know that." Carmen rolled her eyes at herself.

Mark turned his attention to Amy as she started clamping tubes and unhooking things. Carmen distracted Riley with talk.

"Riley . . . It's Riley, right? That's a beautiful name. And you're a beautiful girl. Isn't she beautiful, Mark?"

Mark grinned, trying to focus on Amy's instruction.

"Oh, look," Carmen said. "I've made him blush. Riley, what do you do? Are you from . . . Where is Mark from? Cashmere?"

"Miracle Creek," Riley answered. "I'm a new teacher there."

Amy tied a rubber strap around Carmen's upper arm and removed the tubing from its place above her inner elbow.

"What do you teach?"

"Art." Riley glanced to see Mark take Amy's place next to Carmen, applying pressure at the vein site with his own hands. Amy slid off the stool, and Mark sat down.

As Amy removed the rubber strap, Carmen gasped. They all looked, alarmed at the sound, but Carmen only exclaimed, "You're an art teacher!"

Mark and Amy exchanged smiles, and the nurse made a few more checks and left them.

Riley blinked at the smooth transition of everything, noting that Mark had never once tried to hide his right side from anyone here. She glanced at Carmen, who still waited for a response.

"Yes," she said. "I teach art." *Brilliant, Madigan.*

Mark chuckled, and Riley threw him a glare as she sat in a nearby rolling chair.

Mark leaned closer to Carmen's arm, adding pressure with both hands stacked on top of each other. They moved with a slight *thump-thump* of Carmen's pulse. He looked up at Riley, catching her watching. "Carmen's an artist, too."

Riley looked from him, as he literally held in the woman's life blood, to Carmen. Carmen's eyes were wide as she nodded.

"In what medium?" Riley asked.

Carmen rested her head against her recliner. "Watercolor, mostly. At least, I used to. I had a stroke. My kidneys failed—I almost died—while I was in the hospital trying to—" She looked at Mark.

"Recover."

"Yes, recover from the stroke." She lifted her right arm, the one she'd given Riley when they were introduced. "I lost a lot of muscle control on my right side, so . . ." She looked around, as if searching for the right word. "Umm, partial paralysis. That's why I need someone to come and put pressure on my arm. I can't do it myself like the other patients."

"I'm happy to help," Mark murmured.

Carmen patted his arm. "I'm unable to paint anymore. The stroke is why I don't remember the way I used to. I forget new information quickly. Sometimes I lose words. I had to learn to read all over again! My grown daughter taught me, if you can believe that. I picked up a magazine after the stroke, and I thought, why would anybody give me this magazine? I thought it was written in Latvian or something! I don't know Latvian."

Riley didn't know whether to laugh or cry.

"But I can remember a lot of other things." She took Riley's hand again. "You're . . . Riley."

Riley nodded, and Carmen smiled, pleased.

Riley was struck both by the magnitude of loss this woman

had suffered and by how much joy she still exuded. "I'd love to see something you've painted."

Carmen's eyes lit up. "I have some pieces around town, you know."

"Carmen has done commission pieces for fruit growers all over," Mark said. "Families have had her paint pictures of their homes in the orchards or vineyards."

Carmen nodded. "And I think . . . yes, I'm sure . . . I knew Mark's mother. But you and I didn't know that when we met, did we, Mark?"

Mark shook his head as he adjusted his pressure on Carmen's arm. How long did he have to hold it?

Carmen continued. "Leah Dolan. We were in the artists' guild together. She was lovely. Mark, your mother was lovely. You look like her, around the eyes."

"Thank you," Mark said.

Carmen sighed. "It was so sad when she passed." She reached across and patted Mark's hands. Then she sat back in her chair and closed her eyes for a moment. When she looked at Riley again, she smiled. "Thank you so much for coming."

How was this woman smiling? How was she so grateful? Riley suppressed the welling emotion behind her own eyes. She took a breath. "Do you miss painting?"

Carmen nodded, her smile subdued. "Very much." Pain clouded her eyes for a moment, and then it dissipated. "Tell me about what you do. Do you paint?"

"Riley paints amazing oils," Mark answered for her. "And she did all the backdrops for the school play."

"Oh, wonderful. What was the play?"

"*Peter Pan.*"

"Oh, I bet it was fantastic."

"It was," Mark said. "Your husband took you."

Carmen covered her eyes. "Oh, yes," she groaned. "I remember now. It was wonderful." She dropped her hand in her lap. "Are you a realist, Riley? Or more abstract?"

Riley gathered herself. "A blend of both, I think. I like a lot of color. A lot of contrast."

"Who are your influences?"

"Oh, Caravaggio and Rembrandt. Delaroche."

"Mmm, light against dark, yes."

"Cezanne and Van Gogh, of course."

"Of course, with the color. Brilliant."

"And, um, Samuel John Peploe?"

"Oh, I don't know him, but I want to. Can you get me my bag? I have a notebook in there and a pen."

Riley helped her rummage through a small duffel bag and wrote down Samuel Peploe's name. "There's something about his still lifes that makes me look and look."

"This gives me such an image of your painting, Riley," Carmen said. "Will you bring me something next time you come?"

Riley glanced at Mark, then back to Carmen. "Of course. I'd love to."

"You know, Carmen," Mark said, "Riley's painting reminds me of my mom's work."

Riley nodded. "She's another influence, if you can believe that."

"Is that how you got to know each other?" Carmen asked, looking between the two of them.

Riley remembered that first night, when he'd wanted to ask her to paint the nativity and she'd thought he was a stalker. "You could say that."

Carmen beamed.

Amy returned and checked Carmen's blood pressure against

Mark's hands. If he was tired, he didn't show it. He got the okay and slowly released his hands, giving them a little shake. He removed his gloves and tossed them in a wastebasket.

Amy cleaned up Carmen's arm and applied a bandage, while Mark washed his hands. He helped Carmen walk to the scales to record her weight, and Riley gathered up Carmen's things.

When they were ready to leave, Carmen, weighing about as much as a bird, took both Mark's and Riley's arms and let them lead her out to the car.

As they drove, Carmen asked Riley questions about being a teacher, interspersed with quick bits of trivia about Wenatchee. Mark parked in front of a modest little house with a picket fence. As Mark helped Carmen out of the front seat, Riley slipped from the back seat.

Carmen turned to her once more. "Thank you, Riley. I loved talking with you today. If I don't remember you next time, just remind me. I won't mind at all."

Riley gently put her arms around the woman. "Thank you, Carmen. I think you're remarkable."

The woman brushed the comment away with her hand and a smile, but Riley saw gratitude in her eyes. Acknowledgment, maybe. She took Mark's arm and let him help her into her house.

Later, Mark and Riley drove away in silence. Mark stretched and squeezed his right hand. She wasn't surprised it ached, pressing like he had on Carmen's arm for so long.

"Are you okay?" he asked quietly after they left Carmen's neighborhood.

"Me? I'm fine." She paused. "What will happen to her?"

"She's waiting for a new kidney. She's been waiting for a long time." He glanced at her. "Her chances are good, though."

"Good."

A few more minutes ticked by.

"Does it always feel like this?" she asked. "After leaving her? It's like you don't want any noise."

"That's a good way of putting it."

"I can't imagine never painting again."

He nodded.

"I can see why your therapist wanted you to do this."

"Like you said, Carmen is pretty remarkable."

She studied him, her gaze following the pattern of his scars as they disappeared down his neck. "So are you, Mark."

He didn't answer.

The next traffic light turned red, and he stopped, glancing at her. "Can I take you to lunch? To thank you for your help?"

"You don't have to do that. I liked Carmen, and—"

"Can I take you to lunch, Riley?" This time when she looked up, he was watching her, his gaze unsure but deep.

She nodded. "Yes."

The car behind them honked, and he continued through the green light.

Chapter 13

Mark pulled up to the restaurant, wishing his nerves would settle, and parked. "Do you like Thai food?"

"It's one of my favorites. I haven't had it in a long time."

He'd planned to take her to this restaurant if she said yes to lunch. He wasn't known as the "town hero" in Wenatchee, which meant he was treated like anybody else. No free appetizers or complimentary desserts.

The place wasn't crowded, and the host seated them quickly.

"What's good?" Riley asked, looking over the menu.

"I've had both the Tom Kah and the cashew nut chicken. The spring rolls are really good."

"If I ordered them, would you share with me? I want to order the Thai basil chicken, too, and if I eat them both myself, you'll have to roll me out of here."

"We wouldn't want that to happen."

Mark's hunger peaked just as the food came. Helping Carmen always wiped him out both physically and emotionally. His right hand still shook from the exertion of applying pressure to her IV site. He'd come a long way since he first started at the clinic, but with all the work he'd been doing on the house, he knew he was pushing it. The last thing he needed to do was spill his water or drop the soy sauce.

"You don't use chopsticks?" Riley asked. She snapped hers expertly in the air.

"Show-off," he said, gripping his spoon. The truth was, he'd been great at chopsticks . . . with his right hand. He hadn't even tried with his left.

"Come on," she said, handing him the pair that sat in a paper envelope at the top of his plate. "You're never too old to learn."

"I believe the saying is 'You can't teach an old dog new tricks.'" He scooped another spoonful of curry and rice into his mouth to make his point. "Mmm." He chewed and swallowed. "Mark likes food to make it all the way to his mouth."

"But Mark also said he wanted to try new things." She waved the chopsticks at him again. "Mark could do it if he tried."

He grabbed the packet out of her hands. "If Mark wanted to try, he would, and he'd be great at it."

She raised her eyebrows at him. "Prove it."

He growled but set down his spoon and grabbed the pair of chopsticks. She watched like a kid at a magic show.

Great.

He gripped the chopsticks in his right hand the way he used to hold them. The tremor grew worse, but he just needed to study it for a few seconds. Then he flipped the sticks mirror-like to his left hand.

"Oh, Mark, I'm—"

"Shh," he said. He didn't need to hear the pity in her voice. "You can feel sorry *after* I've made a fool of myself."

He tightened his left-hand grip, the lower stick becoming immobile. He should have been able to move the top stick up and down with his forefinger and thumb. He focused on a slice of carrot in his bowl. It took a few tries, and he might've given up had Riley not been so irritatingly eager. But he finally gripped the carrot, lifted it to his mouth, and took the bite. He chewed and set the chopsticks down on the small plate where half of his spring roll remained.

"Satisfied?" he asked.

"Well, I feel horrible, but yes. Are you? You did it."

He nodded, picking up his spoon. "I'm king of the world."

"I was only trying to help."

"I know."

Several uncomfortable minutes passed, and for the most part, Mark gazed out the window, eating his food and drinking his water and wondering how a great start had led them to this awkward . . . nothing.

"Mark?"

He shifted his gaze to Riley.

"I didn't mean to make you uncomfortable. I wish you understood that."

He gave her a nod and picked up his glass. "I understand it better than you think."

"Okay. Good. And you don't have to do that."

"Do what?" He took a drink, gazing back out the window.

"Give me your left side all the time."

He paused, his glass frozen to his lips. A mixture of anger and humiliation rose in his throat. He set his glass down and stared at it, his face hot. "Why would you say that?" His pulse thumped in his temples.

"I don't mean to upset you."

He made an effort to breathe, to stay in his seat. "Really?

Because you could have said just about anything else and I would've been fine."

"I think you underestimate me."

He flicked a look at her, then rolled his eyes. That was probably true.

"Hey, would you look at me?" she asked quietly. "I'm not done. Please?"

"Why?" He was half angry with her and half frustrated with himself. He managed to keep his voice low. "What else do you want to say?"

"You'll never know until you look at me."

"I don't want to know."

"Fine."

A minute passed, and begrudgingly, he turned her way. He met her calm expression with defiance. "It's a habit," he said. "A 'coping skill' I use to 'make others less uncomfortable.'" Great. He was quoting his shrink again.

She studied him like she often did, but this time he wanted to turn away. He wanted a hole to open beneath him and swallow him up.

She leaned across the table and put her hand on his arm. "I need you to get it," she said, also keeping her voice low. "I don't want you to be constantly worried about how to hold your head or which side of me to stand on. I just want you to know that all I see—no matter which side—is my friend, Mark Rivers. It's the only way I've ever seen you."

How could words be so encouraging and so infuriating at the same time? "Is that right?" he asked, an edge to his voice.

"Yeah, that's right." She sat back. "Take it or leave it. You're stuck with me and my crazy ability to see you—as you are."

He mentally chewed her words, trying to decide what to do with them. "Lucky me."

She looked away, muttering.

"What was that?" he asked.

She looked back at him, her jaw set. "I said—I'm the one who's lucky."

He stared at her.

She shook her head. "I'm the one"—her voice became louder, as if he couldn't hear her—"who is lucky to be *here* with *you*." She waved both hands in the air. "All of you. You *plunk head*."

He glanced around the restaurant, feeling eyes on both of them. The curious onlookers quickly got back to their meals.

He leaned forward. "Plunk head?"

She narrowed her own eyes, challenging him. "Are you going to eat the rest of that roll?"

He reached his hand around the dish and pulled it toward him. He squared himself to her. "Yes."

She took a bite of her Thai basil chicken with her chopsticks, grinning triumphantly.

❄ ❄ ❄

After lunch, Mark turned the car toward Miracle Creek.

"So, what's next?" Riley asked.

"You want to keep going?" he asked, hoping that was the case. "Because I don't know if I can take more of your torment."

"I only torment people I like."

He glanced at her. "That's demented." He wondered if she tormented Dalton Gainer.

Her brow lifted. "I'm a work in progress."

"Okay," he said, sighing deeply. "But I gave you a chance to get out of this. Remember that."

"What, more blood?"

He glanced at her again. "I hope not."

They drove in comfortable silence until they reached a large, boxy city building in the town of Cashmere. Mark parked the car, his pulse already up. He turned off the engine and sat there, turning his keys over in his fingers, his knee bouncing.

"So," she said, eyeing the building. "The fire department."

"Yep."

"What are we doing here?"

"We're going to go into the fire department and talk to someone about volunteering." His keys continued to turn in his fingers.

"Volunteering? You mean . . . to be a fireman?"

He nodded again. He felt her hand on his arm, and his leg stilled.

"Mark, that's . . . that's big."

"Yep."

"Are you ready?"

He shrugged. "I can't just do nothing anymore. This is what I know. I've got my comp pay, but I can't just . . ."

"I get it," she said. "I do. My dad spent a lot of time teaching me what he knew. A camera. A lens. He taught me how to shoot, how to develop. I got to work with the best equipment." She shook her head. "But any other time—most any other time—I was drawing or painting. I can hardly remember a day going by without getting something on paper or canvas. Or a wall."

He watched her, silent, recognizing that it was hard for her to share this about herself. He didn't want to spook her.

"My dad was teaching me, but I was also learning about him. He was demanding. Brilliant, but a perfectionist. Always needing to get the best lighting, the best minutes of the day, the best side—to capture the symmetry, the ideal. It's what made him successful. But he was teaching me that I couldn't be myself. In my young mind, his focus on perfection only emphasized my imperfections. I wasn't the ideal. My mom always worried about being enough for him. And the things I wanted to photograph or paint . . . they were the broken things. Gradually, we grew apart, and though I studied photography, I got my degree in education with a minor in art. The paintbrush won out; I got to teach what I knew and loved best. And then something weird happened."

"What?" he asked.

"My dad offered me a job on a crew, and I took it. I had reasons. And it was good. Until it wasn't." Her expression darkened. "That's when I knew I needed to get back to what I loved. Where I knew I needed to be." The light in her eyes returned. "Like the fire truck in your parade."

He nodded. Nobody had gotten it before. Nobody had understood what he lost.

After a minute of silence, she spoke again. "It's volunteer, right? So only as needed?"

"Yep." He looked out his window. "We really need snow. But it's November, and we've only had a few inches. They'll need volunteers. That's all they've got for Cashmere and Miracle Creek."

"All right," she said, grabbing her purse. "Let's go."

She placed her hand on the door handle. The determined look in her eyes stirred something hungry inside him.

He looked at his door handle and reached for it.

❄ ❄ ❄

Riley's heart beat erratically as they approached the front desk of the Cashmere Fire Department. She wanted to take Mark's hand or hold his elbow—anything that would ease his nerves. She dug through her purse and found a sucker.

"Here," she said, pushing it into his hand.

He looked down at it in confusion.

"I got it at the bank. It's a mystery flavor. It might be watermelon; it might be butterscotch. Who knows?"

He blinked at her, then put it in his back pocket. "I'll save it for later."

"Good idea. I bet all that mystery-flavor anticipation will keep your mind off what we're doing here."

He shook his head. But his posture relaxed as he continued to the desk.

A man with glasses and a goatee got up from his chair and held out his hand. "Mark Rivers. To what do we owe this pleasure?"

Mark shook his hand. "Good to see you, Don. How are things?"

"Quiet. Good. Prayin' for snow."

"Aren't we all?" Mark said.

As the two men made small talk, Riley's heart raced.

Mark's standing at the edge of a cliff and about to jump, she thought. *And I'm at the bottom telling him the water's fine. Who am I to say how the water is? It could be full of . . . not-fine water.*

When Mark set his hands on the desk, pressing down to still the tremors, Riley held her breath. This was the moment.

"Don, I think I'm here to sign on as a volunteer."

Don took his glasses off and studied him. "Are you sure?"

"No. Honestly, I can't believe my feet got me into the building." He glanced at Riley, and she nodded. "But I've got the experience, all the know-how in my head. Even if I'm just training or working here in the office. Running the radio. I can do that. Unless you think . . ."

Don cocked his head. "Unless I think what?"

Mark looked out the window, pressing his lips in a thin line.

He turned back to Don. "Unless you think me being here would be uncomfortable. For the fighters."

Riley's mouth opened, but Don spoke first.

"I think you being here would be one of the best things to happen to this little unit. You have experience, you have nerve, obviously or you wouldn't be at this desk, and you're one of us. We'll put you anywhere you want to be. Anywhere."

Mark held Don's gaze, then nodded. "Thanks."

Don turned to grab some forms, and when he set the papers on the counter, Riley picked up a pen on impulse.

"Me, too," she said.

Don and Mark looked at her.

Her gaze bounced between them. "Women can volunteer, too, right?"

"Of course, they can," Don said. "Do you have any training?"

"Not even a little," she said, smiling broadly.

Don chuckled at her enthusiasm. He picked up another form. "This is the application. You'll need to take a drug test, and there's a physical exam as well. Your application will be reviewed, and we'll let you know if you've been accepted to the program. We train everyone, from the ground up."

Mark put his hand on hers. "Are you sure about this? This isn't like the PTA. It's a commitment to help protect the community. The people. This is a volunteer job, but the program is tough."

"You don't think I can do it?" she asked.

His expression softened. "It's not about that and you know it."

"I want to help," she said, and realized she meant it. "I can at least look it over."

After another moment, he narrowed his gaze and squeezed her hand. "I doubt anyone could stop you, anyway."

She took the papers from Don with a grin.

Mark pulled his own form in front of him. "This is insane," he muttered.

"For your information, the PTA can be cutthroat," she said.

He chuckled as his pen touched paper.

❄ ❄ ❄

"This is the weirdest hooky I've ever played," Riley said. She peeled the backing off the children's "honorary firefighter" sticker Don had given her and stuck it to her shirt.

"Agreed," Mark said, pulling the sucker out of his mouth. He'd lucked out with cream soda. "Have you had enough, then?"

"Is there more?"

"That depends on you."

She tapped her chin with her finger. "Hmm, I seem to recall this guy wanting me to paint something for him for Christmas."

His brow furrowed. "I wouldn't want to keep you from your commitments."

"Ha," she said. "I've been away from my *commitments* for"— she counted on her fingers—"less than six hours, and I think I've piled on even more. How did you manage that?"

"*I* didn't manage anything. Volunteering at the firehouse is all you."

"Oh yeah, like I'm going to let you keep all of your selfless-ness to your . . . self." She scrunched up her nose, and Mark shook his head, putting the sucker back in his mouth.

"I've got a few books you can borrow," he said around the stick. "You can at least read up on procedural stuff and decide if you still want to do it."

"I do want to do it," she said. "Besides school, and the nativ-ity, and the renovations, I don't have anything else going on. I'm strong. I'm smart. My summers are free."

"Are you going to be here this summer?"

Her confidence wavered. "What?"

They were pulling down her street, and he parked in front of her house.

He removed the sucker from his mouth. "Are you going to be here this summer?" he repeated slowly.

She faced forward, smoothing her expression. "I'm not sure, but it's looking that way. I mean, the first year of teaching is probationary in Washington, so if they don't like me, or if I don't really like the school—" She trailed off. She rubbed at the knot forming in her chest. New Orleans rose in her thoughts.

"Riley?"

"What?"

"Just think about it before you commit. Okay? It's real."

"And teaching isn't real?" She'd committed to teaching. She just hadn't committed to teaching in Miracle Creek . . . yet.

"Both are real," he said. "All I'm saying is, think about it."

She took a breath, knowing he was right. But it wasn't that simple. "I've done a lot of different things. Taken a lot of paths. It's how I work. Just because I want to explore another path doesn't mean it wouldn't be important to me. I've considered a lot of important things. And I've left a lot of important things."

He looked away.

"Mostly for the better," she added. "It's life."

A muscle worked in his cheek. "You said you've always wished for a home."

"No, I said I stopped wishing for one."

He turned to her, his brow furrowed. "You're messed up."

She blinked at him, this boy-hero-man who hid from people behind a hood. "You think *I'm* messed up? You stalk people instead of calling them on the phone."

He leaned toward her. "You threaten people in cars with base-ball bats."

"That joke's older than the Stickley."

He glowered at her, and she matched him for a moment.

And then he began to laugh. That rich, deep laugh that first taught her who he really was.

She smiled. And for the first time she considered what it might be like to leave Mark Rivers behind.

She pushed the thought away. "So, plunk head, do you want to see how the nativity is coming along?"

He nodded. "Sure thing, C-fire."

She wrinkled her nose. "C-fire?"

"Trust me." He stuck the sucker back in his mouth. "It fits."

❄ ❄ ❄

Riley watched Mark out of the corner of her eye. He chopped vegetables while she browned hamburger for spaghetti sauce. He was good at it.

"Are you cooking more at home?" she asked.

He nodded. "We've gotten by with mac and cheese, Stouffers, and sometimes Dad's famous tuna casserole, which is not famous for its taste, trust me. Steph goes to Costco once a month and brings us fruit because she's afraid we'll die of scurvy. I told her I'd be better at feeding us."

"Where does your sister live?" she asked.

"Over on Cedar."

"She married someone from here?"

"No, they met at WSU. He's from Richland, but he liked it here and found a job in Wenatchee. Steph never intended to live outside of this valley. She made that pretty clear when they were dating, I think."

"You'll have to introduce me." She was curious to meet more of the Rivers family.

"I don't think so," he said, bringing the chopped onions and peppers over and sliding them off the cutting board with the knife.

"Why not?" She stirred in the veggies, inhaling the scent rising from the pan.

"Because she's a whole other type of fire, and I can only handle one of you at a time right now."

She gave him a funny look, then opened the jar of sauce.

He'd been pleased with her progress on the nativity. She'd finished a sheep and had begun work on the star last night. She'd thought she'd get to work right away on the baby after they'd figured out the face, but she'd only been able to pencil it onto the black board. She'd stood poised over what would be the baby in the manger with her paintbrush for ten minutes before she'd decided to work her way up. After all, she figured, it would be best to work the kinks out on the lesser characters first.

She glanced over her shoulder as Mark poured a bag of salad into a bowl and rummaged through the drawers for serving utensils.

They'd looked at paint sample cards for the front room and discussed her plans for the bathroom. He'd rooted around her art room while she'd readied the paints, and then they'd talked about his mom while she painted. He'd rigged her easel and a large bucket from the garage into an angled support so she wouldn't have to work on a flat surface, which would save her shoulder muscles on the bigger pieces.

The star that she'd dismissed as potentially boring in its angular simplicity took on a life of its own, battling its symmetry and two dimensions as she added color upon fiery color. Riley couldn't say how much time had passed before she noticed Mark had stopped browsing and just watched her.

Then the growl of her stomach told her it was past dinner-time, and she offered him dinner. He hadn't refused.

She returned her focus to stirring the sauce, when the noodles began boiling over, water hissing on the stovetop. Riley grabbed the handles and pushed the pot off the burner.

She yelped as heat blossomed over the palm of her left hand.

Mark appeared at her side, taking her hand and steering her to the sink. He ran a stream of cold water over her hand.

"I think that handle was over the other burner," she said, trying to pull her hand away.

"Do you have any potatoes?" he asked, keeping her hand in place.

"Um, sure, in that cupboard over there. Why?"

He grabbed a potato and cut it in half lengthwise. He pulled her hand from the water and dried it with a paper towel. Then he pressed the potato cut-side down to the skin of her burned palm.

"Is that okay?" he asked.

"I was really hoping for noodles." She could tell from his expression that he wasn't in the mood to joke.

"Rub this around a little," he said. "The juice helps."

She followed his directions with the potato. "It feels nice. Thanks."

He stepped back. "I've got some burn cream in my truck. Do you have bandages?"

"Yes, in the first aid kit. Maybe." She smiled wryly. "Nothing like burning yourself with an ex-fireman around to make you re-evaluate your emergency preparedness."

He didn't laugh. He lifted the potato, examining her skin, and nodded. "Not too bad. The burn cream should take care of it. I'll be right back."

She watched him go, realizing his perspective of something

like a little kitchen burn. The weight of what he'd been through began to settle on her. If it had been her right hand, she'd have a hard time holding a paintbrush or chopsticks—or anything—until it healed.

He came back in with the biggest, most official-looking first aid kit she'd ever seen. He motioned her over to the table and sat next to her, angling so he faced her better.

He opened the kit and pulled out a little blue jar.

"Give me your hand," he said.

She did.

He removed the potato and soaked a cotton pad in alcohol, brushing it across the fleshy part under her thumb. It felt cool across her palm. He waited a second for the alcohol to dry, then applied some white cream from the blue jar.

She felt immediate relief. "Thank you."

"My aunt gets it from Mexico. Good stuff. Apply it again tonight. Let me know if it blisters, okay?"

"Okay." She smiled, but it was subdued. She thought of all the other burns he'd had to worry about. Keeping them clean, wrapping them, applying cream. And the skin grafts . . .

He finished up and repacked the first aid kit.

She reached with her good hand and held him there before he stood. "Thanks. Really. When stuff like this happens . . . it's nice to have someone help."

He nodded. "You're welcome."

And she saw it. His need to help. His desire to use what he knew to protect others. He was a fireman, like he said. He had to be in that red truck.

After dinner was done and dishes were cleaned, they stood in the nearly finished walkway between the front room and kitchen. Riley glanced at the clock on the wall.

"What a day," she said.

"But a good day, though. I hope."

"A *really* good day." She shivered.

"Are you cold?"

"It's this house. Even with the windows sealed, it's drafty. I loved having the fire the other night."

"It's only eight. Were you going to stay up and paint, or . . . ?"

She shook her head. "No more painting tonight. I think I'll let this rest a bit." She lifted her hand.

"Does it hurt?"

"Not much."

"Do you want to build a fire?"

She hesitated, knowing his discomfort around any flame. "Are you sure?"

"Yeah."

So they built a fire, carefully, methodically, and they pushed the sofa in front of it. She sat with her blanket around her shoulders.

"That feels nice," she said, watching the flames.

"Good."

One of the logs sizzled and snapped, and Mark seemed to get lost in the glow from the flames.

"What happened?" she heard herself ask. "When you saved those boys?"

He turned away, and she worried that she'd overstepped her boundaries.

"It's okay," she said. "You don't have to tell me."

"No. It's just . . . it's a long story."

She scooted over on the sofa, pulling her blanket out of his way, and waited, watching him with a mix of curiosity and fear for what she'd just asked him to do.

Chapter 14

Mark studied the space next to Riley on the couch. She'd moved to the left, and he wondered if she'd done it so he'd be less uncomfortable, or if he was just overthinking a girl making space for him. His fight-or-flight response kicked in, and for a second, he froze.

But the desire to tell somebody who wasn't a reporter or an official or his shrink surged through him, and he dropped down next to her before his feet pushed him out the door. Even then, he was unsure how to answer Riley's question.

What happened when you saved those boys?

He focused on the boys.

"We'd been called up into the Chelan Complex." The words came slow off his tongue. Like gears that hadn't turned in a long time. "They were short on fighters. The fires that summer—I'd never seen anything so devastating in my career. Our crew was helping with emergency evacuations." He remembered a few faces. People had been cooperative, but panic was always underneath.

"The fire had turned on this area outside of Chelan. The winds were brutal. We hit this nicer stretch of homes on acreages, and some parents discovered a few of their younger boys were missing. They'd thought they were with other families, but one of the parents guessed the kids had gone to their fort. My gut turned to rock when they pointed in the direction they thought they might be. We barely convinced the parents to follow the evacuation plan. We couldn't spare the crew, so Jay and I took off with one of the dads to look for six boys, aged seven to ten."

He sat back, rubbing his hands together, feeling Riley's eyes on him and the heat of the flames in the grate.

"Forest fire gear isn't the same as standard gear, you know?" He looked at Riley.

She shook her head, her large eyes pale against the dark room.

"The uniform is lighter. A shirt and pants. Smaller helmet and a backpack. Goggles, if the smoke gets bad. Out there, your main worries are heat exhaustion. Dehydration. We approached this stand of old trees in the foothills, clouds of black smoke behind." He shook his head. "I was worried. I could see Jay was, too, but he didn't slow. We just had the crew truck, no road. We stopped about a quarter mile out and booked it on foot."

Riley curled her legs underneath her, and he looked back at the fire. The memory would become more intense now. It always did.

Her hand folded around his, anchoring him to the present.

"We left the dad. Told him we needed somebody there when we brought the boys out. I don't know how we got him to stay. We headed into the smoke, following a trail into the trees—tall old pines creaking in the wind and the heat. We heard a scream, so we ran that way. When we reached the trees, the flames were already there, high in the tops and on the ground. Burning debris falling everywhere. Jay called out, and I followed. He saw what I hadn't. Partway up one of the bigger trunks, about fifteen feet, the kids had built a platform, no walls. The tree above them was lit up and hot. One boy was already on the ground, coughing. I took care of him while Jay called out for the others.

"We heard them, above us on the platform. I don't know how they were breathing up there. The remains of a charred rope ladder swayed from the top. Jay kicked at the part that had fallen, tangled in the burning branches near the boy. I could see Jay's mind working. There wasn't a tree he couldn't climb."

Mark pictured Jay as a kid, scrambling up the tallest pines they could find on his property, smiling and hollering like a lunatic.

"I radioed the crew and then focused on the boy—Zack," he said. "He'd broken his leg trying to jump from the platform to get help. I bound him up best I could and lifted him, running him outside the trees. I signaled to the dad, who was running to meet me, and then I charged back in. Jay had made it up the tree. He'd tied his own rope on and had a boy over his shoulder as he rappelled down the trunk. He handed him off to me, and I ran him outside. Set the boy down, checked him over. His name was Dylan."

Mark paused, his eyes unfocused, watching the flames in the fireplace and in his head.

"Then what happened?" Riley gently prodded.

Mark took a deep breath, still watching the flames dance. "I ran back and Jay was coming down with another boy. That was three. We were only halfway done.

"An older tree on the far side fell with a crash, taking a couple smaller ones with it and spreading flames. I yelled at Jay to hurry as I left with the third boy." Mark's chest knotted up, making it hard to breathe. "Stupid thing to say. He was climbing that tree like a squirrel." He pulled his hat off and ran a hand through his hair. His leg bounced. "When I came back, he'd made it down again and tossed the fourth boy over my shoulder. I yelled at him that I'd go up. He waved me off.

"'Are you kidding?' he said. 'Only two more.'

"When I got back again, things had slowed. He was shouting from above. 'Platform's burning! Be careful!' Yeah, like I was the one who needed to be careful. Jay was coming down with the last two boys, one over either shoulder, and I didn't like the looks of that treetop. The wind was whipping. Flaming branches were falling. The whole stand would be an inferno, and we were right in the middle of it. The heat would get us before the flames did."

He felt Riley's grip on his hand tighten. He was almost done. Nearly there.

"Jay was bigger than me. Stronger too. Not as fast but he powered through and made it down. I caught one of the boys as soon as I could reach him."

He tried to take a breath, but it hitched. In his mind, he saw that exchange again, that nod of Jay's—*We made it. We did good.*

His voice came out husky. "I remember hearing a huge crack, like splitting rock, and I fought to keep my legs under me as we sprinted out of there, lungs choking. Then came this shove. Jay— he'd shoved his boy at me, full force, and it was all I could do to grab the boy's waist as we stumbled back ten feet. 'Go!' Jay yelled. I caught Jay's expression as he went down, the ferocity in his eyes just before the tree fell like a hammer."

The silence in the room engulfed him.

Riley wrapped her other hand around his as he struggled against his emotions. Two. Two small hands keeping him teth- ered. After a minute, he continued, his voice breaking.

"I was dazed—shouting for him. But the weight of the boys and the wave of heat from the fallen tree drove me back, and I had to go. I had to leave him there." He swallowed hard. "I got the boys out and set them down. I somehow missed the emergency vehicles arriving, missed the rest of my crew holding me back as the copse collapsed on itself. Didn't matter. I shook them off and charged back in there. I managed to find the tree, and Jay, in the smoke and heat. He was so still. I pulled and . . ." He shook his head. "Another crack. I heard him again—in my head. *'Go!'* It felt like everything moved in slow motion. I couldn't breathe. I managed to turn and fall, but another tree came down. Smaller. But I was trapped in the burning branches. I tried to get out—had to pull my hand out of my glove, but I didn't get any farther. I was going to die with Jay. Part of me was okay with that."

He paused, trembling, lost in the memory. Something drew him out. The press of her hand on his.

He swallowed, blinking his way back up. "I woke up in the hospital a week later. And then again a few days after that."

"And the boys?" she asked quietly.

The boys. "We got them out. They all recovered." He shook his head. "We'd pulled them all out, and I went back in there."

"For your friend."

He nodded. "That's the one thing—when I realized what I'd done to myself—that could console me. For a long time after." He met her gaze. "He'd have done the same thing." He shrugged, fighting his emotions. "He'd have done the same stupid thing."

She nodded, wiping away a tear. She leaned into him, put her arms around him, drawing him closer. He rested in the cocoon of her arms and blanket and let her run her fingers through his hair. The knot in his chest loosened, and he closed his eyes.

They stayed like that for a long time.

"Who got you out?" she asked quietly.

Some time passed before he could answer. "My crew. All of them. They piled into one of the big rigs and drove in there— hoses, full masks. I wasn't hard to find." He didn't say it was because of his screaming.

She squeezed his hand again. "They risked their lives for you."

He struggled to speak. "They could have died. Because of me."

"They knew that as much as you knew it when you went after Jay."

He breathed that in. After a moment, he slowly sat up, raising his arm around her, tucking her into his side.

"Thanks, Riley," he whispered.

She nodded. Soon, her eyes closed, her skin reflecting the flickering light from the fading fire.

"Mark," she mumbled just when he thought she'd fallen asleep.

"Yeah?"

"I'm no good in relationships."

He rubbed his thumb over the back of her hand as her grip relaxed. "Yeah, I know."

"I'm so glad you got out."

He pressed his lips to the top of her head, breathing in her peace.

She didn't stir.

When he woke, he was more reclined, and she was tucked into his side, between him and the back of the couch. His arm had fallen asleep all the way to his shoulder. The fire had burned out, and the room was dark as coal.

He looked at the desk where he'd set his wallet, phone, and keys, and grimaced. Carefully, he moved so he could see his watch.

The watch blazed, and he blinked.

3:40 a.m.

Inwardly, he groaned. His dad would be worried about him, and his truck outside would spur rumors.

As gently as he could, he eased himself off the couch, pulling his arm from under Riley's head without disturbing her sleep. She sighed deeply, and he froze. When she'd resettled, he managed to free himself without falling.

His fingers tingled as circulation returned, and his eyes adjusted to the dark. Riley's arm dangled over the edge of the couch, her cheek smashed against the cushion, her lips parted as she slept.

She took a sudden deep breath. "That's my fortune cookie . . ."

"My mistake," he whispered, pulling her blanket up higher.

She nodded and settled.

As he collected his things from the desk, his eye caught the shine of one of the glass doorknobs he'd broken off. He took it and returned to her on the couch. He folded her arm up and tucked the knob into her hand. "See you soon," he whispered. He quietly got his coat out of the closet, and then locked the front door behind him.

Before starting his truck, he paused, looking back at the house. His eye roamed over the other dark homes in the neighborhood. He took a deep breath and fired up the engine.

This wouldn't go unnoticed. Not in this town.

❄ ❄ ❄

Snowflakes fell fat and fast as Mark's truck climbed the road to his house. Sure enough, when he pulled up, the lights were on downstairs and a police car was parked in the drive.

Great. He checked his phone and found a dozen texts, missed calls, and several voice messages. The texts had stopped around one a.m. He took a deep breath, then went in to face the blitz.

When he opened the door, though, he found his dad and Lester playing cards at the dining table.

"Hello, son." His dad adjusted the cards in his hand, his poker face on.

Lester nodded. "Hey, Mark." He dropped a card on the table.

"Hey," Mark said. "It's snowing out there, did you know?"

They both nodded. "Hope it keeps up," Les said.

Mark resisted the urge to walk up to his room. "Sorry I'm late."

"You're a grown man," his dad said, picking a card from a pile and adding it to his hand.

"Yeah, but I fell asleep. And I know how you worry, so . . ."

His dad discarded. "Gin," he said.

Lester groaned. He stretched, leaning back in the chair. "That's three in a row. I know when to pack it up and go home." He stood and picked up his hat.

His dad gathered up the cards, smiling. "Thanks for the games, Les. It's been a while."

"Wouldn't know it." He walked toward Mark. "Your dad plays for keeps." He looked over his shoulder and put his hat on. "Thanks for the lemonade, Cal."

"Least I can do." He nodded and kept cleaning up, disappearing into the kitchen.

Lester put his hand on Mark's shoulder. "He had a couple of us out looking. I drove past Ms. Madigan's and saw your truck. He was fine after that. But he's had a scare."

Mark locked eyes with Lester. "Yeah, okay. Thanks."

Lester nodded and moved past him.

"Hey, Les?" Mark asked.

"Yeah?"

"Nothing happened. With Ms. Madigan. She's a friend. We were just talking and fell asleep."

Lester raised his hands. "None of my business." He paused. "But off the record, it was kind of good to find you where I did." He winked and shut the door behind him.

Mark's shoulders sagged. He hung up his coat as his dad wandered into the front room.

"Dad, I'm really sorry. We got talking and fell asleep. I swear that's all that happened." He sounded like a teenager caught out too late after prom. He was almost twenty-seven years old. He shouldn't care what anyone thought. But he cared about scaring his dad. And he cared about protecting Riley's privacy. "My phone was off, and I wasn't thinking about how you'd be worried."

His dad put a hand on his shoulder. He looked at him a few seconds and then pulled him into a hug. "I was worried. But, son? That's the best thing I've heard you say in a really long time." He pulled away from him. "Now get some sleep. We've got a meeting about the memorial at Town Hall in six hours."

Mark nodded, a lump forming in his throat. "Thanks, Dad."

Once in his room, he pulled down the box from his closet and sat on the bed with it. Setting the lid aside, he pulled out a stack of letters and cards. A lot were from family. People from town. He separated out a few, though. Some from Zack. Some from Dylan. Some from the brothers, Ben and Cade, Miguel and Diego. He read through their handwritten letters and looked at the pictures they'd drawn. He unfolded their cards and shook his head at the enthusiasm of young boys with heroes.

He gathered the small stack and rose, crossing the room to his desk. He removed a few old certificates and pictures from the bulletin board and replaced them with the cards and pictures from the boys.

After a moment, Mark added one more photo to the board. The image of two new firefighters smiled back at him, fresh off their first call, arms around each other's shoulders.

Celebrating.

Mark's eyes clouded over. He blinked and pushed out a breath. "We did it, man," he said, his voice hushed. "We did it."

Chapter 15

Riley woke to the morning sun in her face. As she moved her hand to shade her eyes, something hard and smooth shifted under her fingers.

She blinked and turned the object, letting her eyes focus.

The glass doorknob.

She remembered and sat up.

She'd slept on the couch. All night. She looked around, because Mark had been here with her, with the fire. And his story.

The light that had hit her shone from the thin space between the front curtains. She stood, stretching, and then walked over to the window and opened them wide.

She gasped. A foot of snow covered the ground, and the morning sun reflected off it, making everything brilliant. She lifted the glass knob to the light, watching the refracted diamonds of sunlight on her walls.

Her phone rang, and she turned in a circle, trying to pinpoint where she'd left it. Hurrying to the kitchen, she found it on the window ledge above the sink.

"Hello?" Her heart pounded from the quick run.

"Hey, I almost gave up on you there."

"Oh, hi, Dalton," she said, leaning against the counter. "I thought you were somebody else."

"I hope it wasn't Rivers," he said.

"What?"

"Nothing, just kidding. How about this white stuff? It's about time."

"Yes, it's beautiful."

"A beast to drive in, but we sure need it."

"Yes, we do. I thought you were in Seattle."

"Our plans got snowed out. I was hoping I could take you to dinner tonight. We won regionals last night, and the coaches feel like celebrating."

"Oh, I hadn't heard. Congratulations."

"Thanks. Are you feeling okay? I didn't see you at school yesterday."

She pushed her hair back. "I'm just waking up." She glanced at the clock. Nine thirty-four. "Slept in."

"Late night, huh?"

"Mm," she said. "Not really." She had no idea what time she'd fallen asleep, but she didn't think it had been that late. And anyway, she didn't need to report to Dalton. There'd been plenty of days where she hadn't seen him during school. "Just slept hard."

"I'm glad you're not sick. Join me for dinner. I'm the only one without an instant date, if you know what I mean."

"I'm overwhelmed by your offer."

"I didn't say that right, did I? Let me try again. Riley, it would bring me great pleasure if you joined me for dinner with my colleagues as we celebrate our victory."

She hesitated, remembering their last evening together. "I have a lot to do."

"Work all day if you want. We're going to Visconti's."

She'd heard of the Italian restaurant, and knew it was in Wenatchee, not Leavenworth. But she wasn't sure she needed another night out with Dalton.

"Listen, Riley," his said, his voice softer. "I'll be honest with you. I think I might have said some things the other night that came off as brash, and I'm sorry. That crack about the Riverses' nativity—it was art and you're an artist, right? I know I'm a little rough around the edges. I'm hard on people, but I think it's because I'm hard on myself. At least that's what my ex says." He laughed a little, sounding nervous.

She waited.

"You're not arguing the point," he said, "so I'm guessing you agree."

"Dalton, I'm not looking for a relationship right now." Even as she said it, she tasted the lie.

He blew out a breath. "I think we both know I'm not a relationship kind of guy," he said, sounding defeated. "But I've always been honest with you. The fact is I enjoy your company, and I don't want to face these guys and their wives alone tonight."

Riley rubbed her forehead. She knew what that was like. She'd been the fifth wheel a few times with people who wanted to talk about mortgages and babysitters and where they went on their honeymoons. And she wouldn't be alone with Dalton. He'd talk with his staff about the game and championships and plans for next season.

"I can join you for dinner," she said. "But I do have a lot of work to do to meet my deadline."

"Deal. Just there and back. You're a sweetheart, Riley. You won't regret it. I'll pick you up at six."

She hung up and stared out the kitchen window.

She'd gone out with men like Dalton. And that had been fine and safe. Low-risk. They were unattached and fine with it. It had been the same with Gavin in the beginning, but then it had changed. At least, for her it had. She thought it had for him, too, but she'd been wrong. And now she found herself comparing all those men to one man. A man she wasn't even dating. A man who was quiet but drew her out, who didn't demand anything of her but friendship. A man who had battled the depths of hell and still couldn't see how far he'd come out of them.

She turned away from the window, feeling heat run up her neck to her cheeks. She couldn't be falling for Mark. They were just friends. That's all it could be, because she had no idea how long she'd be here. Because she couldn't trust her heart to anyone. She'd told him that.

And yet her heart pounded at the thought of being near him. Traitor.

A car honked twice, and she walked to the front window. Mark's truck was pulling away, his dad lifting a hand to wave as they drove down the street.

She watched them go, her hand lifted in a wave, disappointed they hadn't stopped. More disappointed than she should've been.

Then she saw her driveway. And her walk. All of it, shoveled.

✤ ❄ ✤

Mark and his dad sat at one end of a conference table in one of the city offices with Jay's parents, Nancy and Erik Hendricks. The head of the parks association, the head of the zoning board, and the mayor sat at the other end.

"This is really just a meeting to finalize details," Mayor Evelyn Joffs said, scrolling through her iPad. "Everything is a go. The mason finished before the snow came. Still waiting on the plaque, but delivery is scheduled for the Tuesday after Thanksgiving so that gives us a few days leeway." She looked up and smiled. "Do you have any concerns, Mark?"

Mark shifted in his seat. "I was hoping you or Chief Bennett would be giving a speech, too."

"I'll give the introduction, of course, but I thought we'd agreed to keep it simple."

Erik Hendricks spoke up. "We wouldn't want it any other way, Mark."

Mark nodded.

His dad put his hand on his shoulder. "You up to this?"

Telling his story to Riley, focusing on how they'd saved the boys, instead of how he'd been hurt like he'd had to tell others . . . it had changed the story. It had changed him. The details were still the same, but it was no longer his story of failure. Rather it was his and Jay's story of doing what they could, together. Every one of those boys lived. It still wrenched his gut that he was the only one who'd made it out. But he had to believe Jay was okay where he was. He'd wanted those boys to live no matter the cost.

Mark still had to fight his way through. But maybe he was finally starting to come to terms with that. "I'll do my best."

"Excellent," Evelyn said. "We'll start getting the word out. The volunteer fire department and local businesses have agreed to help us with that."

Mark knew the city council felt the memorial ceremony a fitting lead-in to the firemen's holiday ball and fundraiser the following weekend. He couldn't disagree, but he appreciated the mayor leaving that part out just now.

She nodded at the others. "Chris, Jenny, thank you for your help laying the groundwork. Mr. and Mrs. Hendricks, can we do anything else for you?"

Nancy shook her head. "We're amazed and humbled by all of this. Mark, we can't thank you enough for starting the memorial fund. I know what you two meant to each other. You were pie and ice cream, the both of you." She leaned toward him, with Jay's blue eyes piercing him through. "He would be so proud of you. And not just because of this." She squeezed his hand.

"We all are," Evelyn said, and the others nodded, making Mark want to shrink back into a hood. But he wasn't wearing one.

"I think that's everything," Evelyn continued. "Thank you, everyone, for coming despite the snow. Be safe, build a snowman or two, and barring any hiccups, I'll see you on December third. Happy Thanksgiving."

❅ ❄ ❅

Hey.

Riley smiled at Mark's text. *Hey,* she replied. *Thanks for shoveling my driveway. You and your dad rock.*

Yep.

She laughed. *I mean it.*

So do I. We totally rock.

Shaking her head, she sat down at the metal desk in her art room and stretched. She'd painted all morning, only stopping to eat an apple and refill her water bottle.

She wanted to ask him about last night. About when he left and why he hadn't woken her up, and how he'd put the glass doorknob in her hand and how it had made her feel like he was still there, a little bit. Because maybe then she'd stop wondering about it all. Because she'd been carrying around that dang doorknob all day.

But asking him all that would be showing more interest than

she wanted to. He'd bared his soul to her and then they'd slept. On her couch. She wasn't sure what the boundaries were here, friends or not.

She scratched some dry paint off her arm, then texted him again. *The star's done. I've started the shepherd.*

She switched on an old gooseneck lamp on her desk and aimed the light toward the easel.

Can't wait to see it.

This was what happened when people shared their stuff. Their food. Their couch. Their deepest fears . . . *You left your hat here.*

She waited for his response. She'd watched him pull his hat off during his story, like he was too warm from the fire or the intense memories. His scars were out of her sight, but the fact that he'd taken off his hat at all with her right there was important. His hair had been messy, thick, and as dark as his eyes in the firelight. Just like it had been that day he'd come over and broken her door to get in.

I'll have to come by and get it.

Come by anyti— She paused, remembering her dinner date with Dalton. She squeezed her eyes shut. She should have told Dalton no. But she hadn't. She backspaced. *How about tomorrow?*

Great. I'll come by after lunch.

I'll see you then.

She reread the text conversation and decided it was good. Then she rolled her eyes at herself for needing to do that.

Her phone beeped again.

Thanks for listening last night.

The smile returned to her lips. *Thanks for an amazing day.*

She set her phone down on the desk and leaned forward on her elbows. *What are you doing, Riley Madigan?*

"Nothing," she said aloud. "I'm not doing anything."

Her phone beeped again, and she peeked at it.

Get back to work.

She flipped over her phone and laughed.

✳ ❆ ✳

Dalton followed Riley as the hostess led them to a table already occupied by two other couples.

"Hey, there he is, the man of the hour." One of the men, the oldest of the group, lifted a hand in greeting. The others looked up from their menus.

"Sorry we're late," Dalton said. She felt his hand on her back as he motioned to the older couple. "Riley, this is Rich and Suzanne Derenger. Rich runs my defense."

"And this," Dalton gestured to the younger couple across the table, "is Brian and Stephanie Grady. Brian is my assistant on offense." He nodded to the group. "Everyone, meet Riley Madigan."

"You're the art teacher, right?" Brian asked.

"That's right." Riley took the chair Dalton pulled out for her. She paused as her gaze met that of Brian's wife, Stephanie. The woman's brow arched in a way that reminded her of the women at the bonfire when Dalton had possessively ushered her around. She gently cleared her throat, looking between both men. "Do you work at the high school?"

"No," Brian said, lifting his drink. "In a school as small as Mt. Stuart, finding staff that can teach *and* coach is tough."

"Rich played at UW," Dalton said. "I'm lucky to have him."

"That was more than a few years ago," Rich said, chuckling.

Dalton leaned toward her and lowered his voice. "Rich was

the Huskies' leading scorer his senior year. Went on to play for the Rams for five seasons."

She nodded at the implied importance of that information. "Did you like living in St. Louis?"

Rich chuckled. "They were still in LA when I was playing."

"Oh, my mistake."

He glanced at his wife and winked. "At my age, that's a mistake I'll easily forgive."

Rich gestured to Dalton. "This man here led the Beacons to their first state championship. I never got one of those."

Dalton leaned back in his chair and smiled broadly. He'd already bragged about that achievement to Riley. That and the fact that he'd played for WSU while he got his teaching degree and graduated magna cum laude.

The waiter came to take her and Dalton's drink order and left again.

Riley glanced at Brian, still feeling his wife's unflinching gaze. "And what about you, Brian? What's your football history?"

Brian shook his head. "I played in high school." He shrugged. "Love the game." He looked at his wife, and she smiled at him, genuine and proud. The look of affection they shared made Riley reconsider the earlier scrutiny she'd felt.

"Riley," Stephanie said. "How do you like Miracle Creek?"

Her gaze flickered between her and Dalton as he rested his hand on the back of Riley's chair. The scrutiny returned.

"Well, it's very small, isn't it?" Riley said, meeting her gaze, and the others chuckled. "That takes some getting used to."

"I'm sure," Stephanie said. "Everyone knows everything about everybody. It's a blessing and a curse, really. Isn't that right, Dalton?"

Brian coughed and pushed his open menu in front of his

wife. "Maybe I'll try the Frutte d Mare this time. What do you think, sweetheart?"

Stephanie frowned at her husband. "You're allergic to shrimp."

He shook his head. "What was I thinking?" He leaned closer to her, lifting the menu as if to create a barrier between them and the rest of the table. "What were you thinking of getting?"

Riley watched the exchange half humored and half confused by the undisguised feeling she'd sensed from Stephanie toward Dalton and herself. Was it malice? Whatever it was, her husband was doing his best to block it.

Dalton studied his own menu, his lips pursed in amusement.

She leaned toward him. "Is there something I should know here?"

"Well," he said, his tone hushed, "the ragù has green peas in it. But the chicken parmesan is perfection. And we should definitely share a plate of bruschetta."

Without warning, his warm hand squeezed her knee under the table, which made her jump and wrench away. He grinned, and she felt her face get hot. She pushed her chair back and stood. The others looked up, startled looks on their faces.

"Excuse me," she said, regaining her composure. "I need to find the restroom."

"I'll come with you," Stephanie said, standing before Riley could step away from the table.

Riley paused only long enough to see Brian throw Stephanie a warning glance as he stood, too, and for Stephanie to ignore it.

"Order the short ribs for me, honey," Stephanie said as he pushed her empty chair back in.

Dalton smiled up at Riley. "And what would you like me to tell the waiter?"

She narrowed her eyes. "I'll have the lemon crab linguini." Then she leaned in and whispered through her teeth. "You said you'd behave."

His smile widened. "I am behaving, honey."

The walk to the restroom was tense and silent, and Riley wondered if the woman in front of her really had to use the facilities or if she, too, was using it as an excuse. Riley hoped it was the former.

She was wrong.

The bathroom door had barely closed when Stephanie turned to Riley. "What I said about this being a small town—that's true. It's insane, actually."

"Excuse me?" Riley glanced at a stall, wondering if she should continue with her ruse of an escape.

Stephanie took a deep breath, as though reaching for patience, which only stirred impatience in Riley. "Somebody always knows somebody who is related to somebody." The woman's eyes bored into hers, even in the reflection of the mirror. "The blessing is you have people looking out for you, quick to give you a helping hand."

Riley waited, feeling uneasy.

"The curse is, people talk. They share what they see. Out of genuine concern or morbid curiosity . . . or hope." The woman shut her mouth then frowned. She thrust her hand out at Riley. "We weren't fully introduced. I'm Stephanie Grady. Stephanie *Rivers* Grady. I'm Mark's overprotective big sister."

Riley froze.

"I'd like to know if you're playing games with my brother." Stephanie's voice trembled, but her appearance didn't falter. "Because people are talking. And they'll talk about tonight, too. Dalton will talk."

Riley looked at Stephanie's hand, still held out to her, then at the door as she considered that Dalton had known what Mark's sister's presence here would mean. What Riley's presence here tonight would mean. He couldn't be that conniving, could he? She felt claustrophobic.

Riley took Stephanie's hand and squeezed it. "I'm not playing games with anyone. Your brother means a lot to me, and I've been open with him, just as I've been open with Dalton." She tucked her hair behind her ear. "He's been a good friend to me."

"Dalton?" Stephanie looked doubtful.

"No, your brother. Dalton has been . . ." She searched for the right word. "Attentive."

Stephanie snorted with suppressed laughter.

The action made Riley want to like her. A surprise, considering she was feeling more than a little cornered.

"You know . . ." She chose her words carefully. She cared about Mark. And Cal. And Leah, now that she thought about it. "You don't know me. And I'm feeling judged. I'm getting to know your family, and I like that. I still feel new here. Very new. I shouldn't need to defend myself to anyone, but I can assure you, I think very highly of Mark."

Stephanie's eyes widened. "'Very highly'? He spent the night at your house. Last night. Or have you already forgotten?"

Riley set her jaw, breathing steadily through her nose. This was nobody's business. Stephanie's words came back to her: *Everybody knows everything about everybody.* A blessing and a curse. This was the very thing she'd wanted to avoid by moving here.

Riley's voice was low, but strong. She couldn't believe she was having this conversation in a restaurant bathroom. "Mark was a gentleman. We talked. He talked, actually. A lot. And it was good. And we fell asleep from talking. That's all. So people should shut up. Whether they're morbidly curious or hopeful, or . . ." She glanced at the door. "Selfish." She folded her arms, fighting emotions she didn't want to feel right then. "Mark deserves some peace. He deserves privacy, not a prying posse of small-town hero worshipers. No wonder he's been hiding from all of you."

Stephanie studied her, her mouth tense. Seconds ticked by.

"So," Stephanie finally said, "he's been hiding from all of *us*."

"Yes." She nodded, throwing a hand out. "Duh." Riley would've thought that was clear, especially to his sister.

"So, let me ask you this." She leaned forward. "Why isn't he hiding from *you*?"

Riley blinked. "Because we're friends."

Stephanie's brow lifted. "He has friends."

"Because he trusts me."

"Why?"

"I don't know. Because I don't look at him the way other people do." She didn't owe anyone these answers. But this was Mark's sister. Riley's respect for the family had loosened her tongue.

"Why is that?"

"I don't know. I wasn't here when the accident happened. I didn't know him then." Frustration crept up Riley's neck, hot and irritating.

"And you know him now?"

"No. Yes. I don't know."

"And do you know how Dalton Gainer revels in the idea of me having to watch him cozy up to the woman who spent the night with my brother last night—friends or not?"

The restroom door swung open, and Riley grabbed it from the startled woman.

"Excuse me," she said. "It's too crowded in here." Riley stormed out of the bathroom, but she was too off keel to return to the table, so she took a sharp left and stepped outside to a blast of frigid air. She breathed in deeply, closing her eyes, wishing she'd driven herself. Traffic tires made slushy sounds on the street.

And you know him now? The question rang in her head. She remembered last night. She remembered Mark's smile. She remembered his touch and his words, his fear and his courage. She was trusting him. Just like she'd allowed herself to trust Gavin.

A touch at her elbow pulled her from her thoughts.

"Hey, um, I'm sorry." Stephanie had followed her.

Riley nodded.

"I shouldn't have pressed you like that. I don't know you. And I'm realizing, too late, that my brother would not be grateful for my interference just now."

"He's lucky to have you," Riley said. "But I agree. He would really, really not like what just happened in there." She glanced sideways at Stephanie.

She breathed out a laugh. "Oh, he'd kill me."

"Stephanie—"

Stephanie put her hand up. "You don't need to say anything. You're right. You have a right to privacy just as much as Mark does. I just—I hope I didn't ruin anything between you and my brother. Whatever it is."

Riley sighed, her breath visible in the frosty night air. "It'll be fine," she said, but immediately wondered how it could be.

"Good. Like I said, I'm overprotective. He's been through a lot. But he trusts you." She held her hand out once more. "Start over?"

Riley took her hand, and they shook.

"I'm Stephanie Grady. I believe you know my brother, Mark."

Riley nodded. "I'm having Thanksgiving with him and your

dad." Riley shrugged at Stephanie's look of surprise. "They've been good to me."

"Well," Stephanie said, hugging herself in the cold. "Curiouser and curiouser." She nodded to the door behind her. "We should probably go inside before Brian gets worried. Pretty sure he thought I had plans to take you out."

Riley huffed. "He isn't the only one."

Stephanie grinned. Mark was right; his sister had her own kind of fire.

They turned to go inside, but Stephanie spun back to face her and Riley halted.

"Just . . . be careful with Mark. Okay?" She searched Riley's face with sincere concern.

Riley nodded. "Of course." She left unsaid the words that weighed on her heart: *That's just it, Stephanie. He doesn't want to be treated carefully.*

When they returned, a look of unveiled relief passed over Brian's face. Even Dalton seemed to dial down his touchy-feely possessiveness and let the evening take its course in pleasant conversation between friends.

After dinner, Riley sat in frustrated silence as Dalton drove her home. Every time she opened her mouth to say something about her relationship with Mark or to ask about the fact that Dalton knew Stephanie would be at dinner, she stopped herself. The words "everybody knows everything about everybody" tied her tongue and head in knots.

A year ago, she wouldn't have let any of it get under her skin. A year ago, she'd been in Hollywood, seeing a man she thought she might have a future with, oblivious to the microscopic lens that was even then magnifying and distorting everything when it came crashing down. She thought she'd escaped that kind of scrutiny. Turns out she'd jumped into the hometown beating heart of it.

Dalton glanced at her hands as she wrung them in her lap, and she moved them to her knees.

"So, are you going to tell me about this project you're working on?"

"No," she said, looking straight ahead. The sign for the Cashmere exit passed by.

"Why not?"

"Because Miracle Creek is a small town. And this is a surprise."

"Ah, a mystery," he said.

"No. Mysteries are meant to be solved. This project isn't open for investigation."

He laughed. "Okay, okay. Subject closed. I was just taking an interest in what you do outside the classroom." He cocked his head. "And in that little place of yours."

"There's a lot of that going around," she murmured at her window as he took the Miracle Creek turnoff.

"What's that?" he asked.

"Nothing. Thank you for dinner. The company was . . . enlightening. I can see why you enjoy coaching with your staff."

"I'm glad you had a good time." He passed the park with its towering pines and flagpole. Several trees were draped in lights.

She looked at the Grill-n-Go across the street. Considering what Mark would think of this dinner with his sister unsettled her stomach.

She hadn't wanted these complications. She had rules for this stuff.

Dalton parked in front of her house, leaning toward her as

if he were going to share a secret. "You being there tonight was infinitely better than facing a dinner like that alone."

"I can imagine." She picked up her purse, but Dalton placed his hand over hers.

"I'd be a fool," he said quietly, "if I didn't ask you to join me for dinner again. Maybe somewhere a little less"—he bobbled his head—"crowded. My place? Saturday?"

He looked at her, hopeful.

"I'm busy Saturday," she said, smoothly pulling her hand from beneath his and placing it on the door handle.

"All day? We can get dinner afterward. Take it to my place?"

His lack of receiving her obvious messages was wearing thin. She sighed. "I have other plans. And I have to get back to work now. But thank you for a night out. You were right. I did need the break." *And some perspective.*

He moved to get out and walk her to the door.

"No, I'm fine," she said. "I really do need to hustle. Deadline looming. I'll see you on Monday." She practically leapt out of her seat and hurried to her front door.

Inside, she placed her hand to her head and leaned against the door. She still felt like she needed a break. Or a *bollen,* at least.

A knock at the door made her jump. She opened it to find Dalton looking expectant. She put her hand on her hip. "I thought we said good night."

He cocked his head. "Did we though? The last thing I wanted to do was scare you off."

"I need to get back to work."

He stepped into the doorway. "I'm worried about you, new girl," he said as he pushed past her. "All work and no play makes for a lonely night." He reached to pull her jacket off.

She stepped away, keeping her cool. "I'm not lonely, and I

didn't invite you in. I'm working because it's what I enjoy and because I keep my commitments."

He paused at that last part, then leaned toward her. "And what commitments might those be?"

She said nothing, her grip still on the open door. A car slowly drove past, drawing her attention. He stepped even closer.

"We both know what this is about," he said. "This feeling between you and me."

She turned back to him, shaking her head. "Don't flatter yourself. This is nothing."

He laughed. "It's exactly what you want it to be." Then he hooked his arm behind her and pulled her to him.

She tried to push him away, but he didn't budge. "You know nothing about me. And I'm asking you to leave." Even as she spoke, the truth of his words haunted her. She hadn't wanted anything deep with Dalton, and to men like him, that was a green light.

"I'd like to get to know you, Riley." He arched his brow. "Or does Rivers have the exclusive on that?"

Another car drove past and she glanced at it, distracted.

Dalton slipped his hand around the back of her head, turning her face to him. He pressed his mouth on hers.

She shoved hard, and he stumbled back on his heels.

"Get. Out," she said, widening the door.

He studied her, rubbing his lips with his fingers. "Can't blame me for trying. Maybe I read your signals wrong."

"What signals? I got out of your car and said I'd see you on Monday."

He lowered his chin. "Not those signals." He slowly eyed her up and down.

She straightened her shoulders. "You need to leave. Now."

He nodded. "I'll go." As he brushed past her, though, he leaned close to her ear. "I'll go slow."

She shook her head, disgusted by his persistence.

He paused at the top of the front porch steps and turned. "You know, Rivers isn't the saint people make him out to be."

"And you are?"

He grinned wickedly. "Oh, honey. Nobody makes me out to be a saint." He stepped toward her again, slowly. "I like things uncomplicated. And something tells me you do, too."

She shifted, uncomfortable with how right he was.

"And the way the town is talking about you and a certain ex-fireman . . . Well, that has complicated written all over it."

Her pulse faltered at his words. "Who's talking?"

He tipped his head toward her. "Who do you think? If I were Rivers, I'd have a hard time keeping things to myself, too."

She fought to keep her expression neutral, suspecting Dalton was lying, but then she remembered Stephanie's words from the restaurant. *He spent the night at your house. Last night. Or have you already forgotten?*

Finally, Dalton backed away. "I can go slow, Riley. And with me, what you see is everything you get."

"That's not doing you any favors," she said, and closed the door.

Chapter 16

I don't know if you heard, but there's a ceremony at the park on the third. They're unveiling a plaque for Jay. It has his face on it. I have to make a speech."

Mark winced. His words sounded worse out loud. He took a deep breath, gripping the socket wrench.

"Riley," he said, staring up at the underbelly of his truck, "there's this ceremony for Jay on Friday. I was wondering if you'd like to come with me. There's a ball the next week, I mean a dance—no, that's not it." He tried again. "I'd really like you to be there with me."

That was better. Maybe. He had some time. Maybe.

His phone buzzed, and he scrambled to answer it, sticking the phone between his ear and his shoulder.

"Hey, what's up, Stephanie?" He rolled out from under his truck and wiped his hands with a towel.

She sighed. "Last night I had dinner with Riley Madigan."

He straightened up and switched ears. "What? How?"

"I wanted to—"

"You know," he interrupted, "when you talked about taking Riley out, I thought you meant *me* taking Riley out."

She was silent a few seconds. "Are you gonna let me talk or should I just hang up now?"

He rolled his eyes. "Talk."

"Just know that I wanted you to hear it from me before Dalton starts blabbing about things that didn't happen."

"Dalton?" He tried not to get his hackles up. "What didn't happen?"

"It's what did happen."

His brow scrunched. "What did happen?"

"Brian and I went to a celebratory dinner for the football staff, and Dalton brought Riley as his date. I swear I didn't know."

His jaw clenched. He knew Dalton would keep asking Riley out. He just didn't think—

"Dalton was being all 'Oh, look at my date, I'm going to be all handsy so you know she's my date.'" Steph paused, then said in a rush, "And I may or may not have confronted her. About you. In the ladies' room."

He dropped the towel. "What? Steph—" He didn't know which made his blood hotter, the word "handsy" or "confronted."

"Now, before you go ballistic on me, I think we cleared some things up between us, and I like her."

"You like her." He rubbed his face. "Why are you telling me this?"

"In case Dalton starts talking up the date or whatever. I had the distinct impression he'd asked Riley to the dinner for my sake—or for your sake. Understand? And, in case she brings it up, I did not accost her."

"Did Gainer accost her?" he asked, alarmed.

"I don't think so. Except for possibly something unwelcome under the table just before I followed her to the bathroom."

Mark blinked. "I think you're both nuts."

"Me and Riley?"

"You and Gainer."

"Oh, hey, don't throw me in with that player. I'm trying to help. Just understand that I think Riley is genuine and you shouldn't feel threatened in this friendship or whatever you guys have."

Whatever you guys have. Obviously, Riley hadn't defined their relationship any clearer than that. And why would she, on a date with Dalton Gainer? If he'd felt threatened, he wouldn't have opened up to Riley the way he had on Friday. "You know, I was feeling pretty good until you called."

"Oh, no, now see? I need you to understand that I'm helping."

Yeah, like a shovel to my face. "I really appreciate it."

"I can hear your sarcasm, and I'm choosing not to be offended because I know I may have jeopardized your relationship and I feel terrible about that. Honestly, though, after knowing you spent the night at her place, it was confusing to see her with Dalton. Brian had to practically hold me down in my chair when he introduced her."

Mark frowned. So much about everything she'd just said troubled him. "Relationship" and "spent the night" especially.

"Steph, how did you hear—?" He took a deep breath and let it out slowly. "What exactly did you tell Riley in the bathroom?"

As Steph related what was said, Mark's confidence began to unravel. The idea of seeing Riley again clouded with dread.

"Are you mad at me?" Steph asked, sounding truly sorry.

He paused. "I can't tell if I'm grateful you told me, or sick."

She made a whimpering sound. "I'll make it up to you."

He ran his hand over his face. This shouldn't be a big deal. Right? He had no claim on Riley.

Then why did his insides burn with a lava flow of envy and possession?

Take it easy, Rivers.

"When are you going to see her again?"

He pulled himself together. "I was going to go over later today. I left my hat over there."

"You took your hat off? In front of her?"

"Don't make more of it than it is." Her silence told him she was making more of it than it was. "We just talked. Just—you can't say 'spent the night.' It gives people the wrong idea, and I don't want that for her. We had a good talk, that was all."

She was quiet for a few moments. "Did you kiss her?"

He chuckled ruefully. "No." Just a peck on her head.

"Maybe you should have."

He laughed outright, pinching the bridge of his nose. He'd never wanted to kiss Riley more than after she'd listened to him spill his guts and still curled up next to him. "Doesn't matter."

"For what it's worth . . . it matters a lot."

"Not helpin', sis."

❆ ❅ ❆

Riley scowled at the shepherd's expression, which scowled back at her. Her mood had translated into his bent eyebrows and downturned mouth. He wasn't frowning, really, but he wasn't exactly spreading tidings of great joy.

He was probably distracted, worrying about Mark and his sister and small, small towns.

Little towns. "O Little Town of Bethlehem."

Letting out a growl of frustration, she stomped her foot.

Why had she come here?

You wanted a fresh start.

She sighed and opened the jar of black paint. *Start at the start.* She painted over the face. She'd let it dry and try again. Putting excessive pressure on herself to get these faces right was getting to her. She'd always been a perfectionist, but this was a wooden stand-up nativity scene meant for a lonely stretch of mountain highway.

Not the freaking Sistine Chapel.

A quiet knock sounded at the front door. She groaned and pressed the heel of her hand to her forehead. "Go away," she whimpered. Then she called out, "Just a minute," and washed up in the bathroom. When she finally opened the front door, she stepped back. "Mark."

He smiled at her, his thumbs tucked in his back pockets. "Hi."

"What are you doing here?" She winced, not meaning to sound so abrupt. His smile wavered, and that alone made her try harder. "I mean, hello. Come in, it's cold." She motioned him inside.

He took a step, but then paused. "I came to get my hat. I can just grab it quick, or I can come back later if you're busy."

His hat. From the other night when he'd shared his nightmare with her and he'd still kept her safe and warm on the sofa. She leaned her head against the door as she held it open. "Of course, your hat. I'm sorry. I'm just"—she opened the door wider—"frustrated."

He stepped past her. "I know how that goes," he muttered.

She shut the door and guessed that Stephanie had talked. Or Dalton had. Mark turned and faced her, and the caution she saw in him unsettled her.

She grabbed his hat off the desk and handed it to him.

"Thanks," he said. He squeezed it from one hand to the other. She suddenly wished she hadn't insisted he look at her straight on, because he was. The look burned through her, and her cheeks warmed.

"Are you painting?" he asked.

"Yeah. The angry shepherd."

A look of puzzlement crossed his face, then cleared. "I won't keep you, then."

He stepped around her, smelling like crisp air and sawdust, but before he opened the door, he rounded on her. "Riley."

He was so close to her she looked almost straight up at him. She swallowed.

"I know my sister talked to you—"

"I'm guessing you know about—"

They both paused after speaking over each other.

"Go ahead," she said.

He nodded. "I know my sister talked to you while you were out with Gainer, and I want you to know that I didn't put her up to that. She can be a real hothead, and she's just protective. But it's no excuse."

Riley nodded.

His brows furrowed. "That's not to say if I'd been in her place, I wouldn't have done the same thing."

Her eyes widened. "You would've followed me into the ladies' room?"

"Maybe," he said, a half-smile forming. "I would've looked like an idiot, and I would've had no right, but Gainer didn't have the right to set you up like that."

The lift she'd felt at her own lips faded. "Setup?" she repeated. "You think Dalton was out with me just to get to you?"

"Maybe." He ran his hand over his face. "I don't know." He shook his head, looking down at the floor. He brought his gaze up to meet hers. "Here's the truth," he said. "When Steph told me you were out with Gainer, after the day we'd spent together—I wanted to—"

She swallowed. "You wanted to what?"

His hand came up and gently brushed a lock of hair out of her eyes. Her pulse heightened at his touch. She tried to temper it. Had he really led people on about the other night?

"I know we're friends," he said. "We keep saying we're just friends. But you're important to me, Riley. And I guess Steph picked up on that. So, while I want to wring her neck, I can't blame her." His hands move to her arms, rubbing them softly. "And when she told me you were out with Gainer, I wanted to get over here . . . Remind you of what's . . ."

"Of what's what?" she whispered.

His grip firmed on her arms, and his gaze held hers. "Of what's real."

Her heart shuddered. *What's real.*

He watched her a few seconds, his gaze drifting to her mouth. The heart she was cursing to stay steady pounded far too wildly in her chest.

Mark cautiously took a half-step closer, and she felt her eyes drifting closed.

She didn't know how to attach herself to anyone. No more than she knew how to attach herself to any place. The last time she thought she had, she'd failed.

Dalton's words came back to her: *"If I were Rivers, I'd have a hard time keeping things to myself, too."*

She snapped her eyes open and pulled back.

She swallowed, unable to meet his gaze. "You're important to me, too." Her thoughts whirled up in a defensive cyclone around her. "But I can't say I'd follow you into a bathroom if I saw you out with a woman I suspected of using you." She laughed pathetically. "Dalton was a perfect gentleman the rest of the night."

Liar. A weight settled in her stomach. Her hands shook as she shoved them in her pockets.

Mark was no longer looking at her. "My mistake, then." He put his hand on the doorknob. "I'm glad Gainer treated you well." Then he lifted his eyes. "I'm sorry my sister jumped to conclusions."

She nodded. "I understand. Small town, right?"

He shrugged. "Blessing and a curse. Are you still coming to Thanksgiving?"

She'd forgotten Thanksgiving. "Of course."

When he turned, she reached out and grabbed his hand. He looked down at her fingers grasping his.

"Mark, the other night, that was important, and it mattered to me. That was real."

A smile softened the hardness of his mouth. "Thanks."

She continued, her voice hushed with caution. "I need a friend right now. I'm not sure I'm capable of more than that. Not with Dalton. Not with anyone."

He ran the tips of his fingers quickly along her cheek, then dropped his hand. Even so, her heart shuddered, and she begged it to be still.

"Anything you need."

She breathed a sigh of relief.

He stepped onto the porch. "There's a ceremony at the park on December third, honoring Jay. The day before the tree-lighting in Leavenworth. I'm giving a speech. I could use a friend, too."

She smiled. "I'll be there."

He looked down at the hat squashed in his hands. "Let me

know when you want me to mud that wall. We can paint the room, then. I, um, brought you a present. A gift for the house."

"Oh, you didn't have to—"

He picked up something red and shiny from beside the doorway.

"You got me a fire extinguisher," she whispered, surprisingly touched by the gesture.

"Every home should have one," he said. "I'll install it whenever you want. Maybe while you're at school so I'm not in your way. Anyhow, figure out where you want it and let me know."

"Thank you." He got her a fire extinguisher. She took it from him, buckling a little under the weight. "I love it."

He paused, watching her. "If you come up with anything else—"

Her eyes widened again, remembering. "I think I have wood floors under the carpets."

"Oh," his weight shifted, his expression brightening a fraction. "Yeah, a lot of these houses do. When do you want to get the carpets pulled up?"

"After the painting, I guess. Pulling carpet is my least favorite thing in a reno."

"I don't mind it."

"Really?"

"Don't get me wrong. It's a bully of a job. But tearing up old stuff so you can get what's underneath to shine?" He set his hands on his hips. "I'd think you'd be all over that."

She blinked at him, feeling strangely exposed. "Why do you say that?" It's what she'd been doing. What she'd been doing to him. Maybe what he'd been doing to her, too.

He frowned. "Because of your antiques."

"Oh." She nodded. "Of course."

He studied her a moment. "That looks good on you."

She glanced down at the fire extinguisher in her arms. When she looked back up, he was already down the porch steps.

"I'll talk to you soon," she called after him.

He waved without looking back. She closed the door and set the extinguisher down next to the desk. She eyed the rocker and walked over to it, dropping onto the cushion as Mark's truck roared away. She placed her hands on each mellow oak arm and gripped the wood, rocking back and forth.

Mark. The hero boy who gave her glass doorknobs and fire extinguishers, who brought her not-even-burgers and built her fires when he was terrified of fire—

Had he told people about that night? When he knew her need for privacy? She remembered how she'd felt in his arms then, and just now with that pull between them.

Her hand covered her face, and her rocking stopped. She couldn't do this now. She couldn't fall—

She couldn't fall for Mark. Not in this little town, not now.

She stood and shook away her thoughts. She had a job to do. And she had a lot of hours to spend in Mark Rivers's company yet. It was good that they'd drawn boundaries.

Boundaries kept her heart safe.

❄ ❄ ❄

Mark frowned. What had just happened? He'd gone in there worried Riley would be mad that Steph had talked to him, but then things had gotten pretty close. And then they hadn't.

And then he'd given her a fire extinguisher.

He honked as the Taggart boys crossed the street without looking. They had the decency to look startled and raise their hands in apology.

Mark had meant to ask Riley to attend the memorial ceremony with him—and the firemen's ball, too—as maybe more than a friend, but with the vibe she was giving off, he'd chickened out. Sure, she said she'd be there, but as a friend. A neighbor. Nothing more.

Although, had he asked, and had she said yes, it would have meant she'd be standing next to him on an important day. And the town would see that as more than it was. His family would see it as more than it was.

Who was he kidding? *He'd* see it as more than it was. And it definitely wasn't more than it was. He may as well have been spilling his guts to *Steph* on the couch that night, right?

The sensation of waking up with Riley in his arms returned.

He slammed on his brakes at the four-way stop, and his tires screeched to a halt. This time, the startled looks came from a group of kids wearing birthday party hats waiting to cross the street with Erin Petty, who gripped her son's shoulder.

Mark raised his hand in apology. "Sorry," he said and motioned them across.

He felt Erin's glare through the windshield. He deserved that. Kind of refreshing that she gave it without any reserve.

One thing was certain. Spilling his guts to Riley that night on her couch was *nothing* like spilling his guts to his sister.

Another thing was certain. He had a whole lot of hours left to work on her house with her. It was better that he knew the boundaries. Better that he didn't talk to Gus or Steph or his dad about whatever the town was saying. Better that he didn't get pressured into doing stupid things because people thought their ideas were better than reality.

He'd just been dished a taste of reality.

Bitter as ever.

Chapter 17

Riley rested her chin on her hand, looking blearily over the class outline for advanced art on her laptop. The seniors were allowed to choose their own projects, as long as they were working during class and making progress. But today her sixth-grade art class had asked how to paint snow, and that led to a demonstration of negative space, and now she was thinking of teaching the technique to her seniors, and she maybe had an idea for their final project.

She glanced at her phone.

She hadn't heard from Mark since Sunday, and Thanksgiving was tomorrow. She forced her gaze back to the computer screen.

He'd been busy, she knew that. He'd finished mudding the new wall while she was at school and was gone before she got home. He'd installed the fire extinguisher next to the back door in the kitchen. He'd gotten her a quote for the electrical work. And he was helping his dad. Then there was the whole awkward Stephanie-Dalton-bathroom thing.

Dalton was giving her space, somewhat, but she still felt unsettled.

Truth be told, she wanted Mark's opinion on paint color and to have him visit her classroom and to share a not-even-a-meal so she could tease him about milkshakes named after him. That reminded her that Thanksgiving was tomorrow and she hadn't offered to bring any food.

She picked up her phone.

What can I bring for Thanksgiving? Anything but pie. Or a turkey. I've never cooked a turkey. Or stuffing.

Sorry I didn't ask earlier.

Oh, or yams. I don't know what to do with yams.

She set the phone down and watched it, waiting. She picked it back up.

I could probably find a recipe, though, if you really need someone to make yams.

She went to set it back down again when it beeped.

This is what we've got.

Turkey: check. Mashed potatoes and gravy: check. Stuffing: a big maybe—we'll see how it goes. Pumpkin pie: check. Yams: SKIP. We've got corn and rolls. What do you want to add?

She bit her lip, thinking.

I have a good cranberry sauce recipe. Green beans? I can make apple crisp. That's like pie.

Sounds great. Dad says thanks.

She smiled. *I'll bring whipped cream, too. The real kind, not the stuff in a tub.*

Perfect. Come around 2:00. See you tomorrow.

She stared at the last text, wondering why it felt like a dismissal.

She made a shopping list and closed her office, wishing she knew more about holiday cooking. As she passed her display board of starry nights, she knew one thing.

She missed Mark.

In the hallway she heard her name called, and she turned with a smile. "Hey, Yvette."

"Hey, yourself." Yvette pulled her into a hug. "How're you doing, kiddo?"

"Bleh" was what managed to spill eloquently from her mouth.

Yvette chuckled and stepped back to study her. "You're figuring stuff out?"

"You mean about Dalton being a shallow letch and Mark being a completely decent human being?" She nodded.

"Oh, sweetie, he's much more than decent."

Riley pursed her lips, hiding a smile. "I know. But I don't want to talk about it."

Yvette threaded her arm through Riley's and started walking. "That's fine. I'll be able to see all I need tomorrow."

"Tomorrow?"

"I'm joining you and the Rivers men for Thanksgiving. You didn't know?"

"No. I haven't seen much of Mark the last few days."

"Cal saw me in the IGA the other day, and we got to talking, and when he learned that my plans to see my sister had fallen through, he invited me."

"I'm glad. I'm sorry your plans fell through, but I've been worried about what kind of conversation I'd be up to with just the three of us."

"Well, my youngest son will be at his dad's, and my sister has a couple kids down with strep throat." She sighed. "And no need to worry about conversation. Cal's a great talker, and the way those two men banter is enough entertainment for anybody."

Riley smiled. "True." They pushed the exterior door open, and Riley hunched deeper into her coat despite the midday sunshine. "I just don't know where I stand with Mark, or what the town thinks. I don't want to give people the wrong impression. I already know what some of them believe."

"Who cares what the town thinks?"

Riley did. A lot.

It must've shown. Yvette shook her head. "Okay, maybe that's easy to say. I know my divorce was the subject of enough scrutiny. That sucked."

"I think you just made my point."

Yvette laughed. "I think I did." She stopped and faced Riley. "Only you can judge what really matters. Everything else is just talk."

Riley nodded. Mark had said that, too, in so many words. "Can I ask you something?"

"You bet."

"Dalton told me you were dating Cal when Mark was hurt." Riley lifted her brow, curious how her friend would respond.

Yvette matched her expression. "Is that a question?" She shook her head, smiling. "Okay. Yes. We had only just started dating. And it was . . ." Her eyes got a soft, faraway look. "It was nice. But then Mark had his accident, and Jay was killed . . . and Mark hadn't even known we'd gone out—he'd been living his own life in Wenatchee. We both knew it just wasn't our time. Cal had lost a good part of the orchard, and Mark needed his dad twenty-four-seven." She blinked and refocused. "So that was that."

"And now," Riley said, "Cal has asked you to Thanksgiving." Her brow rose.

"Oh, don't you go there. This is a last-minute thing. That's all."

Riley placed her hands over her heart and batted her lashes.

Yvette put her fists on her hips. "Is that how you want to

play? Because we can have an interesting time tomorrow, Miss 'Mark is a decent human being.' Puh-lease."

Riley's shoulders sagged in good-natured defeat. "Fine. I take it all back." She watched as a mischievous smile grew on her friend's face. "And I'll help you grade tests and I'll wash your windows and I'll shovel your driveway if you will *please* not tease me or Mark about anything tomorrow." She clasped her hands together, begging. "I won't mention you and Cal again. Unless you want me to."

Yvette leaned forward, her eyes dancing. "Lucky for you I believe things work themselves out. As should you. Now, I've got pie and rolls to make. I will see you tomorrow, Smee."

Riley saluted as Yvette sauntered away. "Aye, Cap'n."

❄ ❄ ❄

Mark watched Riley across the dining room table. She laughed, holding her stomach like she would bust if she laughed any more. He didn't blame her. He was as full as he could get. The food had turned out great, and his dad and Yvette had taken the spotlight off whatever was or wasn't happening between him and Riley.

She caught him looking, and he glanced away. His dad was shaking his head, grinning at an old story he'd told a dozen times.

"You remember that, Mark?" Dad asked.

"Gets better every time you tell it."

Riley stood and started clearing dishes.

"Hold on there, Riley," his dad said. "I've got dish duty. Mark and you ladies did the cooking."

Riley put a hand on her hip. "Well, then get in there to the sink, and we'll get the dishes to you."

His chivalrous father didn't even argue. "I like how this one thinks," he said, and hoisted himself up, grabbed some dishes, and left for the kitchen.

Mark and Yvette stood and the three of them began clearing plates and bowls of food.

Yvette gathered goblets. "The turkey was delicious, Mark."

"Thanks. Usually Steph handles the turkey."

"It was as good as any I ever made. Be proud."

His hand brushed against Riley's as they both reached for an empty bowl, and between Yvette's compliment and the touch of Riley's hand, his face warmed.

"Sorry," he said, letting her take the bowl.

"Don't be," Riley said. "And she's right, the turkey was fantastic."

He nodded his thanks.

He hadn't seen her for days. Long days. She'd curled her hair, and her dark red sweater, tight black jeans, and those black boots he liked had made it hard to take his eyes off her since she'd arrived. And she smelled like heaven. Even more so with the delicious aromas still hanging in the air.

He watched her walk into the kitchen. Yvette gave him a nudge, and he followed with his armload.

Riley had set the dishes down on the counter next to the sink, where his dad had hot sudsy water ready and the dishwasher open. He was already scraping plates.

"I can't wait to try your pies, Yvette," Riley said. "The banana cream looks amazing." She stepped back and groaned, hands pressed to her middle. "Well, maybe I can wait."

Yvette laughed. "I haven't eaten like this in a long time. It's different when you're alone, that's for sure." She turned as Mark set his dishes down. "What about you? You don't seem to be in any discomfort."

"Oh, I had plenty. I can barely move." He headed back into the dining room to pick up another load. Being so close to Riley all day had heightened all his senses until he thought his nerves might catch fire.

"You just carry it better than the rest of us, is that it?" Riley followed and reached past him for the bowl of mashed potatoes while he collected the last of the silverware.

She was close. He breathed deeply and shook his head. "Man, you smell good." The words were out before he knew it. "Sorry. Didn't mean that."

"I don't smell good?"

His face grew warmer.

She flipped her hair behind her and looked up at him. "It's the turkey."

He stepped back to give her space. To give him space. "The house smells like turkey. You don't smell like the house."

"You say the sweetest things," she said, smiling.

He shook his head, fighting his own smile.

"So, are we talking now?" she asked.

He glanced over the table, empty but for a few crumbs. "What do you mean?"

"I haven't heard from you for a while. I guess after spending all that time together last week, I got used to having you around."

He nodded, squashing the hope that rose inside him. "Missed me, huh?"

"Mark."

He met her gaze.

"You haven't spoken to me since I got here."

"That's not true."

"Yes, it is."

"Look," he said, stepping around her, "I'm just playing by your rules, okay?"

She followed him back into the kitchen. "What rules?"

"You know."

Yvette and his dad quit their conversation as they entered.

Riley switched tracks. She took a deep breath. "So, do you have any fun Thanksgiving traditions? Besides eating yourselves into oblivion?" She grabbed a dishcloth from the soapy water and started wiping down counters.

"We always had a football game on at our place," Yvette offered. "And some kind of card game at the table after the dishes were cleared."

"We watch the game if the teams are good," his dad agreed. "Sometimes we drive out on the property and pick out the tree. Too early to cut one down yet, but we flag it so we can find it closer to Christmas."

"That sounds like fun," Yvette said. She'd joined him at the sink and was drying dishes. "Riley, what are your family traditions?"

She paused, turning the dishcloth in her hands and staring out the back door. "It depended on where we were. When I was little, we'd go to my grandma's in Bozeman. I'd play in the snow. Once we went to Disneyland. When I was older, it was a formal dinner with one of my dad's colleagues."

"Disneyland sounds fun," Yvette said.

Riley nodded, then rinsed her cloth at the sink. "I'll just go wipe off the dining table."

After she left the room, both Yvette and his dad turned to Mark, motioning him to follow Riley.

"I'm going, I'm going," he growled.

He found Riley wiping the last of the crumbs off the table.

He came up behind her, took the cloth out of her hand and set it down, and pulled her toward the door.

"Where are we going?"

"We're going outside." He grabbed her coat from the hook, and she slid her arms inside.

"Why?"

He grabbed her hat and scarf and smashed her hat on her head as she pulled her gloves on.

"We," he said, grabbing his own coat, "are going to play in the snow."

To his relief, the lost look he'd seen on her face had faded, replaced with a brightening smile. More confident, he found her a pair of Steph's old snow boots. With his own gloves and boots on, he grabbed her hand and rushed her outside.

"Do you have any sleds?" she asked.

He grinned. "You could say that."

He led her around the side of the garage, where he grabbed the corner of a tarp and pulled. "Did they have one of these at your grandma's?"

Her jaw dropped, and she shook her head, staring at the Rivers family snowmobile.

"Riley Madigan, I'd like to introduce you to one of our Thanksgiving traditions."

❄ ❄ ❄

Riley whooped in his ear, her hair flying from underneath her helmet. He grinned as they made another pass up one of his favorite slopes on the property, then down, fishtailing across the old cow pasture. The sound of her laughter did good things to his insides.

"Having fun?" he called back to her.

"Yes!"

"Are you cold?"

"Yes!"

"Do you want to head in?"

"No!"

He laughed and accelerated, spraying snow in an arc as they circled around, her arms tightening around his middle. He tried to ignore how much he liked that. "Wanna try a jump?"

"Um . . . maybe?"

"It's a small jump. Tiny." That wasn't entirely true, but it was a lot smaller than the jumps he'd take with the guys over near Snoqualmie Pass. This was just a couple of slowly decomposing hay bales they kept shaped into a ramp. "Hang on."

He grinned at the sound she made as they approached the white bump along the edge of the pasture. She clasped her own wrists at his stomach and pressed her knees tight against his hips.

Then they hit the jump, and he hollered and she screamed. They were airborne for only a second, and when they hit the ground in a smooth landing, she erupted in laughter.

If she wasn't careful, he'd ask her to do this every weekend they had snow.

He spun the mobile in a circle and pulled to a stop. "How was that?" he asked, looking behind him.

"So great." Her eyes gleamed behind the visor.

"You want to go again?"

She nodded enthusiastically. He didn't need to be asked twice.

✼ ❄ ✼

"You want pie, now?" he asked after he'd put the snowmobile away. He followed Riley on the shoveled path.

"Yes."

"My face is frozen. I'm ready to try that apple crisp you brought."

She glanced at him over her shoulder. "Are you?"

"I meant to say so earlier."

She had the decency not to mention again how he'd barely said a word to her before and during dinner. He hadn't meant to. He'd become so used to being close to her, he wasn't sure how to be distant.

She took a step off the path into the snow. Standing on the gentle slope next to the driveway, she faced him, then fell flat back. She began slowly waving her arms and legs in the snow. "Snow angels."

She hadn't put her hat back on after removing her helmet, and her hair was all messy waves, splayed against the snow. With her pink cheeks and open smile, she was killing him.

"Come make one with me," she said.

"I'd rather watch."

"Get over here."

He trudged over to the clean spot next to her. "Aren't you cold enough?" He fell backward, landing with a whump. He put his hands behind his head and closed his eyes. "I think my angel is a non-flyer."

She laughed. "Please? I'll make sure you get extra whipped cream."

"Well, in that case . . ." He waved his arms and legs a couple of times. "Don't tell Gus."

"My lips are sealed. Let's see what they look like." She sat up but paused at how to get all the way up without ruining the impression she'd made in the snow.

"Just a sec, I'll give you a hand." He pulled himself up and leapt out of his angel, then reached back to take both her outstretched hands. "One, two, three—" He heaved her into the air as she jumped, both of them overestimating the strength needed to get her out of the snow, and she plowed him over. He stumbled, falling backward, and she landed on top.

After a shocked silence, she began to laugh.

"How many of these did you want to make?" he asked, trying to ignore how good she felt in his arms, how good her hair smelled, how the weight of her could have held him there for a good long time.

She pressed her face to his chest, trying to catch her breath.

"You did that on purpose," he said, more for his sake than hers, keeping things light. Because heaven knew his heart was not thinking light things.

"Me?" She met his gaze, grinning. "I'd like to see the replay on that."

"I think the officials would see it my way." He reached with his gloved hand and brushed her hair behind her ear.

"Why is that?"

"Because we've been down here for about thirty seconds now, and you're still on top of me." His breath wavered as she stilled, watching him with those pale green eyes. He couldn't look away. One thing was certain, his face wasn't cold anymore.

He willed his arms to be still, willed his heart to stop thumping so wildly. "Didn't you want to see how the angels look?" he asked, his voice husky.

They were both still breathing hard, her gaze locked on his, when she suddenly scrambled off him, pushing herself up and brushing snow off her legs and arms. He rolled to his knees and took a deep breath. He looked over at their snow angels and stood.

"What do you think?" he asked, feeling cold where she used to be.

She was brushing off her backside, turning in a slow circle as if that would help her get it all. "I think I really need pie."

"No," he said, laughing. "What do you think of the snow angels?"

She stopped her dance and looked over their creations. Two clear snow angels floated next to each other on the slope. "They look good, don't they?"

"Yep."

"I can't remember the last time I made those." She looked up at him. "Thanks. That was fun. All of it." She looked behind him. "Don't forget that one." She smiled before hurrying into the warm house.

He glanced at the mess of an impression they'd made where they'd fallen together. "That one's my favorite," he murmured, and followed her inside.

❄ ❅ ❄

While Cal and Yvette played a game of gin in the dining room, Riley sat on the carpet, warming herself in front of the woodstove as she leaned back against the couch. The football game was on, and two empty pie plates and forks sat on the floor next to her. She was acutely aware of Mark stretched out behind her.

She'd have felt utterly content if it weren't for two things. One, playing with Mark in the snow had turned her inside out and upside down, and even now her heart beat harder with the nearness of him, and two, she couldn't stop worrying about what people might think about her time spent with him, especially if rumors were spreading.

"Mark?" she asked, almost not wanting to.

"Hm?" He sounded drowsy, and she felt his fingers briefly tousle her hair.

She turned and sure enough, his eyes were closed. He lay on his right side, his hat off, his face relaxed. She could almost see him whole, a man without a care in the world.

He rolled onto his back, slowly blinking his eyes open underneath dark brows. They furrowed. "Hey. You okay?"

In that moment, that brief glimpse of before and after, she wanted to tell him he was beautiful, either way. Before and after. Would he ever see that?

She settled on her knees. "I think I should go."

He lifted himself up on one elbow and pushed his hand through his mess of dark hair. "Really?"

"Yeah, it's getting late."

"It's, like, six."

"Six thirty."

His brows rose. "Wow, that's almost midnight."

His sarcasm didn't faze her.

He sat up and patted the space next to him. She obeyed, folding her legs beneath her, the warmth from the woodstove replaced with the warmth of his body heat where he'd been dozing. He placed his arm behind her, resting it across her lower back.

"Talk," he said.

She glanced toward the easy banter coming from the dining room and the commercial on the TV. Mark moved to turn it off, but she stopped him.

"No, I'd rather have the noise," she said. She sighed and spoke quietly. "This has been really nice."

"Why do you want to leave?"

"I don't want to overstay my welcome." That was partly true.

Her determination to keep her distance was a quivering pile of jelly, and she didn't like it.

"It's Thanksgiving. You're supposed to eat all our food and take advantage of our hospitality."

She smiled. "Is that right?"

He nodded, then his gaze swept the room, and he frowned. "You're bored."

"No, it's not that. Like I said, it's been really nice."

"Then don't go." He swept his hand softly across her shoulders.

"Okay."

He chuckled. "That was easy."

It was too easy. The afternoon had reminded her of those few holidays she'd spent as a child in Montana. Easy, family days with shoes off and dirty dishes on the floor and snow falling outside. No fighting.

"What would you like to do?" he asked. "Play a game? Map out the next move on your house?" He tugged at a lock of her hair and arched his brow. "Make more snow angels?"

She smiled. Curse the snow angels. "I thought you were embarrassed making those."

He still played with the lock of her hair. "They weren't so bad. Some of us could use all the angels we can get."

She nodded, unsure if she believed in angels. Hers had been mysteriously absent at the times when she could've used some.

His hand stilled, as if realizing he'd been playing with her hair. His gaze lifted to hers, and he studied her. She wasn't sure what he wanted from her. Her face grew warm. In one move, he could lean forward, lift her face to his, and kiss her. As if he read her thoughts, his gaze dropped to her mouth.

"You kids still alive in there?" Cal called out from the dining room.

Riley blinked, and Mark dropped her hair. "No," he answered. "Pie overdose."

Riley fell back against the couch and drew her knees up.

"How's the game?" Cal called again.

"Somebody's losing," Mark answered. He stood and stretched with his back to her.

Riley pressed her hand to her warm neck. Her pulse flitted like a hummingbird.

"Somebody here is winning," Yvette said. "Gin."

Cal groaned. "Mark, pick a board game and you two get in here. My ego's taking a beating."

"Be there in a minute." Mark faced Riley, his hands at his hips.

She peered up at him, reading the question in his eyes. She spoke barely above the noise. "I'm complicated."

"You're not the only one."

He reached out his hand. She took it, and he pulled her to her feet. Before he let go of her hand, he pulled her closer, leaning down to her ear.

"Complicated or not," he whispered, "I'm thankful you're here."

Riley swallowed, and he turned to a game cabinet and grabbed a few boxes.

"It's a shame, really," he said, "that I'm going to have to mop the floor with you now."

She smiled, her chin lifting. She eyed the boxes he'd chosen. "It's going to be fun seeing you try."

Chapter 18

Mark trudged out to Riley's car, carrying her now-clean dishes she'd brought her food in. He set them in her car, brushed the snow off her windows, then trudged back to the house, where Riley was saying goodbye to his dad and Yvette.

He'd lost. Three games. But Yahtzee was a game of chance, so that one didn't count, right? It felt like it counted. He opened the door as Riley turned to meet him, and just behind her, he caught his dad taking Yvette's hand and pressing a kiss to it.

He froze at the unexpected gesture, then spun away before his dad found him watching. Riley walked past him.

"Walk her to the car, Mark," his dad said, before closing the front door.

"Mark?"

Distracted, he felt a tug on his sleeve.

"Earth to Mark."

He nodded and took her elbow. It had been snowing lightly the last couple of hours, and the walk was slick again.

"Come on, it wasn't that bad." She peeked up at him. "Was it? I mean, you seemed to enjoy my victory dance, at least."

He suppressed the smile that came with the memory of her final Yahtzee, how she'd danced, whooping and bumping her hip into his shoulder as he slumped in his chair. He'd wanted to grab her and sit her down in his lap and kiss her until she retracted her win.

But he couldn't do that.

He looked back at the door.

"What's wrong?" she asked.

She was already shivering. It was late, and he'd kept the wood-stove stoked all night because she'd seemed so chilled after snow-mobiling. But still, she looked at him, waiting for him to explain why he suddenly couldn't think straight.

He began walking again, taking her hand through his elbow. "I think I saw my dad kiss Yvette when he thought we weren't looking."

Her eyes widened. He stopped at her car.

"He kissed her? Just now?"

"On her hand, yeah."

"On her hand?" She smiled. "I can believe that."

"You can?" He couldn't shake the image, or the confusion it was causing him.

She pulled his elbow closer. "They get along really well. It was a good evening. That's all."

He looked down at her in the light from the porch. "You think that was it?"

She nodded. "Remember when you kissed me?"

"Uh—" His pulse ticked up as his brain scrambled.

"You kissed me on the cheek when I agreed to help you. Remember?"

He had. He'd kissed her.

"Your dad's a gentleman. And Yvette likes him."

"She does?" That was news to him.

"Yes. You couldn't see that?"

"I wasn't paying much attention to Yvette."

She turned to him, a smirk on her face. "What were you paying attention to?"

He met her gaze. "Mostly how to keep you from leaving."

"Well, you succeeded. I stayed for all of Thanksgiving."

That wasn't what he meant, but he wasn't in the mood to point it out to her. "I hope you had a good time."

"It was the best Thanksgiving I've had in years." Without warning, she reached up and kissed him on the cheek. "Thank you."

She dropped down in the driver's seat, and he held the door as she started her car.

"Drive safely," he said. "Careful around the curve."

She nodded. "I'll see you tomorrow. Gotta get those walls painted."

"After lunch." He shut the door, still distracted. He watched her drive away, the place where she'd kissed his good side sensitive to the cold.

He drew in a deep breath of air and blew it out slowly. Because he knew exactly what he'd been thinking when he'd kissed Riley on the cheek after she'd agreed to help him with the nativity. And it hadn't been all that innocent.

❄ ❅ ❄

Riley slept hard and woke before dawn with Mark on her mind. Her thoughts cycled between things she'd been told that stoked her fears and her reluctance to trust him, and everything about him that showed her he was genuine.

After an hour of restlessness, she pulled her laptop into bed

288

and distracted herself with lesson ideas. She clicked through web pages with samples of utilizing white space, then sat bolt upright. She grabbed her phone.

Hey, can you take me out to Miracle Creek Bridge? Have an idea for a class project.

She waited.

He answered within seconds. *Why are you awake?*

You're awake.

I am now.

Riley glanced at the clock: seven o'clock. Oops. *I want to catch the morning light. Could you take me?*

There's a lot of snow.

That's kind of the point. Can your truck handle it?

Yeah, my truck can handle it. When?

Ten minutes?

It's a good thing I'm a morning person.

Are you?

Depends on your definition of morning. BRT C-fire.

She smiled. Maybe this excursion would lighten the mood for painting later. Maybe she'd treat him to breakfast to thank him.

Riley had just slipped into her winter boots when she heard the knock at her door. "Just a minute," she yelled and hurried to the art room and grabbed her camera kit off the shelf.

Mark smiled when she opened the door, and a warmth opened up in her stomach. *Stop it already.*

"Hey," he said.

"Hey." He looked good. Sleepy, but good.

"So . . . what are we doing?"

She held up her bag. "Taking pictures."

He frowned. "Of what?"

"Snow," she said brightly, grabbing her coat and stepping onto the porch.

"The sun is barely up," he said.

"That's why we're hurrying," she said, shooing him forward, trying to ignore how good he smelled. "Move."

He chuckled and got moving.

They didn't get too far out of town when she saw the sign for Miracle Creek Trailhead. "How have I been here all this time and not come this way?"

"It's nice to know we still have some surprises for you here in Plunkheadville, Ms. Madigan." He turned right at a road marker and parked in a lot that hadn't been cleared of snow in a day or two. "For somebody who's traveled the world, you're disappointingly unfamiliar with our little valley."

"Give me some time," she argued.

"How much time do you have?" he countered, eyeing her.

Instead of responding to his challenge, she turned to study the view out the window.

The sun had barely come up and light shone across the surrounding peaks. She'd need the perfect angles to get the shots she wanted.

"Is the bridge far?" she asked, hopping down and grabbing her gear from the truck bed where she'd packed it so the camera could acclimatize to the cold. She'd worn fingerless gloves for dexterity and hoped the bite in the air wouldn't fog up her lens too badly.

He shut his door and met her at the back. "You can see the top of the bridge, right between those pines." He pointed, and she stood on her toes, barely making out the tip of a structure.

"Perfect."

Though the air was crisp, the hint of sun felt good on Riley's face. Untouched pillows of snow topped shrubs and trees, and as they rounded a bend in the trail, more snow hugged the roof of the old covered bridge, the railings, and the open window ledges, just as she'd hoped. She dropped to a crouch and pulled out her camera and her favorite lens for this kind of shot, grateful for no fog on the glass.

"You're going to start shooting right here?" Mark asked.

She snapped a few pictures, turning the camera for a portrait angle. "Why not?"

"Well, I haven't even introduced you, yet."

She stood and aimed again at the bridge. "Your dad said there's a legend." She snapped a couple more frames. "When I asked about your mom's painting in the dining room. Something about wishes." She lowered the camera and quickly looked over what she had so far.

"He told you that?"

The doubt in his voice made her look up. "Yeah. What?"

"I'm surprised he mentioned the wishing, that's all."

She moved closer to the bridge, and he followed, grabbing her bag. "So, what's the legend? How did it start?" She scrutinized the structure as if she could coax out its secrets.

"The basic story is soon after the bridge was built in the 1950s, a desperate farmer threw a coin in the water and made a wish that his crop would survive the blight that had been spreading from orchard to orchard that season."

"Did it work?"

"His was the only orchard to yield a full crop. Word spread."

She snapped a few more pictures. "That doesn't seem like enough to start a legend."

"Soon after, a woman made a wish that her boyfriend would

come into enough money that her parents would accept his offer of marriage."

"So, what, he inherited a bunch of money from his great-aunt?"

Mark smiled. "No, but he was offered a job at a car dealership and the two married soon after. After a few years, he bought it. Wade's Miracle Auto."

She'd seen the old sign in front of one of the car dealerships in town. "He got a job." She threw Mark a challenging look. "What else?"

"Ask around. People have wished on everything from college acceptance to babies to protection over their loved ones." He looked around at the trees and the sky and the water. "Some people just come up here to pray."

"But surely not everyone gets their wish?"

He shrugged, but said nothing, watching her.

"You make a broad enough wish, of course it will come true," she said. "I could wish for sunsets for the rest of my life. Voila, granted. To make a specific wish, though . . . Have you tested it?"

"Ah, that's the thing. You only get one wish."

"So if I wished we stay right here on this bridge forever and ever, then we're stuck here? Forever?"

"That would be horrible."

"The worst." Her face warmed from the flirtatious tone in his voice.

She approached the structure, the sound of the creek growing louder with each step. "Have you made your one wish?"

"Almost."

"Almost?" She glanced back at him. "What stopped you?"

"My mom."

She turned.

He shrugged. "She brought us out here that last Christmas. The doctors had done all they could. She came out here a lot to sketch, take pictures. I think she just wanted to be here one more time."

"Did she make her wish?"

"I think so. She just closed her eyes, held Dad's hand. By the end of that few minutes, I don't know . . . It was like this dread came over me. Like I knew she hadn't wished to get better."

"Oh, Mark."

He set her bag on the plank floor of the bridge and, after brushing away some snow, leaned his forearms on the railing over the creek. "She finished with a smile on her face. Peaceful. I begged her to tell me what she'd wished for. I begged Dad to make his wish that she'd live." He shook his head. "I told him if he wasn't going to wish, then I would. I was almost a man, right?"

Riley nodded.

"But my mom stopped me."

"Why? What would've been the harm?"

"She told me that you only get one real wish, and if you make it before it's time, or if you make the wrong one, it'll float up, but it won't come back down. It won't settle. It'll itch at you and wake you at night and leave your mouth bitter."

Riley leaned on the rail next to him.

He stared at the frothing water beneath them. "Dad squared me up to him and asked me if I really thought he hadn't made every wish, said every prayer, to keep Mom with us. That hit me in the gut. Mom said she knew the wish I wanted to make, and that was enough. And you know what I thought?"

He looked at her, and she shook her head.

"I thought that was garbage. I decided I'd wish without them knowing. But when I tried, I couldn't. Because what if she was right? I was scared. And ashamed and angry. I sulked all the way home. Classic teenage slamming-doors-when-I-got-home sulking. Brutal." He shook his head, smiling at himself.

Riley thought about her next words carefully. "But who makes the rules, anyway? As much as we'd all like to believe in wishes coming true, it does sound like nonsense. Would it have hurt anybody to just let you make your wish?"

He watched her. "I don't know. I would have wished for her to live, and she didn't. Later, she found me and asked me to trust her. I told her I'd try. She was gone a month after that. On her terms. She was at peace with everything. More than anything else, *that* gave us peace. Which, knowing my mom, was probably her wish in the first place."

The sound of the creek wove its way around them, a fervent rush and bubble over rocks and under the aged beams of the bridge.

"So it worked," Riley said, hushed.

He leaned against his elbow. "She hoped."

There it was. The hope Riley had scorned so brazenly when they'd first met. It was the very foundation of his family's peace during the worst of times. "Mark, I'm sorry for what I said about hope."

He shrugged. "You had your reasons."

"I wish I hadn't been so careless."

"Doesn't do any good to wish backwards," he said.

"Is that something your dad says? Or are you just wise?"

He turned around and leaned his back against the rail, his arms folded. "I think I've just learned that prayers and wishes don't always work the way you want them to, but eventually you can say, things are okay."

She placed her hand on his arm, and he put his hand over hers.

"That helped," he said. "Later. After the fires. Once I crawled out of my hole and looked around."

"I'm glad," she said. He'd been through so much. And here he was, talking about strength and peace. No wonder he'd defended hope so fiercely. She was almost jealous. "You make me want to try harder."

He made a sound of contempt and shook his head.

She watched him looking out over the water, the wind playing with his hair around the edge of his hat. His silhouette against the colors in the sky.

He spoke to the water. "Last night, realizing there might be something between my dad and Yvette . . ." He shook his head. "That threw me. Just the idea of it." He glanced at her as if needing validation.

"That's understandable. He's stayed single a long time, huh?"

"Yeah. I've thought about leaving, you know, getting my own place, but part of me doesn't want to leave him alone again."

She watched him, grasping for something to make him feel safe. "Yvette's nice."

He smiled out at the trees. "Yeah, she's great."

"She's my best friend here besides you."

He remained quiet.

"I've never known anyone like you, Mark."

He huffed a laugh under his breath. "Yeah. I can believe that."

"Don't do that."

"Do what?"

"Make yourself less than you are." She reached up, running the back of her fingers over his cold cheek. Cautiously, she lifted her other hand to the other side of his face, to where his scars were.

His hand shot up, fingers wrapping around her wrist, stopping her movement.

She held her ground. "You're strong again. Be strong right now."

He gave an almost imperceptible shake of his head.

This is a boundary, Madigan. Are you sure you want to cross it?

She heard the warning in her head, but she felt the strength in his grip give way, and she couldn't back down. She wouldn't. He had to know.

Her fingers touched his skin, and he closed his eyes. He drew in a breath. She paused, but he didn't stop her. Carefully, she trailed her fingers down over his burned cheek to his jaw. She traced the pattern where smooth scar tissue turned to shaved skin. She spread her fingers and slowly moved them down the side of his neck.

She looked up and found him watching her. "How far does it go?" she asked.

He hesitated, his chest rising and falling with his breath. "Down this side, past my hip," he said. "But the graft-harvest scars . . . They had to take healthy skin from the other side so . . ." He swallowed.

She lifted both hands, cradling his face, and he closed his eyes again.

"Does this hurt?"

"No," he said quietly. When he opened his eyes, they were dark and intense. "Not yet." He lifted his hand slowly, as if fighting himself, and touched her cheek.

She shivered. It wasn't from the cold.

He smoothed her skin with the back of his hand. "How far does it go?" he asked softly.

She suppressed a smile, even while losing her breath. "None of your business," she managed to say.

His brow lifted ever so slightly. He moved his fingers down along her neck. "Does this hurt?" he asked, watching her mouth.

She trembled at his touch. "Not yet," she breathed.

They stood like that for a moment, touching and breathing, as the wild creek rushed below their feet.

"Why do you call me C-fire?" she asked.

He held her gaze, his voice soft. "Fire classification. Class C fire is an energized electrical fire. It's tricky." His fingers traced over her jawline. "You have to find the source and de-energize the circuit, and then use carbon dioxide to put it out."

"Sounds simple enough," she whispered.

He shook his head, moving closer. "No way. No one's ever putting you out."

She shook her head, breathless.

As he bent to her, his hands slipping down her body to rest at her waist, she lifted on her toes, melting her lips into his. Her eyes closed, and she let him lead. He took it slow, but her heart sped at his touch.

The voice in the back of her head screamed, *Are you crazy?*

Apparently, yes.

She slipped her arms around his neck, and he pulled her closer. She leaned into him, his lips soft and exploring. He lifted her enough that her toes skimmed over the wooden planks. He turned and leaned her back against one of the bridge uprights. She caught her breath as he dropped his head and kissed her neck, trailing up her jaw and finally returning to her waiting mouth—readily waiting, which was both exhilarating and terrifying at the same time.

"Mark," she said, breathless between slow kisses.

"Yeah?" he asked, his mouth roaming back toward her ear.

"Oh—" she breathed, forgetting what she was going to say. She felt him smile against her skin.

"What was that?" he whispered in her ear.

"Mm—" Seriously, what was she doing trying to think right now?

Madigan, you need to back off right this instant, so help me. Danger! Danger!

"Go away," she whispered, and Mark's head came up.

"What?" he asked, setting her on her feet.

"No, no, no, I wasn't talking to you." She reached for him again.

He watched her, catching his own breath. "Then who were you talking to?"

She swallowed and clasped her hands behind his neck. "The voice in my head."

The corner of his mouth lifted. "What was it saying?" He leaned toward her again, eyes on her neck.

"Nothing important." His lips touched her skin, and her eyelids fluttered. "At least, not at the moment."

"When will it be important?" he murmured.

"Probably later . . . sometime."

He nibbled her earlobe, sending an electric current down her entire left side. "Sounds important," he whispered. He pulled himself away and met her gaze. "Maybe you should listen." He studied her, serious, waiting for a response.

Again, she reached and touched his scars, forming her hand to the contours of his face.

This time he didn't flinch. He leaned carefully into her palm. His words were low and soft. "Why are you doing this, Riley Madigan? When leaving is still on your mind?"

She shook her head, not knowing the answer, not wanting to tell him he'd made it easy to fall for him. His soulful eyes watched, waiting, reaching to hers for an honest response.

"Because you have to know," she whispered. "You're no monster, Mark Rivers. You never could be."

He lowered his gaze, and they stood together for several moments while she wondered if she'd said the right thing. He pulled her closer, resting his forehead against hers. A cold breeze blew around them, pulling at her hair, uncertainty nudging from the corners of her thoughts. But everything between them stayed warm and close.

Finally, he spoke. "So . . . the kiss was okay?"

She smiled at the simplicity of his question. "Yeah, it was okay."

"Just okay?"

"Toe-curling."

He grinned. "I . . . I had to practice, you know."

"What?" She laughed.

He nodded against her head, becoming serious again. He ran his fingertips through her hair. "I worried. Not just about eating or drinking from a cup again." He watched her lips as he spoke. "But about . . . in case I ever . . . if anybody would—"

She breathed, shaking her head. "You didn't have to worry."

His grin returned.

"How did you practice?" she asked, grinning back.

"It was more like—exercise. And I used a straw. Lots of milkshakes."

She laughed, reaching out to trace his lips. He playfully caught her finger in a gentle bite.

"Whatever you did, it worked," she said with a breathy tremble in her voice.

She slipped her finger free and dropped her voice to a whisper. "What about the whole 'friends' thing?"

Oh, sure, Madigan, now *you think to ask that question.*

"You've used that word a lot." He took a deep breath. "I'm finding that I like this new approach to 'the friends thing.'"

She couldn't help smiling. *We're in so much trouble.*

"As a matter of fact," he said, holding her more firmly, "it gives the words 'just friends' a whole new meaning. Don't get me wrong. Jay and the guys were great, but uh . . ."

She arched an eyebrow. "No kissing?"

"No. They didn't smell this good, either."

Her laughter rose, then faded. His fingers stroked her hair again.

"Riley, people will talk. They'll jump to conclusions. Rumors will spread. I'm just saying—"

"I know." She didn't like it. "Small town."

He nodded. "Small town. We'll just have to do our best to . . . keep it real." He looked up at the sky and took a deep breath, letting it out slowly. His gaze lowered to hers. "Thanks for asking me here."

She fought her misgivings; her heartbeat an erratic, bewildering dance. "Thanks for sharing it with me."

His fingers stilled. His voice grew husky. "I'm trusting you, Riley." His lips brushed hers, the weight of his words resting on her thudding heart.

"I'm not sure you should," she whispered.

"Too late," he said with his crooked smile.

She searched his face, recognizing that she was trusting him, too.

"Did you get enough pictures?" he asked.

She nodded, barely noticing the sky brightening over them.

His gaze intensified.

"More practice?" she asked.

"Yeah," he said. "Lots more."

❄ ❄ ❄

They picked up breakfast wraps at the Grill-n-Go and ate in Mark's truck in front of the park. Traffic was nonexistent because of the snow and it being the morning after Thanksgiving. No Black Friday crush in this place. They'd eaten quietly, sharing glances and shy smiles like they were at a middle school dance and her favorite slow song was playing. After the food was gone, he pulled her onto his lap and they kissed until they heard a car drive by.

He dropped her off at her house with a promise to be back later to help her paint the walls.

Until then, she worked on the nativity in a blissfully happy daze. She painted Joseph, but kept pausing, brush hovering over the image, her thoughts wandering to the bridge and Mark's mouth on hers and his whispered words in her ear. She shook the stupid grin off her face, determined to focus, only to wake up from a haze again. Finally, after discovering that Joseph's features bore a strong resemblance to the man who'd been kissing her all morning, she set down her brush, cleaned up, and hauled her camera bag to the desk.

Transferring the images she'd taken at the bridge to her laptop didn't take much time. She hadn't taken many pictures, but she had two or three good ones the kids could choose from for their projects. She downloaded a few more examples from the web as well.

When she moved her camera bag, the volunteer firefighter forms caught her attention. She pulled the paper toward her, remembering Mark's warning that she give it serious thought before committing. Then his other, more recent, words came back to her.

Why are you doing this, Riley Madigan? When leaving is still on your mind?

Her heart spluttered. After this morning, Mark would expect her to stay in Miracle Creek—even if he didn't say so. Would things continue on their natural course? Hopefully. Maybe. She rubbed her chest where a knot grew and tightened. The sticky note with Cheri Matheson's contact information in New Orleans caught her eye. It might as well have been a neon sign flashing *Escape Exit*.

She sat back and pushed both hands through her hair. She hadn't expected this. Hadn't looked for it. Coming here was supposed to help her get away from entanglements. From rumors and the danger of giving your heart away so it could be waved around for everyone to see, even as it was stomped on.

Was leaving still on her mind? Maybe the better question was, was she considering staying? It had always been a possibility. Needing to establish herself in her career. The fantasy of finding somewhere to call home. A little girl's dream. On a deeper level, she'd been seeking that, coming here to Miracle Creek. She glanced at the painting of her grandma's house. It did look like it could belong here.

And the idea of leaving Mark behind, should she move on, was growing more and more difficult to imagine.

Chapter 19

W hat's with all the noise?" Mark's dad wandered into the kitchen.

Mark stopped whistling long enough to answer. "I'm making your favorite breakfast." He flipped the pancakes and shook plenty of pepper on the bacon.

"Where did all this food come from?" His dad looked around. "Is that flour?"

Mark nodded. "We were out of everything but the frozen stuff Steph brought over and salad dressing. Who eats like that?"

"We do."

"Not anymore." He slid the pancakes onto a stack already waiting. He piled the bacon on top and set it on the table. "I didn't learn to cook from the best firehouse company in Washington for nothing." He pulled out a covered dish of scrambled eggs where they'd been keeping warm in the oven. "Could you get the orange juice out of the fridge? Oh, and the syrup's warm in the microwave."

His dad finally moved into action. "Just the way I like it."

Mark resumed whistling, turning off the burners and wiping

down the counters. He tossed the dishcloth behind his back, aiming for the sink. He missed, the cloth hitting the cabinet and dropping to the floor. He didn't even care. He'd spent the best few hours he could remember with a woman, and it had happened with him the way he was now, not the way he used to be. When he'd walked Riley to her front door, he hadn't cared about anything but the feel of her hand wrapped in his and the next time he'd see her. He hadn't been sure he'd ever feel like that again.

His dad picked up the cloth, dropping it in the sink. "What's up with you? Did you take some of those pain pills? The ones that make you want to hug everybody?"

Mark shook his head. "Trust me, if I wanted to hug you, you'd know. Sit down—breakfast is getting cold." He pulled out a chair.

His dad watched Mark closely as he sat across from him.

"I cooked it; you bless it," Mark said.

His dad narrowed his eyes. Mark blinked at him. Then his dad bowed his head and gave a brief blessing on the food. Just before he said amen, he interrupted himself.

"—Oh, and whatever You've done to Mark that's waking him up, let's have more of that."

Mark opened his eyes, watching his dad.

"Amen."

"Amen," Mark echoed.

His dad placed a napkin on his lap and surveyed the breakfast. "This wouldn't have anything to do with a certain art teacher, would it?"

Mark tried to stop the stupid grin that pulled across his face. "What makes you ask that?"

"Some little birdies told me you've been spending a lot of time with her."

"Small town," Mark said, reaching for the syrup.

"So, anything else you want to share with your old dad?" He looked at Mark expectantly.

"Look, it's all kind of new, and we'd like it kept quiet. So that means not telling you anything more."

"Not fair."

"Tell me about it," Mark murmured.

"What's that supposed to mean?"

"Forget it. You've got your network of spies. I'm sure you'll get all the juicy gossip sooner or later."

His dad grabbed some bacon. "Nurse a guy back to health and he shuts you out. Typical."

"Dad."

He paused, a piece of bacon halfway to his mouth.

"I'm not shutting you out. I really like her. I didn't see this happening. Not ever again. I feel like I need to protect it."

Cal nodded. "I get that, son. I do. If anybody deserves something—"

"No, don't say that. It's not about deserving." He pushed his eggs around on his plate.

"Then what's it about?"

"I don't know. I feel like I've stumbled into something that has the potential to kill me. Only it isn't. It's—"

"—waking you up."

Mark nodded. "Yeah."

"To the smell of *bacon*," his dad said, picking up his fork.

Mark smiled as he watched his dad tuck back into his food.

"So, have you asked Riley to the firemen's ball?"

It was Mark's turn to pause. "She's coming to the memorial," he said carefully.

"You didn't ask her to the dance?"

"No."

"Why not?"

"Not sure she'd want that."

His dad raised a brow at him.

Mark shrugged. "Like I said, we're keeping things quiet." Still, the idea warred inside him. On one hand, he'd love to have Riley next to him at the annual firemen's social. He and Jay had gone to the hometown event since they were old enough to take girls, up until year before last. But he didn't want to go to the dance. He wasn't ready, and he hadn't planned on it. Until Riley.

"Don't miss your chances, son. You don't know how many you'll get."

Mark stared at his eggs. "I'm aware."

❄ ❄ ❄

"Hey there, Rivers. What are you up to?"

Mark turned, straightening. "Gainer. Hey. Picking up paint supplies. You?"

Dalton held up a package. "Light bulbs."

"Ah." He still needed painter's tape and moved that direction. "Good to see you."

"I figured something out," Dalton said behind him. "About Riley."

Mark paused and faced him. "About Riley," he repeated.

"Yep."

He sighed, not wanting this conversation but needing to put out any fires Dalton might be setting. "What did you figure out?"

"You know who she dated before, right?"

"Some scumbag actor?"

Dalton chuckled. "Yeah, 'some actor.' Do you ever get on the internet? She dated pretty-boy Gavin-*freaking*-Darrow. *The*

Sounds of War? Sounds like he humiliated her pretty badly. No wonder she's gun-shy. Stringing the two of us along."

Mark held Dalton's pointed gaze while a flare of emotions battled for top spot in his thoughts. "You looked up Riley on the internet?"

Dalton's eyes narrowed a fraction. "Just research."

Riley hadn't told Dalton anything. That idea alone bolstered his nerves. "Here's a tip. Riley's a pretty private person. It wouldn't do you any good spreading around what you find."

"My intentions are honorable, I assure you."

"Hm." Sure they were.

"I'm taking her to the firemen's ball."

Mark fought to keep his expression steady even as his gut twisted. "You asked her?"

He shrugged.

"And she said yes?"

"She's thinking it over. Like I said, gun-shy."

Mark nodded slowly. "Well, good luck with that." He turned, hoping it was enough of a dismissal.

"Painting your dad's house?"

He glanced over his shoulder. "Riley's." He kept walking.

❄ ❄ ❄

Mark waited on Riley's porch holding paint rollers, drop cloths, and painter's tape, his insides turning like gears he couldn't slow, the image of her with movie star Gavin Darrow burning in his brain. She opened the door with a smile so welcoming he immediately nudged her inside, dropped all his stuff, and pulled her close. Before she could say anything, he caught her mouth with his and kissed her until the gears shifted, still turning, but different. Better.

She made a pleased sound in his arms and pulled his coat off, keeping the kiss going. Once his coat hit the floor, she pulled him farther into the room. Together, they dropped down on the couch, continuing from where they'd briefly left off.

"We won't get much painting done this way," she whispered when he broke away to graze his lips against her ear.

"Sure we will," he said. "It's only three walls." He tucked her in closer, savoring the feel of her next to him, deciding where to kiss her next.

She smiled. "It's four walls."

"One wall has a big gaping hole in it." He made for her neck, and she giggled. He couldn't help smiling.

"And you can hardly count the wall with the front window," she said.

He nuzzled her hair. "Hardly. We don't even really have to paint, if you think about it." His lips met hers again, and he felt her shiver.

After a few more minutes entangled on the couch, she slowed the kiss, and he opened his eyes. She blinked up at him, her expression unreadable. He traced the freckles across her nose, his heart beating a rhythm he hadn't felt in a long time. Maybe not ever.

"What is it?" he asked, suppressing the inevitable insecurity.

Her lips and cheeks blushed as she looked away.

His hand smoothed along the definite curve from her waist to her hip, bringing her gaze back to his.

"We're keeping this to ourselves, right?"

He blinked, drawing back. "Yeah," he answered. "Yeah, of course." He frowned, running a hand over her hair, trying to ignore the pang her question shot to his ego. "I mean, I wouldn't mind everyone knowing." He could think of one person in particular he'd liked to shout the news to. "But I get not wanting that right now."

She nodded. "And we're taking this slow, right?" she asked, her eyes searching his.

He exhaled, and dropped his head. "Yes." He'd only just kissed her for the first time that morning. He was barely used to letting her see his face, let alone touch it. As for the rest of him, well . . . He hoped time with her would ease his fears. "We can go as slow as you need." He gave his head a shake and sat up. "As slow as *I* need." He brushed his hand through his hair, a sudden sense of vulnerability making his heart race like a jackrabbit. "With my scars, I'm just . . . Slow is good, that's all."

"Slow is good," she agreed with a sigh. "But it's going to take us a *month* to finish painting."

He shook his head. "A year at least."

She snorted out a laugh. He growled and made a grab for her. She squealed and didn't make it out of his reach. He took some consolation in that it wasn't long before he was wrapped up in her arms again, and it was more than a few minutes before either of them brought up painting. And still he couldn't shake the feeling he was playing a very dangerous game with his heart.

❄ ❄ ❄

The next couple of days were spent focused on the house. Painting, ripping off trim, tearing up carpet. Riley had been right. Solid oak floors were hidden under the old brown carpet—a few scratches and stains, but salvageable. Mark borrowed a floor sander from a friend, and they spent a couple afternoons staining and sealing.

When they weren't at Riley's, they were at Mark's house, cooking meals for his dad and taking the snowmobile out for a turn. And making more snow angels, but the messier kind. Mark said he hadn't been so thankful for snow in a long time. Riley smiled at the thought.

They'd done their best to keep things under the small-town radar. Mark's truck was parked at Riley's for hours, but most people knew he was working on her house, often while she wasn't home. True, people speculated, watched, smiled, but nobody knew enough to come out and say that Mark Rivers and the art teacher were an item.

Thursday night while painting, Riley got a call from Yvette. "How are you doing?"

The concern in her voice confused her. "I'm fine. Why?"

"Have you been watching TV tonight?"

Riley's sense of self-protection knotted in her chest. "No. Why?"

Yvette sighed. "First off, *Eyes on Hollywood* is a guilty pleasure—I admit that."

Riley tightened her grip on the paintbrush in her fingers.

"But they were doing a segment on Gavin Darrow, that actor from—well, I'm guessing you know. Anyway, he's getting married to that actress—again, I'm guessing you know who—"

Riley's heart dropped, and she sat down.

"—and they always do that part about who the actors were linked to in the past and . . . Honey, I had no idea. They said your father's name, and then they showed pictures, and I know you're a private person—"

Riley's head spun as Yvette went on. This couldn't be happening. If Yvette had seen it, then who knows who else had? Gavin could've at least warned her or—

"—my first thought was that you'd need a friend. No wonder you picked up and moved here, after being under a microscope like that. Of course, that show sensationalizes everything. You've obviously wanted it kept quiet, and I just had to warn you that it likely won't be quiet anymore. I wanted you to know I'm here for you."

"Thanks," she answered numbly. How much had been shared on TV? What pictures had they used? She rubbed at her aching chest, her eyes burning. "It's in the past." Gavin was getting married. To the woman she'd caught him with.

"Does Mark know about Gavin?"

Mark. Memories of all the side-glances and scrutiny from the people of Miracle Creek flipped through her mind, all the questioning looks at her and Dalton, all the conjecture about her and Mark were suddenly amplified. She remembered every car that slowed as it passed by, every eyebrow that rose, and every look of judgment from Dalton's admirers, people watching on their porches like they had their own *Eyes on Hollywood*. And now this. It would be a match on a gas leak. A leak she couldn't patch up no matter how far she ran.

And Mark would go up in flames with her.

She struggled to breathe. She didn't want it. Any of it.

"He knows some," she answered. "Not enough."

"Will you talk to him before the memorial tomorrow?"

She dropped her head to her hand, not knowing how to answer.

❄ ❄ ❄

On Friday afternoon, the day of the memorial ceremony at the park, Mark sat on the edge of his bed, staring at the bulletin board he'd covered with cards and drawings and the picture of him and Jay. He turned the glass doorknob over and over in his hands while his speech lay next to him on the bed, read a hundred times.

A knock sounded. "Come in."

His dad entered and sat down next to him. "How're you holding up?"

He cocked an eyebrow, and his dad nodded.

"You'll be fine. I know Jay would appreciate this."

"Are you kidding? He's getting a good laugh. 'Look what I got Mark into.'"

His dad chuckled. "That sounds about right." He patted Mark on the shoulder.

"I'll be okay, Dad."

"Good to hear it." He cleared his throat. "There's something I wanted to run by you."

"You sound nervous."

"Probably because I am. I figured I better start practicing what I preach. I'm asking Yvette to go with me to the dance next week."

Mark arched a brow. "You asking my permission?"

His dad paused and then chuckled. "Heck no. Just wanted to let you know so if I disappear for a few minutes after the ceremony, you'll know what I'm up to."

He gave his dad a smirk. "Glad to see your priorities are in line."

His dad slapped him on the back. "They are. You have a lot to do with that. What do you need me for anyway, right?"

Mark lowered his head with a smile. "Right."

His dad stood up, heading for the door.

"Dad?"

"Yeah?"

"Yvette's great."

"Yeah, I think so too." He cocked his head. "Are you picking up Riley for the ceremony?"

He shook his head. "This is something I need to do on my own."

"I guess I can understand that. See you downstairs?"

Mark nodded. His dad turned to go.

"Dad? Have you heard if Gainer's taking Riley to the dance?"

His dad made a sound of exasperation. "Not that I'm aware of. Yvette asked me why you hadn't asked her yet. I had no answer. Got one for me?"

Mark didn't.

"Hey," his dad said gently. "You'll do great up there today."

The door closed, and Mark thought for a moment, smoothing his fingers over the glass.

He knew of an estate auction Riley would love out near Orondo. Old stuff like barn wood and old clocks and stained glass. Maybe he'd ask her to the dance then.

He reached for his phone to text Riley.

Can I take you somewhere tomorrow? I promise no blood.

He set his phone down and pushed his hand through his hair, the callouses on his palm brushing against his scars. He sighed. What was he doing? He couldn't get her out of his head. He didn't want her out. He craved her like water. But he felt it. Something coming. Something he should be bolting from. He didn't know if it was fear or insecurity or self-preservation.

His phone buzzed.

I'll see you after the ceremony. We can talk then. Good luck today.

He smiled. Riley made him forget he was scarred. And that was worth any storm coming.

Chapter 20

"I know a lot of you think I'm a hero."

Riley wrung her hands, as she'd been doing since Mark had ascended the platform next to the veiled memorial. Miracle Creek had come out in full force, with who-knew-how-many from neighboring towns. Snow in the park had been cleared for the crowds, and most eyes were glued on Mark, though she knew some flickered to her. His hands had a death grip on either side of the podium.

Mark's gaze met Riley's—briefly—but enough for her cheeks to warm. He'd picked her out of the crowd almost as soon as he'd taken his chair on the platform with the mayor, his former fire chief, Jay's parents, and a few other officials. Now he stood, his dress shirt and tie visible under his jacket, a black knit cap not quite covering his dark hair. He lowered his head, as if considering his next words. Riley's heart pounded with anxiety for him.

He lifted his head. "The truth is, that day in the fire, I wasn't thinking about being a hero. I was scared. But I followed Jay."

His eyes met hers again, and she knew he was reaching for her. For a friend. She nodded. He took a breath.

"I followed Jay and borrowed his strength and his courage because he stopped at nothing—*nothing*—to get these boys"—he gestured to the six boys standing in front of the memorial—"to safety. To get them out. He paid the ultimate sacrifice, and I can tell you he'd do it again. I know he would. He was driven to keep people safe." He raised his chin. "'Courage is knowing what not to fear.' Plato said that. Jay lived it. He was my friend. My brother."

He bit his lip, and Riley felt his struggle with his emotions. Then he leaned toward the microphone one more time.

"He's *my* hero." He pulled back from the podium, and the crowd applauded, Riley clapping with them.

Mark lifted his hand to the six boys, who each held a cord attached to the veil. They pulled at the signal, revealing a tall, redbrick pillar with a bronze plaque on the front. An image of Jay in his fire hat had been made in relief above his name and dates, and the quote Mark had just shared.

Mark stepped to the microphone. "I know you're all freezing, but thanks for being here today. The people of Miracle Creek have a way of driving out the cold." He sat, and, after the applause died down, the mayor said a few words.

Riley swallowed when Mark's eyes found her again. She gave him two thumbs-up. He ducked his head, and she knew he smiled.

"He did a great job," came a voice close to her ear.

Riley turned to see Dalton just behind her. "Yes, he did." She suppressed the warning she felt rising inside her. Dalton hadn't made any more advances toward her, and any interactions at work had been respectful.

He folded his arms, leaning forward to speak quietly as the mayor wrapped up. "Must've been tough for him."

"He missed the funeral. I think this was something like that for him."

"Oh, yeah, that too."

She looked at him. "That, too?"

Dalton frowned. "Oh, of course. I was thinking of, you know, being in front of a crowd like this. I mean, there are a lot more people here than in line at the bakery."

"I don't follow you." She suspected she did, but he couldn't be saying what she thought he was saying.

"He's just come a long way. You know, in showing himself."

The rising warning turned to irritation.

He shrugged. "I suppose that has a lot to do with you. You have a way of making people want to be better. Try harder."

She narrowed her eyes at him, and he smiled, almost humbly.

People were starting to mill around now, the ceremony over. She noted a few people watching her and whispering behind their hands. "Speaking of making people want to try harder," he said. "I was hoping I could make good on that promise I made you."

She searched for Mark in the crowd. He was surrounded by the rescued boys and their families. "What promise?"

"To get to know you better. Sort of a do-over."

She turned to him, genuinely surprised.

"I meant what I said that night, Riley." He took a step closer. "I'd like to do less talking, more listening. Maybe take you to the firemen's ball next week?" He raised his brow expectantly, his confident grin growing.

Riley took a step back. As much as she suspected his sincerity, the idea of sharing the things in her head and in her heart with Dalton made her wall go right up. "The do-over is that we're still civil after that night. I believe you mean well, Dalton, but I don't think it's a good idea to be anything other than colleagues."

His grin faded. "You don't."

She shook her head. "Thank you for asking."

He frowned but nodded. "I understand. Maybe I'm a little relieved. It's hard to measure up to someone like Gavin Darrow."

Riley froze.

"Explains a lot about your interest in Rivers, too."

She spied Mark talking to Jay's parents and to Nate and Gus. He caught her gaze and tossed her a wink. She swallowed.

"I don't even want to know what you mean by that," she said to Dalton.

"I mean that Rivers is your rebound. He's safe. I'm hoping you'll consider me as someone on a level between movie star and . . . ex-fireman."

She frowned at him. "Mark isn't a rebound. And I'm starting to think you're more on the movie star's level."

Dalton studied her. "It's true, then."

"What's true?"

"You and Rivers being a thing."

Her pulse picked up. She didn't want this. She didn't want his speculation. "Are you listening to small-town rumors, Dalton?"

He laughed. "It's true you've got the town buzzing. But, no. I know better than that. This came from the man himself."

"What do you mean?" A knot tightened in her chest, and she glanced around, noting they'd drawn some judgmental looks from people in the crowd.

"Mark made it pretty clear to me that you and he had been getting on *very* well, if you know what I mean. I just had a hard time believing it."

She swallowed hard, trying to wrap her head around what he was saying. "Can you be more specific?" Except she didn't want him to be more specific, and the knot in her chest was making her jaw clench.

Dalton looked shrewdly over the crowd and then shrugged,

meeting her glare. "Oh, just dropped hints, really. How he's 'painting' your house. How you've spent hours together on a 'secret project.'" He kept using finger quotes. "Even claimed to know that you slept with a baseball bat under your bed. And everyone knows he's stayed over at your place."

She stared, frozen in place, replaying any scene at all where Mark would be justified in making such an announcement. They'd slept on the couch. *Slept.*

"Was he mistaken, then?" Dalton asked.

She wanted to slap his innocent look off his face. She clenched her fists, anger and frustration and foolishness whirling inside her like a cyclone. Why was this bothering her so much? It shouldn't. Half of that was true, though she didn't know why Mark would share any of it.

But this hurt. They'd agreed to go slow. To keep things quiet. Friends. Friends and maybe something more. She'd trusted him.

❄ ❄ ❄

Mark worked his way down from the platform, putting as much distance between himself and the podium as he could. He just wanted to find Riley and get out of the spotlight.

Finally, after a few more handshakes, the crowd broke up around him.

He spied her immediately. She was talking to Dalton Gainer, and when she spotted Mark and didn't smile back, a warning shot up his spine. Whatever Dalton had said to make her look like that had Mark picking up his pace.

"Hey," he said as he reached her. He looked between Riley and Dalton. "What's up?"

Riley's frown deepened. She was upset. Ticked-off upset.

"Are you all right?" he asked, genuinely concerned.

"Dalton just told me something very interesting," she said.

"Really?" He turned to Dalton. "You stay up all night practicing what to say?"

Dalton smirked.

Riley didn't laugh. She clenched her jaw and didn't meet Mark's eyes. "He says you told him that you and I are sleeping together."

Mark's stomach dropped at the underlying anger in her voice and the hush that fell over the crowd around them. Of all the things he would have guessed she was going to say, that wasn't one of them. He looked at Dalton. "What the—"

Riley interrupted him. "Dalton said you made sure he understood that you and I were intimate."

He couldn't help the laugh that found its way up and out. He would never have said anything like that to anyone, let alone to Gainer. But the look of smug triumph on the man's face quickly dowsed any humor in the situation.

Fury roiled inside Mark. He was already fighting emotions from the speech. He'd made it through. And he'd wanted nothing more than Riley's smile, her hand—anything she'd allow. Not this.

He turned to her, his head spinning. "Why would I—I didn't—I didn't say that."

"You certainly did, Rivers," Dalton said, his manner cool. "Just outside the school when I helped you with those boards you were taking to the shop. Claimed your territory pretty clearly."

"You helped me with—?" Then it hit him. He remembered that day, how he'd felt defensive of Riley and had thrown out that stupid comment about her baseball bat. "Why you sonuva—"

"It's true, then?" Riley gazed at Mark, hurt evident in her eyes. Disappointment. Betrayal. "Has this been some kind of game to you?" She looked between them. "To both of you?"

Mark rubbed his hand over his face, chuckling but without humor. "Yeah. Yeah, it's true. I told him I knew you slept with a baseball bat under your bed. And I let him think whatever he wanted because he's Dalton Gainer and who cares?" His anger took over. "Do you know why I told this lying, *cheating* piece of work about your bat, Riley?" He held up a hand. "Shut up, Gainer."

Dalton shut his mouth on whatever bull he was going to dish out. More people were gathering, but he wasn't going to let this land in his lap. Not after what he'd just done. Not today.

"He was telling me to back off. Of *you*. He was comparing you to points on a scoreboard and claiming he was going to win." He breathed hard.

Dalton opened his mouth again.

Mark pointed at him. "Don't think I can't take you *right* now."

"Mark," he heard Steph say from behind him.

In his peripheral, he saw Gus and Lester take a step closer.

He focused on Riley. "I've treated you with nothing but respect. I told him about the bat, Riley, because he was talking about my *friend* like a high school record he wanted to break. I told him to be careful, because I knew if *you* heard about it, *you'd* end up swingin'." Mark backed away, watching her watch him, her eyes big and green and watery. "I just didn't think you'd be swingin' at me."

He glanced around at faces and shrugged off his dad's hand on his shoulder. He stared at Riley. "I get it, though. Why on earth would you be with me? Wouldn't want that rumor spreading. So you just let Dalton keep playing you. No rumors to fear there." He turned and stalked toward his truck on the other side of the park, his insides hardening like poured concrete.

❄ ❄ ❄

Riley watched Mark stride away through blurry eyes, her lungs on fire.

Dalton stepped closer. She felt his hand on the small of her back. "I'm sure he'll be all right. Today was rough on him, poor guy. What a scene. How the hero has fallen. Are you okay?"

As his hand slid lower, she stepped away and slapped Dalton Gainer across the face. Pain burst through her palm.

"What the—" He held his face and spit out blood.

"Imagine what I could do with a bat." She turned.

"You'll be hearing from my lawyer," Dalton called after her.

"Oh, sure," she heard Gus say. "Because no woman has ever slapped you across the face before, right, Gainer? Officer Lester, what do you think?"

"Clearly self-defense."

Yvette touched her arm, but Riley pulled away, her feet taking her after Mark as she fought her churning emotions. She'd been a fool. Why? Why had she so readily believed what Dalton had said? What he'd implied? Mark had done nothing but respect her in every way. Was he right? Was she afraid to be linked to him in the public eye as anything more than just friends?

Just friends. Tears spilled down her face. They were more than that. From the beginning, they'd been more than that.

"Mark!" She picked up her pace as he reached his truck. "Mark, please stop."

He halted, his shoulders rigid, his head held high. Slowly he turned. He didn't meet her gaze, his jaw working tightly.

She slowed and stopped several feet away, afraid to scare him off. "I shouldn't have believed him."

He shifted his weight, stiff.

"When he said you'd told him—"

"You are such a hypocrite," he said, interrupting her.

She faltered at the accusation in his voice. "What?"

"You're angry at your parents for moving you around so much you don't know what to call home, but you won't commit to stay in one place long enough to plan your summer. You go out with a man who *cheated* on his wife and left his children, then, after he takes you to *Leavenworth* and makes you cry, you go out with him again?"

He stepped toward her. "I get it. Dalton's all shiny—but it's smoke and mirrors. Like that idiot actor you dated back in California. I thought you could see through that. I've done my best to show you what's real in this valley. I wasn't near done yet. While I was on that platform, scared out of my mind, it hit me that I didn't care who saw us or who didn't. I didn't care about small-town rumors anymore. I just wanted you by my side any-where. *Everywhere.*"

She stepped toward him. "Mark—"

He stepped back. "And at the same instant, you jump on the first excuse you can find to believe the worst of me."

She shook her head, wiping at a tear.

He didn't slow down. "You're making the same mistakes your parents made, and you don't even see it. You say you can see me, Riley, but you can't even see yourself. You can't even see what it might be like if you stayed. It might be amazing." He shook his head in frustration. "It *has* been amazing. When are you going to realize that I'm not your father, Riley? I'm not some guy who couldn't see what he had right in front of him." He threw his hands out at his sides. "What part of any of me says that I'm going anywhere?" He laughed, half-crazy. "That I won't be here for-freaking-ever?"

He closed the distance between them in a few steps and took her arms, his dark eyes sparking with a mix of anger and desperation. "You make me feel *real*, Riley. What do I make you feel?"

She couldn't breathe.

His grip tightened. "What do I make you feel?"

A car rolled on the gravel behind her and a door opened. "Riley, baby?"

Her head jerked at that voice. "Mom?"

Determined footsteps came around from the driver's side of a large SUV. "Get your hands off her!"

"Dad?"

Mark dropped his hands, turning their way.

Her mother gasped, and her dad halted in his tracks. Then fury clouded his face. "What are you doing to my daughter?"

Riley wiped quickly at her tears and stepped in front of Mark. "Dad, what are you doing here?"

He pulled his eyes away from Mark. She'd seen the moment his anger had turned into distaste. Her mother still held her hand over her mouth in revulsion.

"Is this man hurting you?" her dad asked.

"No." She sucked in a breath, which was difficult considering her chest was caving in. "The other way around," she whispered. She dared a look at Mark.

He was watching her, his expression dark, reminding her of that man in the hood at the backstage doors so long ago. He addressed her parents, keeping his right side away from them. "I'm sorry if I've made you uncomfortable. Excuse me." He gave Riley one last look, then walked back to his truck, kicked up the engine, and drove away.

Chapter 21

R iley drove blindly on roads so familiar now she could draw a map and name them, even with the snow falling hard enough she had to use her wipers.

She'd asked her parents to return to their hotel in Leavenworth with a promise to call them.

"We decided that since you weren't coming to us for the holidays," her mom had explained, "we were coming to you. I hear there's a big tree-lighting tomorrow."

Surprise.

The look on Mark's face haunted her. His anger had shielded his hurt, but she was the girl who could see him. And she'd hurt him. Betrayed his trust. He was right. She'd taken the first chance she was given to push him away and made it spectacular. *Congratulations, Madigan. It worked.*

You make me feel real. What do I make you feel?

He'd been open and vulnerable, and then her parents had shown up and reminded him that there were those in this world who saw scars walking around as people.

She wiped the insistent tears from her eyes, realizing that

she'd been climbing the winding roads to Rivers Orchards on autopilot.

She slammed on the brakes.

She'd hurt Mark. Because she didn't know how to commit. She didn't know how to put down roots and give them the chance to grow.

She gripped the steering wheel.

It wouldn't stop there. Now that people knew about her and Gavin, they'd be curious and questioning and watching. He didn't need someone like her leading him on or using him. Because that's all she'd been doing. She hadn't meant to. She'd wanted to believe everything he said about hope and belonging . . .

But how could someone like her know how to trust? How to love?

At the thought, she crumpled forward, fighting more tears as they came anyway.

She'd told him she could see him. But at the first real test, all she could see was a reason to run.

She wiped at her tears again, then backed up, angling the car so she could turn around on the narrow road banked by snow. She had to get out of there. As she whipped the car around, she heard a horn and slammed on her breaks just as a truck slammed on theirs. Both vehicles slid to a halt, only a few feet from each other.

Mark stared at her from his truck.

Her hands stayed on the steering wheel. He got out and approached her door.

"What do you think you're doing?" he shouted at her through the window.

She clamped her mouth shut and looked away.

"Open the door," he said, knocking on the glass.

"Just let me pass," she said.

"If you don't open this door, I'm going to wrench it open myself."

"With your bare hands?"

"Fireman," he said. "You've got a bat. I've got an ax."

She looked up at him, her eyes raw from dried tears and a headache blooming. He scowled, his hands at his hips. With a sound of exasperation, she pushed her door open and got out.

"Are you okay?" he growled at her, his breath making puffs in the cold air.

"Why wouldn't I be okay?" she answered. "Your truck didn't even hit me."

"My truck didn't hit *you?*" he asked. "You were the one coming at me like a maniac."

She didn't know what to say to that, and the way he looked directly at her with such ferocity and pain made her unable to look anywhere else.

He studied her for a minute, a steely wall between them.

She desperately wanted to leave. "I'm sorry I ruined your ceremony."

"Forget the ceremony." He glanced up the road toward his place, breathing heavily, then back to her car. "Where were you headed?"

She shook her head. "I don't know."

He waited for more. She didn't give him any.

"Fine," he said. "I'll pull off the road so you can get past."

"You don't have to do that."

"Yeah, I do. The snowplow didn't clear it wide enough for two cars. There's a pullout back where the road splits up to Harriman's. I'll back up to that point, and you can pass me and head home." He stepped away.

"I'm leaving, Mark," she said, staring at her feet.

"Not until I move my truck, you're not."

"No. I'm leaving Miracle Creek. I've been invited to teach at an artist residency in New Orleans." Even as she said it, she could see it like a golden light in front of her. An exit door wide open. "I'll leave as soon as the school can find me a replacement. I'll need that time to get the house ready to sell."

He'd stilled. "New Orleans."

"Yes."

"Sell the house."

"Yes."

His voice was forced. "Is this about what Dalton said?"

"No."

"Because that was a load of—"

"That's not it. I shouldn't have believed him."

"Then is it—"

"It's an opportunity. That's all."

"What about—"

"I'll finish the nativity. Don't worry."

He stayed put. "How long have you known about this?"

She stared at nothing. *From the beginning*, she thought. "It's something I've kept in mind, in case I might want to leave."

"You want to?"

She didn't answer.

"I thought you liked it here."

She met his gaze. "I've liked a lot of places."

He searched her face, his expression stony. He backed up a bit, looking toward his house, then back down the road, his breaths of air coming harder and faster now in the cold.

"I trusted you," he said, his voice strained. "You couldn't trust me."

Her gut twisted. She almost went to him. Almost wrapped her arms around him. To tell him she'd never leave.

He nodded. "I guess you've answered my question."

His words jerked her back to reality.

"I make you feel like running."

Heart stuttering, she couldn't argue. He was right. From the beginning he'd made her feel like running.

With her silence, he strode to his truck, got in, and shut the door. He looked behind him as he drove smoothly back down the road, disappearing around the bend.

When she passed him, his truck pulled off to the side, he kept his head down, as though messing with the stereo.

During the drive back to her house, she nearly convinced herself she'd done the best thing for both of them. For him.

❄ ❄ ❄

Mark plowed up the front steps of the house and slammed the door behind him. Inside, he took the stairs two at a time.

"Mark?" his dad called.

He didn't answer. He shut the door to his room, leaving the light off, looking around blindly. He pulled off his tie and unbuttoned his shirt. He stripped it off and threw it across the room at his closet door.

He ran his hands through his hair and sat down on the bed.

He'd trusted her with . . . everything.

And now she was leaving. She'd be gone.

He couldn't wrap his head around it. Before her, he was surviving. But with her? How could life be *something* without Riley in it?

He pictured Dalton's smirk, and the look on Riley's face. As if he were as despicable as Gainer.

He fell back on the bed, humiliation washing over him. Twice this had happened. First with Caylin. Now with Riley. She couldn't even look at him. She'd just faded away, as if he wouldn't notice her not coming around anymore. But that was nothing compared to this. Riley . . . she'd looked. She'd made him let her see, and he'd thought she could feel something for him beyond pity.

Fool.

All the frustration, all the anger and jealousy and rage he kept locked down reached up and dragged at him, tore at him until it broke free. His low growl grew into a yell. He clenched his fists, the skin on his face and hand stretching painfully. He drew another breath to yell again.

His dad opened his door, and a beam of light fell across him. "Mark?"

"Get out!"

"Son—"

"Just get out!"

The door closed, and Mark rolled over onto his stomach, gripping the pillow to the point of almost tearing it. He yelled again, muffled in the covers, every muscle in his body tight, his head pulsing. Fear was strong. It was always strong when it had its way, and it had been boxed up for a long time. A burning sensation started up his hip like a fiery ghost, and Mark sucked in a breath. The fire burst across the side of his torso and up his arm.

He was past this. He thought he was past this.

He knew what would come next if he didn't get a grip: the very real memory of piercing-cold knives carving waves of searing heat through his body. The side of his head. His face.

Sweat beaded along his brow.

Get out, Mark.

Go.

He drew in deep breaths, pushing beyond the haunting memory.

With his eyes squeezed tight, he saw Jay. Just Jay. He saw him smile.

Get yourself out, Mark.

He pressed himself into the pillow, calm pushing against the fire.

"Mark." He felt his dad's arms lift him, a cold sheet pressed around the right side of his body. A cool wet cloth on his forehead. "It's out. The fire's out, son. It's gone," his dad said quietly, holding him as best he could.

Mark drew in a ragged breath, his face damp from the cloth and sweat. "Didn't get me this time."

"Good. Hold on."

Mark nodded.

"Been a while. But you made it. Proud of you." His dad rubbed Mark's shoulder.

"She's leaving, Dad." The words were sharp in his throat. He swallowed, as if that would get rid of the hurt.

"We'll figure it out, son." He pulled him into a hug, and Mark didn't fight it. "We'll figure this out."

Chapter 22

A week had passed since the memorial ceremony. Riley's parents had approved of the renovations she'd made to her house and agreed that just a few more key updates would make for a great investment return when the house sold.

She'd explained that Mark was a good friend helping her with the house, and she'd let him down on an important day. They'd wanted to make it up to him somehow, but she'd convinced them to leave it alone. The last thing Mark needed was her mom's well-intentioned pity.

Her parents mentioned Jeremy the orthodontist again, but when Riley brought up the artist residency, her mom changed gears and talked about New Orleans for an hour. Before her parents returned to California, her mom bought Riley a set of Sennelier oils and a wreath for the front door. Both reminded her of her time with Mark and tore at her heart.

In the meantime, Riley finished painting Mary for the nativity.

She'd managed a nearly exact likeness from Mary's image in Mark's photos. As she looked over the virgin's face, she wondered what Leah Dolan would think. It couldn't be anything good.

Riley had let the entire Rivers family down. Yet Mary appeared perfectly content.

Her phone buzzed, and she picked up. "Hi, Yvette."

"Have you changed your mind about the firemen's ball tomorrow?"

"I can't. You know why."

Yvette sighed. "I know. I actually called to ask you a favor. I'm heading to Yakima for my nephew's birthday, and I wondered if you could pick up the cookies I ordered for the ball. Lette Mae needs them picked up at ten tomorrow morning, and I won't be back until four."

Riley put her hand to her forehead and grimaced. "Sure. I can do that." Going out meant seeing people, and after *Eyes on Hollywood* and the scene she'd made last week, she hadn't been too keen on going anywhere but her classroom. Even those who hadn't witnessed things firsthand knew the story. She couldn't tell if the looks from the residents of Miracle Creek were of pity or derision. Probably both. School was hard enough, but at least Dalton slunk away quickly whenever their paths crossed. He'd received plenty of backlash for his despicable behavior, but she hadn't behaved much better. She'd believed him—on the day of the hometown hero's memorial of his best friend's life. She couldn't call Dalton a coward without calling herself one, too.

Yvette's voice pulled her thoughts back. "Thank you, Riley." She paused, and then said carefully, "Are you sure you know what you're doing?"

Riley heard the same worry in her voice that had been there when they'd first discussed her move. Only Yvette, Mark, and likely Cal knew she was leaving. She'd give the school her notice after Christmas break.

"No, I don't. I never have."

"And how far has that gotten you?"

Her belief that she knew what she was doing, that she held the reins, had gotten her in trouble. Lesson learned. "I won't hurt Mark anymore."

"Is that what you think you're doing by leaving? Not hurting him?"

Yvette's question sat like sharp rocks in Riley's stomach for the rest of the day. Her advanced art students were tackling the final project she'd assigned, so now wherever she turned, depictions of Miracle Creek Bridge in negative-space snow filled her vision.

Brilliant idea, Madigan.

She'd just stepped into her house when her phone rang.

"Hello?"

"Hello, this is Sheila from West Wenatchee Dialysis Center. Is this Riley?"

Unease settled over her. "Yes. How can I help you?"

"Today is Mark's day to come in for Carmen, but the time has changed. I've tried contacting Mark, but he's not answering his phone. I've left a message, but Carmen will be coming in soon, and we have a full house today. She'll need help getting off the machine and getting home. I could call a taxi, but I thought I'd check with you first, since you were here before and she seemed to like you."

Riley turned in a slow circle, her phone to her ear, looking for some reason she couldn't go. But it was useless, because she could picture Carmen and the way she smiled.

"I'm sorry for asking," Sheila said. "I know it's last minute."

"No, that's all right," she said. "I'll be there." She got the address of the clinic and the approximate time Carmen would be coming off the machine. She skipped changing out of her clothes, piled her hair on top of her head, then threw her coat back on. She opened her front door, keys in hand, and stopped short.

"My paintings," she said aloud. She'd promised Carmen she'd bring her paintings the next time she came.

She grabbed a large tote bag from the closet and hurried back to the art room. She selected the only finished canvases she hadn't taken to her classroom and nestled them into the bag between pieces of cardboard. Then she grabbed her portfolio and a few of her favorite art books. Anything to make Carmen smile.

Then Riley dashed out to the car.

❄ ❄ ❄

Mark had parked among a few other vehicles and hiked up the groomed trail. The volunteers for the Washington State Trails Association didn't clear it much beyond the bridge this time of year, so he'd gone as far as he could and brushed snow off a boulder. Taking a seat, he looked back down at the bridge through the trees, squinting as the sun reflected off the snow. He was grateful to have this spot to himself.

The creek rushed by as he stared at the red beams. Last time he'd been here was with Riley. The thought of that day pulled at him, and he felt the warmth in his face even as his gut knotted.

This is so stupid.

He'd done his best to keep his head down and work. No more episodes. He'd left the numbers for a plumber and a window guy on Riley's kitchen table, along with her house key. Wasn't much more he could help her with until the weather warmed up. He didn't even know how much more work she wanted done on the house before she planned to put it up for sale.

He pulled in a deep breath, thinking of the time they'd spent on that house together. The time they'd spent *in* it together. But this had been her plan all along. To fix it up and leave. She'd warned him over and over. He just hadn't wanted to see it.

That morning he'd made the mistake of wandering up to his mom's attic studio. The bright winter sun had lit up the workspace. Taking in his mom's easel and desk and unused art tools, he couldn't help thinking of how dark and cramped Riley's art room was at her place, and how easy it was to picture her up there in her element. He'd almost offered the attic to her the first time he'd taken her up there. But he'd stopped himself, because he'd barely known her, and it wasn't his to offer.

When he'd gone back downstairs, he'd paused in the dining room, staring at the painting of Miracle Creek Bridge, hit with the overwhelming need to come up here. To make his wish.

His dad had caught him staring at the painting. "Thinking about doing something crazy?"

"I tried to get her to stay, Dad. I don't know what else to do."

"Sounds to me like you've got no other choice."

Mark looked at him. "I'm not going to make a wish."

His dad patted his arm. "You've got a couple hours before you go see Carmen. Couldn't hurt to get up there and think awhile. Let that mountain air clear your head."

So here he was, head as clear as October fog.

Mom, tell me this is stupid. I'll go home right now.

He waited. Nothing.

What was he supposed to wish for? For Riley to change her mind? For her to stay when New Orleans had so much to offer her? And what then? She'd changed her mind about him. And the way her parents had looked at him? He'd nearly forgotten those kinds of looks.

You could wish for sunsets for the rest of your life and you'd have them. But what if I wished we were stuck here forever?

He tried to lose himself in the surrounding beauty, the snow-brushed evergreens and the sound of the icy creek, the view descending toward town. It was all home to him. And he hated that he couldn't make it Riley's. She'd seen him, but no future with him.

After a while the sound of cars pulling out of the gravel lot drew his attention. The tourists had left, and he'd have the bridge to himself if no one else showed up.

He stood and willed his boots to take him back down the trail. Too soon they made a hollow thump as he walked over the bridge beneath the red-beamed roof. He stopped at the railing, watching the water gurgle toward him before it headed under the bridge and down the mountain. Snow still mounded boulders here and there in the water and along the edges, but the sun had melted most of the snow on the bridge.

With the way things had ended, the last thing he wanted was to be stuck here forever with Riley Madigan.

So why are you here?

He shook his head. If he was honest with himself, he knew exactly what he'd wish for. He'd wish for Riley to want him.

To love him.

But everything about that seemed wrong. To wish her to bend to his wants—his needs? No. All he'd wanted from the start was to make her smile. To bring light to her moss-green eyes. To hear her laugh even during her worst time of the year.

I wish for Riley to find peace at Christmas.

The wish broke out of his thoughts like a fortune out of a cookie.

Really? Peace at Christmas? It was like he'd sent up a generic Christmas card to the powers that be. *Happy Holidays, from Mark.*

Mark turned away from the railing and walked to the opposite side as if watching the water flow away from him would bring him some sense of reality. Would empty him of this nonsense. Because really, what was the worst that could happen?

He knew exactly what could happen. His mom had spelled it out for him all those years ago.

Endless torment.

Like he wasn't already there.

But at the same time, no other wish came to mind. No other idea tried to replace his one wish.

God, if you can hear me, just let her find peace.

❄ ❄ ❄

Riley tied the front of her gown and hoisted her bag over her shoulder. She signed in at the clinic's front desk. Nobody greeted her. Like Sheila said, almost every station was occupied. A handful of nurses moved purposefully among the chairs. Riley pulled on her gloves and headed to station number ten, where Carmen rested with her eyes closed, her blood coursing through tubes, into the machine, then back out. Cycling her life-source so she could live.

Riley rolled a nearby stool to Carmen's side. A timer beeped loudly at the next station, and Carmen opened her eyes.

She smiled. "Oh, hello. I didn't even see you come in. How are you?"

Riley smiled back. "I'm pretty good, Carmen. How are you?"

"Happy," she said. Her blue eyes shone with such contentment that Riley almost believed her. "It's so good to see you. Where's Mark?"

Carmen remembered their previous visit. That was a nice surprise. "I'm not sure. They couldn't reach him, so they called me. I hope that's all right."

"Of course. I hope nothing's wrong. Mark's never missed an appointment. I worry about him. He's so lonely." Her face brightened. "But he was so changed with you."

Riley swallowed, not answering.

"Tell me your name."

Riley breathed out a small laugh. "I'm Riley Madigan."

"Yes. Riley Madigan. You're an art teacher."

"I am. I brought you some of my paintings to look at." She pulled out a few of the canvases from the tote, and Carmen gasped.

"Oh, look at the robin. He's beautiful. You've captured him perfectly. The males are given all the beautiful colors to attract the females, you know."

"Maybe that's because they don't have much else going for them."

Carmen laughed. "Oh, that's terrible." Her blue eyes focused on Riley. "But you're able to see all that Mark has going for him. I could tell. And you—he eases your pain."

Carmen's machine beeped loudly, and Riley backed away as a nurse hurried over and started working to get Carmen unhooked.

All Riley could do was watch until it was her turn to press her hands over Carmen's IV site. *He eases your pain.* She replayed their last visit. She'd only focused on Carmen's incredible attitude and Mark's care for her. What had the woman seen?

The nurse signaled to Riley. "Have you done this before?"

Riley shook her head.

The nurse took in her size. "You might need to stand at first. Here." Riley stood, and the nurse helped her position her hands over a gauze bandage, her stacked palms directly over the insertion site. Riley glimpsed deep bruising on Carmen's arm. "Press very firmly here. You'll feel her pulse."

Riley nodded. "Feeling the pulse" was an understatement. No one could say Carmen didn't have a strong heart.

"Keep the pressure steady. You'll be able to ease up after about ten minutes, but just a little at a time. You'll feel it. It takes about fifteen minutes for the veins to close. Got it?"

Riley nodded. The nurse removed the tubes and the IV, working around the pressure site.

Riley's hands pulsed with the rhythmic flow of Carmen's blood. Holy cow. This was important.

"Thank you for doing this," Carmen said.

She pulled her gaze from her blue-gloved hands to Carmen. "You do this twice a week?" she said in wonder.

Carmen nodded. "And the rest of the week I get to live."

"You're set," the nurse said. "If there's a problem, push this button." She pointed to a red "help" button on the machine.

It didn't make Riley any less overwhelmed.

The nurse was about to go, when Carmen spoke up.

"Oh, Janet, this is Riley. Riley, this is Nurse Janet. All the nurses here are so nice. Janet, Riley's an art teacher. She brought me her paintings to look at. Aren't they wonderful?"

Janet looked at the painting Carmen held—a colorful street scene in downtown Denver. "It's beautiful."

Carmen pulled out another painting.

"Are these for sale?" Janet asked.

Riley's brow rose. "I hadn't thought about it."

"Well," Janet said, "let me know if you decide to sell. My sister would love that robin for Christmas." She wrote her number on a pad of paper from her pocket, gave the note to Carmen, and left.

Carmen sighed and settled back into her chair. "I should be your sales rep. I'd work on commission."

Riley laughed, then focused on her hands. "Is this okay?"

Carmen nodded, looking up at her like she had just handed her a dish of ice cream. "That's perfect. Thank you so much."

Riley studied her, noting the way the light from the window

softened the lines around her eyes. There was something about her eyes. Like all the misery had burned away and let you see what was left. Carmen was fragile and pale, but she had that light in her eyes, a knowing of things.

A certainty.

Carmen shook her head. "I loved watching you with Mark. It's still new, isn't it?"

Riley smiled, but it felt like a lie. "Oh, we're not—" The smile faded, and she swallowed. "What did you mean, he eases my pain?"

"We all carry pain. Those of us who've carried the most can recognize it in others. Maybe that's why you see his. And perhaps because of his pain, he sees how to heal yours. You're lucky to have found each other."

Riley felt a lump in her throat. "It's not like that . . . it can't be. I'm going to teach art in New Orleans. Mark and I . . ." She looked out the window, not wanting to watch the delighted expectation in Carmen's eyes turn to confusion. "I don't think it's good for anybody to rely on someone else to make them whole. It's not fair."

"Yes, I think that's true." Carmen said. "But are you talking about Mark? Or you?"

Riley looked back at Carmen and felt heat fill her cheeks. "Does it matter?"

Carmen smiled softly.

Riley lowered her gaze. "Mark can handle himself." She adjusted her hands, taking care to keep the pressure steady. Her muscles burned, and she realized why Mark's hand shook after this. "He's stronger than he knows."

She glanced up to find Carmen still watching her, the smile in her eyes dimmed.

"We don't always have to be strong. It's exhausting, isn't it?" She looked around the room, then out the window. "I think it's okay to be tired. Or scared." She turned to Riley. "But here's a secret I discovered." She leaned toward Riley. "Sometimes we think we want to run away. Disappear. When all we *really* want is to be found."

Riley stared, transfixed.

Carmen cocked her head, studying her. "Have you been found?"

Flashes of memory lifted before her like birds unsettled from their rest. Mark, swinging Ivy in his arms. Mark, grinning next to his truck when he didn't know his hoodie had fallen back. Mark, kissing her quick when she said she'd help him. Mark, sitting with her in front of the fire. Mark, holding her where they'd fallen in the snow. Mark, kissing her like he never wanted to stop. Mark, holding her gaze like he would never let her go . . .

Riley blinked away the sting behind her eyes and swallowed. "I was found. For a little while."

"What happened?"

"I ran." Worse. She'd thrown Mark out even though she'd known he was a Stickley.

"You're human, sweetie. But it's never too late to try again."

Riley smiled, but it faded. "Sometimes it is."

Carmen leaned back. "Where would I be," she said, her eyes glassy, "if I thought that way?"

❄ ❄ ❄

That night, Riley worked on the figure of baby Jesus. She sketched the paint lines on the black board with graphite and opened several of the sample-size jars of exterior house paint she'd been working with, giving them a stir. And still she hesitated.

The other characters stood in a line against the closet doors, watching her.

No pressure, guys.

She dipped her brush in the paint and began, working lightly and building up layers. The quiet of the house blanketed her thoughts, with only the sound of a tap and swish as she cleaned her brush in a mason jar of water. She'd gone through a lot of paint fast with this project, and Mark had found her a large pane of safety glass to use for mixing colors. It covered a sheet of black poster board on the desk next to the easel. She could mix large puddles of paint to work from and clean up easily when she was done.

He'd just showed up with it. Like when he and his dad had shoveled her driveway. Or when he'd given her the fire extinguisher. Like so many other things.

The framework of the manger and the hay forming the bed took shape first, followed by the soft bundle of white cloth wrapping the bulk of the baby's body, save for one chubby arm reaching up to his mother.

She rinsed her brushes again and changed out the water. She mixed the baby's skin colors and again built up layers against the black: the lifted arm and bare shoulder, the infant head and ears, adding dimension and the subtle glow this baby had. She found herself humming and paused. Not so much at the fact that she'd been humming, but more at what song had been rolling through her head.

What Child Is This . . .

She lifted her gaze to the figures against the closet and swallowed hard. She focused on Mary, who looked content. She rubbed her eyes with the back of her hand. Selecting a smaller brush, she mixed the darker colors she would use for the baby's facial details. She glanced again at the sketch she'd studied a hundred times.

Taking a deep breath and blowing it out, she touched brush to wood. Unbidden, the song came back to her as her brush followed the strokes she saw in her head, the idea once scratched on paper coming to life. She added more color to her brush, and her heart thumped a gentle tempo as she painted bowed lips, added depth to eyes and curls of hair, all the while that melody coursing through her senses.

At last Riley sat back, taking in the work. Taking in the face that said, *I just want to be loved. Like everyone else.*

To be loved. Even when she didn't know whether to stay or go. Even when she was so afraid, she hid. Even when she was so sad and confused, she broke things, smashed things on the floor.

Grandma?

Grandma, what do I do?

She wiped a tear, but more fell. She let them fall, unsure what to think but knowing what she felt.

This is real. Dirty and imperfect and real.

Real is what stays.

She inhaled a slow, deep breath, and exhaled as the room stilled around her.

"Real is what stays," she whispered.

Later, as she cleaned up, exhausted by the early morning hour and the emotional wringer she'd just been put through, she halted in front of the grouping against the closet.

They watched her, waiting.

"Don't think I don't know what you've been trying to do," she mumbled, the smallest of smiles on her lips. She clicked off her lamp and walked away. "I hope you're all proud of yourselves."

Chapter 23

Mark opened the door to the bakery mid-Saturday morning, the familiar bell jingling above him. The room was packed with people picking up their orders for pies, rolls, and pastries for the firemen's ball. His dad had sent him for two pies, but it felt like a bigger job than that.

Mark had promised he would make a showing at the dance to support the fire department. He was a guest of honor. But he wouldn't stay. And he wouldn't dance. Surprisingly, his dad had agreed without argument.

A few customers turned his way.

And then they stared.

He ducked his head and stepped inside. "Excuse me," he said as he reached for a number. The closest woman nodded, looking uncomfortable.

He hadn't realized how much his self-consciousness had faded until that moment. When he lifted his head again, the entire bakery had stilled, all eyes on him.

But not only him. The way parted to where Lette Mae stood

behind the register, bag lifted, staring. He frowned, and she moved her eyes to the spot behind the paying customer.

Riley Madigan stood there, glancing at him, fidgeting under the gaze of the customers, which oscillated like an electric fan between the two of them.

Lette Mae got the paying customer's attention. "Your change, Jeff. Tell the twins I said hi. Merry Christmas."

Jeff nodded. "Merry Christmas." But instead of leaving, he moved to the back of the room, standing awkwardly behind a couple eating their breakfast at one of the small café tables, and turned back to watch whatever unfolded.

Lette Mae sighed. "Number twenty-seven."

Mark watched Riley step up to the register. He hadn't seen her since the day of the unveiling, and there had only been one text from her letting him know she'd nearly finished the nativity and would tell him when he could pick it up.

After his trip to the bridge, he'd seen the messages from the dialysis center about Carmen. He called to check, and they'd said Riley had taken care of it. He hadn't known what to think. It had been easy not to see her all this time. He'd just stayed up at the house and shoveled snow, chopped charred apple trees down to nothing, hauled loads of salvageable wood away to people who needed it. Anything. Everything.

So maybe not so easy.

Then his dad had made him come here to pick up pies.

"Here are Yvette's cookies, already paid for." Lette Mae passed over a pastry box to Riley. "And two cream *bollen* for you. That'll be $5.86, darlin'." Lette Mae glanced in Mark's direction.

So did everyone else.

He could leave. He could turn around and leave the bakery and nobody would think the worse of him. There would be plenty of pies at the dance. But then he remembered his wish. He sighed. "A person can get their pastries without being stared at, can't they?" he said to the crowd.

"Y'all can look at me," said Freya Hines toward the front. "I just got my hair done for the firemen's ball tonight."

"Save me a dance," Bill Bushman called out from the back.

"Oh, Bill," Freya said. "You can't be asking a girl to a dance from the back of a bakery."

"Can I ask her to the dance from the *front* of the bakery?"

"You could try," Freya answered.

The room shook with laughter.

Mark turned away, relieved to have the prying eyes elsewhere, just as Riley's shoulder brushed against his arm as she attempted to exit the bakery. The simple touch sent shock waves through his body. He knew that coat, the give of it around her as he'd held her close. Her scent and the way her hair parted through his fingers. Her determined kiss on his mouth . . .

His jaw clenched as Riley slipped out the door. He caught Lette Mae's eye. She lifted her brow and motioned him to go.

Everyone watched. Again.

He rolled his eyes and pushed through the door; it closed on a loud cheer that went up as he left.

He may or may not have growled.

His feet were bricks as he followed Riley, who was already in her car by the time he spotted her.

Why was he following her if she was in such a hurry to get away from him? Because a roomful of people buying sweets said he should?

Riley was backing her car out of her parking space when he reached her spot.

"Wait," he called. "Just wait."

Whether she heard him or saw him he didn't know. What he did know was that she was rolling down her window and he didn't know what to say next.

She spoke first. "I should have said hi to you in there. I didn't know—I don't know if you want me to—"

"Can I see the nativity today sometime?"

She looked up at him, squinting from the sun. "Oh. Yes. Of course. It's yours, after all." She paused as if waiting for him to say something more. When he didn't, she nodded. "I'll see you later, then." She started rolling up the window.

"Wait. Riley—" He took another step toward the car.

She rolled down her window again, her expression pained. "If I give you a *bollen* will you let me go?"

He paused, uncertain if she was serious or not.

"I bought two because, honestly, buying one seemed pathetic, but now that I think about it, buying two was even more pathetic, especially since I only bought two because I wanted one so desperately and I didn't want to look desperate."

He paused again, still uncertain. "Are you bribing me to go away," he said carefully, "with *bollen*?"

She grimaced. "That's what it sounded like, didn't it? I'm sorry." She leaned forward and put her head on the steering wheel. "This is all my fault."

Mark took a few steps closer to her car. "If you want to throw blame around, throw it at Gainer. He's a manipulator." He shrugged. "We've all got voices talking at us. Sometimes it's hard to hear who's talking truth."

He glanced behind him. "On the other hand, I've got a whole bakery full of people watching out the windows, and I need to go back in because if I come home without Lette Mae's pies, my dad's going to know something's up and I really need a few hours of peace and quiet. So who am I to talk about throwing off manipulation?"

He didn't really know what more to say. His toes started to freeze in the cold. "I understand if you want to roll that window up and get going, so I'll just back off now." He took a step back.

"Wait," she said, and he halted.

That dimple had appeared next to her mouth. The one that meant he was making her head spin.

"It would be good to just . . ." She bit her lip, as if searching for the right words.

"Get past this?" he offered.

She nodded.

He shoved his hand forward. "Friends."

Slowly she took his hand, her gaze on his compression sleeve, her grip firm. She lifted her eyes. "Friends."

He couldn't help feeling both relieved and disappointed by how easily she'd accepted him back in that capacity. He let go of her hand.

"I'll come by at three?" he said.

"Okay. Oh—" She rummaged next to her and then held out a white paper bag. "Your *bollen*."

He frowned. "You don't have to buy me off. I'm leaving now."

She shook her head. "Take it." Her sunlit green eyes watched him above her spray of freckles and determined mouth. "It's yours."

He held her gaze for a moment, fighting a surge of the thing he'd tried to bury concerning Riley Madigan. He took the *bollen* from her without a word.

She rolled up her window and backed out of her space, then drove away.

❆ ❄ ❆

Riley's doorbell rang at three. She wrung her hands as she approached the front door. Despite the awfulness at the memorial and what came after, Mark had kept his word in helping her with the house. And after this morning, she knew he was willing to be civil and show that they could move on with their lives despite the rumor mill in this small town, or maybe because of it. And now he was coming to see the nativity, unaware she'd finished it the night before.

Her bare feet padded on the satiny wood floor. She paused with her hand on the doorknob, then pulled it open, shivering from the rush of cold air.

Mark quickly stepped inside so she could close the door, glancing at the giant fresh fir wreath with the big red bow on her door as he did so. He pulled off his hat as if that's what he always did when he entered a house.

Her brow lifted. "You got a haircut."

He nervously ran a hand over his scars. "Steph did it."

"She did a great job." It was no lie. The smooth lines of the cut accentuated the angular planes of his face, his eyes, and the softness of his mouth.

His smile revealed relief. "Thanks."

After another awkward pause, they spoke over one another.

"I'll take your coat—"

"I wasn't sure if I should—"

They stopped again. How had they come to this? Unable to make decent conversation? Oh, right. Because she was an idiot.

"The nativity figures are in the art room," she said. "Go ahead. I'll meet you back there in a couple minutes." This was her plan. To let him view them alone first.

He nodded and headed to the art room.

In all honesty, she was chickening out. She'd fretted all day over what he'd think of the nativity figures now that they were done, and she didn't want to be there when he first laid eyes on them. It might have been ridiculous, but wasn't she a coward, anyway? Isn't this what she did?

She sat down on the couch and rearranged some books on the new coffee table she'd found at one of the thrift stores in Wenatchee. Her mother had suggested she get one for the front room, but Riley doubted her mother meant the multicolored tramp-art piece that complemented her green couch. Her eyes lifted to the paintings on the wall, the middle one in particular, and she realized something. The thing that made her grandma's house feel like home wasn't the house. It wasn't Montana. It wasn't even Christmas.

It was her grandma.

And she'd felt her grandma in this house right here in Miracle Creek.

It was *people* who had the potential to make a house feel like a home, no matter where it was or what time of year.

Had her parents been that lousy at it? Had she? All this time? She suddenly felt very drained.

After a couple of minutes, Riley stood. She listened for any sound coming from the art room as she warily made her way back. She hesitated at the partially opened door, then knocked quietly and pushed the door open.

Mark turned, his posture straight, his hands in his pockets. He watched her approach even as her gaze bounced between him and the figures leaning against the closet doors, the baby Jesus figure still on her easel.

Unable to stand the silence any longer, she opened her mouth to ask him what he thought, but he put his finger to his lips, and she stilled. He held out his hand, and she took it, a touch she didn't deserve. He pulled her to him until they stood shoulder to shoulder. She closed her eyes, not wanting to be this close to him, missing being this close to him.

"Thank you, Riley."

A shiver slid down her spine at the gentle timbre of his voice. She opened her eyes. "Thanks for asking me."

He scrutinized her as if he were about to ask her a question, but she didn't feel up to answering anything.

"Shall I keep them here until you're ready to give them to Cal?" she asked, heading him off.

He let go of her fingers and folded his arms in front of him. "Yeah, that would be great, as long as you don't need this space."

"It's not a problem. I've gotten used to having them around."

He nodded, watching her curiously. "Well, I better get going." He followed her out of the room and back to the front door.

"They really are incredible, Riley. More than I hoped for."

"I'm glad you like them. Just let me know when you want to pick them up."

He placed his hat back on his head and nodded. Then he was gone.

She thought she'd been so careful with everything and everyone. Not just here. All of her adult life. She'd had to be. Because every time she let her guard down, every time she trusted someone, it ended in disaster. She'd obeyed her rules with Gavin, heck even with Dalton. Look where that got her. And Mark had come in around a side door. A door she didn't even know she had.

Ha.

When had her rules *ever* applied to Mark?

The sound of his truck fading down her street left her standing at the window, wishing he hadn't had to go. Wishing she could have shared more about finishing the nativity. Wishing he would have kept her hand a little longer. Wishing she'd had a reason to make him stay.

❄ ❄ ❄

Mark stood next to his dad and Yvette, no easy feat with the lights low and the disco ball spinning in the center of the high-ceilinged room. Some guy from the forties crooned over the sound system and a cluster of older women in sequins kept eyeing him with coy smiles and waves. Mark clung to his plate of peach pie and fork like it was the only thing keeping him afloat in the sea of swaying bodies on the dance floor.

He nodded politely at Mrs. Polk, then turned to his dad. "Remind me why you made me come to this, again?"

His dad snickered. "I'm not the one who made you guest of honor. You came out of your own sense of duty. Can't help it if I raised you right."

Mark grimaced, and the song ended to light applause. "Jingle Bell Rock" followed, and the floor stayed full. The community spirit at these things was always high.

One night a year, Miracle Creek Vineyards donated their small events lodge to the Annual Firemen's Holiday Ball. The dance gave the fourteen-years-and-older people of Miracle Creek a reason to get dressed up and celebrate for a good cause. On top of that, word of Mark's application to the volunteer fire department had surfaced, and he was getting a lot of premature congratulations tonight. At least nobody dared ask where the art teacher was, though sometimes he sensed it right on the tips of their tongues.

Mark wanted to go home and crawl into bed.

He was about to say so when the music changed again, and

his dad promptly set down his and Yvette's drinks and led her out to the dance floor.

"Hey. Don't leave me," Mark whisper-shouted in their direction, flickering a glance toward the widows' corner.

His dad only arched his brow in return, and he and Yvette faded into the crowd on the dance floor.

Traitors.

Steph and Brian danced by, and she waved. He lifted his pie plate in response. But she waved again, this time nodding her head toward the heavy double doors at the entrance. He frowned and looked in that direction, then promptly forgot all about his pie.

Just entering from the cloakroom, Riley stood in a dress he could only describe as miraculous with her dark hair piled in big curls on her head, looking hesitantly around the room, gathering turned heads of her own. When her eyes found Mark's, she stopped.

She wasn't going to come to the dance. Yvette had said she wasn't coming. But here she was. Walking toward him.

Friends. Just friends. That's all they could be.

I'm in trouble, he thought, reminding himself to breathe.

❄ ❄ ❄

Riley walked across the room toward Mark at a pace she hoped appeared relaxed because her heart was hammering and her legs shook. He wore a well-cut suit and a burgundy tie, holding a plate of pie and a fork, staring right back at her. He wasn't the only one. She could feel the eyes of everyone on her, watching to see what the art teacher would do or say to the fireman.

She swallowed and kept walking in her three-inch strappy heels and a dress she'd worn for one of her dad's premieres—a deep teal taffeta with a plunging sweetheart neckline, fitted waist, and a full pleated skirt falling to her knees. The dress made her feel beautiful and strong, and that's how she needed to feel right now.

He turned away abruptly, and she faltered. But then she saw he was just setting down his pie on the nearest table. He pivoted back to her so quickly she heard a few chuckles from nearby observers.

Gathering her nerve, she took the final few steps to him. "Hi."

"Hey." He shook his head, his gaze never leaving hers. "You look incredible."

She flushed. "Thanks. You make the suit look good."

"This old thing?" he asked, still not breaking eye contact.

She smiled, and he returned it.

Good. This was good.

"I brought you something," she said. She held out a gift bag from behind her back.

He took it and peered inside. "Mini candy canes?"

"They're to throw at people. To hit them in the—"

"—Christmas spirit," he finished with her. He studied her, clearly mystified.

The music changed, slowing down.

"Want to dance?" she asked before her courage fled.

His gaze flickered to the dance floor. He nodded once, and set the bag down next to his dessert, grabbing a handful of candy canes and shoving them in his pocket. The simple act gave her courage, and her legs didn't shake so much when he took her hand and led her to the dance floor.

He chose a spot and pulled her into a standard dance position. His hand at her waist kept her at a safe distance. Although "safe" was a fluid term at the moment. Her heart rioted.

"I didn't think you were coming," he said as he swayed them slowly side to side. "Or that you'd even want to come."

"Because it would be awkward?"

"Because it would be Christmassy." He nodded to the lights and tree in the corner. The main portion of the room was backed by a bank of tall windows overlooking the river valley. "But awkward works."

"I expected it," she said. "The Christmassy, I mean. It's okay."

"Are you sure? I know you have rules and stuff. Santa's going to visit—"

"I'll be fine."

"You will?"

"I kinda made friends with Christmas."

He stopped dancing. "How?"

She made a little shrug like it was no big deal, her eyes lowering. "I did something for someone else."

He drew her closer. "Who was that?"

She looked up, meeting his intense gaze. Then she lifted her hand from his shoulder, pointed at both her eyes, then pointed at him.

She'd expected him to nod. Or smile. Maybe even laugh.

Instead he took her hand and led her off the dance floor mid-song, pulling the gazes of a dozen or more people with them. She followed as best as she could in her heels out through a door and onto a dark deck overlooking a vineyard hillside. The shock of cold enveloped her as Mark let go of her hand and began to pace, running a hand through his hair.

"Mark?" She wrapped her arms around herself, shivering.

He looked at her, then pulled off his jacket and set it around her shoulders. He rubbed her arms, watching the space between them.

"What are we doing here, Riley?"

"Freezing?"

That drew his eyes up to hers, anyway.

"Sorry," she said. "I know what you meant."

"I can't do this." He shook his head. "I can't pretend to not feel things I do, and I can't even feel about you the way I want to because you're leaving without any plans to come back. So, tell me, why did you come tonight? To tell me you're friends with Christmas? I'm happy for you, Riley. I really am. Nobody could be more relieved for you than I am." His gaze searched hers, begging her for answers. "But is that really why you came?"

"I've been doing a lot of thinking," she said. "'Courage is knowing what not to fear.' You said that."

"Plato said that."

"Then you said it."

He shook his head in frustration, but she continued before he could say anything.

"All this time, I thought courage was putting up walls against the things and people that hurt you. That courage was anticipating how you might be hurt and preventing it before you got close. Even with my grandma, I thought it was strength to push away this thing, this holiday she loved so much, to protect myself from feeling that pain year after year—"

"You were just a kid."

"I'm not a kid anymore. You were only a couple years older than I was when you lost your mom. You didn't shut out the best things about her."

His gaze intensified. "No, but I shut out almost everything when I lost Jay."

She paused. Her voice wavered. "I think I've been doing this wrong. I've been afraid of the wrong things."

He waited, watching.

"I want to be brave," she said. "Will you help me?"

His piercing gaze never left hers. "Since the fires, I've been trying to work my way around the idea of living again. Then you came and threatened me and laughed at me and ordered me around, and I stopped trying to work my way around living and just started . . . living. Waking up and making plans for how to spend time with you, how to make you smile, how to make a life, how to make you love me—"

He'd stopped himself as her breath caught.

Her voice softened. "You love me."

"That's not what I said."

"Yes, you did."

He stepped closer, his complexion mottled. "I said make—"

"—you love me," she finished.

"I said you—"

"You."

He pulled her close. "Love."

Her pulse raced. "Love."

His lips neared hers. "Me."

"M—"

His mouth met hers, and she wasn't able to finish her argument—or win it. Or maybe she had won, because this kiss warmed her all the way to her toes, and she forgot snow and sky and mountains or maybe felt them all at once—

He broke the kiss, his hands cradling her face. "If you hate it here, if you can't stand this place, then yes, leave. Find somewhere that makes you happy. I'd follow you. I'd take all the looks and stares and follow you anywhere, if you'd let me."

She swallowed hard, knowing what that would mean for him.

"But, Riley"—his eyes pled with hers—"if you like this place? If you love this place? If you love me—" He stopped, his chest rising and falling.

"If I love you," she whispered, searching his eyes, begging him to trust her.

"If you could be happy here, then stay here. Stay with me. Make more memories with me."

She saw a thousand hopes in his eyes. And more courage than she'd ever known.

She was out of arguments. "I'll stay. With you."

He smiled his beautiful, breathless smile. "Then get used to more of this."

She laughed as he picked her up, kissing her again.

In an instant, the deck space flooded with Christmas lights as indoor curtains were drawn back on the wall of windows behind them, revealing one side of the dance area and plenty of eyes.

They heard a shout, and somebody whistled.

"Way to go, fireman!"

"Get her inside—she's gonna freeze!"

Mark's deep laughter pulled a smile from her. "We better do what he says."

"I kind of like it out here," she said, still looking down at him.

He set her feet on the deck.

"Kiss her again!" someone shouted.

"I know where I'd like to throw a few of those candy canes," Mark grumbled. He lifted his head and shouted back, "I'm trying to!"

"Mark?"

He turned back to her, frowning. "Hmm?"

"My lips are cold."

He slowly smiled. "Ms. Madigan, I am going to love keeping you warm."

Chapter 24

Mark closed his eyes under the blindfold as Riley pulled it tight. "Ouch."

"Can you see anything?"

"My eyes are closed."

"Good." Riley grabbed his hand and led him out of the house and down the porch steps.

"Hey, slow down. I can't see, remember?"

"You know this place like the back of your hand." She didn't slow.

He did his best to keep up with her. "Are we going to the storage building to make out?" he asked. "'Cause if we are, I'm kind of digging this blindfold idea." He grabbed for her with his free arm.

She laughed, evading his grasp. "Not this time. It's a surprise. Be good."

"Oh, I'm good."

She laughed again.

They left the path to the storage building and began tramping into the snow.

"This isn't some sort of survival test, is it? You leave me with

---

a knife and duct tape? Like you said, I know this place like the back of my hand. I'd be back before dinner. I'd even keep the blindfold on."

"I'm sure you would. Now shush."

"Hey." He planted his feet. Her hand pulled hard in his, but he held on, and she stopped.

"What?" she asked, a little impatience in her voice.

He smiled. "Come here." He pulled on her hand, and she gave in.

He wrapped her in his arms, smelling her scent mixed with winter air, knowing exactly where the top of her head reached his nose, exactly where her lips would be if she looked up at him. Her arms wrapped around his middle.

"Do you know how much I love you?" he asked.

"Not as much as you'll love me a few minutes from now?" she answered, her voice soft.

He grinned, his breath hitching at the ease of her answer. He pulled her to him and kissed her, lingering as long as she'd let him, which, thankfully, was longer than he expected.

The blindfold was a great idea.

Finally, she pulled away. "You're making us late, Mr. Rivers." He loved the breathless smile in her voice.

"I wasn't exactly working alone."

She didn't argue and pulled him again. "Follow me."

"Anywhere."

Finally, after a half-mile or so, they stopped walking.

"What took you so long?" his dad asked. His dad?

"He, uh, really liked the blindfold," Riley said.

His dad chuckled. "You ready?"

"I think so," Riley answered.

Mark let himself be pulled into position, facing south.

360

Wait a minute. He knew exactly where they were. Two weeks ago, they'd made this same trek with his dad on Christmas Day. The man had been rendered speechless by the nativity and had crushed both him and Riley in his arms.

Riley untied his blindfold and let it drop. He blinked at the brightness of the spotlights aimed at what stood in front of him.

"The nativity," he whispered. He looked at Riley, who watched him with a hopeful smile, then back to the figures she'd painted.

"I know it's not the same," she said. "But I had this idea—"

"Shush," he said softly. She shushed.

She'd added a resting donkey and an angel in white, wings glowing like the baby's swaddling.

"Well?" Riley asked.

"You made an angel."

She nodded. "It's a snow angel."

He grinned at her. "It's perfect. How did you do all this?"

He scooped her up out of the snow and kissed her mouth. Her hands drew around his neck as she kissed him back.

"It's perfect," he said again. He couldn't believe she'd done this. For him. "Thank you."

She smiled. "You're welcome. But I had help."

"I'll thank Dad in a minute."

"A handshake will be fine," his dad said.

Riley's eyes sparked. She drew her arms closer around him. Resting her cheek against his scars, she whispered in his ear. "Merry Christmas."

He closed his eyes. "Be warned. I'm never letting you go."

"I'm counting on it."

Acknowledgments

Thank you, Heidi Gordon, Lisa Mangum, and everyone at Shadow Mountain for taking this story on with enthusiasm and determination. Thank you, Lisa, for your editing prowess and encouragement. It's an honor to be able to tap into your wisdom. Thanks for getting my voice.

Thank you, Sam Millburn, for your patience and encouragement, for your support and honesty, always.

Thank you, Natalie Cooper Clark and Sachiko Burton, for being my alpha readers and steering me onward.

To Melanie Jacobson and Robison Wells—I'm not sure I would have had the courage to find this story a home without you. My respect and gratitude for both of you is deep and shiny.

Thank you, My Suzy, Bear Lake Monsters, and Columbia River Writers. Love, love, love.

To Sara Ditto, Laura Ridd, Shannon Carlson, Molly Neal, and Diana Layton—thank you, ladies, for lending your ears, shoulders, hugs, and getting my body outside and moving. You are my own Yakima cheer squad and the epitome of friendship.

To Chelsea and Matt, Braeden, Jacob, Maren, and Will. Thank you for supporting your determined and goofy mother through such a crazy few years. I love you all more than I can describe. Way more.

Thank you, Brandon—my partner, love, and fierce defender of my writing time. Together, we are home. XO

Photo by Rooted Souls Photography

About the Author

Krista writes contemporary romance, historical romance, and fantasy. She has lived in lush Oregon and rugged Wyoming, but Washington is her beloved home state. She likes to choose familiar settings for her stories and is grateful to have such inspirational places to choose from. She is a mother of six, gramma of three, a gardener and cook, loves to travel, laugh, and hike, and lives to make the best of what she's been given.

Find her on Instagram @kristajensenbooks.